THE
BOOK
OF
BEGINNINGS

Sally Page is the *Sunday Times* bestselling author of *The Keeper of Stories*, which has now sold over half a million copies.

After studying history at university, Sally worked in a number of different jobs, including running a market research company and a flower shop, which inspired her series of non-fiction flower books.

Later, Sally founded her pen company, PLOOMS, when she could not find the fountain pen that she wanted. Her passion for stationery partly inspired her second novel, *The Book of Beginnings*, which is set in a small stationery shop in London.

Sally now lives in Dorset. Her eldest daughter, Alex, is studying to be a doctor, and her youngest daughter is the author Libby Page.

www.sallypage.com
🐦 @SallyPageBooks
📘 /sallypageauthor
📷 @bysallypage

Also by Sally Page

The Keeper of Stories

THE
BOOK
OF
BEGINNINGS

SALLY PAGE

HarperCollins*Publishers*

HarperCollins*Publishers* Ltd
1 London Bridge Street,
London SE1 9GF

www.harpercollins.co.uk

HarperCollins*Publishers*
Macken House,
39/40 Mayor Street Upper,
Dublin 1
D01 C9W8

First published by HarperCollins*Publishers* 2023
1

A catalogue record for this book is available from the British Library

ISBN: 978-0-00-861287-0

This novel is entirely a work of fiction.
The names, characters and incidents portrayed in it are
the work of the author's imagination. Any resemblance to
actual persons, living or dead, events or localities is
entirely coincidental.

Typeset in Berling LT Std by Palimpsest Book Production Ltd, Falkirk, Stirlingshire

Printed and bound in the UK using 100% Renewable Electricity by CPI Group (UK) Ltd

For Rev. Anne Heywood
Always an inspiration

Prologue

Sometimes a heartbeat is all the time it takes to reach a decision.

It may not even feel like a considered choice. Just the veering away from the prospect of more misery – a final spur to movement. The room remains unmoved. A silent witness. But loyal in its way to the woman who has just left it. The chair pushed out from the table tells no tales. The plate of half-eaten roll and cheddar (extra mature) with leftover Christmas pickle (eight months old, but still going strong) lies in mute defiance.

The man calls her name, and without pausing to be invited in, pushes open the door that leads from the hall into the kitchen. And why would he pause? He has already let himself in the front door without asking.

He huffs and puffs his way around the kitchen, opening the fridge, flicking through the diary left open on the table.

The diary doesn't give her away either. Its record of parish meetings, choir practice and a planned visit to a local garden with her curate; a testament to a seemingly blameless life. Maybe there is something in the handwriting? A neatly formed hand, precise and clear, apart from a kink in the S's that look as if they would like to escape from the regularity of the line.

Opposite him, the back door to the garden (which always requires a doorstop) for once stands half open, half closed. Stilled, as if in anticipation, like the rest of the room.

Then, very slowly, it swings on its hinges and quietly clicks shut.

Ninety miles away, off an alleyway in North London, another door is pushed open. A different woman, a different life. The mail piled up in the entrance slithers aside and the broken bell clinks its tinny welcome. First across the threshold is a solitary leaf. A twist of orange, sent spiralling by a late August wind that holds within its warmth the piquant tang of autumn. The woman watches the leaf's spinning progress into the quiet darkness of the shop within. For her, autumn has always been a season of beginnings; punctuated, in her childhood, by the anticipatory thrill of new shoes, crayons and pencil cases.

Now she only thinks of endings.

1

Out of place

Jo stoops to retrieve the post and, as she does so, she picks up the stray leaf. It lies in her open palm like a coloured-paper 'mood fish' that as children they would hold in their hands to tell their fortune. The leaf trembles and then is still. She wants to ask it, does this mean that one day she will be happy? She wants the orange leaf 'fish' to tell her, if when she is thinking about James, is he ever thinking of her? During all those minutes that stretch into hours, she wants to believe that if at some point he is missing her, this would constitute a connection between them. A thread of hope that she could twist around her little finger and gently pull on. Jo closes her hand around the fragile substance of the leaf, cocooning it in the hollow of her hand, and tucking the post under her arm, she pushes the door wider.

Stepping inside, her suitcase wheels rumble in rhythm over the tiles that mark the entrance to her Uncle Wilbur's shop. Taylor's Supplies is a premises not much bigger than an elongated cupboard, selling a mixture of hardware and stationery. This has been her uncle's business and home for the past fifty-two years.

Looking around, it is much as Jo remembers it. From the front of the narrow premises, one aisle leads away from the door, turning left at the back of the shop (where there is an archway to a small kitchen, a toilet, and stairs to the upstairs flat). A second narrow aisle returns back to where Jo is now standing. This is all there is to her uncle's shop, apart from the small area at the front where a glass-topped cabinet sits, set at a right angle to the window. This old-fashioned oak cabinet (which, in a former life, Jo imagines, had displayed handkerchiefs or gloves) comprises of a top shelf given over to fountain pens and, underneath, a series of broad drawers containing the larger sheets of paper that Uncle Wilbur sells.

A place for everything and everything in its place.

Jo can hear Uncle Wilbur's voice echoing in her head; and studying the shop, she can see that he has held true to his favourite maxim. The shelves may be more sparsely stocked than in previous years, but everything is neat, everything is in its place.

Apart from her uncle, she thinks, who is miles away from here.

And apart from her.

Jo glances at the gap between the counter and the wall. Here, suspended by string on a wooden pole, hang the brown paper bags. Bags that, miraculously, seemed to accommodate everything Uncle Wilbur sold, from a few screws and nails (bag twisted at the top to secure them) to a long metal saw with gleaming teeth.

And here is where Jo played 'post offices' as a child, tucked away in her secret spot. (*A place for everything and everything in its place.*) Standing behind the counter, shielding her from sight, her uncle appreciated that a busy postmistress needed a ready supply of stationery. As a little girl, one of her greatest joys had been when her uncle had beckoned her over and presented her with a brown paper bag bulging with some intriguing shape. Inside might be a notebook with its cover missing or a receipt book with a scrape in the carbon paper. Uncle Wilbur had told her (and more importantly, Mrs Watson-Toft, his bookkeeper with the basilisk's stare) that he only ever gave away 'damaged goods'. But when she was older, Jo began to suspect that when Uncle Wilbur had seen her younger self gazing covetously at a new batch of receipt books, he had run his broad, flat fingernail over the carbon paper on purpose.

Looking up, Jo notices a small, square calendar pinned to the large noticeboard on the wall behind the counter. This is all that is displayed there. The month is now August, but it still shows July's date. Fleetingly she wonders what her Uncle Wilbur used to use this noticeboard for – she can't recall it being here on her visits to the shop as a child.

Leaving the post and the leaf on the counter, Jo takes her suitcase to the back of the shop and mounts the stairs. From the first-floor landing, a half-glazed door opens into a small entrance hall. A low bench sits under a row of coat hooks, on which her uncle's dark grey winter coat still hangs.

Off the hall is a bathroom. This has an ancient suite in brilliant white, and is heated by a small, ineffective blow-heater. Jo is not looking forward to using this room. She knows from experience that even when the bath is full of hot water, the outer edge is still ice-cold to the touch.

The hallway opens up into a living room, beyond which is the kitchen. Both have long sash windows overlooking the alleyway. Opposite the first window are two doors to bedrooms. Jo wavers for a moment, undecided whether to use her uncle's room or the box room she slept in as a child when she visited for a few weeks each summer. She opens the door to the smaller of the rooms and is soon unzipping her case. Most of the clothes she flings onto a chair. What she is looking for is at the bottom of her bag.

She pulls out the dark-blue denim dungarees, their fabric stiff in her hands, like card. Jo stares down at them, unsure why it was so important for her to bring them with her. Her best friend, Lucy, left them in her cottage after staying over one evening – oh, it would have been months ago now – vintage Fifties, high-waisted, wide-legged dungarees. Lucy is a lover of all things vintage. As a teenager, and still now, as a 38-year-old woman, she wears the dresses that she begged off their grand-mothers. Jo sees her own passion for stationery as an echo of her friend's quirky connection with the past, and clings to her love of newly sharpened pencils, knowing it makes her feel closer to Lucy. Even at primary school, the two of them were attuned and in step – without fail and without effort, winning the annual three-legged race at the school's sports day.

Jo sits on the bed, holding the dungarees to her. And now? Now she thinks that even if someone tied her and Lucy's legs together, they would not be able to keep in rhythm. She has never felt more out of step with her best friend, and she cannot clarify in her mind exactly why. She knows there are probably many reasons, but whichever way she stacks and rearranges these reasons – her point of view; her perception of Lucy's point of view – it never gives her a sense of truly understanding what has gone wrong between them. They rarely text each other now; and when they do something jars, and Jo can't put her finger on what or why. She just knows that if she and Lucy were to try a three-legged race now, rather than emerging as the natural victors, they would both fall flat on their faces.

Jo's far-off gaze gradually refocuses on the precise tidiness of the small room. She should really put her things away in the chest of drawers. (*A place for everything and everything in its place.*) It doesn't take long. Less than ten minutes later her possessions are stowed away and her empty suitcase is stored under the single bed.

There is just one thing she doesn't have to unpack, or to put away. There is no need. It is not something that she can hide away at the back of a drawer. However much she would like to.

Jo knows she has no option but to carry her broken heart around with her, wherever she goes. James saw to that when he left her four months ago.

2

I do

Jo sits behind the old oak counter looking up at the sliver of sky that she can just spy – if she leans out far enough on her tall stool. This is where she has perched for the past six weeks, minding the shop, watching the pedestrians who move in an intermittent stream through the alleyway, and scanning her sliver of sky for signs of change. Today, the sky is a troubled grey and the rust-coloured brickwork of the alleyway wall opposite gleams wet from squally, October rain.

Whatever the weather, Jo finds her small slice of sky strangely soothing. She knows that beyond the alleyway (its entrance between a hairdresser's and a café), the same sky is a canopy to a larger world: Highgate High Street, with its broad avenue of shops and restaurants. A mixture of the enticing and the functional – at times managing to combine both in one establishment. Like the shop papered with old newspapers that sells cherrywood-handled knives with sculpted steel blades, or the haberdasher's that displays on its door a wreath made from ribbons, the colour of autumn fruit.

Beyond the High Street, if she were to walk up the hill to the left, she would reach the expanse that is Hampstead Heath. There, the same sky she can glimpse from her stool sweeps across a landscape that is part parkland, part pleasure garden, part wilderness. It is good to know this larger world is out there, but also that her slice of sky is contained, bordered by a wall and a rooftop – giving definition to her place in a city that, to Jo, is an alien world.

She has tried to imagine this same sky stretched out, flapped like a huge bedsheet or tablecloth to cover her old home: the terraced cottage on the outskirts of a Northumberland village. But they had different skies up there. Broader, bigger, and more magnificent in their changing moods. She cannot imagine ever being able to capture a slice of those skies.

But then, she never needed to. It was enough to walk out onto the fells and gaze up at them.

Today, as usual, Jo is wearing Lucy's dungarees. Vintage is not really Jo's style (she's not quite sure what is), but it seems fitting to wear borrowed clothes, sitting here, in her borrowed life. Jo reaches for the dungarees each morning, her jumpers underneath changing from green to orange to yellow to red, depending on the weather, her mood and the washing pile. Sometimes she feels like a traffic light, solid and static, glimpses of colour recycling, as life moves slowly past her. The high, fitted waist holds her tight just under a heart that aches for her friend's company.

Since living in London she has tried to text Lucy more regularly, but it has been hard to find the right words. The words that do keep returning to her are from their final conversation before she left. She'd always known Lucy didn't like James, but never until that conversation, just how much. Jo knew her best friend's outburst was fuelled by Lucy seeing how hurt Jo was, but she wonders why Lucy thought she would want to hear it, or in what way she imagined it could ever make her feel better. Not while she held onto that slender thread of hope. She hadn't told Lucy about this. But now she wonders if she needed to. Wasn't that part of what made Lucy so furious?

And James? Jo spends most of her time trying *not* to text him. It has been hard. Texts written and then deleted. Only one thing stops her pressing send. The thought that James's phone might be picked up and the texts read by his new girlfriend, Nickeeey. Jo can never think of her old work colleague, Nicky, without extending her name with a whine. They had only worked together briefly, but Jo won't forget her endless complaints and whinging in a hurry

Jo glances up at the small, square calendar that is still the only thing pinned to the large noticeboard behind her. At the close of each day, she crosses a date off. Sometimes she does this well before the end of the day, as if urging time to hurry up.

Six weeks on, Uncle Wilbur is still in the home that he moved into (temporarily) for some respite care. It is near to her parents, and Jo's mother visits her brother most days. What started as confusion (that her mother put down to a 'very nasty tumble') has revealed itself as something else. The doctors talk about the things they can do to manage the progression of dementia. Jo's mum talks to her about how Wilbur is feeling much better and it won't be long now before he can come back to the flat and the shop.

Her dad rarely talks to Jo on the phone, leaving all that to his much more talkative spouse.

But when he is the one who answers her call, he says quietly to Jo, 'Just give her time.'

So this is what she is trying to do.

Jo turns her attention to the sole customer in the shop. It is late morning, and the woman has been lingering by the reels of parcel tape and rolls of brown paper. Jo is about to ask if she can help when another customer walks in.

The first customer is extremely tall, the second one short and rounded. As they browse, the smaller women obscures the taller woman, giving the illusion of double-decker heads. Jo's mouth edges towards a smile.

The taller woman moves away and the tableau is broken. She approaches the counter.

A pause.

Jo looks expectant and, she hopes, keen to please.

The woman glances down and frowns.

'Of course, no one writes with a fountain pen these days.'

She says this with composed certainty. She is not trying to be rude or to imply that Jo is a simpleton for selling them. In fact, she does not seem to have made the connection: she, customer, one side of the small wood and glass-topped counter;

Jo, shop assistant, the other side, with a range of fountain pens on sale underneath this same glass-topped counter.

'The thing is, we don't write, do we?' The woman looks up, but doesn't wait for an answer. 'It's a lost art.'

Jo has been here before. She would like to say, *I do. I write with a fountain pen.* But she knows she would be wasting her breath.

The tall woman in front of her frowns uncertainly, as if Jo is somehow in the wrong place (which Jo thinks is not far from the truth), then she moves on to handwriting: 'They don't even teach them to write in schools.'

Jo wonders what this woman does for a living. She is thin and neat and precise. Pharmacist? Dentist, maybe?

'I mean, what's the point of all of this, really, when you think about emails and social media?'

Jo contemplates what this woman would think if she sat in her dentist's chair and said, *Well, of course, there must be something wrong with you, if you want to spend all your time rooting around in other people's mouths.* But it's not the sort of thing she would ever say. Well, certainly not to a woman with a drill in her hand.

Jo glances over the 'dentist's' shoulder to the small woman in an overlong raincoat who is now waiting patiently in line, and she gives her a tiny nod of acknowledgement. The woman lifts both eyebrows and rolls her eyes, and Jo is surprised into stifling a laugh.

The 'dentist' gestures a vague dismissal towards the back of the shop and repeats, 'I mean, what's the point?'

'Well, I think some—' Jo tries.

But this woman hasn't come to the shop to hear what Jo thinks.

'It's terrible how these things are changing,' the woman reflects, as if she really has no choice in the matter.

Jo's eyes stray to the customer waiting in line. The woman's expression is completely deadpan; a mild, open face; middle-aged; with mouse-coloured hair squashed under a rain hat. Then she winks at Jo.

The gesture is so fleeting, but it breathes warmth into her. And something else creeps into her mind: does she know this woman from somewhere?

'Do children even know how to hold a pen or pencil any more,' the 'dentist' continues. Again, not a question – a querulous reproach, as if somehow Jo is at fault.

Jo rallies – well, at least in her mind. She would like to ask this woman some questions. *Do you have children? Do they see you writing a letter? Writing a list, even?* But she knows there is simply no point in saying these things. Her eldest brother's family live in a house with barely a single book in it (unless you count agricultural catalogues and tractor manuals), and her sister-in-law's frequent complaint is that the twins never pick up a book. 'Can't get them to read at all. Well, they're just not interested in books, are they?'

Then, like now, Jo keeps quiet.

'Is there something I can get you?' Jo eventually enquires, politely. She glances again at the woman in the raincoat, trying to catch her eye, trying to tease out the memory of why she seems familiar. But now the woman is gazing out of the shop window to the alleyway beyond. She appears miles away from this tiny shop in North London. Distanced, in some way, from the wet October day.

Jo rather envies her.

'Just some Sellotape if you have it.'

Jo gets the woman what she needs, takes the payment and then wishes her a pleasant good morning. Even to herself, her voice sounds over-friendly.

The woman looks sharply at Jo, as if unsure if she is being sarcastic. In that look, Jo thinks the woman actually sees her for the first time. An unremarkable-looking woman, apart – she allows herself this – from her eyes. A woman on the brink of forty, wearing denim dungarees over a yellow jumper.

The 'dentist' turns quickly away. She runs her hand over a set of envelopes and writing pads on one of the shelves as she heads to the door. As she opens it, she says, carelessly, 'And of course, no one writes letters any more.'

Jo mouths silently after her, 'I do.'

It doesn't seem worth adding sound, either for the 'dentist's' benefit, or for her own. Of course, she is right. Writing could soon be a lost art. That is the reality. Jo may make lists, send cards, write letters to her mum and to her Uncle Wilbur; she may rejoice in that particular squeaky sound of a fountain-pen nib moving over paper; but she is not going to be able to stem the tide of change. She may take comfort from connecting with other stationery lovers via social media, but she is not a campaigner or a denier; she is not prepared to stand Canute-like, holding her hand up to the inevitable. And what would she be defending anyway? This is not even her shop.

Not even her life. The niggling thought wriggles in behind.

The rain-coated woman steps forward and hands over the exact money for the pack of envelopes she is holding.

'No one believes in God any more.'

Jo looks at her in confusion.

There is a pause, and the woman half-smiles at Jo, her eyes glinting.

'But I do,' she adds.

The three small words fill the space between them. And then, with another smile, as if they are sharing a joke, she turns and is out the door.

3

In black and white

Jo is left staring at the closed door. Why on earth had the woman said that? And *why* does she feel she has seen her before?

Jo's mind is a complete blank.

Her attention is caught by a figure walking past her window; a man, almost petite in his build; he is on his phone. One of her neighbours.

Her uncle's property is one of three identical shops positioned some twenty metres into the small alleyway. First comes her uncle's shop: the indecisive, ineffectual hardware-cum-stationery shop. Next door is an optician's run by a very efficient-looking Spaniard by the name of Lando Landaidas – the man who has just strolled past. Lando came in to introduce himself as a neighbour within a week of her starting in the shop. A neat man, in his late thirties, with short dark hair and a grey goatee, he bought a plug and a pencil sharpener, neither of which she suspected he needed. She would have liked to return the compliment, but she knows she doesn't need glasses and doesn't want to waste his time.

Next to the optician's is a tattoo artist, whom Jo just knows as Eric. And she only discovered this because she once heard someone call after him down the alleyway. Eric waves to her as he bounds past the store each morning (usually around 10.30 a.m.), grinning cheerfully. She finds it harder to guess at his age – is he even thirty? At the end of the summer, he wore black shorts and orange flip-flops, his legs a swirl of inked crescents and stars. Now the weather is colder, he is in jeans and short furry boots, but with arms still exposed, displaying an array of complex symbols in black ink. Eric has a short beard and messy ash-blond hair – hence Jo's nickname, Eric the Viking. When he had started to wear furry boots in the colder weather, she experienced a feeling of satisfaction that he was living up to his nickname. They have never spoken, but he always waves and he always smiles.

For three such close neighbours, it surprises Jo how little interaction there is between them. She wonders if it is because each is looking out onto a brick wall, and so the day-to-day lives of the shops carry on as if in isolation. She also suspects that Lando and Eric the Viking are an awful lot busier than she is. They probably have little time for socializing, judging by the number of people who walk past her window to reach their shops.

It also occurs to her that when you feel most in need of new friends, is often the time when you feel least capable of making them. She appreciates the irony of this, but the realization does little towards encouraging her to call on her neighbours. She thinks back to articles she has read in the past about how to kick-start your way to a new life/new friends/new interests. These still have the power to ignite her sense of inadequacy, even though she now recognizes their naivety.

Her reflections are interrupted by a bump against the shop window. A young woman has just steered the side of her pram into the low windowsill. The girl holds up a hand apologetically and calls through the window, 'Sorry!'

Jo heads outside, wanting to reassure the girl – the pram only lightly grazed the paintwork.

'Sorry!' the girl repeats, pulling the pram back to straighten the wheels so she doesn't veer into the shop again. 'I'm new at this,' she says laughing. 'They don't give you lessons when they sell you one of these!'

Jo looks into the pram at the baby. A tiny, sleeping bundle completely oblivious to the fact its mother is a poor driver. She wants to say something about how lovely the baby is, but it isn't really. It is small and squidgy and blotchy. Despite this, Jo feels what she recognizes as jealousy spreading through her veins. She catches the young mother's expression as she gazes at her infant and there is a knot tightening within Jo that takes her breath away.

The girl does not seem to register Jo's silence and continues, cheerfully, 'You know the last time I pushed a pram, it had a doll in it and I would have been about six.' Looking past Jo into the shop's interior, she exclaims, 'Oh, you sell stationery. Do you have invitation cards for christenings? Although Guy thinks we should go for a naming ceremony rather than the church stuff. I guess he's right. It was bad enough with the wedding. His family are Catholics and my mum's not bothered. I don't think his mum and dad really care, but I'd say his granny will kick off. She certainly did when we got married . . .'

Two things come to Jo at exactly the same moment – a double distraction from the knot of pain. This women sounds like friends she has known with new babies, who have been stuck on their own for too long with no one to talk to. Secondly, and more importantly, she now knows exactly who it was who was in the shop talking about God.

'Sorry,' Jo explains, apologetically, 'we don't sell that sort of stationery.'

She is tempted to say the next statement out loud, but stops herself.

You will never guess who I just sold some envelopes to.

The girl smiles and nods, then heads off on her erratic course down the alleyway and Jo returns to the shop.

She is sure she is right.

The comment about God.

A black-and-white photograph. But wearing a very different outfit from the long raincoat. A clerical outfit. Jo is now sure of it. It had come with the mention of christenings and weddings.

She has just sold some envelopes to the 'Runaway Vicar'.

Jo immediately reaches in her bag for her phone to start Googling.

The 'Runaway Vicar' sobriquet had been the inspiration of a journalist who was reporting on the disappearance of a country vicar. Jo remembers first seeing the story deep in the inner pages of the paper she was skim-reading as she sat in the café on the corner.

The vicar had left her vicarage in the manner of the *Mary Celeste*; chair pushed back, meal half eaten. A churchwarden had raised the alarm. No sign of forced entry, back door left ajar. Car still in the drive. The parishioners were 'flummoxed'. Jo wondered at the time if anyone actually said this any more, or, indeed, ever had. She remembers that the vicar was described as someone that, 'No one had a bad word to say about.' Which, Jo reflected, told her very little about the woman. The same woman, who she is now certain has just been in her shop.

Thinking back to the first article, she doubts if she would have remembered all this if the headline of 'Runaway Vicar' hadn't appeared the following day on her news app. But, even then, it was the merest ripple in a tsunami of other news. Would she even have spotted it, if she hadn't felt the conspiratorial empathy of a fellow runaway? She now wonders whether – if she had said something to the bad pram driver – she would have any idea of who Jo was talking about.

The question now is: should Jo do anything? Tell somebody? Does anyone know that the vicar is safe?

Jo stares out of the window to the brickwork opposite. Really, is it any of her business? The Runaway Vicar was here in the solid flesh, buying a pack of envelopes; she was not teetering perilously close to the parapet of a bridge.

Jo turns back to her phone and follows more links. The Runaway Vicar (who she now knows is called Ruth Hamilton) has not been in touch with her extended family . . . they seem to be in Glasgow. A longer article from a Warwickshire paper gives more background on Ruth, a 57-year-old vicar (divorced); her parish covered a large village and several hamlets near the town of Rugby. The article includes a couple of photographs of Ruth: one by the cake stand at a village fete; one of Ruth outside a church, with a crowd of children and animals gathered around her. In the pictures, she is smiling.

Jo enlarges the images on the screen. It is definitely the woman who was in the shop. She wonders how long ago the photos were taken. The woman buying envelopes looked older, more careworn. Or is she imagining that, now she knows she's the Runaway Vicar? Jo scans the screen once more for a clue as to why this woman walked out on what looks like an idyllic parish. The woman has a nice face; broad-browed and open. She is the sort of vicar Jo would have liked to marry her and James.

And there it is. The barb that catches her. Just when she has been experiencing the peace of not thinking about him for an hour or so. And once the hook is in, she knows that conscious thought will not dislodge it, only dig it in deeper.

With a supreme effort, Jo tries to focus back on the Runaway Vicar. She studies her face once more, looking for some clue. She wonders if she will ever see that face again. And if she does, whether she will say anything to the Reverend Ruth Hamilton.

4

A man called Malcolm

An hour later, thoughts still drifting occasionally to the Runaway Vicar, Jo starts on her daily stocktake. Like studying her measured portion of sky, this mundane ritual gives her comfort. It has become an important, if unnecessary, part of her day.

Business is slow – some days she only has a dozen customers in the shop – so there really is no need to check the stock so regularly. Anyway, she could always calculate the stock from the computerized till that her Uncle Wilbur had invested in. She suspects that by this nod at modernity, he somehow hoped to revolutionize his sales. That didn't happen. What did happen was the opening of a massive DIY store, less than a mile away. For over fifty years, her uncle's business has been based on a combination of hardware and stationery. Since the opening of the superstore, the stationery – mainly functional items that appealed to her uncle's practical mind – have come to occupy more and more of the shelf space.

Jo begins her stock-check by glancing briefly at the few remaining shelves of hardware. An embarrassed nod of acknowledgement, rather than a careful study of the desultory mixture of screws, picture hooks, nails, plastic washing-up bowls, brushes and extension leads. Each item is lined up neatly, but this regimentation cannot hide the truth; it is an undeniably motley collection.

She moves quickly on to the shelf of writing paper. Here, simple pads of white and pale blue paper are displayed with packets of matching envelopes. Old-fashioned stationery that would not have looked out of place when her uncle started the shop. Flicking through the nearest pad of paper, she pauses to run a finger over the line guide and to stroke the single sheet of blotting paper. The 'dentist's' words come back to her.

'No one ever writes with a fountain pen these days.'

'And of course, *no one* writes letters any more.'

Her finger hovers momentarily over a pile of envelopes, similar to those bought by the Runaway Vicar. Well, the vicar is clearly writing to someone . . .

Jo moves on from the writing pads to the notebooks, pushing these thoughts away as she focuses on the simple pleasure of bound pages of pristine paper. Here there are large notebooks covered in brown kraft paper; smaller black ring-bound books; exercise books in a range of primary colours; and her favourites, the receipt books with their virgin navy carbon sheets. Next come the ink-pads and stamps.

A sudden memory produces a genuine smile. Her best Christmas present ever – and this includes the diamond earrings that James gave her on their last Christmas together – was a small handheld stamp from her Uncle Wilbur when she was ten years old. On it were the words, 'Paid' and 'Due', along with numbers for the date that could be rotated into place. Once the numbers were adjusted, it would be pressed with satisfaction into the accompanying pad of red ink. Next came the exquisite 'thunk', as she brought the stamp down hard on the top page of one of her receipt books.

Jo is loitering by the pencils, rolling the shaft of a 2B pencil between her thumb and forefinger, as if it were a fine cigar, when the shop door opens.

'Malcolm!' She turns with pleasure towards the approaching figure.

Malcolm was the first customer Jo ever served when she started work in her uncle's shop. He introduced himself slowly and politely. He was pleased to meet her; his name was Malcolm Buswell and he lived a few minutes' walk away. Their interaction is fairly limited, but she often finds herself looking out for his tall, rangy figure from her vantage point in the window. It makes her smile to see his long legs striding down the alleyway, arms swinging. When she first met Malcolm she was reminded of Roald Dahl's character, the Big Friendly Giant. Malcolm may not have the large protruding ears, but he has the hooked nose and the same benevolent expression.

'Ah, good afternoon,' Malcolm says, as he turns to study the display of notebooks, as Jo expected he would. Malcolm buys a new one most weeks. He is writing a book. As yet he hasn't said what his book is going to be about, and he is clearly reluctant to discuss it with Jo. She has tried polite enquiries and has also drawn Malcolm into conversation about the books they are both reading, but his answers are always vague and noncommittal, and she hasn't liked to press him.

Jo has gradually discovered that Malcolm has lived near the heath since he was a young man and that he is a retired tax analyst. (This didn't surprise her; Malcolm is always formally dressed in grey, even his most casual clothes looking remarkably like a suit.) He was a specialist in wills and legacies. He has an interest in local history. And literature. Since his mother died, he has continued to live in the small house they shared together. Each piece of information is offered to her with polite formality, usually once the transaction of purchasing his latest notebook has been completed.

Jo has found herself selecting pieces of information to reciprocate with. It seems only polite, and Malcolm is always polite, holding the door open for other customers and bowing them in or out with a slight incline of his long, narrow head. Jo has told him that her family have always been farmers, her mother's family in the Lake District, her father's family in North Yorkshire. She has explained she went to university in Bath, but returned to work in the North after a few years of travel. She worked in Newcastle but lived in a village in Northumberland. She was employed by a national bank, working at their headquarters, until she left nine months ago.

She does not offer Malcolm an explanation as to why she left. Nor does she intend to. Sometimes the words she might say fill her mind, but they never find their way out into the space that sits between them.

25

You see, I wasn't good enough, Malcolm.

In the end, whatever I did, and I did try (probably too much), I wasn't what he wanted.

So that was it, he left me, and is now with a younger, much more beautiful woman.

Nickeeey.

I'm sure his friends don't blame him.

And my friends? Well, my friends were never really his friends. It turns out that Lucy, my best friend, hated him.

I guess I didn't really realize to start with. She and her husband, Sanjeev, had moved away for a few years with his job, but when they came back, oh, I could see it then.

I tried hard to keep everyone happy . . . I really did . . .

And so it would go on.

Today, before the internal monologue can start, she fills the void with a question.

'Malcolm, can I help in any way?'

'I'm sorry, Joanne? You said something?'

Malcolm always uses her full name.

'Can I help?' Jo repeats.

'No, it is a simple process. A new week. A new notebook.'

Maybe Malcolm is writing a diary, not a book? His reticence makes it impossible for her to ask.

'Ah, this will do. A5, blue, ring-bound. Perfectly adequate.' He brings the notebook to the counter and presents his debit card.

Jo suddenly remembers something she has been meaning to say to Malcolm.

'Malcolm, I know you often ask how Uncle Wilbur is doing,

but I wanted to ask, were you a friend of his?' She thinks that Wilbur, at eighty, is probably older than Malcolm, but not by much.

'I wouldn't say a friend, Joanne, but we did sometimes sit here and have a cup of tea together.'

Jo is aware she has never thought to offer Malcolm a drink, let alone a seat.

'What did you talk about?' she asks.

'Oh, the area. How it has changed. And Wilbur was very keen on chess; we chatted a bit about that and the chess club he was in.'

'Are you a member too?'

'No, no. Not really for me, clubs and societies.'

Jo wants to ask why not, but Malcolm's next words forestall her.

'I can't think why not, really. Just something I never did.' He continues, 'Your uncle is a good man, Joanne. You must remember me to him.' He adds, rather wistfully, 'But no, I wouldn't say we were friends.'

Before he gets to the door, he turns back to Jo. 'I think I would have liked to have been his friend.' He pauses, and continues more slowly, a puzzled note creeping into his voice, 'There were times, you know, when he was the only person I spoke to for many weeks.'

They look directly at each other and something passes between them.

Jo knows that Malcolm doesn't want her sympathy. Any more than she wants his. But she knows she wants to give this gentle man something.

'Oh, I would say Uncle Wilbur thought of you as a friend,' she offers.

Malcolm accepts the words with a slow nod.

As he turns away, Jo notices that his expression is more hopeful, even if his brow is still furrowed.

5

A Viking called Eric

It is a week since the Runaway Vicar was in the shop. There has been no further sign of her (Jo has been on the lookout), but now she has a new, unexpected visitor.

'I need one of those folder things. You know, black . . . portfolio, I guess . . . but not huge . . . A4 . . . clear plastic sheets.' Eric the Viking is waving his arms in the air.

When Jo doesn't answer, he starts to use his hands to draw out a large rectangle in front of him, as if he and Jo are playing charades. She knows exactly what he is looking for and she has them in stock, but she still says nothing. She just can't get her head around the fact that Eric the Viking is from Birmingham.

He has the furry boots on, the tattoos on his arms that look like ancient Nordic symbols; his hair is so blond it is nearly white. He has the beard, the blue eyes.

But his accent is nasal and clearly from somewhere in the Midlands.

She wants to say, *But I thought you were a Viking*. Instead she says, 'I know exactly what you mean,' and she comes out from behind the counter. She squeezes past him so she can go and fetch him one. He is even built like a Viking.

'Here you go,' she says, returning with an A4 file and laying it on the counter. 'Is that for your designs?'

He looks a bit confused, as he flicks through the plastic sheets.

'You know, so people can choose the design they want?' she repeats.

'I'm sorry?' he says, looking up, but before she can answer, he adds, 'This is perfect, except, you don't have any in brighter colours, do you?'

'Sorry, we only have them in black.'

'Never mind. I guess I could always put stickers on the front. I don't suppose you sell those?' he enquires, looking vaguely towards the rest of the shop.

'What kind of stickers?' Jo has no idea why she is even asking. All they have are a few packets of sticky dots and white address labels.

'The sort of thing children would like. I want this to be something children can look through.'

'But you can't tattoo children!' The words are out of her, and because there is no going back, she adds, lamely, 'It's against the law.' All the time thinking, of course, Eric the Viking would know you have to be eighteen to get a tattoo.

Eric the Viking starts to laugh, and she decides it suits him. His laugh is deep and rich and rolling.

'What do you think I do for a living?'

'Aren't you Eric the Viking, the tattoo artist?'

He issues a huge bark of a laugh. She imagines it is what a walrus might sound like if it were to meet someone as stupid as her. Why on earth had she said her nickname for him out loud? He leans across the counter and grabs her hand, shaking it, while all the time grinning delightedly at her. 'Why haven't I been in here sooner? This is perfect. Tell me, what's your name, Stationery Girl?' He lets go of her hand and steps back to study her.

She can feel her hackles rise. 'I'm Jo Sorsby,' she says with as much dignity as she can muster. 'This is my uncle's shop. I'm just looking after things while he . . .' She has no desire to share her uncle's troubles with Eric.

'Ah, yes,' he says, suddenly looking more serious. 'I'm sorry. I've been keeping up with how Wilbur's doing through one of his friends from the Legion.' An image comes into Jo's head of an old soldier with an arm of tattoos.

Eric is now back to standing and smiling at her. It is as if she once told him the best joke and he is remembering it fondly. She isn't even sure what he found so funny in the first place. Her inner voice answers for her: *You called him a Viking, you idiot.*

'You know I should have come and said hello sooner.' He makes it sound like he is talking to himself. Telling himself off. 'No excuses.' He then leans across and grabs her hand again for a brief but exceedingly firm shake.

'Eric Sv . . .'

She does not catch even a fraction of his surname; it seemed to start with an 'S', there is a 'V' in there somewhere, and a 'J'.

'. . . very pleased to meet you, Jo Sorsby,' he finishes.

'How do you spell that?' she asks, faintly.

'That's not going to help you at all,' he laughs. 'It's Icelandic, although I was brought up in—'

'Birmingham?' she offers.

'No, Brighton.'

'I see . . .' she says, not seeing at all.

He shakes his head, laughing once more, 'Oh, that was far too easy. You're right; I grew up in Birmingham. Was there until I was eighteen. But you're also right – and God, would my dad love to meet you – we are descended, way back, from the Vikings. My dad's favourite subject when he's had a few.'

'I thought Vikings came from Scandinavia.'

'Ah, and you were doing so well with my dad up to that point, Jo.' He hangs his shaggy blond head in mock sorrow.

She is still struggling to equate the Birmingham accent with this solid, tattooed bulk in front of her.

'Mum and I try and tell him that Iceland was settled by the Vikings, but he won't have it. He insists they started there.' He shakes his head again. 'And now I'd better go. I've got someone due in for an appointment. What do I owe you for this?' he asks, patting the black portfolio.

She tells him, and he pays, shoving the receipt she gives him deep into the back pocket of his jeans. As he lifts the folder up, he glances down into the glass-topped cabinet and spots the fountain pens. 'Ah fountain pens! You want to get those out, Jo. They're no good to you in there. Fountain pens like to be used. Every day. Or they get lonely, they feel like no one loves them . . .' He pauses for a long moment, and she experiences a churning mix of embarrassment that he has guessed that she is equally unloved, and a stir of something else disquieting that she can't quite identify.

She thinks he is going to say something else, ask her something, but instead he puts his hand into the pocket of his black short-sleeved shirt, and pulls out a fountain pen. It is the colour of pewter, has a short broad body and a shiny silver clip. She looks up at him – taken aback. Then, she thinks, why should she be surprised? After all, Eric the Viking (she's decided he has earned his nickname) works with ink himself.

She is about to say something, but Eric is not looking at her; he is scribbling something on a small pad of paper he has also pulled out of his shirt pocket. Eventually he looks up and smiles. 'Lando's your ink man. And very good he is too,' he says, glancing down at the script on his forearm.

'So you're—'

He tears the top page from the pad of paper and hands it to her.

'Eric the Optician.' He heads for the door but, as he opens it, he grins back at her. 'But *you* can definitely call me Eric the Viking.'

She looks down at the piece of paper in her hand. On it is an ink drawing of a Viking wearing ridiculously large glasses. She laughs, and looks towards the window.

But Eric the Optician has gone.

She is still smiling as she pins the picture to the noticeboard next to the lone calendar. Jo is aware that her face feels strange, slightly stretched and achy. And she wonders exactly when it was that she last laughed.

6

Mr James Beckford & Ms Jo Sorsby

The previous evening, buoyed up by the memory of the laughter, Jo texted Lucy. Nothing significant, just the story of Eric the Viking. Lucy immediately responded with a row of laughing emojis. It felt natural, more like their old selves.

But this morning, Jo doesn't feel much like laughing. The postman has just been.

It is an official letter, nothing more. An oversight. An old water bill that needs paying. Inside, James has scribbled what she owes. No further message.

Yet the familiarity of his handwriting unravels something in her. She tries to fight the feeling, to gather herself. As she pins the letter on the noticeboard – she will deal with it later – she notices a blotch by the postmark on the envelope and realizes her face is wet.

That is the trouble with tears: they catch you unawares.

* * *

Jo might not have left her job in the bank if she hadn't cried.

She cried in the stationery cupboard at work, sitting huddled on the floor, tears forming welts in the letter-headed paper that no one used any more. Maybe there was a certain ironic symmetry in her now running a stationery shop in London. A shop hardly bigger than that cupboard.

The crying didn't start in the stationery cupboard. She might have got away with that. It started in the conference room. It was April and her mother had just called to tell her that she was worried about Uncle Wilbur. He had locked himself out of the shop and he seemed to think his keys were in the Lake District – which made no sense at all. Jo had been distracted, but it was a meeting she had to attend, and really, it shouldn't have been too difficult; she was only there to field questions about the bank's database – her area of expertise. Others had to deliver the bulk of the presentation.

One of the people who spoke was her boyfriend of six years, James. As he took the room full of people through the year's forecast, she sat with one arm resting along the table, the other propped up, her thumb and forefinger gently fingering the diamond earring in her right ear. James had given her the earrings for Christmas and she wore them most days. She remembers thinking he looked good: tall and athletic; nice white shirt, charcoal-grey jacket. James was a confident speaker. And he had every right to be; he was good at his job. He held the attention of everyone in the room, not because he was loud or amusing, but because he was reasonable. Everyone liked James. She loved him.

But did he love her?

She had no idea where the thought came from. She pressed her thumb more firmly into the prong at the back of her earring, as if pushing home the point: yes, of course he did.

But all that did was to take her back to Christmas Eve and she relived her blushing, crushing disappointment when she had opened the small leather box to find not an engagement ring but a pair of tiny diamond earrings. At the time she had not been able to look at James, but had lowered her head, audibly whispering, 'Oh, they are *so* beautiful,' while her mind had shouted, *How could you do this to me? How could you? In front of my family!* It was another hour before she had been able to look at her mother, and even then Jo refused to meet her eye.

In the conference room, she pressed harder on the back of the earring, until pain and emotion were focused into a tiny spot on her right thumb. *James does love me and one day we will get married.* She had been planning it for several years. Not in a Pinterest, mood-board kind of way; but images would flash into her mind now and again: the flowers she might carry; where they would get married; where they might go on honeymoon. And so it had gone on, until she had collected a series of mental images, like Polaroid snaps, of their future life.

She sat in the conference room wondering what her colleagues would think if she asked them to clear the coffee cups and bottles of sparkling water, if she laid her imaginary photos on the conference-room table. Would they have nodded reassuringly and said, *Yes Jo, of course. We always knew you two would marry?*

At this point she recalls she looked at James – now barely hearing his voice – and she knew that, above all things, there was one thing she wanted to say to him.

That is when he caught her eye; his voice faltered for an infinitesimal moment, and in that fraction of time, she knew. *He is never going to ask me. He doesn't love me any more.* And as she had started to cry, she knew she would never tell him that one thing:

I really want to have a baby, James.

She was not aware of the unnatural silence in the room until someone touched her arm, forcing her to stand. Then she was conscious of this person putting her body between Jo and her colleagues who were now frozen, as if in suspended animation. She remembers thinking, *I didn't expect this from Jemima.* Jemima, who could be scathing in her dismissal of others; Jemima who, going by the photos in her office, seemed to like dogs more than people.

She left Jemima at the conference-room door, walked straight to the stationery cupboard and shut the door.

'Joanne? . . . Joanne?'

It is some moments before Jo realizes that Malcolm is at the counter. She has her back to the shop and has been staring at the letter pinned to the noticeboard.

'Sorry, Malcolm,' she says, turning to face him.

'Joanne . . .' Now Malcolm sounds concerned, and a little shocked.

She didn't realize that her face would give her away so completely.

'Not bad news, I hope? Your Uncle Wilbur is all right?'

Not really, Malcolm; often he can't remember what he did five minutes ago. Jo doesn't say this; instead she tells him that Wilbur is fine and offers Malcolm a cup of tea.

The old man's face falls. 'That would have been very pleasant, Joanne, but I do have an appointment at the bank . . . about my pension and so forth,' he finishes, still looking worried.

'Another time,' Jo suggests, summoning a smile.

Malcolm glances at the noticeboard. 'Is there anything I can do to help? *Anything* at all?'

She wants to say: *Please could you make James love me and make him realize he has made a huge mistake.*

She says this in her head often enough and at times out loud in the quiet of the flat. Sometimes she even believes it could happen.

She wants Malcolm to explain to her why, after nearly six months apart, it still hurts so much. She tells herself it is a lot to do with pride, but this does not quite equate to the visceral pain that squeezes the breath out of her, when she is curled up in a tight ball in bed at night.

Jo is suddenly conscious she hasn't actually said anything, and she feels she owes Malcolm something for his concern. She volunteers, 'It's a letter, well, a bill from my old boyfriend. We lived together for four years and broke up before I came down to London. It just brought it all back.'

Malcolm nods, as if this is making sense of things.

'We were going out for two years before we moved in together.' Jo wonders why she feels the need to mention this. To underline it *was* a serious relationship? That it *did* matter?

'It's been hard, I guess, on both of us,' although she wonders if this is true. She adds, somewhat irrelevantly, but feeling she doesn't want Malcolm to think badly of James, 'Everyone likes James.'

Ah, except Lucy. And – it comes to her – *and* Jemima. Jemima, who rescued her in that meeting. No, Jo would bet a sizeable amount on the fact that Jemima had never liked James. Had never fallen for his charms.

Her ruminations are interrupted.

'Indeed, indeed,' Malcolm continues to nod, 'and that is why you came to London?'

'Yes,' Jo admits, 'I heard that he'd started seeing someone else. A girl who I used to work with.' She tries to smile, 'So, I ran away.'

'No, no,' Malcolm exclaims, and Jo wonders if the repetitions are there as a double dose of reassurance. 'Not at all, not at all – you came to the aid of a favourite uncle. I am sure your family and friends do not think you have run away. I am sure they all miss you very much.'

'Oh, Malcolm,' is all Jo can muster.

Where does she even start?

7

Average Jo

Later that evening, sitting by the gas fire in her uncle's chair (deep-seated and remarkably comfortable), Jo revisits her conversation with Malcolm. She knows her family misses her (well, maybe not her brothers, but her parents certainly do); however, when she thinks of her friends, she feels uncomfortable to the point of queasiness.

It had happened slowly. She barely noticed it. They always seemed to end up doing what James wanted to do. Went where he wanted to go. But then he did have good ideas. A man so reasonable, it seemed petty to create an argument just because she fancied doing something else. And there were other people to think about. James had a circle of friends who often joined them. For once in her life she felt she was part of the 'popular crowd', even if she was only there on sufferance as James's girlfriend. That had been novel and mostly good. Plus she had been lonely when they met. Lucy and Sanjeev had just moved to Amsterdam with his work – a posting of two years that eventually stretched into four. She had been happy to throw herself into her life with James.

She knows with a wave of guilt that, in doing so, she let some older friendships drift. She got swept up in being with this new crowd. The bank paid well. James kept telling her that they worked hard, so should play hard. It was one of his favourite sayings. So they went away for weekends, went skiing, out for expensive meals with the 'friends' that she no longer sees or hears from.

She doesn't miss these people – even back then she could see that some of it was a bit much – but James was always different when it was just the two of them. Especially after his dad died from a heart attack and he was broken by his sudden loss. She held him together, had been the one in charge. Looked after his mum, too.

During all of this, Jo had tried to keep faith with Lucy, to visit, to call, to make time for her, especially in the last two years when she was back in the UK and living nearby. Whatever James said. She had, hadn't she? Tried so hard to get their friendship back on the old footing? Never reminded Lucy that she was the one who had left.

Then why does the thought of her friendship with Lucy only add to her queasiness?

Her phone starts to vibrate and Jo grabs it with something like relief. It's her mum. Jo holds it to her ear and is talking for a moment before she realizes her mum has video-called her – this is not her usual style.

As Jo looks down into the screen, she can see the top half of her mum's head, wavy dark hair threaded with grey; the rest of the screen is ceiling. It doesn't seem to be the farmhouse: there are ornate scrolls on the cornicing and she spots a green 'Exit' sign above what looks like a door.

'Hi, Mum, where are you?'

'Jo, I think I've got this. Elaine, one of the carers, showed me how to switch to video on WhatsApp. Can you see me?'

'Yes,' Jo laughs, 'well, half of you.'

'Oh, there you are. Ah, it is a treat to see your face. You look tired – are you okay? It's not all too much for you?'

Jo feels a twinge of guilt. She calls her mum every now and then, but she hasn't been home for a weekend since she got here. 'I'm good, Mum.'

'I'm here with Wilbur.' Her mother's head dips even further off the screen. 'I've got her, Wilbur. I'll show you.' And with this the screen blurs and Jo is suddenly looking at her Uncle Wilbur. He is sitting in a winged chair uphol-stered in burgundy fabric. He is wearing sandy-coloured trousers and a blue jumper, but the clothes look loose on him, like they are a size too big. Jo's heart aches; her uncle has never been tall, but he was always a solidly built man. This man looks as if he is fading away. He is not looking at the screen, but at a point somewhere in the distance – maybe at her mother?

She can hear her mother's voice. 'Can you see him, Jo?' She then says more quietly, 'They said it might be nice for him to see faces from the past,' then more loudly, 'Wilbur, it's Jo.'

'Jo?' His voice sounds hesitant but as he repeats her name it gains more certainty. 'Our Jo?'

Jo breaths out. It is still her uncle.

'Give me that phone, woman – you have no idea what you're doing,' and with this Uncle Wilbur grabs the phone and Jo laughs. Oh, that's her uncle all right. Now she is looking full at her uncle's face. 'Hello Jo, where are you? Still with that bollox James?' Jo gasps. 'He's a right fart, Jo. How's uni going? Where is it again?'

'Bath,' Jo says faintly, at the same time wondering – *you too?* Was she the only one who liked James?

Jo can hear her mother's voice in the background. 'Wilbur, you know Jo left university years ago. She's in London looking after your shop for you. You know she is.'

Jo wonders who her mother is trying to convince.

'You're in the shop? What, playing post offices?' Her uncle's face is grinning at her.

'Certainly am, Uncle Wilbur,' Jo tells him.

'You having fun, lass? Keeping out of trouble?'

'Good as gold,' she assures him, then on the spur of the moment asks, 'Uncle Wilbur, do you remember Malcolm, from the shop? Tall man, buys notebooks.'

'Malcolm . . . ?' Her uncle sounds uncertain, and Jo can't help feeling disappointed. 'Should I?' he asks her, and doubt has threaded its way into his voice. Jo can see that he is starting to look worried, so she changes the subject. 'I met a runaway vicar in the shop the other day,' she tells him.

'Did you now?' Uncle Wilbur perks up. 'What was he running away from?'

'It was a she, and I don't know.'

'A she? You don't say. Well, you know the answer to that one, don't you?'

'No?'

'A place for everything, and everything in its place. This runaway vicar of yours just needs to find her place.' Wilbur then repeats, 'A female vicar, you say?'

Jo can see her mother's hand trying to take the phone, but Wilbur is having none of it. He pulls away and swivels the phone around, showing Jo the rest of the room. 'Quite fancy here, lass, look at this. It's a hotel they've got me in. No sea, though. Bit disappointing that.'

Jo can see a bed-sitting room, chintzy and comfortable-looking. It could almost be a hotel, apart from the number of sturdy-looking horizontal bars screwed to the walls, presumably to stop Uncle Wilbur from falling again.

Jo smiles, 'It looks really nice, Uncle Wilbur. And with all those bars you could do ballet.'

Uncle Wilbur's face suddenly appears on the screen. 'Don't be ridiculous! I can't do ballet,' he barks.

Jo can hear her mother making soothing noises as she takes the phone. But before she loses sight of her uncle's face, she sees it crumple into confusion.

'Can I?' he asks her.

Jo's mum laughs as if Wilbur has told a good joke. But Jo knows that her uncle is completely serious.

After Jo hangs up, she sits for some moments thinking about Wilbur and her mum. Her uncle's quick descent into confusion makes her feel like crying. It is the threat of tears that reminds her: she wouldn't be here in London now if her mother hadn't cried. Again, tears had a lot to answer for.

It was nearly four months after she had broken up with James. She had opted for voluntary redundancy and he had moved out of the cottage they were renting. James divided the money they had been saving up as a deposit for a house. She got a little less than half. He explained this was due to the extra contribution he had made at the beginning. It was only later she remembered she had matched this when her bonus came in. She had tried to raise this, but James talked of timings and interest rates, which ended up sounding reasonable. And James was always reasonable.

Throughout all this, Jo visited her mum weekly, finding respite in her large, undemanding presence. Her mother was an uncomplicated woman; she loved her daughter and wanted her to be happy. She didn't have much idea of what Jo did for a living, nor did she enquire into the intimate details of her relationships. Jo was grateful, and in her mother's simple platitudes she found comfort and relief.

Her parents still lived in the farmhouse near Northallerton, which had been in her father's family for generations. Each year, more and more of the management of the farm was being passed on to her eldest brother, Chris, who lived with his family in one of the larger farm cottages. She imagined that one day Chris and her parents would swap houses. She liked Chris, in a vague kind of way, but she wasn't sure how she would feel about this.

Her younger brother Ben ran the local livestock market, but still maintained an active interest in the farm, much to his elder brother's annoyance. Chris and Ben could not have been more different: Chris, as solid as a hay bale, was round and squat; Ben was lean and tall, like an elongated scarecrow. Jo's mum often shook her head over the boys (who did not have the easiest of relationships). They in turn barely noticed Jo, so focused were they on their brotherly rivalry. If they did spot that she was around, they both teased her, calling her 'Average Jo': neither tall like Ben, nor solid like Chris and, in their opinions, never really amounting to much. Her mother would then pull her daughter to her in a huge hug, laughing, 'Thank goodness for my Average Jo.'

And she was average: neither tall nor short, neither fat nor thin; her hair somewhere between blonde and brown. She did pretty well at school, never winning any prizes but never the bottom of the class. At university she achieved a 2:2 degree in Human Geography. She had never been in trouble with the police or contemplated doing anything that was extraordinarily adventurous. She left university, travelled for a brief while to safe places around the world, then found a position in a bank where she worked with databases. She had expected to marry her long-term boyfriend and have an average number of children.

Now, she realized that she envied those women who had more of a plan, who had taken control of their lives – or, she had to admit it, Lucy, who had no plan, but who ambled through life dressed in the clothes of the past, living entirely in the moment.

Jo was considering this – and wondering whether to ring Lucy about something she had just seen on Instagram – when she arrived at her parents' house for her weekly visit and found her mother sitting on the floor between the wall and the kitchen table, crying. The family dog was on the floor beside her, his nose wedged into the crook of her arm.

She dropped to her knees and hauled her mother to her feet, steering her to a chair by the Aga. She instinctively reached for the kettle, with an anxious, 'Mum, what's wrong?'

Jo had only ever seen her mum cry twice before in her life. Once at her grandmother's funeral, and once when she had fallen while helping to move a sheep pen and had broken her ankle. On that occasion her dad (as short as Chris and as thin as Ben) had run full pelt across the field, before lifting his wife into his arms (and her mother was not a small woman – it is where her sons had got their height and bulk from). He had carried her to the farmhouse as if she were a mere featherweight. Jo still thinks it is one of the most romantic things she has ever seen.

But when her mother was quietly crying in the kitchen chair, this image was very far from her mind. She was thinking of cancer (her mum or her dad?) and of whether Uncle Wilbur had died.

It turned out that her Uncle Wilbur was the source of the tears.

He couldn't manage that shop.

He'd had a nasty fall.

He needed proper care until he could get back on his feet.

And now, look at her, tripping over the dog.

Bloody dog.

No, she didn't mean that, Winston.

She was that worried.

Wilbur wouldn't come and stay with them (was there ever a more stubborn fool), but she thought they could get him into a good care home nearby. He might be persuaded to come North for a bit, but what to do with the shop and the flat? He was fussing about leaving them empty.

Would there be any chance . . .

Jo immediately said, 'Yes.'

There was no other answer to the woman who loved her so well and asked so little.

Afterwards, Jo thinks she would always have said 'yes' to her mum, but maybe the fact she had just seen James and Nickeeey on Instagram made the decision easier. At least in London there was no chance of bumping into this new, brightly smiling couple.

8

Dear Giana

The Viking is back. This time he is not drawing rectangles in the air; instead he is snapping his fingers and thumbs together like two hungry mouths.

'You know, big thing, like . . . holds things together. Clippy thing . . .'

Jo knows exactly what he wants and has a selection of bulldog clips, but this is too much fun. She frowns. 'No . . . not really with you . . .'

The 'mouths' are now frantically chomping.

'Clippy. Not a paper clip.' Eric the Viking looks frantically around him like he might find them on the walls or in the air.

Jo looks vaguely around as if she might find them there too.

'Bigger than normal clips. Metal.' The mouths are now going like castanets.

Jo takes pity on him and pulls out a sheaf of papers she has under the counter, held together with a bright yellow bulldog clip. 'Like this?' she asks, simply.

Eric the Viking eyes her suspiciously. 'Yeah,' he says. '*Exactly* like that.'

'Just the one?' she asks, innocently.

Eric is still eyeing her. 'Just the one,' he says, slowly.

Jo hands the clip to him. 'That's on the house.' She laughs. 'You earned it.'

'Hmmm,' Eric the Viking says, grinning as he takes it from her, before turning to leave.

Jo returns to sweeping the floor, which is what she had been doing before Eric came in. That, and worrying about Uncle Wilbur (it had been so good to see him yesterday), and also trying to marshal her thoughts about James.

The doorbell sounds its tinny welcome and, looking up, Jo sees a figure disappearing down the first aisle. She recognizes that raincoat. There is no doubt about it, the Runaway Vicar is back. It has been two weeks since she was last in the shop buying envelopes and talking about God. Jo has kept an eye out for her, but until today she has seen nothing of her. Malcolm has been in a few times, and it suddenly occurs to her that he is coming in more often than normal. Is he keeping an eye on her since their conversations about friendship and James?

She surreptitiously studies the Reverend Ruth Hamilton's profile, now part-hidden by a display of padded envelopes. It strikes her that the vicar has done something strange with her hair. It is set in a longish, auburn bob that stands out from her head. Startled, Jo realizes that the vicar is wearing a wig.

She is about to ask if she can help when the shop door opens and a woman who looks to be in her early thirties, wearing a bright yellow coat, breezes in.

'Lovely day,' the woman says cheerfully, nodding sideways at Jo's sliver of sky, which today is the brightest of blues. 'I love the autumn,' she adds.

Jo gazes skyward for a few seconds, and then returns to the front counter. 'Yes, it's my favourite season,' Jo tells the young woman, her mind suddenly filled with memories of pencil cases, crayons and new exercise books.

The girl at the door is now shaking her head to free some curls that appear to have got snagged in her scarf. Her long hair is the colour of caramel toffee. She steps closer to the counter.

'Oh, are those proper pens?' she asks, spotting the fountain pens.

Jo feels a mix of pleasure at her interest and anxiety in case the Runaway Vicar leaves without her being able to . . . well . . . she's not sure what.

'Whoa! I haven't written with one of those for years.'

'Would you like to try one?'

'Can I?'

The girl looks at her as if she is being offered a rare treat. She radiates an open friendliness that sweeps aside Jo's preoccupation with the Runaway Vicar. With a sense of shock, she fears that this keen warmth is going to puncture something in her. She hadn't realized until that moment just how lonely she was. With a jolt she thinks that she would like this woman, with the smiley, freckly face, to be her friend.

She misses Lucy with a sudden longing.

She busies herself, unnecessarily straightening the pad of paper on the counter so the girl can try a fountain pen. Since Eric the Viking had made his comment about fountain pens liking to be used, she has kept a selection of tester pens out for people to try.

'Take your pick,' she says to the woman, relieved that her voice sounds normal, and grateful that the moment has passed.

The caramel toffee curls lean closer. 'They all look very grown-up.' She tilts her head to one side. 'Maybe that one.' She selects a simple grey pen with a silver band around the centre of the barrel.

Jo thinks this girl is right: they are all very serious-looking pens. The sort of pens her uncle might choose. Perhaps there are other options – more colourful, more modern fountain pens she could sell? She wonders if they even exist. She is surprised that she doesn't already know. Jo often connects with other people online who love stationery, but fountain pens aren't even that popular amongst *them*. And James had always laughed at her 'stationery habit'. Conscious of the implication that hers was a childish pleasure, she had tried to put it aside when she was living with him.

'Why did I do that?'

'I'm sorry?' Caramel Toffee Girl asks, bewildered.

Jo hadn't realized she had muttered the words aloud. 'Sorry. No, nothing.'

'What shall I write?' the girl asks, doubtfully.

'Anything you like.'

As the girl stares into space, considering, Jo's eyes flick towards the back of the shop where the Runaway Vicar is still browsing.

The curly head leans over the counter, yellow spotty fingerless mittens abandoned by the rack of fountain pens. 'Oh, this takes me back,' she murmurs over the paper. When she stands up straight, Jo sees the words, *Dear Giana*, and then two lines written in a foreign language. The girl's writing has loops and rounded curls, rather like her hair.

'Are you Italian?' Jo asks, making a guess.

'No, but I used to have an Italian pen pal and we wrote to each other for years. I still have all her letters in a drawer under my bed.' She strokes the top of her finger over her pen pal's name.

'Oh, I've smudged it!' She sounds crushed, like a disappointed child.

Jo rushes to reassure her.

'Do you still write to her?' Jo asks.

'No,' she says, gazing down at the smudged name. 'We text sometimes.' She adds, softly, 'I used to love getting Giana's letters.'

'You should write to her again.' –

It is not Jo who says this. It is the short, bright-eyed woman in a wig who has stepped up to the young woman's side. Jo has the fleeting impression of a wren coming to settle by the counter.

The girl in the yellow coat glances at her, smiling. 'I suppose I could.'

'I think it's rather lovely when we tell our friends that they are dear to us,' the Runaway Vicar says, gently touching the paper just above the smudged words, *Dear Giana*. Jo notices her hand is delicate and fine-boned. 'That is the lovely thing about a letter. It is probably one of the few times we call our friends "dear".' She looks up at Jo. 'May I?' she asks, pointing at the fountain pen that is now lying on the counter. Jo notices for the first time that her accent is softly Scottish, as though it has been a long time since she lived there.

'Of course,' Jo says, and the Runaway Vicar gives her a slow, steady look. Her eyes are the colour of chocolate, flecked with gold – and Jo gets the impression the woman is trying to communicate something.

Now it is the auburn wig that is bent over the paper. The Runaway Vicar does not pause to consider what to write.

'Oh, that is lovely,' the younger woman says, reading it first. She turns the pad of paper around so Jo can see it.

The writing is even and regular. Only the S's twist and sweep, as if trying to escape the formality of the rest of the writing.

I have known the silence of the stars, and of the sea.
And the silence of the city when it pauses.

Jo doesn't say anything. Is she being told something? Stay silent? Say nothing?

Caramel Toffee Girl asks, 'Is that from a poem?'

'Yes, I forget who wrote it, but it seemed to fit. It feels like, here in this shop, the city pauses. Life pauses.'

Jo has no idea what to say; it is like this woman sees her here suspended in time. Caught in her limbo. 'Do you write with a fountain pen?' she asks, unable to think of anything else.

'I do. I used to sign documents that would need to last for hundreds of years. We used a special ink that would darken over time. I rather like that idea; the names, not fading with age, but growing stronger. Living on.'

'What, like legal documents?' Caramel Toffee Girl asks.

Registers of marriage, signed by a vicar, Jo thinks, not saying anything.

'Yes.' She turns towards the young woman beside her. 'You should buy that pen.' Then, looking self-conscious and less sure of herself, adds, 'I'm sorry – that sounded very bossy. I just think that Giana might like to receive a letter from you.'

'No, don't worry, you're right.' She picks up the pen, smiling. 'I came in for some Post-it notes. I had no idea I was going to buy a fountain pen.'

The Runaway Vicar waits patiently as Caramel Toffee Girl chooses between two pens and then selects some ink cartridges. Jo throws in the Post-it notes for free.

After she has called a cheery goodbye from the doorway, the shop falls silent. *The silence of a city when it pauses*, Jo thinks.

The Runaway Vicar does not look at Jo but lowers her head. She rummages in her bag for her purse to pay for the small notebook she has selected. Jo wonders if she should say something to her. But what?

In the end, the Runaway Vicar silently holds out her debit card towards the machine.

They look at each other for a long moment.

'Thank you,' Jo adds, '. . . Ruth.'

'Aah.' Ruth lets out a small sigh. Her hand moves briefly to her neck, where Jo presumes there once used to be a clerical collar. And then she smiles at Jo. It is a ghost of the smile she had worn in the newspaper photos. It seems she is about to say something more, but just then there is a light tap on the window.

Walking slowly in front of the shop as if he hasn't a care in the world is Eric the Viking. He doesn't look at them, but Jo knows he is watching them out of the corner of his eye. His face looks serious, apart from a slight dimple at the corner of his mouth.

Jo stands back to take him all in. On his head is a metal helmet (well, it might be tin foil) with large horns. Around his shoulders is a type of sheepskin rug. It is the same as the one her mum has in the guest room, and it is held in place across his chest by a bright yellow bulldog clip. When the Viking reaches the far side of the window, he turns his head slowly towards them, face expressionless. He raises his hand briefly in salute. 'Afternoon,' he calls, and is gone.

A gurgle of laughter erupts from Reverend Ruth, making her wig shimmy. 'And that was . . . ?' she says, between laughter.

Jo is grinning broadly. 'That would be Eric the Viking.'

'Of course it is,' Ruth says and, still chortling, heads for the door. For once the broken bell decides not to sound its tinny farewell.

Jo is still smiling as she pins *Dear Giana* and the few lines of Italian to her noticeboard.

Then it comes to her what she should do.

She should write a letter to Lucy.

9

Dear Lucy

The next morning, when Jo wakes, it takes her a moment to remember where she is. A couple of weeks after moving in, she took the decision to move from the small spare bedroom into Uncle Wilbur's room. The single bed was just too narrow. She bought new bed linen for Uncle Wilbur's double bed; a duvet cover scattered with tulips. It's the last design her uncle would choose and, by adding this to the sparse, masculine surroundings, she hoped to imprint something of herself upon the room.

However, she still wakes, startled, some nights, thinking her uncle has walked into the room. Whatever she does with the bedroom, by way of opening windows, adding scented candles and diffusers, the room still smells of the old man. It isn't an unpleasant or strong fragrance, but it lingers.

For the past few weeks, she has taken to wishing her Uncle Wilbur a 'good night' before she switches off the light, and she has found she sleeps more soundly. Since the last video-call with her uncle, she has spoken to his carer, Elaine, and followed her suggestion of sending photos in her letters. She also included some seashells and some sand (stolen from the toddler play park) as she remembered Uncle Wilbur's comments about not being by the sea. On a call to her mum, she told Jo how pleased Wilbur was to receive this parcel, even if Jo could tell by her mother's tone that she was worried about her brother.

This morning Jo decides to wish Uncle Wilbur a good morning, because something is troubling her – although as she says the words, she realizes it is nothing to do with her uncle. She recognizes the essence of what is not right, has burrowed for it before. Not James (this time). Not being away from home. Not being in limbo, unsure what to do with her life. Not the yearning for a baby, which is more like a constant ache within her.

Lucy.

When she digs into this feeling of unease, this is what she finds at the root of her sadness. Jo reflects that it is like having a virus you can't shake; never feeling quite right, off-colour, anxious, unsettled. Could an out-of-step friendship make you feel ill? Now, she thinks it can.

Jo lies there, staring up at the ceiling. What should she write to Lucy?

Instead of answering this, her mind flips back to when James told her that he wanted to move out. It was the same day as the stationery cupboard tears.

'Did you really have to cry in front of everyone?'

Then later.

'It isn't me, it's you.'

He quickly corrected himself. 'Sorry, I mean, it isn't you, it's *me*.'

Even in her despair (and something that felt a lot like panic), she had thought – *Really? You are really going to use that cliché. And didn't you get it right the first time you said it?*

He followed this with. 'There's no one else.'

She hadn't asked.

She also thought: *Why would you think that there not being someone else makes me feel better? You are simply telling me that I alone am not good enough.*

Over time, she has persuaded herself that James not being unfaithful was a good thing. She can hold on to what they had. Think of the good times.

That used to be easy. But over the past few weeks?

He moved on pretty easily, didn't he? Hooked up with Nickeeey at work, a woman ten years younger than Jo, one of the graduate trainees. But then James was five years younger than she was. This thought, like nails on a blackboard, still makes Jo flinch. At first, James seemed to delight in the age difference – the older, sexy woman. He had been twenty-eight when they met; she had been thirty-three. But then . . .

Jo doesn't want to go there, so refocuses on Lucy.

Lucy was certainly there for her when she split up with James. Jo pulled hard on her lifeline to her best friend and it held firm, as she knew it would do, despite their . . . would she even call them differences? Lucy and Sanjeev had been back from Amsterdam for about eighteen months, and she thought during that time they had got back into the old familiar ways. But had they, really? With James needing so much from her, especially when his dad died.

Well, despite all that, Lucy had definitely looked after her when James left. Had her to stay for days on end, more or less let her move in with her and Sanjeev. Lucy had comforted her, held her tight, then poured them both wine, telling Jo she would die alone surrounded by cats. It felt like the old times; Lucy had always been able to make her laugh.

It was only later – when Jo sobbed and hiccupped her longing for a family – that Lucy asked Jo: hadn't she and James talked about the future; the life-crap stuff? It was then that Jo made another discovery.

She had thought theirs was a relationship of equals; James was not a man to put words into her mouth. Yet now, she realized, that she had followed where his conversations led them, and that he had somehow managed to avoid discussing the future.

Looking back, perhaps she had been waiting for him to catch up. At twenty-eight, when they'd met, she knew he wasn't interested in settling down – and then time moved on but it seemed James didn't.

As she saw more of Lucy, her friend became increasingly open about what she thought of James. And none of it was good: *twat*, *selfish* and *tosser* featured quite a lot. But it seemed she saved the biggest tirade for their last night together before Jo headed to London. Jo particularly remembers Lucy declaring:

'Always thought you were too good for the manipulative wanker. For fuck's sake, who gives his girlfriend a ring box on Christmas Eve with sodding earrings in?'

Jo resisted the knee-jerk reaction to defend James. Experienced the familiarity of being caught between the two of them. She couldn't help feeling that this was the last thing she needed on their final night together, and that it wasn't fair. What was she supposed to have done when Lucy moved to Amsterdam? There was no option but for Jo to get on with her own life. And if Lucy really thought Jo had been manipulated by James, what did that say about what Lucy thought of her? Foolish? Easily led? Certainly nothing good.

It was at this point Jo noticed Lucy was only pouring one glass of wine. When she commented on this, Lucy admitted with a slight awkwardness that she and Sanjeev were having a baby. Jo's grievances fell away, as if she had opened her arms and simply dropped everything she was carrying. She leapt to her feet and hugged Lucy like her heart was about to burst with happiness (which it was), and she buried her anguish so deep that even Lucy couldn't find it. With the anguish she buried something she had never told her best friend. She had thought she could tell Lucy anything. It seemed she was wrong.

And now she wants to write to Lucy. What on earth can she possibly say that could unravel all of that?

Jo is in the shop staring at a blank page. She has tried writing to Lucy, but her attempts lie in (and littered around) the waste-paper bin. Her mind keeps drifting back to that last evening, and one thought emerges that she cannot seem to shift. Lucy had been furious with James – for sure – but there was also a suppressed anger. It unsettles her, as Jo can't help feeling that this barely contained rage was directed at her.

The broken bell above the door clinks and Eric the Viking steps into the shop (minus the tin-foil helmet). 'Morning! I need to get some more ink.' He nods approvingly at her display of tester pens. 'Told you they like to be out and about.'

Jo reaches for the cartridges that she knows fit his pen. 'Black or blue?' Before he can answer, she adds, 'Or we have lots of other colours?'

'No, I'm good with black,' he tells her.

'Yes, probably best to avoid green. I had an MP in this morning who told me that the rudest complaint letters are always written in green ink. Then, out of the blue, he started telling me all about the love letters he used to write to his wife, and about how much he loves her.' Jo nods. 'I'm glad I got the pens out . . .'

'Thank you, Eric the Viking,' he murmurs.

Jo smiles, but doesn't respond. 'It's amazing what people tell me when they are writing.'

'What other things have you heard?' Eric asks, taking the packet of black cartridges from her.

'Well, the same MP told me that admirals always write in green ink.'

'I wonder if that's true,' he comments, looking interested.

'No idea. And an old lady came in and told me all about a handwriting competition she won when she was nine. Oh, and that when she was in her twenties, her father's curate had written to her and, when he went on a trip to the South of France, he bought her a bottle of mimosa perfume. Her father wouldn't allow the marriage, but sixty years on she still buys mimosa for herself sometimes . . .'

As Eric the Viking listens, he leans down and picks up the scattered paper from around the wastepaper bin. Absent-mindedly he smooths one of the sheets out on the counter.

Jo watches his hand. The fingers are broad, but nicely shaped with neat nails. She thinks if she were to stretch out her hand, the back of his hand would be warm to touch; her fingers would slip in easily between his fingers, and rest there quite happily. She imagines the feel of his thumb stroking the side of her little finger.

She looks up at him in shock.

His head is still down.

Even so, she feels caught out. Her heart is racing.

'I'm sorry,' he says, glancing up and handing her the paper. 'I can see it's a letter. I didn't mean to pry.'

Jo looks down at the only words on the page: *Dear Lucy*

'Not much to see there,' she admits, still feeling flustered. 'I've been trying to write to my best friend.'

'Tricky letter?' he asks.

'That's just it,' she says, trying to regain her composure, 'it shouldn't be. We've been friends since primary school, but just now we seem to be in different places.' She smiles. 'Literally.' Jo then sighs. 'It's more than that. For the first time, I can't think what to say to her.' Had it been like that when Lucy was in Amsterdam? Not really. There had been a steady stream of texts and Jo had visited every few months. More often than not, without James. It was the coming home that hadn't worked like, Jo suspects, either of them had imagined. James was always there then.

'"Dear", is a good place to start,' Eric the Viking suggests, breaking in on her reverie. He is looking down at the words on the page, and Jo thinks of the Runaway Vicar, who said it was always a good thing to tell our friends that they were dear to us.

'Tell her about this,' Eric the Viking continues.

For a startled moment, Jo wonders what he means. Did he notice her staring at his hand? She feels her colour rise. There is no *this*. Is there? Now even her ears are pink. It is then she sees that Eric the Viking is staring around him.

'The shop?' Jo queries, and she can hear the relief in her voice.

She thinks Eric the Viking must have heard it too as he says, 'Yeah, what did you think I meant?' He is now smiling at her in a way that does nothing for her colour. 'Well, maybe not a description of the shop,' Eric continues, quickly, and Jo sees that he is blushing too. 'That wouldn't take long,' he grins, glancing down one of the narrow aisles, 'but about the people who come in. The things you were telling me.'

'Yes, I could do that,' Jo concedes, thankful to be back on solid ground. It would be a safe place to begin, and isn't that what she needs, a fresh place to start with Lucy?

A place for everything and everything in its place.

Dear Lucy,

I'm missing you and I know texts aren't always great, so I thought I would write to you and tell you a bit about some of the people who come into the shop. It was Eric the Viking's idea. So if you find it strange or boring you can blame him.

One of my favourite customers so far is a massive police officer (who looks ridiculously young – how old did that make me feel?). He gazed at the fountain pens for a long time but wouldn't touch them. I told him he could try one without buying it, but he still wouldn't, although I could tell he was dying to. In the end he confessed that he was ashamed of his handwriting. I tried to say it didn't matter, but he then looked even sadder, and said that he thought handwriting represented a person.

I thought that was interesting. Another time I'll tell you about the Runaway Vicar and how some of the letters she writes look as if they would like to spin off and escape. Bit like the vicar herself!

Anyway, I ended up telling the police officer that I would look out some books on handwriting from the library and he should call back in, once I'd had time to work out what he needed to do.

That's why in the evenings I am now practising my letters. Uncle Wilbur had some old-fashioned exercise books in the store cupboard. Do you remember those from school? The ones with two rows of lines to show you where to place the letters. I can't tell you how much I enjoyed opening the first page of the book, smoothing the cover back and writing my name on the top line. Since then, I've been reading handwriting books and watching some YouTube clips – one with a fierce American woman. It seems there are a few simple rules and I think I'll make a list of them (in my best handwriting) for the police officer.

I'll let you know how I get on.

Hugs to you, Sanjeev and the bump.

With lots of love,

Jo x

10

The list of good intentions

Jo takes a glass of wine and a handful of nuts and settles into Uncle Wilbur's chair. It has been a long day. The room is still and quiet and Jo feels completely alone in the city. She wonders where the Runaway Vicar is tonight. Is she curled up with wine and snacks? Is she on her own, like Jo? Or did she run away to someone? She wonders if Malcolm is alone too. She has a feeling he will be.

Her eyes flick to a card that is standing on the mantelpiece above the gas fire. It shows an image of a young woman carrying a large bouquet of flowers – a card from her mum. These turn up every so often, just hoping Jo is well, sending her lots of love.

She wonders when her mum will realize that Uncle Wilbur is not coming back home. But would he really think of this as his home? Hadn't her Uncle Wilbur run away too? In his case, he had run from the country to the city.

Well, it had been more complicated than that. Her mum has told her a lot more about her brother since he was moved into the care home. Uncle Wilbur left their parents' farm in the Lake District to join the army, and after that he moved to London. He worked as a salesman, and then as a handyman, when he found he was completely unsuited to persuading young couples to buy insurance policies they neither needed nor could afford. His work on the farm, as a boy, had given him good practical skills but no love of the land or of farm work. Her mother confided that she thought Wilbur had left, and stayed away, because he could not bear the look of disappointment on his parents' faces.

Jo holds her wine glass up and stares into the ruby liquid. Is she like her uncle? A runaway? Yes, of course she is. She thinks of James. Ever since Eric the Viking's visit this morning, she has tried to focus on James and think of the good times. She wants to feed the tiny bit of hope she has that they will get back together; convince herself that he and Nickeeey won't last.

It hasn't worked. Instead of thinking of James, she has replayed the image of Eric the Viking's hand stroking the crumpled page. It unnerves her.

A sudden thought comes to her: what would have happened if James's dad hadn't died? (Oh, he needed her then.) Her wayward brain adds: Or, if you'd got pregnant? And slipping into her mind is a thought she wants to fling away from her as soon as it sidles in. *Aren't you running away from Lucy's baby?*

Please, no. Not that.

She reminds herself how much she is looking forward to meeting her best friend's first child. Then she worries she shouldn't have had to remind herself of this.

Jo shifts in her uncle's chair. Why does it now feel, when she thinks about James, as though a thick layer of confusion is settling like dust on her past life? Was James really a 'manipulative wanker'? An image comes into her head of Lucy, Jemima and Uncle Wilbur – arms folded, lips pursed, nodding to each other and her. She doesn't know whether to laugh or cry.

Then all thought of laughter dies. If they are right, what has she been doing for the last six years? She doesn't want to have wasted six precious years of her life. She doesn't think she can cope with feeling that foolish.

She gets up and goes into the kitchen, looking for something for supper. There isn't much in the fridge, and she decides she will make do with the rest of last night's pizza. She puts it in the oven to warm through and stands at the window, looking down on the alleyway below. It is deserted. Her position, high above the pavement, accentuates her sense of being suspended in time.

It feels as if she is stuck in a limbo she would like to move on from. But to what?

Later, having finished her sparse supper, and once more tucked up in her uncle's chair, nursing a coffee, her eyes come to rest on an unsent postcard to Uncle Wilbur. It shows an old image of the alleyway, including his shop, taken in the 1960s. Jo had fallen on it when she had spotted it in a junk shop. There is a blurry figure inside the shop who she thinks might be her uncle. She wishes that the picture was clearer and that she could rid her mind of the idea that her uncle, like this image, is fading away.

Next to the postcard is her letter to Lucy. She is conscious that this letter is a form of atonement for something she has done that Lucy knows nothing about. Yet another thing she hasn't told her best friend. The list is getting quite long. She thinks back to Lucy's suppressed anger. Does Lucy already know about this other thing? Jo stares fixedly at the letter, as if it will provide her with an answer to that all-important question – does Lucy know about Finn? Is that why she is so upset? The trouble is, Jo doesn't dare ask.

The letter remains mute, but the more she looks at it, the more it seems that the paper she has used for the letter to Lucy is all wrong. She took some of the old-fashioned stationery from the shop. It doesn't seem large enough or colourful enough for a woman who meanders through life with such bold and easy grace.

Jo stops and mentally raises her eyes to the heavens. She is a woman running a stationery shop who doesn't have the right stationery. She thinks of the bad pram driver asking if she sold invitations. The answer is blindingly simple: she can order more stock for the shop. She can buy the type of stationery she loves. It needn't cost her uncle anything; she could use some of her redundancy money. She can't believe she hasn't thought of this before.

Jo is up from the chair in one swift movement. This is something she can do (and at least she won't be thinking about Lucy).

She leaves her coffee on the table and goes in search of her laptop and a notebook. She smiles and shakes her head, her spirits immeasurably lifted.

She feels like a child who has only just realized that the keys to the sweetshop were in her pocket all the time.

The next day is Saturday and it is quiet in the shop, which gives Jo the chance to continue ordering her new range. She also sends messages out to her fellow stationery lovers for their thoughts of what else she should stock.

So far she has ordered: correspondence cards, invitations, notecards, some new journals and, best of all, a more modern fountain-pen brand. She thinks this will complement the classic pen designs that Uncle Wilbur favoured.

Soon messages are pouring in, and she adds the ideas she likes to a list pinned to the noticeboard. One stationery lover suggests a journal she has come across, entitled, *Letters I would write to myself.* Jo pauses.

What would she write to herself?

Not to waste time dreaming about marrying James? Jo lets out a long breath. She is trying so hard to move on. So far she has resisted texting him; she only occasionally succumbs to looking for him on Instagram. But she knows every time her text alert sounds, she still wants it to be James, saying that he has made a terrible mistake and that he can't stop thinking about her.

But, something *has* changed. The pain isn't as raw. Maybe it isn't James himself, but the loss of her dream of them growing old together, which crushes her in the middle of the night? Perhaps what she is missing is not James but the thought of them as a family? That extra person, who sits in the corner of her consciousness, so that if she turns her head quickly enough she thinks she will catch sight of them.

She is facing downhill to forty, and her whole being feels this like a strong gravitational force. She fights it, tells herself that many women cannot have babies or choose not to have children; she knows she shouldn't allow this biological act to define her. In the cold light of day, she has some chance of squashing these feelings, but when she wakes up in the middle of the night? Then she experiences the clammy panic of time running out. Wasn't she reminded often enough by James that she was getting old?

Jo stops herself there. She has no desire to dig up and examine a whole lot of pain she would rather leave buried, so instead she concentrates on what the Runaway Vicar and Eric the Viking said – that friends are dear to us. She would definitely write and tell herself to make more of an effort with her friends (whatever James said).

There is a tap on the window and, looking up, she realizes with a start that she is hoping to see Eric the Viking. It is Malcolm. He is wearing a grey trilby which he tips to her, before striding off down the alleyway. She half waves to his retreating back then, telling herself to stop trying to double-guess what James is thinking, she turns the radio up loud and sets about cleaning the shop.

It is late into the afternoon before she has finished, but she is pleased with her efforts. The stationery stock is better organized and she has created spaces for the new items she is expecting. (*A place for everything and everything in its place.*) Plus the shops smells richly of polish.

Keen to tackle the oak counter that sits in the window, Jo pauses, wondering where to put all the odd bits of hardware that she has piled there. In the end she takes four deep plastic washing-up bowls, fills them with various items and carries them outside. She props them up against the outside wall of the shop and fashions a sign saying, 'Free to a good home.'

She frowns as she thinks of Uncle Wilbur. Would he mind her doing this? Then she thinks of the man who gave her damaged stationery in brown paper bags and believes that this man would understand and forgive her.

Then she returns to the job of bringing a new sheen to the old cabinet.

It is early evening before she finishes, and she is just sweeping the floor when she spots something half hidden under the counter. She pulls it out and frowns down at it. It is one of the notebooks she sells, but this one has a creased cover with a corner missing. For a moment she thinks of damaged stationery and of her Uncle Wilbur.

In the next instance, she realizes what she is holding in her hand – surely this is one of Malcolm's notebooks? Hadn't she seen him with it when he came in yesterday? He must have dropped it. Instinctively she opens the notebook, simultaneously thinking she must return it, while conscious of a childlike glee that she can now see what he's writing. On the inside cover of the notebook is the name *Malcolm Buswell*. The first page is covered in neat copperplate handwriting and on the top line, *William Foyle* is underlined. The name means nothing to Jo.

A rap on the window makes her jump. She half expects to see Malcolm and looks up, guiltily, feeling caught out at reading his notebook. Instead, Eric the Viking pokes his head around the door.

'Sorry, Jo, didn't mean to creep up on you.'

Eric is wearing a shaggy kind of jumper (very Nordic) and carrying a black drill case.

'You're doing some DIY?' Jo asks, and then wishes she hadn't stated the obvious.

'Yep, I've just moved into my own flat. Forgot I left the drill in the shop.'

I, Jo thinks, not *we*.

Before she can stop herself, the words are out of her mouth. 'How old are you, Eric?'

'Thirty-three,' he replies, clearly puzzled. When Jo doesn't say anything else, he continues, shaking his head. 'I know, I know, you're thinking I should have stopped living like a student years ago and got myself a place of my own.'

She isn't thinking that. She is thinking, six years. She is six years older than this man. She was five years older than James, and she can't bear to think where that took her.

She reminds herself that it doesn't matter, that she and Eric are just *friends*, that she barely knows him. It suddenly feels ludicrous to be thinking like this.

They stand silent and awkward, the buzz of traffic in the distance. It is Eric who fills the gap.

'Anyway, I'm glad I've caught you. I wanted to ask you if you were free for dinner sometime . . .' He rushes on, and Jo notices his face is flushed. Hers is too. '. . . That is, Lando and I wanted to take you out. An apology, a meal . . .' He now sounds embarrassed. 'You know, to say sorry that we've been such useless neighbours.'

When Jo doesn't immediately respond, he adds, 'What d'you say?'

Jo thinks of the letter she imagined writing to herself. This is what she had in mind, wasn't it? Being a better friend, making new friends. Why is she now so anxious that her jaw is clamped shut? She knows she should simply say, *Yes*, and go with them. But all she can think is: *I can't do this*. She feels an almost physical pull back to the Jo who sat on the shop stool grieving for James. It was miserable there, but it was safe.

Eric seems to sense some of her anxiety (if not the reason for it) and, shifting his drill case to his other hand, says more gently, 'Look, it will be fun, very casual. And you've got to eat,' he says encouragingly, smiling at her.

'Yes, there is that,' she says, trying hard to sound light-hearted and join in with this game.

'Look, where would you like to go?'

'I don't know many places round here,' she admits, thinking she could just as easily say, *I don't know* any *places round here*.

'Well,' Eric says, looking brighter, 'me and my man Lando, can help you there. What kind of food do you like?'

Jo pictures the newest, the latest, the award-winning res-taurants and pop-ups she used to go to with James. She doesn't want Eric to see how vulnerable she is, and she wants to let him know that she does know something about food. So she tells him with as much confidence as she can manage, 'Newcastle, where I used to work, had some great places, where new cooking techniques were combined with a more eco-approach and naked ingredients were sourced from woodland foraging.' She knows she must sound ridiculous; she wonders why the James in her head is now speaking for her, spouting words like a pretentious food critic.

The walrus laugh is back. 'Jeez, Jo, I know I'm a Viking, but do we have to go traipsing across Hampstead Heath gathering lichen?'

'I really like Italian food,' she blurts, with perfect truth.

He waves a triumphant finger in the air. 'Got you! We can do that for sure. There's a great Italian near my new flat. Thursday night be good for you?'

Jo nods. She doesn't trust herself to open her mouth again.

11

In case of emergency

'That is very pretty. Is it Italian paper?'

Jo looks up in surprise. Standing in front of her is the Runaway Vicar – minus the wig. Her mouse-coloured hair, looking freshly washed, is curling in a short bob around her ears. Today she is not wearing the overlong raincoat, and once more Jo is reminded of a small bird.

'Ruth,' she says – as much to herself as to the person in front of her; a reprimand to stop thinking of this woman as a tabloid headline.

'Yes, that's right,' Ruth says, as if amused and waiting for more.

Jo reaches out her hand. 'I'm Jo.'

Ruth pauses for a moment before holding out her own slim hand and grasping Jo's.

The physical contact shocks Jo. Ruth has been existing predominantly in her head: she has researched her; mulled over the reasons she might have run away; invented a few scenarios for what might have happened. Now the small hand she holds is warm and solid, and she experiences the substantive humanity of it with a jolt.

'Pleased to meet you, Jo,' Ruth says, releasing her hand. 'Italian?' she repeats, nodding towards the box Jo is unpacking on the counter.

'No, I think the company is American, but I know what you mean. This reminds me of a paper shop I once visited in Florence.' She holds out the pack for Ruth to examine. The clear-lidded box contains correspondence cards – pale cream in colour with a design at the top in red and purple, reminiscent of seashells. A thin gold line runs around the edge of the cards.

Unnerved by the handshake, Jo keeps on talking, pulling more cards from the brown cardboard box. 'I thought I would get some new stock in, try some different things. My uncle—'

For an instant, Jo is reluctant to talk about her uncle's private affairs, and then she remembers that this is a vicar in front of her. Flotsam from Sunday School bobs to the surface of her mind. *You should always tell the truth to a vicar.* So, she says, honestly, 'This is my Uncle Wilbur's shop. He started to trip and fall and at first we thought he just needed to recover from those. But then it became clear that other things weren't right. He's struggling with dementia.'

Ruth nods. 'My mother went the same way. It is hard. So, what's going to happen to the shop?' Ruth asks.

And Jo is relieved at the lack of pretence that all will be well.

Instead of answering, she asks her own question. 'Did your mother end up in a home?'

'Yes, in the end,' Ruth says, picking up another pack of cards and turning them over slowly in her hands. These are the palest duck-egg blue, with bumble bees along the top and three pastel-coloured beehives pictured at the bottom. 'So pretty,' she says, under her breath.

'Uncle Wilbur is in a home near to my parents in North Yorkshire. But at some point we're going to have to think about what to do with the shop. Just at the moment, my mum . . .'

Ruth glances up at her. 'Not got her head round it yet?'

As Jo grimaces, Ruth nods in understanding, and Jo realizes she hasn't spoken like this to anyone for months. Really talked about what is going on in her life.

'Your uncle's had this shop for quite a while then?' Ruth remarks, looking around.

'Over fifty years. I used to come and stay here as a child.'

'He lives above the shop?' Ruth asks, glancing upwards.

'Yes. That's where I'm staying now.'

'Quite a lot to sort out then,' Ruth comments. 'I wonder if it will still feel like this when the shop eventually changes hands. Unless you think you might stay?'

'No, no, I want to go back up North.'

'Ah, so it will be sold.'

'I expect so. Do you ever want to go back to Scotland? It is Scotland you're from?'

'Yes, Glasgow. And no. Never,' Ruth says, with such finality that it makes Jo wonder about her childhood.

Ruth has gone back to perusing the shop. 'You can tell that this shop has history.' She smiles. 'If you don't mind me saying, you suit it, somehow.'

'My dad always calls me an old soul,' Jo says, mirroring her smile.

'Perhaps that's why I find it so . . .' Ruth doesn't finish. 'I hope you don't mind me calling in,' she says, looking directly at Jo. 'I find it helps—'

The shop door suddenly crashes back on its hinges, and as the metal handle hits the wall, Jo braces herself for the sound of breaking glass. There is the scrunch of metal burying itself into plaster but, despite rattling ominously, the glass stays in place.

The tall figure of Malcolm staggers through the door, blood trickling down over his right eye. He is blinking rapidly, but does not appear to be able to focus. One hand is holding onto the doorframe, the other arm is limp by his side.

Ruth moves like a greyhound out of the traps, and before Jo can even step towards Malcolm, Ruth has inserted her small, bird-like form under Malcolm's arm, her own arm around his waist. It looks as if she is tucking herself under his wing. Ruth readjusts her hold and heaves at Malcolm, just as his body starts to slump. With a grunt she drags his body into a more upright position.

With one hand reaching behind her for the shop's stool, Jo's legs start to move. She whisks round the counter to get to the two figures. Between her and Ruth they half drag, half carry Malcolm to where Jo had dropped the stool.

As he slumps onto it, he reaches out both hands to grasp

the edge of the counter, steadying himself. Jo spins on the spot and locks the shop door, flicking the *Closed* sign over, before whirling back to the bowed figure.

'Malcolm?! What happened?'

'I'm sorry. I'm so sorry, Joanne – I felt so faint and then all I saw was your shop.'

Being seated seems to bring Malcolm back to some sense of where he is, although the blood that was running down his face is now dripping onto the counter and the new packs of cards. Ruth leans forwards and whips them out of the way, placing them on a shelf behind her.

'I saw your shop and headed to it, like a beacon in the storm.'

Jo feels a surge of relief at hearing Malcolm's voice regain some of its lyrical, measured rhythm.

'Well, let's get you sorted,' Ruth says briskly, stepping closer to Malcolm, but not touching him. 'Do I have your permission to look at that cut?'

'Are you a doctor, madam?' Malcolm looks at Ruth as if seeing her for the first time.

'No, I'm a priest.'

'As bad as that?' Malcolm says, looking at her with a slow, rueful shake of the head.

The smile that Ruth gives Malcolm lights up the shop. 'Now, Jo, would you get me a bowl of warm water, a towel, and if you have them, cotton wool, lint, bandages and scissors.' Ruth asks, calmly.

A place for everything and everything in its place. Jo can immediately picture where Uncle Wilbur keeps his first-aid kit.

She dashes into the back of the shop and returns a few moments later, carrying everything Ruth has asked for.

'. . . and so you have found yourself visiting this shop too?' Malcolm is speaking, head held up, whilst Ruth gently wipes his face with a large white handkerchief – Malcolm's, Jo presumes.

'Mmm,' Ruth murmurs, then dips the handkerchief into the warm water Jo has brought with her and goes back to her task. Jo has such a sense of being in safe hands that she dismisses all thought of calling 999.

'I can see that you have done this before, madam,' Malcolm comments, leaning forward so Ruth can more easily reach the wound.

'Oh, it comes with the territory. Blood, poo and vomit are the vicar's lot.'

'But hopefully not all at once. A very unholy trinity,' Malcolm suggests, and Ruth, eyes not moving from her work, makes a small snorting noise.

'But you must introduce us, Joanne – I can't keep calling this kind lady "madam".'

'This is Ruth,' Jo explains, repeating in her head – do not call her the Runaway Vicar. Then she remembers the newspaper article. 'Ruth Hamilton,' she adds. 'Ruth is originally from Glasgow.' Then it strikes her: perhaps she shouldn't have disclosed her full name.

Ruth's expression doesn't change as she continues to bathe the gash on Malcolm's head.

Malcolm says formally, 'My name is Malcolm Buswell. I am very pleased to meet you, Reverend Hamilton.'

'Please call me Ruth.' Glancing at Jo, Ruth continues, 'Don't look so worried, Jo – it's not as bad as it looks. The flow is slowing now, and I really think if we can patch you up securely, Malcolm, you will be okay.'

'People in the street did offer to call an ambulance,' Malcolm explains to them, 'but I really thought it was only a graze. It only started to bleed as I walked along.'

For the second time Jo asks, 'What happened, Malcolm?'

Malcolm continues to stare at a spot somewhere above Ruth's head, as if his mind is miles away.

Ruth's eyes flick downwards as if trying to read his expression and then she continues, 'The wound is in a tricky spot, Malcolm. I am going to have to secure the bandage underneath your chin.' She smiles at him. 'I'm afraid it's not going to look very beautiful, but it will stay in place.'

'Oh, never fear, Reverend Ruth. No one has ever accused me of being beautiful.'

'All God's creatures are beautiful, Malcolm,' and Jo is shocked by the power of Ruth's obvious sincerity and her own uneasy embarrassment. She cannot imagine anyone else she knows saying something like this. She is reminded of their first meeting; the *No one believes in God any more.*

'And you really believe that?' It is Malcolm who voices this. He sounds totally bemused.

Ruth pauses for a moment. 'I do,' she says, and then she grins. 'It rather comes with the job.' As she reaches for a bandage she adds under her breath, 'Along with the unholy trinity of blood, poo and vomit.'

Malcolm smiles.

As Ruth carefully secures the dressing in place, Jo watches with fascination. 'You have definitely done this before,' she comments.

'Oh, yes. I'm fully trained in first aid.'

Malcolm, who is no longer having to lean on the counter, makes a movement with both hands as if using a defibrillator. 'What, even the "Stand clear!"?' he booms.

Jo smiles and Ruth laughs. 'Oh, yes. I did it once on a horse.'

Jo makes a choking sound, completely baffled by the image conjured up in her head. 'But how?' she exclaims.

'It wasn't difficult,' Ruth tells her.

'But where did the legs and hooves go? Didn't they get in the way?'

Both Ruth and Malcolm turn and stare at her. Then their laughter fills the small shop. In between gurgles, Ruth splutters, 'I said, I did it once on a *course*.'

Jo laughs so much she struggles for breath.

When the laughter dies away, something has changed. The shop is silent but it feels full of something. Jo might even call it promise.

'Tea!' she declares with decision. As she heads to the small kitchen at the back of the shop, she can hear the sound of Ruth and Malcolm's voices joined in conversation. She experiences a feeling of relief.

But why, she's not quite sure.

* * *

It is only as Jo is closing up that she realizes she never turned the door sign around from *Closed*. That would explain why the shop had been so quiet that afternoon. She has no regrets, though, as it gave the three of them a few hours to chat and drink tea. The feeling of relief she felt seeing Ruth and Malcolm chatting by the old counter has stayed with her. It's wrapped itself around her, insulating her from thoughts of James, Lucy and Eric the Viking. Another name slips in too: Finn. No, she had not had to think about any of them.

After a while, the first-aid kit was stored back under the counter, bloodied cloths cleared away, and Malcolm sent on his way. Ruth did not exactly insist on accompanying him home, but just made vague noises about going the same way, even though Jo is pretty certain that Ruth had no idea where he lived. Which in turn makes her wonder, where is it exactly that Ruth is living? Where or who did she run away to?

Alone in the shop, Jo contemplates these two people who have now been thrust into her world. She can't recall precisely what they talked about as they sipped their tea and ate the lemon and white-chocolate cookies Jo brought down from the flat, along with a couple of stools. Hampstead Heath? The shop? The seasons changing?

Before Malcolm left, Jo handed him back the notebook he had dropped by the shelves. She was on the verge of confessing she had read his notes about William Foyle – who she now knows started the bookshop chain, Foyles – and was going to enquire (once again) what Malcolm's book is about, when Malcolm quickly turned the conversation. It seems Malcolm is still as reluctant as ever to talk about his project. Another thing Jo is equally sure of, is that Reverend Ruth was quite as reticent to answer Malcolm's mild enquiry about her parish.

However, over tea, Malcolm did open up a bit more about how he got the gash on his head (not a bump, he reassured Reverend Ruth, who made noises about taking him to hospital in case he was concussed). No, just a scratch. He had slipped by the side of the road and had almost gone under a bus. He had been saved by a courier who was cycling past and who had swerved, reached out and saved him. It was the edge of the courier's bag flying up into Malcolm's face that had inflicted the wound.

It is only as Jo is pinning the leaflet from the first-aid box ('In case of emergency') onto the pinboard that she wonders more about what Malcolm had meant by his last muttered words. 'And I was very grateful, as I didn't want to die.'

She studies her noticeboard for some moments – the calendar, the pieces of paper, and now a leaflet that fill about a quarter of the board – and she considers those last words: 'I didn't want to die.'

It was the way he said it, much more than the actual words. Malcolm sounded . . . well . . . he sounded surprised.

The question she can't help asking is: was there a time when Malcolm *did* want to die? She thinks back to Reverend Ruth and the slight movement of her head as Malcolm said those words, and she wonders if the Runaway Vicar is thinking about them too.

12

La Biblioteca

Jo is still dwelling on Malcolm's words, days later, as she gets ready for her night out with Lando and Eric the Viking. She is also conscious that over the past few days she has retreated into what now feels like a self-indulgent, self-pitying splurge of missing James.

Maybe she is just tired of wallowing (and realizes that it had been quite hard work), but her pulse quickens as she reaches for a wrap-round dress in emerald green, and she feels a rising anticipation. Perhaps it is the chance to wear something other than dungarees. And this is a dress that James never liked. She then adds a defiant finishing touch of bright pink lipstick. He didn't like that either.

The Italian restaurant that Lando and Eric are taking her to is within walking distance, but it is in an area of London she hasn't explored before. As they make their way there, Jo is reminded of how little of London she has seen.

On one of her first Sundays there, she braved a bus ride into the centre of the city. After the initial elation of watching the streets from the top deck, she became increasingly conscious of her lone, purposeless self, seated amongst a busload of Londoners and earnest tourists. Later, after struggling to find the right bus back, she tried the Underground, and got lost trying to decide which branch of the Northern Line she was meant to be on. She stood on the platform, staring up at signs that made no sense to her, battling a rising panic that left her feeling foolish, and robbed her of the confidence to ask for help.

The memory squashes the dress-induced confidence out of her, along with any conversation, and she walks along beside the two men in silence: Lando, neat and dapper; Eric the Viking rolling like a ship in full sail. When a text sounds on her phone, she takes the chance to look at it to buy herself some time. It is from Lucy.

Like the idea of you teaching the police to write. Tell me more about these people. L x

So the letter has gone down well. Something eases within her.

Jo thinks of Lucy's innate ability to talk to people. She will strike up a conversation with anyone she meets, including posing random questions to strangers. Jo recalls how she has borrowed this trait from her best friend in the past (rather like her dungarees), especially when she has found herself in awkward situations. Has thought – what would Lucy say now?

It is bonfire night, and as a firework explodes over a building in front of them, she throws a question out into the cold November night air.

'What three things in life do you think are completely overrated?'

The men leap on this, and by the time they have reached the restaurant, the conversation is flowing and the question has been thoroughly thrashed out.

Lando: fireworks, breakfast in bed (Eric is not buying that one), and God.

Jo thinks Reverend Ruth might have something to say about that, but thinks Malcolm would probably slap him on the back (if she could imagine Malcolm slapping anyone on the back).

Eric the Viking: caviar, shopping and emojis.

Before she can stop herself, Jo thinks: *I can live with that.*

She offers up: macaroons (controversial from Lando's point of view), turkey (controversial from Eric's point of view) and football (controversial from both men's point of view).

Once inside the restaurant, it is apparent that the building is a former library – the walls are still covered in books, all in their thick, clear plastic covers. Jo guesses the name, La Biblioteca, is also a clue. Sitting down at their table, Jo experiences a momentary pang, realizing that this library is now filled with books that no one will ever read. The feeling doesn't last long. It is impossible to feel low, sitting between Lando and Eric.

They clearly know each other well and alternate between insulting the other and then praising them in some way. Lando tells her about the travels that helped him develop his skills as a tattoo artist (and during which he had met his Bulgarian wife, Sacha). At this point Eric insists Lando show Jo some images on his phone of his tattoo art.

And it really is art.

Eric continues, explaining that the best artists become known for a particular style, some using more colour, realism, or taking inspiration from a particular theme. Anything from Japanese anime or Māori symbolism to pirates or Disney. Lando's art is mainly black ink work with the occasional splash of colour.

Jo comments, 'It reminds me of Banksy.'

Eric roars out loud, 'There you go, mate,' and slaps Lando on the shoulder.

Then Lando takes over, deploring everything about Eric from his size to his dress sense, and his inability to open up his shop on time. And then in the next breath he is telling Jo that Eric is the first man he would go to if he was in trouble, and that Eric always spends Christmas Eve with the charity Crisis, providing eye-checks and glasses for the homeless.

Eric interrupts Lando at this point and starts insulting his goatee, telling him he needs to grow himself a proper beard.

It is at this point, several glasses of wine in, that Jo interrupts, 'But I saw you!' she cries.

They both look at her.

'I saw you,' she repeats, looking at Lando, 'in the optician's. *That's* why I thought it was your business.'

'Poor bloke needs my help. Blind as a bat,' Eric says, shaking his shaggy head.

'Not as much as you need the help of a proper barber,' Lando retorts, before declaring. 'And Eric, here, wears contact lenses. At least I'm not too vain to admit I need glasses for close work.'

'I have to wear contacts. It's all the sport I play,' Eric says, seriously.

'Really? What do you play?' Jo asks.

They both laugh uproariously at this and she is left feeling foolish and caught out.

Lando leans nearer, 'And he always insists on coloured lenses. You don't seriously think his eyes are that blue, do you?'

Jo isn't going to be taken in a second time, but as she looks into Eric the Viking's very blue eyes, she can feel herself blushing just as much as if she had been.

As they are leaving the restaurant, Jo makes a quick detour to the front desk to pick up one of La Biblioteca's business cards.

'For your pinboard?' Eric asks, as Jo rejoins them, card in hand.

She nods, surprised he has noticed that she is building – what? her new life? – on the board. Fingering the card, she wonders if maybe she could come here with Ruth and Malcolm.

'You're a magpie,' Eric jokes.

She thinks he could be right; the bits and pieces that she is collecting are precious to her – especially all the words people write when they test out the fountain pens. Perhaps she has started collecting new friends too? It's been easier than she expected with Eric the Viking. She has repeated to herself – he is *just* a friend, a neighbour – and it's working. As long as she doesn't look at his hands.

'My wife, Sacha – now she *is* a magpie,' Lando declares.

'Is she?' Jo is happy to be diverted.

'Well, maybe not in the way you think,' he says, opening the door for Jo. 'Sacha, she collects the things people tell her. That woman is a mine of useless . . .' he pauses, '. . . and sometimes really useful information. I don't know how she remembers it all. That woman will talk to *anyone*.'

Like Lucy.

And as if somehow her best friend knows she is thinking of her, Jo's phone pings. It used to be like this all the time. They would just be thinking of each other and suddenly, simultaneously, it seemed they would text or ring.

When Jo glances at the message, she wishes she hadn't. The text reads:

Finn's coming to London. I gave him your address. Said he might call in and say hello. L x

There is no reason why Finn shouldn't have her address.

She wonders if Lucy is puzzled that Finn didn't text Jo himself. But then they weren't really that close.

Were they?

13

What the magpie collects

This is not the time for a list. As much as Jo normally welcomes the calmness that comes from curating a good list late at night – tasks and thoughts brought to order on a page – now is definitely not the time.

Firstly, she is lying down, cocooned in a nest of pillows and duvet. Secondly, she is a little drunk. And thirdly, she does not want to record what is ricocheting around her mind. So much harder to laugh off a midnight brainstorm if those thoughts have been crystallized into enduring ideas by the simple application of ink.

What she really wants is the oblivion of sleep, but she can tell that this is as far away as Northumberland. So instead she tries to focus her mind on just one thing. She thinks of Lando's comment about Sacha 'the magpie'. Does she do the same? Collect things from friends? Well, doesn't she borrow from Lucy? Not just taking clothes, but trying on part of her character to help her when she's feeling shy? She knows she does.

Jo thinks of Malcolm's notebook all about William Foyle. That feels like something she has borrowed. The story of an East Ender, who tried for the Civil Service, but when he failed the exams was left with a load of unwanted textbooks. Except William discovered that there were people out there who wanted second-hand books on a startling array of subjects. So his failure was turned into a thriving book business. Jo frowns into the darkness. Would she really call this borrowing? She hadn't actually been invited to read Malcolm's notebook.

But then didn't magpies steal too?

She moves swiftly on. There are other memories – things that friends have said to her in the past that have stayed with her. These *are* precious, representations of the friend who gave it. A gift worth keeping, even if some snippets of information are odd or seemingly irrelevant.

Cézanne had a huge influence on other artists, and his work was the beginning of cubism. (Her cousin Alice, now working in New York)

Shocking pink was first made popular by the Italian designer Elsa Schiaparelli in the 1930s. (Lucy)

It is best to harvest beans when the weather is not too dry; otherwise they bounce everywhere. (Adam from Young Farmers – her first crush)

The pollen in lilies is poisonous to cats. (Georgia from university, who gave up on Maths and became a florist – just one of the friends she has lost touch with)

The Festive 500 is a 500-km bike ride that has to be completed between Christmas and New Year. (Finn)

And, she is back to Finn.

She pushes against this intrusion but is only rewarded by a splatter-gun of other thoughts exploding in her brain:

Eric the Viking is a bit weird.

And messy.

But he doesn't eat noisily which is a very good thing.

I bet he snores. It's the sort of thing he would do.

He has the most amazing eyes.

And body.

I don't really mind the teasing.

I do mind the teasing. I felt stupid.

Lando likes him.

I like Lando.

What would Mum think of the tattoos?

Lucy would like them . . . and she'd like him.

Those hands.

Forget it.

He's far too young for you.

Then come the whispery words, worming their way in:

I don't want to live in London.

He's an optician, he could work from anywhere.

Will we tell our children about tonight?

She doesn't want any of these thoughts. They make her feel desperate and out of control. Like her yearning for a family has taken over.

And yet, there, lying in the dark, within the confusion and anxiety, there is a glimmer of something. A spark.

Jo closes her eyes tight and tries to grasp it.

Then it comes to her.

She could almost believe she could hate James right now.

What he did *was* wrong. Long before the 'It's not me, it's you.' She wasn't being unreasonable. Telling herself it was a small thing, not worth making a fuss about had been a mistake.

Jo swears, very loudly, into the stillness of the room.

It is only as she is dropping off to sleep, having said goodnight to Uncle Wilbur (and apologized for the swearing), that a stray thought drifts in, twisted in with the first tendrils of sleep. Isn't she also running away from Finn?

Finn, Lucy's youngest brother.

14

Finn comes to town

Dear Lucy,

Since you liked the story of the police officer, let me tell you about another of my customers. He's a boy of about thirteen who sometimes comes into the shop on his way home from school. He's always on his own and at first he seemed too shy to admit to his passion for fountain pens. But over a few visits, he's started to talk a little bit more to me. He told me he has a collection of fourteen pens.

We had a bit of a breakthrough when two of Uncle Wilbur's chess club mates were also in the shop. With a chance comment from one of them, it emerged that Ranbir likes chess almost as much as he likes fountain pens. But the thing is, he doesn't have any friends to play with. Well, he muttered, he didn't have many friends, full stop.

The two old men and Ranbir then started discussing the Sicilian Defence and the Ruy Lopéz Opening. The upshot was, the two men recruited Ranbir for their Thursday evening's chess club.

That was a week ago. Ranbir has just come in to tell me all about it and has brought his selection of fountain pens for me to look at. He stores them in a beautiful silk kind of roll-up cover that his mum made for him. He looked so much happier that I wanted to cry.

With love from,

Jo x

Writing to Lucy is all that Jo can think to do. Since the text about Finn, she has felt the weight of guilt like a solid mass between them. Not for the first time, writing a letter feels like a secret act of atonement. And she is revisited by the thought that the list of things she hasn't told Lucy is becoming quite long.

It is three days since her outing with Lando and Eric the Viking, and Jo is back in her normal spot in the shop. The woman in front of her has not stopped talking for the last five minutes.

'. . . that was when I found out he had spent three hundred thousand pounds on a stripper in Madeira.'

Jo is less surprised that this woman is telling her every intimate detail about her life than that there are strippers in Madeira, a place she associates with her ageing godparents, who always visit the island in the spring.

'We've had one of those on-off relationships – you know how it is,' the woman says earnestly, staring at Jo, as if willing her to understand.

Before Jo can think of an answer, the woman continues, 'And the funny thing is, I had decided this was the last time, and I'd stopped calling him. Now I think he realizes what we had and he keeps texting. Maybe I should give him another chance. It's his birthday on Friday. Do you think he would like a fountain pen? It seems like it would be his sort of thing.'

What can Jo say in reply to this? She pictures herself leaning over, taking the pen the woman is testing from her hand, and writing, *What are you doing buying this idiot a present?*

'You know how it is,' the woman says again, looking hopefully at Jo.

The doorbell sounds its tinny clink and, looking up, she is actually relieved to see Finn walk into the shop. The relief is short-lived; embarrassment and confusion follow. He raises his left hand in greeting; his other hand is grasping a large holdall. Oh God, is he expecting to stay with her? He nods slightly towards her customer who is still looking at her expectantly.

For once, Jo doesn't want to sell a fountain pen. This woman's on-off man clearly doesn't deserve it.

'You know what. If he can afford to spend that sort of money . . .' Jo doesn't want to say *on a stripper*, in front of Finn. It is not his business. Nor is it hers, but she has found that when people start to write with the fountain pens, they start to tell her things. 'If he can afford to spend that sort of money . . . in Madeira,' she amends, 'I'd say he could afford to buy his own bloody fountain pen.'

The woman giggles in surprise, and Jo grins apologetically. She hadn't meant to swear.

And then I would block his number. Jo doesn't say this last bit out loud.

'So you think I shouldn't get him one?'

And Jo realizes with a sinking heart that this woman will always be led by whoever is currently in front of her. She has no doubt that On-Off Man will be enjoying a birthday drink, and probably more, by the end of the weekend. Well, at least he won't be writing with one of her fountain pens.

'Thank you. Thank you,' the woman says, waving the pen around as if uncertain what to do with it.

Jo takes it from her and Finn steps aside to let her get to the door.

'Right, Right, I should go then,' the woman says, as she picks up her handbag. Finn holds the door open for her. Jo notices the woman give Finn a speculative look. She doesn't blame her. She too thought how good he was looking the first moment she saw him: sandy-red hair slightly dishevelled, clean-shaven, clear-eyed. Lithe, fit. And tall. Six foot two of him. He looks like a man who, if he wasn't taking part in the Tour de France, should certainly be commentating on it.

Finn closes the door behind her and stands looking at Jo.

The moment stretches on, and Jo realizes she is holding her breath.

His face inches towards a smile.

Jo smiles tentatively back at him.

Finn grins.

Jo finds she is grinning back.

Then Finn starts to laugh.

Jo feels the answering laughter brimming up within her and it spills into the shop carried on a huge wave of relief.

'Come here, Sorsby!' Finn declares.

Jo heads round the edge of the counter and straight into his open arms.

They stand locked together in a huge hug, rocking slightly and laughing.

'Oh Finn,' Jo says, giving him a final squeeze, before letting go. She thinks how good it is to hold him, to just hug someone. She finds herself wondering how long it has been since someone gave Malcolm a hug.

'We good?' Finn asks, releasing her and looking down at her.

'Yeah,' Jo says, and she knows that they are. 'Coffee?'

'Yep,' Finn replies, dragging his bag over towards the counter and pulling up a stool.

When Jo returns with two mugs, he is doodling something with one of her fountain pens. 'You've been ignoring me,' he says accusingly, but with the laughter still in his voice.

'Well, you weren't exactly getting in touch with me,' she responds, tartly, looking down at the cycle Finn is drawing. 'Have you told Lucy?' she asks him.

He looks up quickly at this. 'Are you kidding?! You know what Lucy's like – she's more like my mum than my sister.'

Jo knows this to be true. Their mother was an erratic presence in their lives, coming and going as the drink took her, her life reflected in the maudlin and tragic country-and-western songs that she sang so well. Lucy ebbed and flowed to her father's side, picking up where her mother left off to help him

103

raise their bevy of boys, none of whom had inherited much from their mother, except her strawberry-blonde hair. Certainly none of them could sing. It was Lucy who was given that one gift by her mother.

So Finn, the youngest of the brothers, was someone always referred to as if he was still barely more than a teenager. And what is he now? Thirty-two? A respected environmental consultant. Still dressing like a surfer and into his bikes, cycling miles most days. But still, to her, Lucy's younger brother.

Out of bounds.

'And that makes that night what? Like sleeping with your mum's friend?'

'Ah, go on, Jo. It was good.' He looks up at her and smiles softly. 'Was always going to happen, ever since Reading Festival.'

'Yeah, I guess,' she agrees.

She always knew Finn had liked her. From thirteen, when she was nineteen, it had been as obvious as the pimples and blemishes that had covered his face. Not a spot in sight now though, Jo thinks, with a half-smile. Oh, there had always been something between them. Nothing ever said, Jo always acting the older sister. Apart from that one time at the Reading Festival. She had been twenty-seven, Finn turned twenty-one. That kiss. Jo smiles slowly at the memory. It was so good. So long in coming. But she knew it was wrong. Called a halt to anything else.

It was a memory she would cherish. But nothing more.

Until that night in Newcastle. It was two weeks before she left for London. She was out with old friends from work, saying goodbye. The database, geeky crowd. At work it was always so good. The in-jokes and teasing. But in that neon-lit bar, they all felt like strangers, struggling to find conversation.

A place for everything and everything in its place comes into her mind.

Then Finn wandered in, the old friends left and, well . . . they drank way too much. Talked about old times. Reminisced about Reading Festival.

Still, she is not sure who was more surprised when they woke up next to each other the following morning.

'Unfinished business,' he says, winking at her.

Rebound, Jo thinks, she had been missing James and had just found out about him seeing Nickeeey. But she doesn't disagree with Finn that it was also unfinished business. 'But no more sleeping with your mum's friend?' she teases.

He looks slightly startled, and she takes pity on him. 'No, we're good as we are,' she reassures him. And they are. She hadn't wanted more, but had been worried he might have done. (Another reason to leave.) It also did not sit easily with her and all her thoughts of Lucy. Lucy, who was like a mum to Finn. And a fiercely protective 'mum' at that.

'So Lucy doesn't know?' Jo persists.

'Of course, not! And I'm not telling her. I wouldn't hear the last of it.' Finn mimics his sister's voice. '. . . *You're taking advantage . . . she's been through enough . . .*' He looks up from his coffee. 'And don't you start spilling the beans either. You don't have to tell her everything.'

Jo is about to say, *But she's my best friend,* when she remembers the other things she has never told Lucy about. 'Believe me, I don't.'

'Anyway, this is my private stuff too.'

He has a point: it's not just her secret to share.

But if Finn isn't behind Lucy's anger, then what is? After all, this is what has stopped her asking Lucy outright. The fear that she knew about Finn, and that she would think *Jo* had taken advantage of *him*. All six foot two, thirty-two years of him. Jo wishes she could smile, but she finds she is too anxious.

'How is she?' she asks.

For the first time, Finn frowns. 'Oh, you know. Bit cranky with the pregnancy. You know the jazz club she sings in sometimes? Well, they let her go. Seems they didn't want a singer with a huge belly entertaining the after-work crowd. Imagine that. Yeah, she was well pissed off with them.' Finn pauses. 'Things okay between you two?' he asks, airily.

Jo pounces. 'She's said something, hasn't she?'

Finn shakes his head. 'Not really. You know Luce and I don't talk like that . . .'

He stops mid-sentence, watching a woman in a yellow coat walk past the window.

Jo follows his gaze. It is Caramel Toffee Girl.

'Nice,' he says, appreciatively.

'Enough of that,' Jo pokes him, feeling that she *is* more like his mum. And also that she doesn't blame him: Caramel Toffee Girl does look nice. Hadn't she wanted the woman to be her friend?

Finn looks back at Jo. 'Oh, I don't know. Lucy's just been a bit weird when it comes to you. Have you fallen out?'

Jo has no idea how to answer this, so instead asks, 'Did you like James?'

Finn shifts on his stool and takes a while before saying, 'Truth?'

'Truth.'

'Thought he was a right tosser.'

'Oh, Finn, not you too.' She leans her head on his shoulder and he puts a consoling arm around her. A picture comes to her of Lucy, Jemima, Wilbur and now Finn lined up, arms crossed, lips pursed, shaking their heads at her.

'I feel like such an idiot. I didn't see it . . . still not sure I do . . .'

'Well, he was a fit, good-looking bloke, who was doing really well. Isn't he what a lot of women want?'

Like Nickeeey, Jo thinks. But Finn's words do make her feel better. He had been all that, and there *had* been good times. Especially when it was just the two of them.

Jo glances down at Finn's bag that is still by the counter. 'Want to stay?' she asks.

'No, you're good. But can I leave the bag here until later? I've got some meetings this afternoon. Should only take a few hours.'

Jo nods.

'I'm staying with Matt from school. Remember him?'

Again she nods.

'He liked you too,' Finn says with a laugh, and Jo grins.

He then grabs her hand and kisses her wrist with a loud smack, 'But when I was fourteen, Jo Sorsby, I proper loved you. And don't you forget it.'

15

In need of an optician

They are on their third coffee when the door opens and Eric the Viking walks in.

Before she can say anything, Finn rises from his seat, 'I'd better get going Jo – I've got a couple of companies I need to call in on. Possible new business leads.' He leans down and kisses her on the cheek, 'See you later.'

As he heads for the door, Jo is conscious she should make some sort of introduction. But what? Her relationship with Finn is too complicated for a one-liner. So in the end she simply says, 'Eric this is Finn. Finn, this is Eric who runs the optician's next door.'

She watches as the two men shake hands and fall into conversation about the upcoming weekend. It seems Finn has a ticket to England's rugby international against Australia, which he is going to with Matt. 'Not my normal sport, but a good crowd are going,' he adds.

'Not into rugby, Jo?' Eric asks, casually, as if assuming she would naturally be going with Finn if she were.

'Working,' is all she can think of to say. She can hardly say, 'He didn't ask me. It's not like that.'

Finn glances back at Jo and then again at Eric. 'Right, see you later, Jo. I'll text you.'

Jo busies herself checking the tester fountain pens. She unscrews each pen to check the level of ink, even though she did this first thing this morning. She finds she is reluctant to start talking about Finn, it's too complicated and she is also aware that a tiny part of her wants Eric the Viking to think that this man (who is younger than he is) likes her.

'Seems like a nice bloke,' Eric offers.

Before Jo can reply, the doorbell sounds. She looks up, hoping for a distraction. Maybe it will be Ruth or Malcolm? She hasn't seen either of them since Ruth escorted Malcolm home several days ago, and she has been worrying about how he is recovering. But it is neither the tall, lanky figure, nor the short, bird-like one; instead a woman in a yellow coat pokes her head around the door. Caramel Toffee Girl.

'Hi, I just wanted to say hello. I don't know if you remember me?'

'Of course – Giana's pen pal. Come in.'

The girl steps into the shop, 'That's it. Well remembered.' She is clutching an envelope that she holds up. 'I just wanted to say thank you. I did write to Giana and she wrote back. I can't tell you how nice it was to get her letter.' She grins delightedly at Jo, her smile also taking in Eric the Viking.

'Oh, this is Eric . . .' Jo very nearly says, 'the Viking'; instead she adds, '. . . the optician.'

Eric flings out a hand and the girl grasps it. 'Really? You're an optician?'

'Certainly am.'

And Jo thinks he holds her hand for a bit too long.

'That's amazing. I need to get my eyes tested. Is your shop around here?' Caramel Toffee Girl spins her head from side to side as if looking for the shop. The sun streaming through the window catches the gold in her curls, like an advert for organic shampoo. The young woman smiles up at Eric the Optician, her freckles crinkling across her nose. And Eric smiles back down at her.

In that instance, Jo sees Eric as if through this girl's eyes.

He is startlingly attractive. It's not just the tall, ash-blond immenseness of him; his face has a simple, uncomplicated openness, with a twist of humour, that Jo can now see is pretty irresistible. Jo realizes with a sickening punch to her guts just how much she likes this man.

Looking at Caramel Toffee Girl smiling up at him, Jo has never felt more average in her life. She feels old, acutely aware of every one of her thirty-nine years. Caramel Toffee Girl is younger than she is, she is sure of that. Much closer in age to Eric the Hand-Holder – who only now lets go of Caramel Toffee Girl.

'I'm next door. Do you want to come in and we can book you in for an eye test. I might be able to fit you in today if you have time?' Eric suggests, holding the door open for her.

'Did you want something, Eric?' Jo tries, even though, to her, this smacks of desperation.

'It can wait,' he says briefly, turning once more to Caramel Toffee Girl.

'Great!' the young woman says, pausing briefly to wave the envelope at Jo, 'and thank you *so* much.'

With a final smile, she is gone. And so is Eric the Viking.

Jo stands completely still for some moments. The relief and pleasure she had felt chatting to Finn drains away. The shop feels hollowed out; completely silent except for the distant thrump of a helicopter somewhere over the city.

Did something just happen there? She thinks it did. She is sure it did.

Jo looks at her reflection in the shop window. A shadowy ghost in borrowed clothes. She continues to gaze in silence. Something definitely connected between Eric the Viking and Caramel Toffee Girl.

Jo feels as if something has just slipped away from her. She would like to rewind time. Why didn't she say he was Eric the Viking, not Eric the Optician? Then maybe the girl might have left and she could have explained about Finn.

She turns to stare at the pens lined up on the counter. Why hadn't she seen things more clearly? She's been wallowing in James-soaked self-pity and fretting about Eric the Viking's age, and she missed the sign. A sign that now feels like it was written in large letters. In black ink.

Eric the Viking was a man who liked fountain pens. How could she have missed *that* sign.

She should have just talked to him – properly – then maybe he might be here.

Instead, Eric the Optician is now leading Caramel Toffee Girl into a darkened room, where Jo imagines he will soon be gazing deep into her smiley eyes.

16

How to improve your handwriting

The afternoon has been dragging and Jo found it hard to concentrate – until the appearance of the police officer with the bad handwriting.

His dark head is now bent towards hers, concentration writ large on his face. 'That looks like a series of waves. So they're not actual letters you have to practise?'

Jo begins to write slowly across the page of the exercise book. 'No, these are just shapes, like these circles here, or these lines.' She points to the strokes she has made across the paper. 'The idea is to teach yourself to form regular shapes. That way, when you come to write, you will be used to forming letters about the same size, and your writing will be more legible.' She knows she's not a campaigner, but maybe, little by little, she could encourage more people to write.

Jo continues. 'The woman I've been watching on YouTube says no more than ten minutes' practice a day.' She shrugs at the police officer. 'No idea why. But she wasn't a woman I'd mess with.'

'Bit like my wife,' the young man discloses, grinning.

He doesn't seem old enough to be married. She has to remind herself that this man actually has the power to arrest her.

Her thoughts flit to Eric the Viking. Then another memory rises to meet it: James and the joke he often told about being with an older woman. What started as a throwaway comment, delivered with a certain amount of pride, laughing about being her 'toy boy', was later aimed at her with more deliberation.

'Lean back a bit, Jo – your face looks saggy when you sit like that.'

She was reaching out towards him over lunch, telling a story. Nice restaurant. Window table. She withdrew her hand as if scalded.

And sat back.

He muttered, 'Don't take it like that, Jo, I'm just saying. None of us are getting any younger.'

She didn't say anything more, just pushed back into her seat as far as she could. The friends at the table with them, James's friends, carried on as if nothing had happened.

At the time she told herself she was making too much of it. He had said 'us', not 'you'.

In front of her, the police officer waits patiently, as Jo slowly turns the page of writing around so he can see better.

A change of perspective. That's all it takes.

What if she wasn't the one who was at fault? Somehow it had always felt as though she must be the one in the wrong, not quite fitting in. But James had definitely meant 'you' and she had felt awful. It *was* a horrible thing to say.

'Okay, I think I could do that,' the police officer comments. 'What else?'

Jo tries hard to concentrate.

'Find some letters in the alphabet that you like to write. It might be the first letter of your name. Now practise writing those with a bit more of a flourish. What you're aiming for is regular writing with the odd fancy bit. Then you can read it, but it's more stylish.'

'And this really works?'

'Yep.' Jo's confidence solidifies. 'That and the things I was telling you about earlier.' She hands a copy of her handwriting tips across the counter to him and pins another one to the noticeboard next to the 'In case of emergency' leaflet. Something of the afternoon spent with Malcolm and Reverend Ruth comes back to her. The feeling it brings is an unexpected gift.

She hands the police officer an exercise book. 'Here, take this to practise in.'

He looks down at his unexpected gift. 'Really?' he asks, hesitatingly. He flicks through the pages of the book. 'I feel I should buy something,' he says, looking around.

'If it works, come back and treat yourself to some stationery or maybe a fountain pen.'

His face clears. 'I could, couldn't I? My mum won't believe it if I actually wrote her and Dad a letter.'

'I am sure your parents would be delighted.'

It is Reverend Ruth that says this. She is standing in the doorway.

Jo feels a rush of pleasure and something like relief at her presence.

The police officer smiles at the diminutive figure and, with renewed thanks, picks up his handwriting guide and exercise book and leaves.

'I caught some of that. What are the other tips?' Ruth asks.

Jo pulls forward a seat for her. 'Would you like a tea or coffee? Then I'll show you,' she suggests, smiling warmly at the Runaway Vicar.

'A coffee would be lovely,' Ruth says, sitting down on the stool and unwinding a scarf, patterned with multicoloured stars from around her neck.

'Nice scarf,' Jo comments, as she heads towards the kitchen at the back of the shop. She calls over her shoulder: 'If someone comes in, sell them the most expensive fountain pen.'

'Will do.'

Oh, Finn! She had almost forgotten about him. She adds, hurriedly, 'And if a guy in a blue cycling jacket comes in looking for his bag, that's Finn and his bag is behind the counter.'

When Jo returns with coffee and flapjacks, Ruth replies as if there has been no break in their conversation. 'Finn?'

Jo sees the beady, bird-like eyes watching her keenly.

'A friend.'

'Boyfriend?'

'Oh, not really. We just . . .'

There is a silence.

Part of Jo feels the urge to put her head on the counter and tell this woman all she is feeling, about how some days she wants a baby and a family so much that it hurts. How troubled she is when she thinks of Lucy . . . and Eric the Viking. How ashamed she is of jettisoning her old friends for James. How she still misses him, but how confused she now is when she looks back at her life with him.

All this swirls through Jo's mind. Yet, another part of her is gripped by a reticence born out of a sense that the Runaway Vicar has enough troubles of her own. She doesn't need to hear this. And she doesn't want to admit what a crap friend she has been. She doesn't want Ruth to think badly of her.

After a wait of some moments, Ruth suddenly looks stricken. 'I'm so sorry. That really is none of my business. I should never have asked. It's nothing to do with me.'

Jo rushes to reassure her, confused by the change in Ruth. 'Really, it's fine. Finn's my best friend's brother. It's . . . complicated. Would you mind if I asked you a question?' she says, changing the subject.

Some of Ruth's humour appears to seep back, as she answers, 'If you must.'

'Does anyone, I don't know . . . in the church, know where you are?'

'Ah, I thought you were going to ask something else,' Ruth says quizzically, head on one side.

Jo thinks Ruth must have been expecting her to ask her why she ran away. She does want to ask this, but she doesn't feel she has any right to. Not yet. It's too personal. There is also an instinct underlying her caution; she senses that if she were to say the wrong thing, she might never see Ruth again. After all, she has form; she is the Runaway Vicar.

'No,' Ruth eventually replies.

'No one?' Jo queries.

'To answer your question correctly: my bishop does not know where I am.' She pauses. 'But he does know that I'm safe. And now, I'd like you to show me how to improve my handwriting. I heard what you said about practising so you have regular writing and adding the odd flourish—'

'You have that already,' Jo interrupts. 'When you wrote the lines from that poem, your S's looked as if they wanted to swirl off and escape.'

'Hmmm,' is all Ruth says, eyeing Jo.

'No, I didn't mean that!' Jo blurts. 'No, I just meant you already have good writing.'

'But it could be better. What are the other tips?'

'To be honest, the rule everyone talks about, which makes the biggest difference, is that we all need to slow down.'

'Just when we write?' Ruth asks, over the top of her coffee mug.

Jo suppresses a smile. 'Well, we are talking about handwriting here.'

'I hoped we were,' Ruth says, unsmiling, but with a gleam in her eye.

Is that it? Had this woman just needed to slow down? Had it all become too much for her? 'And we need to relax.'

'When we write?' Ruth repeats slowly, the gleam becoming more pronounced.

'That is what we're talking about,' Jo retorts, smiling openly now. 'Most people write too fast and hold their pens way too tight. So it's a case of slowing down and relaxing.'

'Is it indeed?'

They look at each other in silence. And Jo feels they are sharing more than just coffee and flapjacks.

'And now,' Ruth says, putting her mug down, 'I want to talk to you about Malcolm.'

'Have you seen him?' Jo enquires, anxiously.

'No. I was going to ask you the same thing.'

Jo shakes her head. 'When you walked home with him, did he say anything else?' Jo is searching for how to mention the 'I didn't want to die' comment.

'About finding out that he didn't want to die?' Ruth supplies.

Jo nods.

'So, you noticed that too. He really did sound quite astonished, didn't he?' Ruth muses, then continues, more decisively, 'We should go and visit him.'

'Do you think he'd mind? He might not want us barging in.'

'I wasn't suggesting we batter his door down. I was thinking of calling around with a bottle of wine.' Ruth pauses, gazing into the air. 'Or do you think he would prefer gin?'

It strikes Jo that the vicars she has known, which she admits aren't many, were more likely to arrive carrying the church magazine rather than alcohol. On impulse she asks, 'Did you do this in your parish?'

'What?'

'Turn up with a bottle?'

120

'Of course. If someone is bereaved, has lost their job, their dog's been put down, or they've been diagnosed with cancer . . . who on earth would want a cup of tea? On the other hand, I have never been turned away with a bottle in my hand.'

Jo laughs. 'No, I don't suppose you have been.'

'It's what you would do for a friend, isn't it?'

It is, of course, but she had always seen vicars as distant characters, dispensing strictures about kindness from the pulpit, rather than knocking on people's doors, wine or gin in hand. 'Did you do a lot of that?' Jo asks, distracted for a moment from the worry about Malcolm.

'What? Drinking?' Ruth asks, innocently.

'No, the visiting. It's just, as you started to list what goes wrong in people's lives, it struck me it must have kept you busy.' She wonders: *did it keep you too busy, take too much out of you?*

'It was the thing I liked the best,' Ruth says, simply.

Jo senses she does not want to say more, so she moves on. 'I think Malcolm would like a single malt whisky. Now I think about it, Uncle Wilbur has a couple of unopened bottles upstairs. I think people have given them to him over the years, but he hasn't touched them. He only drank beer. When were you thinking of going?'

'When do you close the shop? We could go then.'

Jo looks out at the darkening sliver of sky. She feels battered by her day; wrung out with relief at it all being well between herself and Finn, caught out and exposed from watching Eric meet Caramel Toffee Girl. 'You know what – I think I could close up early. It's been really quiet.' She stands up, ready to clear the mugs away, then she catches sight of Finn's bag. 'Oh, I'd forgotten, Finn's coming back for his things.'

Ruth peers over the counter at the bag. 'Is there anywhere you could leave it for him?' she suggests. 'Or we could wait,' she says, slowly, and she sits up straighter on her stool. Ruth's eyes are starting to glint, and Jo can't help feeling that Reverend Ruth has decided she would quite like to get a look at Finn.

Jo studies her warily as she contemplates asking Eric to hold onto Finn's bag for him. He tends to work different hours to her – starting later and finishing later. But his shop, like hers, is small. He might not welcome the addition of a large holdall. Jo is also aware of a battle going on within her – she really wants to see Eric the Viking, yet at the same time cannot face the prospect.

'I tell you what,' she says, pushing herself to make a decision, 'I'll ask my neighbour, Eric, to give Finn my spare key. Then I can just text Finn.'

'Ooh, is that Eric the Viking?' Ruth says. 'Can I come?' She gets up from the stool and starts the job of rewinding the long, star-patterned scarf about her.

Jo grabs the mugs, dumping them in the sink at the back of the shop. As she sprints up the stairs to collect the whisky, she feels the rush of pleasure of a child being let out of school early.

When she returns to the shop, she realizes that Reverend Ruth is on her mobile.

'Yes, thank you for calling. I am delighted you rang.'

Jo pauses, halfway down the aisle, unsure whether to go forward or back. She doesn't want to be caught eavesdropping.

'Yes, certainly.'

Jo takes a cautious step backwards.

'No, I'm glad you rang. I'd really like to talk to you. I think it would make a big difference to you . . .'

Jo stands stock-still. She can't help herself; she wants to hear more.

There is a long pause, before Reverend Ruth continues, 'Yes, it's a good time now. It is always the right time to bring the love of our Lord, Jesus Christ, into your life. Please just open your heart . . .'

This wasn't what she had been expecting – or hoping for.

'. . . the Word will fill your soul with love and wonder . . .'

Jo is crippled with embarrassment. But what had she expected? The woman *is* a vicar.

'Oh, if you must, okay then.'

The shop falls silent. All apart from a low cheerful humming that is coming from the Runaway Vicar.

'You can come out now,' Ruth calls.

Jo edges around the end of the aisle, the bottle of whisky clasped tightly in her fist.

Ruth nods at her phone. 'Scam call. Usually does the trick. Can't wait to get rid of me.'

Jo is still laughing as she and Ruth head towards Eric's shop. She holds the laughter close; it helps combat the nervousness she feels about seeing Eric again. As they open the wooden and glass door (a replica of her own), Jo is aware that this is the first time she has visited Eric the Viking in his own shop. It occurs to her that she has been a bad neighbour too.

Inside, the shop is starkly different from her own: the interior is panelled in pale wood, with glasses suspended in rows around the walls. In front of them is a small, modern reception desk, behind which is a door, presumably leading to the consulting room. Jo is disconcerted not to find Eric behind the desk. But is there relief there too? Mixed up with disappointment? It hadn't occurred to her he might be with a patient. Instead, they are met by the smiling face of a woman who strongly resembles the cook from *Downton Abbey*.

Like Mrs Patmore, Eric's receptionist is quick on the uptake and she is soon storing the key in an envelope and writing Finn's name on it. Jo glances once more towards the inner door, before thanking her and turning to leave.

As they close the main shop door behind them, Jo can't help wondering if Eric the Optician still has Caramel Toffee Girl in the consulting room with him.

17

The exceptional Eve

Ruth had been right. People welcome a visitor (or in their case, visitors) when they arrive with a bottle.

'Come in, come in. This is most kind of you.' Malcolm ushers them in, his long grey cardigan swinging as he flaps his arms in welcome. Jo is pleased to see his colour is much better than when she last saw him, and that the bandage has been replaced by a medium-sized plaster.

Malcolm's house is a small brick cottage, squeezed between two rather grand, white-painted Georgian houses. The bright red front door opens straight into a sitting room and Jo feels as if she has stepped into a softly lit woodland. The chairs and sofa are covered in ivory linen patterned with ferns, the carpet and table lamps are pale green, and the walls are lined with faded botanical paintings. In the small grate, a fire burns.

Catching her looking at the paintings, he says, 'Those are my mother's work, Joanne. She became quite an accomplished artist in the end, and even if it really wasn't what she wanted to do with her life, I do believe she found solace in painting.'

Before Jo can ask what it is she had wanted to do, Malcolm is circling them, encouraging them to take off their coats, and to take a seat, whilst exclaiming over the gift of whisky. He really does seem delighted to see them, and Jo wonders how often he has visitors.

Ruth settles into a chair by the fire, casting Jo a look that so eloquently says, *I told you so*, that she wants to laugh. She takes a seat on the sofa, leaving the chair opposite Ruth's for Malcolm. It is clear it is where he had been sitting, and Jo spots one of his familiar notebooks resting on the arm.

'Now, make yourself at home, and I will get glasses.' Malcolm disappears through a door that leads into the kitchen.

As she and Ruth wait in silence, Jo looks around the room. White-painted bookcases are set either side of the fire and, on the bottom shelf of the right-hand bookcase, she spots a long row of notebooks. There must be forty or fifty of them. Jo catches Ruth's eye and nods significantly towards them. On the walk to Malcolm's house, she told Ruth about the mystery of the book Malcolm is writing (although not about reading the notebook that Malcolm left in the shop). If nothing else, she is determined to find out what Malcolm's book is about.

Ruth, who had also been gazing around the room, now bobs up from her chair and heads towards a small group of black-and-white photographs displayed on a mahogany side table. These are the only photographs or ornaments in the room.

'Oh, my goodness me. No wonder she found life dull.' Ruth glances up from the photographs to the botanical paintings.

Jo has no idea what she is talking about and, before she can ask, Malcolm is back, carrying a silver tray loaded with cut-glass tumblers, the whisky bottle and a plate of biscuits.

'Best not drink on an empty stomach. I thought some shortbread might be a nice accompaniment.' He puts the tray down on a low ottoman, which is covered in a faded green and cream tartan blanket. 'Ah, I see you have spotted the photographs of Mother.'

He leans down and picks up a glass, already generously filled with whisky, and hands it to Jo. He takes the other two glasses and walks over to Ruth. 'Here you go, Reverend Ruth.'

She takes the glass from him and half turns back to the photos. 'Your mother was a Spitfire Girl?'

A warm smile spreads over Malcolm's face. 'She was indeed.'

Jo is now on her feet. The first picture she looks at shows a young woman in flying gear climbing out of what is clearly a Spitfire. 'That's your *mum?*'

'It is indeed, Joanne. And here we have her beside a Short Stirling.' He points to an image of a small figure standing underneath the nose of an enormous aircraft. Another photograph shows a group of women in uniform being presented to a dignitary, who is instantly recognizable as the woman who would become the Queen Mother.

'Wow, so she was . . . did she fly these planes? Was this in the war?'

'Yes, she was in the ATA. Air Transport Auxiliary,' Malcolm says, settling into his chair and stretching out his long, grey-corduroy-trousered legs towards the fire. Jo is startled to see bright purple and orange striped Moroccan-style slippers peeping out from beneath them. They are embroidered all over with tiny golden birds. As if aware of her glance, he tucks his feet quickly out of sight.

'To start with, the ATA was made up of men, perhaps those too old to be fighter pilots, who would ferry aircraft to where they were needed around Britain. Eventually they started recruiting female pilots, and then they advertised for novices and began training a small number of women. My mother was one of those. The upshot was, I think my mother had a rather marvellous war. She said afterwards she was one of the few people who was sad when the war ended.'

Malcolm picks up a shortbread biscuit and stares at it for some moments. 'Yes, it must have been a very exciting time.' He looks up at them. 'You see, fighter pilots would be trained on just the one aircraft. Mother, now, she had to fly anything she was given. It could literally be any one of ninety or so planes.'

'But how did the ATA women know how to fly all of those?' Jo asks.

Malcolm leans over and offers her some shortbread, 'Sometimes they didn't.' He shakes his head as if in disbelief. 'All they had was a ring-bound book, with one page for each aircraft. Mother said you sat in the cockpit, read that and then crossed your fingers. Some of the girls offered up a prayer, but Mother had given up on God, after her father was killed in 1939. She said God should have known he was too ancient to fight again, and that losing part of his face and most of his belief in humanity in the First World War should have been enough for any God.'

Malcolm glances at Ruth, 'I do apologize.' He pauses and adds, 'But maybe you too have lost your faith?'

It seems Jo is not the only one who knows that Ruth Hamilton is the Runaway Vicar.

'Not that,' Ruth replies, softly. 'There have been times, but no. Not now.'

There is a long pause, then Malcolm continues, 'The women were not taught to fly with instruments, and they had no radio either, so it was a case of following the roads and rivers, and trusting that the weather didn't close in. Mother lost friends that way,' he reflects. 'A sudden storm or mist coming in off the sea and it was easy to become disorientated.'

'Malcolm, she must have been the most amazing woman,' Jo says, in awe.

'Ah, Joanne, she was.'

'You weren't tempted to take up flying yourself, Malcolm?' Ruth enquires.

'Oh, no,' Malcolm says, a little sadly. 'I'm afraid I have led a very dull life in comparison.' He pauses, and adds, 'No, I am not a brave man.'

There is a brief silence.

'What was your mother's name?' Jo asks.

'Eve. She was called Eve.'

Ruth rises to her feet and, taking up the whisky bottle, she tops up all their drinks. 'I give you a toast to Eve. A courageous and exceptional woman.'

Jo thinks Malcolm is going to cry, then he pulls back his shoulders and stands up straight (his bright purple and orange slippers peeping out from under the turn-ups of his corduroys). He raises his glass in salute.

Jo scrambles up from the sofa and follows suit.

As they all sit down, Ruth turns to Malcolm, 'And now, I think you should tell Jo and me all about the book that you are writing.'

Reverend Ruth then adds, for good measure, 'Nice slippers, by the way.'

18

When animals speak

Malcolm blushes and coughs and then glances towards the row of notebooks on the bookshelf. He doesn't look exactly enthusiastic, but he does look resigned. Perhaps he feels it is best not to argue with a vicar.

The silence stretches on, as if Malcolm is searching for the right words. Jo looks at Ruth, who simply gazes at nothing in particular. Jo is not fooled; her eyes are gleaming.

'I worry you will think I am rather foolish,' Malcolm eventually confesses, looking down at his clasped hands. He turns towards Jo. 'And I also feel I should apologize to you, Joanne, as I know you have asked me about this before and I have been very rude in not answering you. But where to start . . .' he muses, contemplating the row of notebooks.

'At the beginning?' the vicar suggests, innocently.

'Of course, you are perfectly right,' and Malcolm takes a deep breath. 'I could very well start there.' He sits up straighter in his chair and looks at Ruth. 'I do not know if Joanne has told you, but I have an interest in local history. As a result of this, some years ago, I started attending a number of lectures at Highgate Cemetery. In the early years, my mother came with me.' Malcolm now turns his whole body towards Jo. 'Have you ever visited the cemetery, Joanne?'

Jo shakes her head, feeling she wears her ignorance of London like a badge.

'You have been there, I expect, Reverend Ruth?'

'Of course. Vicars and cemeteries go together like—'

'Blood, poo and vomit?' Malcolm suggests, helpfully.

Ruth laughs, while Malcolm looks calmer. The handwriting 'tips' float into Jo's mind – *you need to slow down and relax.*

'It really is the most marvellous place. Victorian Gothic at its best. To wander in between the tombs, discovering the names of those buried and interred there, is like walking through history. You will find the famous and the great, lying alongside local people, who may not have made such a splash in their lives, but still will have made a difference to those who loved them.'

Jo notices that Malcolm's eyes flick towards the table of photographs. Her mind meanwhile drifts to William Foyle. She has a feeling she knows where that particular bookseller is buried. Another thought occurs to her. 'Is that where your mother is buried?' she asks.

'No, Mother chose to be cremated, and she wanted her ashes scattered on the heath near the swimming ponds. She was a great one for outdoor swimming. They do still bury people in Highgate Cemetery, but only about thirty or so souls a year.

'Well, as I say, I have been visiting the cemetery now for many years. And not just for the history and atmosphere of the place. The wildlife is also a great attraction for me. Between the plots there is such an abundance of growth, one is reminded of the impermanence of human life, of its frailty, compared to the power in nature.' He pauses and says, softly, 'Now nature is a god I could perhaps believe in.'

Malcolm appears lost in thought, so Jo asks, 'Would I know any of the people who are buried there?' She doesn't add, *Apart from William Foyle.*

'Why certainly, Joanne. The two most famous – shall we call them "residents" – are Karl Marx and George Eliot.'

'Really?' Jo remembers studying the Victorian female novelist who wrote under the name George Eliot at school, but realizes she knows very little about Karl Marx, apart from the fact he was involved in the start of Communism.

'Who else is buried there?' Ruth asks.

'The painter Lucian Freud, Charles Cruft who started the annual dog show, the poet Christina Rossetti, the actor Sir Ralph Richardson. Frederick Warne, Beatrix Potter's publisher, the singer George Michael – oh, my goodness, so many. There are over one hundred thousand people buried there.'

'You're kidding?!' As Jo says this, she wonders why she has worried about sensing Uncle Wilbur's presence in her bedroom, when there are that many dead bodies lying just down the road.

'Indeed. Not all of them are famous, of course. There is a man called Ernest, who died when the *Titanic* sank, and a

133

woman called Elizabeth who assisted at Queen Victoria's many confinements.' Malcolm rubs his hands together, warming to his subject.

'And you are writing a history of the cemetery?' Ruth enquires, glancing at the long row of notebooks.

'Ah, not exactly. Oh, this is more difficult to explain. I rather think you will consider me a foolish old man.'

'Would you like another wee dram?' Ruth asks, her accent now more pronounced.

'Yes, indeed. I think I may need it.'

As she tops up their glasses, Ruth starts to look worried, and Jo is reminded of her previous changes in mood. Ruth says in a much more serious voice, 'Malcolm, I do hope you don't think I'm badgering you. Which, of course, I am.' She pauses. 'The trouble, and the privilege, of being a vicar is that you become very closely involved with people's lives. I sometimes think it has made me rather nosy and a bit pushy. Or maybe that came before I was a vicar.' She sits down, still holding onto the bottle. 'If you would rather not tell Jo and me about your book, we will quite understand.'

Speak for yourself. Jo tries to keep her face looking noncommittal and understanding.

'No, no. I have come this far.'

Jo cannot look at Ruth. She thinks the vicar will know she is suppressing a grin.

'Now how to put it?' And Malcolm takes a big slug of his whisky. 'I want to write a ghost story,' he says in a rush. Malcolm looks up at them. 'You don't think that is a ridiculous undertaking?'

'Not in the slightest,' Ruth reassures him, placing the whisky bottle on the floor by her chair. 'It is in the best tradition of Victorian Gothic.'

'Yes, I suppose it is,' Malcolm agrees, perking up. 'I think I have spent too much of my life dealing in hard facts, so it seemed rather fanciful to me. To be honest, I felt embarrassed to talk about it. My work as a tax analyst was all about establishing the truth hidden in the numbers . . . nothing so nebulous as ghosts . . .'

His voice trails off, and Jo and Ruth glance at each other. Malcolm appears lost to them. Jo thinks about their conversation on the way over here, which had touched on the implication of those words, *I didn't want to die.* They hadn't reached any conclusions, but Jo had told Ruth about the slight unease she sometimes feels when she thinks of Malcolm.

To draw Malcolm back, Jo says, encouragingly, 'Well, maybe it's about time for a ghost story.'

Malcolm takes another sip of whisky. The tip of his nose is almost as bright as his slippers. He crosses one leg over the other and one beautiful embroidered slipper swings gently up and down in the warmth of the firelight. Malcolm seems to have completely forgotten his out-of-character footwear.

'Maybe start with where the idea came from,' Ruth suggests.

'Yes, you are right, Reverend Ruth.' Malcolm rubs his hands together. 'The idea came from a story that my mother told me. Something from her childhood. And when she died, I remembered it.' He pauses, and Jo thinks they have lost him again, but he continues, 'She passed away in December, five years

135

ago, just before her ninety-fourth birthday, and she is always very much on my mind at Christmas time. Now, when she was a child, her father had told her that Christmas Eve was the one night of the year that animals could talk. He regaled her with stories of their family's dogs and what they got up to each Christmas Eve night, visiting the other animals they owned: the horses, the ducks and the chickens. As well as speaking to the local wildlife – the barn owls and the foxes . . . ah, yes, the foxes . . .'

Malcolm pauses once more. Jo has no idea why he is dwelling particularly on foxes, but when he starts speaking again she has the distinct impression that there is something more he might have told them but decides against it.

Malcolm continues, 'Ah, well . . . now I hope you don't think I am taking things too far, but I began to wonder what would happen if some of the people who ended their days in Highgate Cemetery were to appear in ghostly form? But just for one night of the year. And that night would be Christmas Eve. What would they talk about? What secrets would they share?'

He looks anxiously at the two women.

'Oh, I love it,' Jo exclaims.

'Malcolm Buswell, you have been hiding your light under a . . .' but Ruth can't finish for laughing.

'Under a Bushel? . . . Or would that be a Buswell?' Malcolm suggests with a slow smile.

19

The art of conversation

An argument has broken out. But as Jo watches them, she realizes that Ruth and Malcolm are thoroughly enjoying themselves. She is reminded of Eric and Lando squabbling in the Italian restaurant.

Malcolm is leaning forward in his chair, his long, slim hands clasped around his knees. In the opposite chair, Ruth is bent towards him, her small feet planted firmly on the floor. While Malcolm's hands pull tight on his knees, causing him to rock back and forward with each point he makes, Ruth is using her hand to swipe at the air, as if batting each point back to him, like a skilled table-tennis player.

'Who's to say just because George Eliot and Karl Marx are the most famous people in Highgate Cemetery that they would necessarily start chatting?' (Swipe)

'Who you end up talking to is so often a matter of chance.' (Swipe)

At this point Reverend Ruth scores a winning point: 'Well, I mean, just look at us three.'

Malcolm holds up his hands, conceding the point. 'That is undoubtedly true.' He nods at Ruth. Both sit back in their chairs and turn to Jo.

Jo hasn't taken part in the argument that sprung up after Malcolm confessed that, so far, he hasn't actually got around to writing a single word of his book. He pulled all the notebooks from the shelves and laid them out on the ottoman (removing the tray for the whisky and returning with coffee). Each of the notebooks, he told them, represented a different person who was buried in the cemetery; they recorded his research into their lives.

Malcolm had been holding tight to the two notebooks that represented George Eliot and Karl Marx, suggesting they should meet within his story and discuss topics ranging from politics to philosophy to religion. He suggested Karl and Mary Ann (as George Eliot had been christened) would enjoy debating George Eliot's translation of the German philosopher, David Strauss's *Life of Jesus*, and her unravelling of Ludwig Feuerbach's *The Essence of Christianity*.

At this point, Ruth had said, somewhat acidly, that the two of them might very well enjoy it, but she wasn't sure any reader would. Jo thought Ruth had a point. But she had also agreed with Malcolm, when he had fired back, that a woman who was considered the 'cleverest woman in London' should not be confined to talking about needlepoint.

Now, argument suspended, they both seem to be expecting something from her.

'Well, Joanne, what do you think?' Malcolm eventually asks her.

Jo looks at the two flushed faces.

'I think,' she says, considering for a moment, 'that we should order a takeaway.'

There is a small grunt of laughter from Ruth.

The remnants of the pizzas have been cleared away and the ottoman has been dragged closer to the fire, so all three of them can rest their feet on it. The notebooks sit in a pile on the sofa beside Jo. Each of them holds a glass of red wine, which Malcolm insisted was essential to go with Italian food.

Jo watches the firelight catch the wine in her glass, turning it from crimson to silver. Ruth and Jo have taken their shoes off and Jo can see their socks through her glass: hers, with navy and cream stripes; Ruth's, red with penguins on. Malcolm has tucked his slippers away out of sight and now his feet, in soft grey socks, rest – one crossed over the other – on top of the faded tartan blanket.

'I believe I need to make another confession,' Malcolm says, sipping his wine. For a moment Jo thinks about those beautiful slippers. 'I strongly suspect the reason I have made so little progress with my book is that I myself do not have the gift of natural conversation.'

Like Jo, Malcolm has been stuck in his own limbo – always researching, never writing.

He continues, 'I have always found it hard to hit on subjects that might be of interest to others. I'm afraid I make rather slow work of it. I fear I'm rather a dull dog.'

'Not at all,' Ruth says, swiftly, 'we have only just met, but you've already introduced Jo and me to a whole different world. I may have visited Highgate Cemetery, but you have made me see it in a completely new light.'

'I have?' Malcolm says, and the trace of hope in his voice touches Jo.

'And look at the conversations we've already had,' Ruth insists.

'It has been *quite* a to-and-fro,' Malcolm admits, brightening. 'And I suppose conversation is so much a matter of practice.'

'I know you must miss your mother, Malcolm. And I'm not at all sure people are right when they say that time makes it easier.'

Malcolm's gaze is fixed on Ruth, and Jo is conscious of this woman's palpable empathy. She is someone people want to confide in – hasn't she felt that herself? Hasn't she wanted to lay the problems of her life down in front of her? Ruth's lack of embarrassment in talking about subjects that others might veer away from comes as a refreshing relief. Does it open the door to confidences that Ruth would rather not have? Is that what had made her run away?

As she watches her, Jo begins to imagine a time when she might ask Ruth why it was she left her parish.

Malcolm doesn't say anything, but looks away from Ruth towards the table of photographs. In the firelight his face is deeply etched with sorrow.

'Malcolm, I don't think you are alone,' Ruth says, gently. 'The art of conversation, like most things in life, is a matter of practice. As a young curate I was often overwhelmed by the prospect of talking to people. I would find all manner of things to do in the vestry rather than join people for coffee after the service.'

'How did you get over that?' Jo asks, finding it hard to imagine Ruth as a shy woman.

'I watched how others did it and copied that . . .'

For a moment Jo thinks of Lucy.

'. . . and, once you start, you usually find something to talk about. Even if it's that you both like dogs.' Ruth smiles at Malcolm, the man who thinks he's a dull dog.

'Right,' Jo says, with sudden decision. 'I have an idea. Move your feet.'

They look at her in surprise but do as they're told. She is surprised too. This is not the behaviour of the woman she has become; the woman who is now living in limbo; the woman who tried so hard to do everything James wanted and who followed where he led (well, rather like a faithful dog). But she wasn't always like this. She may have envied Lucy for her way with people, but she was the one, out of the two of them, who usually came up with the ideas, the one who solved problems.

Jo takes a deep breath and gathers up the notebooks that are piled up beside her and spreads them out on the ottoman.

She gestures to the notebooks containing his research on Karl Marx and George Eliot. 'Now, Malcolm, you can only keep one of those,' she says.

Malcolm frowns at her. 'I'm not sure—'

'One of them has to go.'

'I'm not sure I quite understand, Joanne.'

'Karl or George?'

'Well, if you put it like that, I think I will keep George.' And he holds his Karl Marx notebook out towards her.

'No, give that to Ruth,' Jo instructs, kneeling down on the floor and moving the pile of notebooks around on the ottoman until they are all muddled up. Taking charge has the refreshing feeling of revisiting something in herself, something half-forgotten.

Ruth, who is now holding the Karl Marx notebook, is watching her with a fascinated eye.

'I think we should pick a notebook at random – in my case, two notebooks, as you already have Karl and George. And then, once we've read them, we can come back together and say what we think these people, or rather these *ghosts*, might chat about, when they bump into each other on Christmas Eve. I think it *would* be random, Malcolm – both who actually meets and what they talk about. And the initial chat might lead to things that really mattered to these people. After all, they've been dead for a while and have probably had time to dwell on their lives. What they talk about might surprise you. Well, us.'

There is a moment's silence, then Malcolm bursts into speech. 'I think that is a truly marvellous idea,' he enthuses.

'Brilliant,' Ruth echoes.

'It doesn't mean you have to take up our ideas,' Jo says, suddenly made anxious by their praise. 'It's your story, after all,' she adds to Malcolm.

'No, not at all. I can't wait to begin,' Malcolm says eagerly, surveying the books.

Jo feels her confidence return.

'Oh, we're going to have to blindfold you, Malcolm,' Ruth laughs. 'Don't kid us that you don't know who is behind each cover. You go first, Jo. It's your idea.'

Malcolm is watching her; Jo wonders if he has already guessed what she is going to do. She reaches out and, at random, picks a bright red ring-bound A4 notebook. Then she plunges her hand back into the pile to retrieve the notebook with the torn cover. If she is going to follow this through, she wants the spirit of William Foyle by her side. A man who certainly got things done. As she touches the damaged cover, she feels there is no harm in having Uncle Wilbur by her side too.

She catches Malcolm's eye and he gives the shadow of a nod.

Suppressing a smile, Jo turns to Ruth, 'You next.'

'So I keep Karl Marx, and just pick one more?'

'Yes. I think Malcolm has a point about wanting to include the two most famous ghosts. I think readers *would* be interested in them. I know I'd be interested to see what Karl had to say to a stranger he might bump into as a ghost – and what they would have to say to him.'

'Okay,' Ruth nods, 'here we go,' and she reaches out and grabs a yellow and white striped notebook.

'Now, your turn, Malcolm,' Jo says, beginning to enjoy her new role.

'And you have to promise to close your eyes,' Ruth insists, leaning forward and shuffling the notebooks around some more.

Malcolm reaches out his long arm, eyes tightly shut, and digs under the pile for who George Eliot will meet. He pulls out a shiny blue hardback notebook and opens his eyes.

'Oh my!' he exclaims and he starts to laugh. 'Oh, my! Oh my!' And he brings this new notebook together with his George Eliot research with a clapping sound. 'Now, what are you two going to have to say to one another?'

'Who is it?' Jo and Ruth ask together.

'Issachar Zacharie.'

'Who?' they ask, once more in unison.

'Issachar was Abraham Lincoln's chiropodist.'

'Oh, my,' Ruth echoes.

'Indeed,' Malcolm says, his eyes as bright as hers. 'This will need *some* thinking about.'

Feeling rather overwhelmed Jo says, weakly, 'Ruth, who is Karl Marx meeting?'

Ruth opens up her yellow and white striped notebook and frowns. 'I'm not sure I've heard of her either.' She looks enquiringly at Malcolm. 'Leslie Hutchinson?'

'Leslie was actually a man, and you might have heard of him by his stage name, Hutch.'

'Hutch? That's more familiar. Why am I thinking of Nat King Cole?'

'You are heading in the right direction,' Malcolm assures her, looking positively bushy-tailed. 'He was a cabaret star, originally from Grenada, but eventually he settled in London. He was performing a few years earlier than Nat King Cole. Maybe "Cole" came to mind because you recalled he was Cole Porter's lover for some time. As he was, of Edwina Mountbatten, Earl Mountbatten's wife.'

'Oh my!' and Ruth is really laughing now. 'So Hutch and Karl Marx . . .' Ruth grins, 'This is fascinating. I can't wait to start reading your notes.'

'How about you, Joanne, who have you got?' Malcolm asks, with all the appearance of someone who does not already know the answer.

Jo opens the damaged notebook. 'William Foyle. Founder of the bookshop,' she says without reading a word of what is written there.

'Oh, you will enjoy his story,' Malcolm says. 'He was a great character. When he was in charge, Foyles was the most famous bookshop in the world. They called him the Barnum of booksellers.'

Jo hurriedly opens the red notebook. 'John Lobb?' she says, looking enquiringly at Malcolm.

'Lobb, you say?' And with this he ducks his head down and, picking up his purple and orange slippers, he disappears through a small door set in the wall to the side of the mahogany table. Ruth and Jo stare at each other as they listen to Malcolm's feet running up the stairs.

A few minutes later, Jo and Ruth hear a heavier tread descending the stairs and Malcolm reappears in the sitting room.

Instead of the exotic slippers, he is wearing a pair of smart black brogues. He walks over and, lifting his trouser legs slightly, clips his heels together.

'I give you the work of John Lobb.'

Then, as if regretting such a theatrical entrance, he colours and, looking flustered, quickly sits down. 'Although these shoes were not of course made by the great man himself. John Lobb died in 1895.'

'Lobb. Yes, I *have* heard of them,' Ruth admits, smiling. 'Don't they have a very smart store in London?'

'Oh yes, their shop is on St James's Street, where they continue to make handmade shoes. I bought these shoes there when I was twenty-five. So that makes these shoes forty-eight years old.'

Jo does a quick mental calculation of Malcolm's age: seventy-three. So seven years younger than Uncle Wilbur.

'Well they are in amazing condition,' Ruth says, peering at Malcolm's feet.

'Oh, they are built to last. Oh, please excuse my pun,' Malcolm chortles. 'Every customer's foot has their own wooden last – a piece of wood that has been carved to the customer's exact foot dimensions, so that their shoes can be made to fit perfectly. They have a store of these personal lasts, going back over more than a hundred years.'

Jo wants to ask how much these shoes cost, but doesn't like to.

'So how much would it cost me to have a pair of handmade shoes?' Ruth enquires.

Jo suppresses a smile.

'I'm afraid to say that, these days, it would be quite a few thousand pounds, and it takes several months to make them. So many highly skilled craftsmen and women are involved.'

Ruth studies Malcolm's feet, head tilted to the side. 'Well, that is definitely beyond my budget, but if they last that long I can see why you might invest in them.'

'What did make you buy them?' Jo asks, emboldened by Ruth's directness.

'My father always wore Lobb shoes and boots, and when I came into a small inheritance at twenty-five, I decided to invest in a pair myself.'

'Did your father take you to buy them?' Jo asks, envisaging this tradition being passed down from father to son.

Her romantic imaginings are brought up short by Malcolm's answer.

'No, my father died in a car crash when I was twelve. As did my younger brother.' He hesitates, his voice wavering. 'They had been on their way to get the Sunday papers, my brother had gone along in the hope of sweets. The money I received at twenty-five was from a small trust fund my father had set up when I was born.'

'Oh, Malcolm, that's terrible. I'm so sorry,' Jo says.

'I would say those shoes have been worth every penny. I imagine you remember your father every time you put them on,' Ruth says quietly.

'I certainly don't need a pair of shoes to remember my father,' Malcolm says, brusquely, then taking in a sharp breath, rushes on, 'I do apologize, Reverend Ruth. That was uncalled for.' He adds, dryly, 'But you will perhaps understand why I gave up believing in God before I turned thirteen.'

'I can indeed,' Ruth replies, with composure. She reaches for her shoes. 'But now, I really think I need to be heading to my bed.'

Jo sees that the clock on the mantelpiece is showing past midnight.

Ruth rises to her feet, gathering up her two notebooks: Karl Marx and Hutch. Jo does the same, slipping John Lobb and William Foyle into her backpack.

'We'll take Jo to Highgate Cemetery on Sunday,' Ruth says, decisively.

Before either Jo or Malcolm can say anything, Ruth rushes on, 'You see, there I go again. You may worry you say too little, Malcolm. I feel that I say too much, just bustle in and take over. You worry you're a dull dog. I worry I'm a bossy bitch.'

'No!'

It is the 'bitch' that makes Jo react so instantaneously. Ruth is the last woman in the world she would ever call a bitch.

'Well, I hope not a bitch,' Ruth concedes, seeming to register their shock. 'But definitely bossy.' She smiles.

Jo thinks that she could give Ruth a run for her money in that department, if tonight's behaviour is anything to go by. 'Highgate Cemetery, Sunday,' she says as she leaves, 'it's a date.'

Which makes her think of Finn. Has he collected his bag? Had he been expecting to see her this evening?

She hasn't as much as glanced at her phone since Malcolm opened the whisky.

It is then that she remembers the key. Will Eric the Viking simply think she has left the key so Finn can let himself into his girlfriend's flat?

20

John Lobb's boots

The following day Jo is hanging fairy lights around the top of the wooden shelving. It is mid-November and this is her first nod towards Christmas. She also adds a small table lamp to one of the shelves that she has cleared to make it look like a desk, set as if ready for someone to start writing. She places a half-written letter on the blotter and tucks an envelope underneath it. This gives her an idea.

Returning to the counter, she takes a packet of the old-fashioned envelopes that no one (except a Runaway Vicar) appears to want to buy, and opening them she writes random names and addresses on the front of each (in her best handwriting). She starts to have fun with these and includes fictional characters, friends and a Viking called Eric. Jo then searches out Uncle Wilbur's old philately album and, selecting colourful stamps from the packet of loose stamps he hadn't deemed worthy of mounting, she sticks these to the letters. Next she cuts lengths of different-coloured ribbon and hangs the envelopes from these across the window, like multi-layered envelope bunting. Left with a short bit of ribbon, she creates a small strip of envelope bunting for the top of her noticeboard.

She has just finished when the door gives an ominous rattle and Eric the Viking steps into the shop, carrying a parcel in one hand, and trying to close the door against a sharp wind with the other. When the wind blows from the East, the alleyway becomes a wind tunnel, and Jo has often watched pedestrians battle their way up the alley, hair streaming back, eyes watering.

'A courier dropped this off yesterday,' Eric says, finally winning the battle with the door. 'I think it might be fountain pens, going by the brand name. I was very good, I didn't sneak a look,' he grins, 'but I think it's only fair that you open it now. Do you fancy a coffee?' he offers, before dumping the package on the counter.

'Cappuccino would be good, thank you,' Jo says, grateful for the time it will take for Eric to go to the café and back. She hopes she can get her head and heart in order by then.

Eric leaves to get the coffee, acting like nothing happened yesterday. And maybe nothing did, and she is reading far too much into his meeting with Caramel Toffee Girl? Then she remembers Eric the Hand-Holder. Jo stares out of the window, replaying it in her mind. She's not sure what to think. But maybe it was easier this way. Just put him out of her head.

She tries to retreat into thoughts of James, but she finds this just makes her feel weary and slightly sick. Instead, she revisits how heart-thumpingly pleased she had been to see the Viking coming through the door. And then, once again, she remembers Caramel Toffee Girl's smile, and feels her stomach twist.

Things are so much simpler with Ruth and Malcolm. Despite the mystery surrounding Ruth's sudden flit, Ruth and Malcolm's spats (which they seemed to thoroughly enjoy), and the worry about Malcolm's words, 'I didn't want to die', everything is definitely easier.

She was tempted to tell Ruth about Eric, James and Lucy, and oh, so much more, on their walk home last night. Jo was just about to open her mouth, when Ruth said cheerily, 'Well, this is me,' and after a 'goodnight', veered off down a side street at the very top of the High Street. Earlier she had told Jo she was renting a studio flat that was particularly reasonable as it was no bigger than the vestry back in her old church.

Jo is just finishing a text to Finn (*Have a good time at the rugby. Glad you got your bag OK. Sorry not to be here*), when Eric arrives with the coffees. Jo puts her phone away.

'So you met Mrs Patmore?' Eric says, making himself at home on the stool in front of the counter.

'She's not *really* called Mrs Patmore?' Jo says, laughing.

'Yes, she is – what's wrong with that?'

'Have you never watched *Downton Abbey*?'

Eric shrugs.

'You mean she really *is* called Mrs Patmore?' Jo repeats. 'That's amazing.'

Eric shakes his head, grinning. 'It's like taking candy from a baby.' Before Jo can respond, he adds, 'Thanks for introducing me to Clare, by the way.'

'Clare?'

'Met her here yesterday. Thought she was a friend of yours? Needs new contacts and has ordered glasses too. So cheers for that,' he says, raising his coffee cup in salute.

Clare? So it's Clare now. What can she say? She knows what she wants to ask, but she can't think of any combination of words that wouldn't give her away.

'I didn't know her name. She's just a customer.' Then, thinking this sounds dismissive, adds, 'She seems really nice though.'

'Oh, she is. She's great. We had a good chat while I got her sorted.' He nods towards his shop. 'Just one of those genuinely warm and straightforward people. You don't meet them that often. Really open and smiley.' He grins again. 'So I owe you one. Well, more than one.'

Jo wishes he would just shut up and drink his coffee.

To distract him from how great Clare is, she starts to unpack the parcel he took in for her. Inside are twenty pastel-coloured fountain pens, short and compact, with lids that are hexagonal rather than rounded. They are amazingly light to hold. Jo takes a blush-coloured one and unscrews the top; the lid clips perfectly onto the end.

'Nice,' Eric comments, 'but a bit too small for me.' He holds out his hands in front of him and Jo wishes he wouldn't.

'You've been getting a lot of new stock in,' he says, glancing around. 'You expanding your range?'

'Yes, stationery is something I've always loved, so I thought why not buy some bits that I really like.'

'I can see that,' Eric says, with an approving nod at her window bunting.

Jo concentrates on unpacking the pens and moves the empty box aside to open the top of the cabinet. As she does so she knocks her coffee with the edge of the box. She catches the cup before it spills, but Malcolm's notebook spins off the counter and falls open on the floor. She was reading all about John Lobb earlier this morning.

Eric leans down and picks it up for her. 'Great handwriting,' he comments. 'Yours?'

'No. It's a friend's. I'm helping him with some research. He's investigating some of the people who are buried in Highgate Cemetery.'

'I love that place!' Eric responds, with enthusiasm. 'Couldn't believe it when I first visited it. Just went there because I thought my dad might like to see it. But it's crazy. Those Victorians sure knew how to do death.' He hands the notebook back to Jo. 'So, who've you been reading about?'

'It's a guy called John Lobb. He was a boot-maker.'

'Lobb? Yeah, I think I've heard of them. Traditional, cost an arm and a leg?'

'Yep, but John who built the business started with nothing.'

'When was this?'

Jo flicks through Malcolm's notes, 'He was born in 1829.'

Eric settles down on the stool, like he's not going anywhere soon, 'Go on.'

'He came from a poor Cornish farming family, but he struggled to work on the farm after a run-in with a donkey left him with a load of broken bones, and eventually a limp. So he trained as a boot-maker. When he was a teenager he decided to go to London to make his fortune but, as there was no money to pay for the journey, he decided to walk.'

'Jeez, that would have been tough, even if you didn't have a leg injury.'

Jo nods. 'Anyway, there were thousands of boot- and shoe-makers in London at the time, but John decided he only wanted to work for the best, so he walked straight into Thomas's, on St James's Street, demanding to see old man Thomas.'

'What happened?'

'Thomas threw him out on his ear.'

'Shame. Thought you were going to say he won him around.'

'Nope, John ended up out on the side of the road. And he's there roaring and shouting that Thomas would be sorry and that he would build a firm that would knock him sideways.'

Eric grins. 'Which presumably he did?'

Jo grins back at him, thinking how good it is to share this with him.

'Long story. But, yes. Anyway, at this point he's in London, on the side of the road, with barely any money. So then he decides to get himself to Australia as he's heard that people are growing rich finding gold.'

'As you do. And did he find gold?'

'No. But he found a lot of prospectors wearing really badly made boots.'

Eric laughs. 'Don't tell me . . .'

'Yes, John started making them new boots. And he invented something called the Prospector's Boot. It had a space in the heel where prospectors could hide their gold, where no one would find it if they were robbed – which happened quite a lot.'

'Great idea,' Eric says, appreciatively, and his enthusiasm reaches something within Jo and she is conscious that she would like to share more stories with this man. And to hear his stories too.

She picks up her thread, 'That *did* make him rich – because many of his customers paid him in gold nuggets as they didn't always have ready cash.'

'This is great stuff, Jo. What happened next?'

She continues, smiling warmly at him, relaxing into his encouragement. 'He entered some boots he'd made for the Great Exhibition in 1851.'

'So, was he back in England for that?'

'No, still in Australia, but he won a gold medal. And he was only twenty-two at this stage . . .' Jo wonders, looking at Eric, why age is such an issue with her? She knows the answer to this, but then she remembers sitting in a woodland sitting room with a Runaway Vicar and a man in embroidered slippers. Had age mattered then?

'What next?' Eric prompts.

'Oh, well, he then decided to make a pair of boots for Queen Victoria's son, the Prince of Wales.'

'Was that Bertie? The womanizer? Am I getting that right? Science was more my thing at school than history.'

'Yes, that's him. How John did it, I have no idea, as they must have been made to his exact measurements and John was still in Australia. Anyway, he sent him the boots as a gift and Bertie loved them. Then John writes and asks if he can have a royal warrant.'

'Why doesn't that surprise me,' Eric drains his coffee, and Jo is conscious that she doesn't want him to go.

She carries on quickly. 'Well, at the time Queen Victoria was giving Albert and Bertie a hard time for handing out royal warrants, as she thought she was the only one who should do this. So, maybe Bertie gave John one to annoy his mother, or maybe he thought it wouldn't really matter as this was an Aussie boot-maker that he would never hear from again.'

'But I have a feeling that wasn't the last he heard from Mr Lobb.'

'No. That's when John came to London, with his gold and his royal warrant and set up a shop on Regent Street.'

'Ah, I thought you were going to say he set up next to old man Thomas on St James's.'

'He did,' Jo grins, 'but that came a bit later. I've seen photos of the shop on Regent Street. I looked it up after reading Malcolm's notes.'

'Malcolm?'

'The friend I'm helping. The amateur historian.'

'What was the shop like?' Eric asks.

'Very traditional, but above the door was the biggest royal warrant I have ever seen. It was simply enormous.'

'I wonder what Bertie thought.'

'Maybe he laughed,' Jo says. 'He certainly went on ordering boots from John. So did other members of the royal family and, oh, sultans, and a huge number of other famous people.'

'Not bad, for a poor lad from Cornwall,' Eric sounds impressed.

'That's what I thought,' Jo says, but what she is really thinking is just how much she likes this Viking from Birmingham, who writes with a fountain pen.

A man who listens to her.

Had James ever *really* listened to her?

They are interrupted by a light tapping on the window.

'Ah, it's Clare,' Eric says, getting up. 'Better be going.'

Clare waves at them both, her caramel toffee curls twisting in the wind. As Jo watches her, she doesn't know if she is imagining it, but Clare looks slightly uncomfortable. She looks like a woman who is embarrassed to see her.

Jo reflects she may have got away with it with Eric. He may not have guessed how much she likes him. But she's not so sure she's fooled Clare. Clare is doing a good impersonation of a woman who suspects she may have stepped on Jo's toes. She may be happy that it is she, not Jo, that Eric is now leading towards his shop, but she is also clearly discomfited.

More evidence – that Jo could well do without – that Caramel Toffee Clare is a nice woman.

21

Highgate Cemetery

The light is extraordinary. Above her Jo can see where the branches of the trees splinter the late afternoon sunlight, diffracting the rays so that in places the light is firefly bright, in others, diffused and softened, turning the stone angels golden. Everywhere she looks there are tombs and grave-stones. And growth. Greenery shrouds the tombs so it appears like the leaves have become part of the carvings. In places it seems the monuments are growing out of the tangle of ivy, and in others like the ropes of intertwined leaves are reaching up and pulling the stones into the earth, reclaiming them. Underfoot, the pathways are mottled terracotta, and old leaves lie scattered among the graves like curling flecks of rust – a reminder that the year is ageing, as is everything around them.

They had met at the entrance to the Western Cemetery – the cemetery being divided into two halves, positioned either side of a steep, narrow lane. Malcolm was back to his sombre self, dressed entirely in grey gabardine. Ruth was wrapped up warmly, her star-spangled scarf coiled around her neck and chin like a jolly python. Malcolm had passed Jo a map of the cemetery, commenting, 'One for the pinboard.' She looked up quickly, surprised and touched that he has noticed her growing collection.

Now Malcolm is guiding them along paths that lead upwards through the ancient Western half of the cemetery, pointing out graves of particular interest as he goes: a Regency bare-knuckle boxer who had the largest funeral London had ever seen; a monument topped by an elephant for the man who started the first zoo in England.

Jo gazes at the marble elephant and wonders if Uncle Wilbur ever visited the cemetery. He had never brought her here as a little girl, their favourite outing on a Sunday being to London Zoo. She had thought about revisiting the zoo when she first came to London, but wasn't sure she would enjoy it without her uncle there, retelling his favourite story of the zoo keeper who ran a sideline opening the reptile house at night for his neighbours from the East End – until two of his visitors were killed by a Black Mamba snake.

Jo hurries to catch up with Malcolm and Ruth, who have just disappeared along the Egyptian Avenue, an ornate curved channel that leads to the catacombs. From here they descend the hill, crossing the road to start exploring the Eastern side of the cemetery. Broad avenues bordered by tombs lead into smaller byways, and then into narrow paths that eventually became impassable in the tangle of growth and gravestones. Jo loses count of the names she has read or tried to read on the headstones.

She is just turning quickly away from a small gravestone for a baby when she spots a red stone monument for an industrialist from Birmingham. Hadn't Eric the Viking said he brought his father to the cemetery? She tries to dismiss the thought. It is enough that she is constantly looking for Eric every time someone walks past her shop window. She doesn't want him invading this time with Ruth and Malcolm, which is such a respite from all that troubles her.

She moves further along the path to join Ruth. She hears the Runaway Vicar murmuring words under her breath, and she wonders if she is praying or just passing the time of day with the dead. They are both crouched down studying a grave of a young woman who died in the 1850s, when Jo remembers something she has been meaning to ask her.

'Ruth, I get that vicars go with cemeteries, but I've been wondering, why do vicars go with blood, poo and vomit? Did you work in a particularly tough area?'

Ruth bobs up from where she had been crouching, 'Oh, you don't have to live in a rough area to come across those three.' She studies Jo for a moment, 'You must have seen it, where you used to live and where you grew up. You can be in the most beautiful spot in the world but there will always be people in trouble.' She nods towards a bench, 'Shall we sit here for a bit? I think Malcolm may be a while.'

Jo glances towards the tall figure of Malcolm, who is

examining a tomb further up the path. He is busy making notes in a small book.

As Ruth sits down she proclaims, 'Dr and Mrs Claybourne.'

'Who are they?' Jo asks, looking about her for a tomb.

Ruth shakes her head. 'Oh, no, not from here. John and Sonja Claybourne were from my last parish. Lovely couple. Lived in the sort of cottage you see on Christmas cards. Their son, Paul, died of . . . well, they say it was a drug overdose. But in the end, who knows. I believe it might have been exposure or malnutrition. They found his body in their garden on the seventh of January, six years ago.'

'That's awful.'

She realizes, without having to be told, that Ruth had stood beside Paul's parents in that wintry garden.

Jo thinks back to her own childhood. 'I was aware of some problems growing up, but not that many, if I'm honest. Maybe that was because we were on a farm, and I was young. I think my parents would always help people they knew were struggling, I'm pretty certain of that. But they didn't talk about it.'

'Quite right,' Ruth says, briskly. 'When your right hand gives, even your left hand shouldn't know what the right hand is doing.'

'Who said that?'

'Jesus,' Ruth says, raising an eyebrow. 'I wish more of my congregation followed it. Quite a few spent a great deal of time advertising their Christianity to the world. I sometimes thought they should just have had done with it and worn a sandwich board: *I'm a Christian and I enjoy gossip and philanthropy.* It would have saved an awful lot of breath.'

'Were there many like that?' Jo asks.

'A few. And some skipped the philanthropy part,' Ruth says, with a grin.

Jo is about to laugh when she sees that, once again, Ruth is looking anxious.

'No. No, that is unfair of me. I shouldn't say that. Many, *many* of the people I knew did a great deal of good.'

Ruth's frown clears and suddenly she laughs out loud.

Jo looks expectantly at her.

'I'm sorry, I was just thinking of my curate, Angela. I do miss her. She was a quiet thing, but had a wicked sense of humour. Our churchwarden, Colin Wilkinson, now he was quite the opposite: a large, bluff, angry kind of man. I don't think he was always very kind to Angela. Instead of "Wilkinson", behind his back she used to call him, "Mr Will-kill-soon".'

Jo joins in Ruth's laughter, wondering if Colin is one of the people Ruth imagines wearing a sandwich board.

Ruth pulls a packet of jelly babies from her pocket and offers one to Jo, 'Are your parents churchgoers?'

'Christmas and Easter, and not so much at Easter these days.'

Ruth nods and says nothing more. Jo notices that Ruth hasn't asked her directly about her own faith, and also that Ruth is not the one who usually introduces religion into the conversation – unless it's a scam call, she remembers, smiling. If anything, it is Malcolm who is the one who tends to lead the conversation in that direction.

'Anyway, you were asking about the blood, poo and vomit,' Ruth recalls, returning to Jo's original question. 'Well, a vicarage and church can be magnets for drunks, addicts, vandals and thieves. They may well be the people who need your help the most, and that is fine, but there will always be one or two who take the piss. And in some cases deposit their piss and shit on your doorstep or in the aisle of your church.'

'God! How did you cope with that?' Jo asks, then wishes she had skipped the 'God' part. Talking to a vicar brings with it a self-consciousness that she isn't used to. Is that a problem for Ruth? Is she aware of people treating her differently?

Unperturbed, Ruth replies, 'Usually with a bucket and bleach.'

'But how did you work out who you could help and who you couldn't?'

'I don't think I ever did. You have to try, but you also have to accept that you can't always make a difference.'

This reminds Jo of something, 'Last night, I was reading more about William Foyle. When he'd become rich and successful, people would write him begging letters. He knew that some people would be trying it on, but he replied to them all, including money in the envelopes. When people told him he was a fool, he asked, how would he know he was reaching the people in real need if he didn't help them all?'

'I'm looking forward to hearing more about him,' Ruth says, leaning back on the bench and looking up through the trees to the last of the afternoon sunshine.

'Weren't you ever frightened? I mean of people turning up at the vicarage and church?'

'Sometimes I was, especially as I was a woman living on my own.' Ruth looks back towards Jo. 'I was married for a short time, but it didn't last. So, being alone, I had to be sensible about who I would invite in.' She goes back to studying the trees above her. 'I may believe in God,' she says, with the trace of a smile, 'but I'm not stupid.'

Jo grins.

'I did think I was being broken into once,' Ruth goes on, meditatively.

'What happened?'

'I kept hearing noises on the stairs – it was first thing in the morning. I called out a few times but no one answered. Then I started getting really worried, so I jumped out of bed and grabbed the first thing that looked like a weapon.' Ruth starts to laugh.

'What? What?' Jo says, starting to smile herself, without knowing why.

'Then Angela, my curate, appeared at my bedroom door carrying a breakfast tray and a bunch of flowers. It was my birthday.' Ruth is rocking with laughter by now.

'And you?'

'Well, I was stark naked, pointing a hairdryer at her, like one of those community support people who stand by the road with a traffic gun.'

Jo gives a shout of laughter. 'But without the high-viz jacket.'

'Or anything else,' Ruth agrees. 'It took quite a while to calm Angela down.'

Ruth is wiping her eyes now. 'I don't think she'll forget that sight in a hurry.'

Jo continues to laugh, thinking how much she likes this woman.

'But where were we?' Ruth says, looking around. 'Oh, the people you try and help, well, we were never short of them.' She waves a hand towards the tombs, 'Still, we wouldn't want to go back to this.'

'To what?' Jo asks, puzzled.

'To the Victorian age of only helping the "Deserving Poor". You just have to look at how women were treated. Nobody was less deserving of help and pity in society's eyes than a fallen woman.'

Jo shakes her head. 'I've never really hung out with a vicar before. Are they all like you?'

'Oh, we're a mixed bag,' Ruth smiles. 'What would you have expected?'

'I guess I might have expected you to ask me about my beliefs.'

Ruth's laugh rings out into the still November air, 'Oh believe me, I don't normally have to ask. People are more than happy to ambush me and tell me what they do and don't believe in. And usually, where the Church – and I personally – have gone wrong.'

Ruth is still chortling to herself when Malcolm comes to join them.

22

Coming or going

Malcolm addresses them. 'Now, my dears, the light is beginning to fade and I think before we leave we should pay our respects to Karl Marx and George Eliot.' He swivels on the spot, the stones on the path screeching under the sole of his Lobb brogue, and he strides away. Jo and Ruth are left to scurry after him.

A few minutes later, they are standing in front of the monument to Karl Marx. It is a huge rectangular block of stone, on top of which is an enormous, bulbous head. Karl Marx stares down at them from under shaggy brows – a complement to his flowing locks and beard.

Malcolm is bending down, examining the tributes that have been placed at the base of the tomb: a holly wreath, some wilting scarlet roses, and a bunch of red plastic carnations.

'I've been reading up about Karl,' Ruth says in Jo's ear. 'I think that enormous lump of stone rather suits him. He was a huge bear of a man with hair coming out of every orifice.'

'What was he like as a person?' Jo asks.

'Difficult to say at this stage. There's some good stuff in there, but I'm having to wade through an awful lot of politics and pontificating. He seems to have fallen out with most people he met.' Ruth grimaces, 'But I suppose I wasn't expecting the father of the Communist Manifesto to be a bundle of laughs.'

'William Foyle, you know who I was telling you about, he wrote a kind of manifesto – but it was all about books.'

'Really?'

'Yes, I don't think he called it a manifesto, but it read like one. I rather liked it. I can't remember all of it, but there was something about supplying the greatest number of books to the greatest number of people.' Jo steps forward to join Malcolm, who is still studying the flowers at the base of Karl Marx's tomb. The tall figure is bent at a right angle, as if folded at the waist. 'Malcolm, do many people leave tributes here?'

Malcolm slowly unfolds until he is standing upright, 'Yes, indeed. Although when Karl died, only a handful of people attended his funeral. Since then it has become a place of pilgrimage for many. Not all of whom wish him well. Over the years a fair few have tried to deface or destroy this monument.'

'But no one's succeeded?' Ruth asks, looking more bird-like than ever as she hops up the shallow step in front of the tomb.

'No, not completely. But someone did once put a bomb under it.'

'Wow! Was there a lot of damage?' Jo asks, staring up and reading the inscription underneath the stern face: *Workers of All Lands Unite.*

A slow smile spreads across Malcolm's face. 'I'm not sure the bombers achieved quite what they intended. The device didn't destroy the tomb. It just made it tilt a bit more to the left.'

'Oh, Karl would have liked that,' Ruth says, appreciatively. 'Now where is George Eliot? My feet really are beginning to freeze standing here.'

'Oh, yes, yes, indeed. One more stop and then I think we should get some tea.'

Jo isn't convinced by the idea of tea; she has been dreaming of a warm pub for the past half-hour.

Malcolm leads them up one of the side paths to a much smaller grave. At the head of a shallow rectangular trough is a simple monument. Underneath the stone edifice are the two names: George Eliot; and also, Mary Ann Cross; and the dates, 1819–1880.

'Why did she write under the name George Eliot?' Jo asks, thinking of Jane Austen and the Brontë sisters. Hadn't they paved the way for female novelists?

'At the time she really started to write she was living with a man who was already married. George Henry Lewes, her partner, was accepted in society regardless, but George Eliot was an outcast. So writing under her own name would have been difficult. I believe she chose the name "George" in honour of her lover.' Malcolm explains.

'A fallen woman,' Jo comments, remembering her earlier conversation with Ruth. 'So was George Eliot shunned for the rest of her life?' she asks.

'No, fame changed that. She really was quite a celebrity. Then she became a much more palatable proposition, especially once it was known Queen Victoria liked her books. And then eventually George Lewes died and so she was no longer living in sin. But I think it is fair to say the world judged her harshly, despite her prestigious talent. On the other hand, I think it is also fair to say that she could be tricky, and did not always have an easy relationship with those who surrounded her.'

Malcolm taps the edge of the grave with the toe of his brogue, 'As a result of which, she upset some very influential people, and I believe that was the reason her request to be buried in Westminster Abbey, alongside other writers – like her friend Charles Dickens – was refused.' He sighs, 'And so here she lies.'

'It's good to know that she's still famous and that things have changed, compared to her day. People have more freedom to live the way they want,' Jo suggests.

Malcolm gives her a long look, but says nothing. He turns his attention to Ruth. 'And the sad thing is, George Eliot would have had no hope in death. She gave up believing in God as a young woman, and consequently was treated appallingly by her family. No. She had been brave enough to live outside the conformities of society, but all the comfort the Church had to offer her was the prospect of everlasting Hell.'

'Oh, I don't believe in Hell,' Ruth says, breezily, flapping her arms about her as if to warm herself.

'You, a vicar, don't believe in Hell?' Malcolm sounds incredulous.

'No. I thought about it and decided against it,' Ruth says, cheerfully.

Jo smiles to herself. Ruth certainly isn't like any vicar she has ever met.

'But surely you can't just pick and choose?' Malcolm presses. 'You *are* ordained into the Church of England, I presume?'

'Oh, yes.'

'But surely, the doctrines, the Bible—'

The Reverend Ruth nudges the tall man beside her in the ribs. 'Malcolm Buswell, you stand here by George Eliot's grave and tell me I have to believe every word written in the Bible? A book compiled solely by men?'

Malcolm stares at her for some moments, then makes a humphing noise, close to a guffaw. 'You make a good point,' he says, and bows his head slightly. It is the same gesture he uses when he opens the door for customers in Jo's shop.

As they make their way back towards the entrance of the cemetery, Ruth links her arm into Malcolm's. Jo hears her say quietly to him, 'I know it can take a lot to step aside from convention, but I think God favours the brave, even though in saying so I know you think me a fool.'

Malcolm stops and turns towards Ruth. Jo can barely make out their faces in the gloom, but she glimpses a look of – she is not quite sure what – pass between them.

'Well, well,' Malcolm says briskly, picking up pace, 'it really is getting dark now, and I for one am feeling the cold. Tea? Or shall we find ourselves a pub?'

'Pub,' Jo answers without a pause, still wondering about that look.

* * *

In an alleyway off Highgate High Street, a tall figure in a shaggy jumper pauses by the darkened window of a small stationery shop. From where he is standing, he can just make out the noticeboard behind the counter. Hanging there, underneath a ribbon of envelopes, are drawings, handwritten words, pamphlets – and he spots a card for the restaurant, La Biblioteca. A small calendar sits in the centre of the board. Some of the earlier dates have been crossed off, but in more recent weeks the dates have been left unmarked. The board is half full and half empty, and the Viking called Eric wonders whether this is a sign that Stationery Girl is coming or going.

23

The ghosts and a fox

They are writing a list of rules for the Highgate Cemetery ghosts. Jo is doing the actual writing; happy to get her fountain pen out of her bag and to have an excuse for using it; but the compilation is a group effort. She, Ruth and Malcolm are gathered around a table, close to the pub fire, discussing Malcolm's book. Earlier, Ruth had made the problematic observation that not all the ghosts could appear every Christmas Eve – there would just be far too many of them. In the end, over mulled wine and cheesy chips, it had been decided that readers would allow Malcolm a bit of artistic licence and that it would be okay to focus on a few characters in particular. Other points on the list include:

Christmas Eve night lasts from 10 p.m. until dawn.

This would give them more time to enjoy themselves, rather than ending their existence on the stroke of midnight, as was perhaps more traditional. Jo suggested that Christmas Eve might start earlier than 10 p.m., but Malcolm was worried about his ghosts bumping into children, and he didn't want the possibility of them being scared. Jo wasn't sure if he meant the ghosts or the children being frightened, but said no more, thinking that, after all, it was Malcolm's book.

The ghosts cannot walk through walls but could get on a bus.

Ruth particularly wanted them to be able to make the most of their night out in London.

The gathering is an annual occurrence.

This would mean that, in some instances, the ghosts might have met before (and could hope to meet up the following year).

The ghosts can be seen as solid forms, not as diaphanous spectres.

As well as this, they have decided that because it's Christmas Eve – and anything can happen at Christmas – people who see the ghosts (presumably dressed in the clothes of their time) won't perceive them to be unusual.

As they discuss this last point, Jo wonders what James would say if he could see her now? She is sure he would dismiss it all as nonsense. A ridiculous preoccupation – rather like her childish 'stationery habit'. Well, her 'stationery habit' was now helping her to improve the running of her uncle's shop. And this? Jo hasn't felt so relaxed in ages, and she smiles at the two very different figures sitting beside her.

She is not just bound to her family and friends in the North-East any more; she has real friends in London too. Home has always been in the North, but sitting in this London pub with Ruth and Malcolm, Jo feels a tug of something close to an ache when she thinks of leaving them. She pushes the thought away, for once happy to settle into her limbo.

Ruth is still chatting about the ghosts when Malcolm relapses into silence. He looks sad, and Jo is reminded of other times when she has felt anxious about him. Ruth's words trail off, and both women watch him as he fiddles with one of the beer mats on the table.

Looking up, he turns from one to the other and says, 'Would you mind me asking you both something?'

'Ask away,' Ruth encourages, and Jo nods.

'Do you believe in ghosts?'

'What, apart from the Holy Ghost?' Ruth replies, and Malcolm gives her a shadow of a smile.

'I don't think I do,' Ruth says, more seriously. And then she asks the question that had sprung into Jo's mind. 'Do you, Malcolm?'

He stares at Ruth for some moments then, patting the table with both hands says, 'I think it is only fair that I tell you and Joanne a bit more about how I came up with the idea for my book.' He gazes at a point above their heads.

Ruth and Jo glance at each other and wait in silence. Jo's thoughts return to the time that Malcolm first told them about his book, and how hard he appeared to find it to tell them where the idea came from. She had thought then that there was something he wasn't telling them.

'I sometimes feel like such a foolish old man,' Malcolm starts, shaking his head. 'My mother was a wonderful woman, and we were very close, especially after my father and brother's death.

She understood me like nobody else ever has.' He pauses. 'Well, maybe one other very dear person.' He stops talking, and Jo wonders if they should say something, but after a few seconds, Malcolm picks up the thread. 'Yes, she was a very special woman, and it is true to say that I never felt I measured up to her. My goodness, when I think of what she had done with her life. And what had I done?' Malcolm opens his hands outwards, palms empty.

Jo is about to say something to try to reassure him, when he turns his whole body towards Ruth. 'Reverend Ruth, you once said that loss didn't always get easier with time. My dear, you are quite right.' He nods his head vigorously. 'It must be about two years ago now that I found, well, that life without my mother felt barely worth living. And, I know, I know, that I should have been able to cope; it was the natural order of things, she was a very old woman when she died, but oh, how I missed her.'

Jo can see the sadness etched into his face, just like she had when she'd watched him looking at photographs of his mother.

'Again, I feel so foolish confessing to this . . .'

Ruth reaches out and strokes one of Malcolm's hands. 'There is nothing shameful about loving another human being and missing them,' she says, gently.

He sighs and continues, 'I told myself I should have got over her loss, but all I really felt was a desperate loneliness. It was worse than when my father and brother died, and I felt guilty about that, too, because they had died so young and she had lived to a ripe old age. But I missed her terribly. I tried to busy

myself with some research into Highgate Cemetery, but . . .'
Again he holds his hands out, palms empty.

'And the ghosts?' Ruth asks, and Jo remembers where this
conversation had started: Malcolm's question, *Do you believe
in ghosts?*

'Ah, the ghosts, or rather a ghost.' Malcolm's tone suddenly
becomes earnest. 'Now, I am not for a moment saying that I
saw a ghost, but I can't help feeling that there was an occasion
when my mother . . . reached out to me. You will no doubt
think me even more of a decrepit and senile old man.'

Jo is certainly not thinking this. 'What happened?' she asks.

'I was in the cemetery. It was last winter, a cold afternoon
that turned into a bitter night.' Malcolm glances towards one
of the windows in the pub, which is now dark, apart from the
glow of streetlights that look like baubles suspended across the
panes. 'I was sitting in a quiet part of the cemetery; I often
found myself there, thinking about my life. But on that evening,
a feeling of desolation burrowed into the heart of me. I crept
in behind a large monument so that nobody could see me, and
just sat on the cold earth, hidden from the world.' Malcolm
shakes his head very slightly, and tries to smile. 'I have been
hiding from the world most of my life. A man in grey.'

Jo thinks for an instance of purple and orange slippers
embroidered with golden birds.

Malcolm continues. 'I could see no possible reason for going
on. I wanted to die. It wasn't a big decision; in fact, it hardly
seemed to matter, but I thought if I just sat there long enough,
the cold and the night would take me.'

Ruth reaches out and holds Malcolm's hand. 'I understand that, Malcolm. People often think suicide is a massive decision, which of course, in its way, it is. But when someone is in the depths of despair, it can seem as irrelevant a choice as, well, shall I go to the shops or not.'

'Yes, yes,' Malcolm says, urgently, and Jo is aware of how much the small, bird-like woman beside her will have seen in her life. And also that it is typical of her new friend that she called it by what it was: a suicide attempt.

'What happened, Malcolm?' Jo asks, reaching out and taking his other hand.

'Well, I sat there. I even took my coat off, to speed things along. I heard the church clock strike one, and then I remember hearing it strike four. Maybe I had slept. I was beyond cold by then, feeling rather numb and light-headed. I particularly remember the silence. I felt isolated from the city beyond the cemetery walls, and I suppose no longer really part of life. I thought it couldn't be much longer, and that if I fell asleep again I wouldn't wake up.' When Jo makes a small noise of distress, he squeezes her hand. 'That was when a fox walked round the edge of the gravestone next to me. It stopped in its tracks and just stood and stared at me.'

Ah, the foxes. Jo remembers Malcolm's mention of them when he related the tale of the Christmas Eve animals.

'I have no idea how long we looked at each other. Its form was mainly shrouded in darkness, but there was a smudge of red, and oh, how bright its eyes were. That is when it came to me, the story that my mother told me . . .'

Jo can see Malcolm's eyes sparkling with tears.

'It was close to Christmas – I cannot recall the exact date – but I thought, if this was Christmas Eve, then maybe you would speak to me. And I know it sounds foolish but, in that instant, I knew what the fox would say.'

The two women beside him nod encouragingly. A tear rolls down his long nose.

'It would say, "Malcolm, all you need to do is to keep putting one foot in front of the other and things will get better. But maybe you could help yourself by finding a really good hobby."' Malcolm gives a watery chuckle. 'Mother was always trying to encourage me to take more interest in things.'

Jo goes to speak, but Malcolm interrupts her. 'Most of all I felt that the fox was there to reassure me, to tell me what my mother always told me. That I, Malcolm Buswell, was enough.'

Jo can feel her own tears gathering.

'When the fox turned tail and left, it came to me what I should do with all the research I had been doing, and that is how the idea for the book based on the meeting of Christmas Eve ghosts was born.'

'Well, I do not doubt for a moment that it was Eve coming to give you some encouragement and a bit of a talking-to,' Ruth says, releasing Malcolm's hand and picking up her glass of mulled wine.

'You really think so?' Malcolm asks, his voice a mixture of incredulity and hope.

Jo reaches for her wine too, 'Of course,' she says. And she means it. For once she is very glad that James is not with her.

He would pick something like this apart and scoff at it. But for Jo it makes perfect (if inexplicable) sense.

Malcolm smiles at them both, and another tear runs down his cheek.

'Tissue!' Ruth declares, rummaging for a packet in her bag.

As Malcolm accepts the tissue, he adds, 'I have had no one to share this with, and to be honest I have made so little progress with the book that I did sometimes feel like . . .'

'Going back to the cemetery full-time?' Ruth suggests, and Malcolm laughs.

It is a good sound, Jo thinks.

'Well, there have been moments. But since nearly going under that bus, and meeting you two dear people . . .'

There it was again. *Dear*.

Malcolm puts the tissue away and reaches out and takes Jo and Ruth's hands again, '. . . it has made the world of difference to me. You have made me feel that I should do things differently in my life. That I should be braver. I cannot thank you enough for what I hope isn't presumptuous to call *our friendship*.'

Jo leans across and takes Ruth's hand in her other hand – the three of them connected in a circle around a small pub table. 'Friendship' is exactly the right word for it. She knows that she has undervalued her friendships in the past, and she silently promises her new, *dear* friends that she will never do so again.

24

The silence of the city when it pauses

'Now who would like another mulled wine?' Ruth is on her feet gathering their glasses.

'You must let me help you,' Malcolm says, half rising.

'No, you stay and keep Jo company, I'll only be a minute.'

Left at the table with Malcolm, Jo realizes that he looks more relaxed, but tired. He starts to say something, then stops.

'Yes, Malcolm?' she prompts.

He checks over his shoulder and leans forward in his seat. 'I have been unsure whether to raise the subject, but I fear that curiosity has got the better of me. And I do worry about her. Has Reverend Ruth ever told you what it was that caused her to become what they're calling the Runaway Vicar?'

Jo shakes her head. 'Not a word. And I haven't liked to ask. She told me that her bishop knows she's well, but I don't think he realizes she's in London.'

'Ah.' Malcolm sits back in his chair, his fingertips joined together to form a steeple in front of him.

'Do you think we could ask her?' Jo enquires.

'Ask her what?'

Ruth is back at the table, carrying three steaming glasses.

'Ask her what?' Ruth repeats, setting the glasses down.

Jo thinks she and Malcolm must look like children caught stealing chocolates from the Christmas tree.

Jo decides to take the bull – or rather, the Runaway Vicar – by the horns. 'Ruth, we don't want you to think we were discussing you behind your back.' Which she thinks, *we were*. 'But Malcolm and I wanted to ask you why you ran away.' Worried this is a bit too direct, she adds, 'I hope you don't think we're being nosy . . . and if you don't want to tell us . . . well . . . that's okay too . . . of course we'll understand . . . it's just that we . . .' And now she wishes she had stopped talking some time ago.

Malcolm comes to her rescue. 'Joanne and I wondered if we could help in any way?'

'I don't think you can.'

'Aahh.' Malcolm looks down at his hands, now clasped on the table.

'And I didn't,' Ruth says defiantly, sitting back down.

There is a silence. Jo wants to ask, *Didn't what?* but is reluctant to open her mouth after her earlier ramblings.

Again, it is Malcolm who picks up the slack. 'Didn't what, my dear?'

Ruth is glaring at them now. She seems very different from

the woman who was so reassuring to Malcolm. 'I didn't run away.'

'Oh, so the press got it wrong,' Jo blurts, relieved. 'It was all . . .' But she can't finish, thinking: there must have been something in it. It can't all have been a fabrication. Why the hints at staying quiet? And *why* the wig?

'A storm in a teacup?' Malcolm offers, blowing over the top of his mulled wine.

A mulish look comes over Ruth's face. 'I didn't run away. That's all.'

Jo can't help herself. 'But the newspapers? The "leaving the house with a meal half eaten"? No one knowing where you were?' She doesn't want to upset Ruth, but she wants to know. Plus, having seen the relief so evident on Malcolm's face, she can't help thinking that Ruth would feel better if she confided something of her story. So she persists, 'Was none of that true?'

Ruth sniffs. 'Some of it was. But I didn't run away,' she repeats. Then, looking down into her glass of mulled wine she says, sulkily, 'I just didn't go back.'

Jo is now completely confused. So Ruth left – for some reason – and then what?

It is Malcolm who seems to have made some sort of mental leap. He leans towards Ruth. 'Ah, going back, finding the will to do that – now that is a much more difficult endeavour.'

Jo suddenly thinks of Uncle Wilbur. Perhaps he hadn't run away, when he was a young man. He had needed to leave home to join the army. But then? Was it just impossible for him to find his way back to a farming family who he felt were disappointed in him?

Ruth looks up a little sheepishly, a hint of a smile returning. 'Maybe the wig was a step too far.'

'Ruth, you don't need to tell us, but are you still, I don't know . . . in hiding?' Jo asks.

'The press were very persistent. They rang everyone, tried to find out everything they could about me.' Ruth's face is distressed now. 'I just need some space and time to think.'

Malcolm nods his understanding.

'"I have known the silence of the stars and of the sea, And the silence of the city when it pauses",' Jo quotes, recalling what Ruth once wrote with one of her fountain pens. That piece of paper is now pinned up on the noticeboard next to a drawing of a Viking wearing overlarge glasses.

Jo still finds the words intriguing and rather poignant. It also makes her think of the quiet of Highgate Cemetery.

Perhaps the three of them are like the ghosts who meet on Christmas Eve – feeling their way. New friends, finding a way to know each other better, through conversation and through silence. And Jo senses what Ruth needs now, from her and Malcolm, is silence.

Dear Lucy,

I have spent today in a cemetery (and a pub) with a Runaway Vicar and a retired tax analyst called Malcolm. That doesn't really do them justice, and I'd love you to meet them one day. Malcolm has the most wonderful handwriting

– oh, and now the police officer does too. Well, maybe not as beautiful as Malcolm's, but he wrote me something for my wall of words (I'd like to show you that too) and it was very stylish. It was a limerick about a policeman and was extremely rude, but so beautifully written!

My favourite customer last week was a man called Barnaby Postlethwaite. He is the owner of more than forty fountain pens, and he told me that he hides his new pen purchases from his wife, in the same way that she hides her new shoes. He gave me some good advice about ink and now I have a shelf filled with different-shaped glass bottles containing inks of all colours. There is vermillion, lemon, verdigris, scarlet, sepia – and a turquoise one that reminds me of the sea we once swam in in Croatia – do you remember?

Barnaby says he always writes in purple ink because he thinks of it as a regal colour, and that in another life he'd have liked to have been 'of royal descent' rather than the son of a welder from Huddersfield.

Hugs to you all, with love from,
Jo x

Jo seals the letter and tucks her feet further under her hot-water bottle. She is propped up in bed and every part of her is warm. She wonders what Lucy will think of her hints about seeing her. She's not sure why she doesn't just ask her to come down (or go back home for a visit herself) but she still has a sense of feeling her way to a better place with her best friend. (*A place for everything and everything in its place.*)

Jo never expects to get a letter back from Lucy – writing was never her thing – but in her texts Lucy often refers to the stories of the people in the shop. In her last message she also mentioned Finn. Nothing to suggest that Finn had 'spilled the beans', but just that Finn was okay and 'loved-up' and that he enjoyed his brief visit to London and seeing Jo. Jo thought it was typical of Finn (and men), that in all the things they chatted about, he hadn't thought to mention his new woman. Or maybe he was a bit self-conscious because of their fling?

Her mind drifts back to Malcolm. She hopes that she and Ruth have been able to help him in some small way. She only wishes that she and Malcolm could do the same for Ruth.

So Reverend Ruth hadn't run away. Does Jo really believe that? Frankly, no. But maybe the prospect of going back to her parish had assumed greater significance, compared to her *Mary Celeste* flit. And what was it she couldn't face? The blood, poo and vomit? No. These seemed to be things that Ruth took in her stride. Even the tragedies she encountered were an accepted part of her life.

So, maybe, some of her congregation? Not all of them obviously – Ruth had made it clear that many people had been a help, and didn't she say she had enjoyed visiting people? Declared it was the thing she liked the best. So no, not everyone, just people like Mr Will-kill-soon.

Perhaps it was the fact that people treated her differently because she was a vicar? Ambushed her with talk of religion. And didn't people feel that it was a vicar's job to be nice to everyone, to put up with anything? Jo may not agree with this point of view, but she is aware that she expects Ruth to be interested in her troubles. Even if she has held back from dumping on her, isn't she self-conscious when she talks to Ruth? She draws in a sleepy breath, thinking of the conversation in the pub. Well, maybe not now. It occurs to Jo that she would like to see where Ruth came from, to visit her parish and talk to the people who knew her there, and especially to meet her curate, Angela.

And Malcolm? Jo is taken back to that look in the graveyard. What was it that had passed between Ruth and Malcolm? Some acknowledgement of something hidden? Jo thinks of the pair of bright, embroidered slippers. So unlike everything else Malcolm wears.

These contemplations lead her nowhere. Instead she thinks of the three of them in the pub talking about ghosts and she smiles into the darkness.

An unlikely trio. A believer, a non-believer, and . . . what is she? She doesn't believe in God, she knows that. But on the other hand, she thinks there may be more to life than this. And she does believe that if you think about friends in trouble, wish them well with all of your being, that in some way that does some good. It's not praying exactly, but it is not the act of someone who believes there is nothing more out there. And she had no trouble believing that the fox had come to Malcolm just when he needed it.

So, a believer, a non-believer and there she is, Average Jo, somewhere in the middle.

Jo remembers Malcolm's mother, Eve, who had wanted her ashes scattered on the heath by the swimming ponds.

An exceptional woman. She recalls Malcolm's statement: *I am not a brave man.* She wonders if any of the ghosts would be brave enough to go for a dip there on Christmas Eve night.

Her phone pings. It is a text from Ruth.

I was thinking about Malcolm's mum and I'm sure it must be this time of year that she died. Maybe we should go for a swim in Hampstead swimming ponds in memory of her. What do you say?!

This is just plain spooky. Maybe Ruth isn't a vicar. Maybe she's a witch.

Jo falls asleep before she gets around to replying, her phone lying abandoned on the duvet beside her letter to Lucy. She dreams of playing in a rugby match in which everyone is dressed as either a vicar, a witch or a Viking.

25

Breath comes slow

'Sometimes I can't seem to get it to write.'

The young police officer is back. He is now the proud owner of a fountain pen (and his parents the astonished recipients of two handwritten letters). But he admits he is having problems.

Privately, Jo is not surprised. There is a reason that ballpoints were invented: they are less trouble. It still doesn't make her want to write with one, though. Since looking after her uncle's shop, she has fallen more deeply in love with fountain pens than ever. But, despite all this, she has to admit, fountain pens can be tricky. 'Is it when you first try to write with it?' she enquires.

The dark head nods.

'There might be some dried ink on the end of the nib.' She can see he is looking worried. 'It's easy to fix,' she reassures him, 'I keep a glass of water on my desk. All you need to do is dip the tip of the nib into that and it will get going again.'

'I use my cup of tea,' a twenty-something girl suggests. She's been standing apart from Jo and the police officer, looking through the Christmas cards Jo is selling for a local charity. Jo is not surprised by the interruption; she has discovered that people who love stationery tend to be a helpful bunch.

'I could certainly do that.' The police officer sounds relieved. 'I've always got a brew on the go.'

As he leaves the shop, two more customers enter – a mother and daughter. Jo recognizes them from a previous visit. More Stationery Lovers. Word is out that a small shop off an alleyway in North London is expanding its stationery range. Jo feels a burgeoning pride that her efforts are making a difference to the business. She wishes she could tell Uncle Wilbur, but on her last phone call to him, he had struggled to register where she was. Still, she wonders if here in his shop she might have found a new beginning.

The bad pram driver has been back to visit, this time manoeuvring her precious charge in and out of the aisles with consummate skill. When Jo peered in the pram, the baby was awake and studied her seriously from a pair of clear blue eyes. Jo yearned to pick her up, and breathe in that intoxicating baby smell, but didn't like to ask.

With the upturn in business, Jo has been able to expand her product range even more. She now also stocks: a range of traditional, heavy fountain pens that come in glorious colours; terracotta pots filled with crayons (that look like they are growing there); soft leather covers, perfect for one fountain pen; and colourful hand-held blotters with chrome tops which, when pressed with a rocking motion over newly written words, stop them from smudging.

When she first saw the rocker blotters, Jo thought of Caramel Toffee Clare, and pictured the smudged words, 'Dear Giana'. She has seen Clare a few times, heading past the shop. She hasn't yet had the chance to show her the rocker blotters, as Clare appears reluctant – or maybe is too busy – to come in. But Clare always waves and smiles, although Jo still thinks she detects a certain embarrassment in her look.

It is nearly closing time when Eric the Viking comes in, and the shop is finally quiet. Jo is so conscious of his presence it feels like a large and noisy crowd has stepped over the threshold.

'How's your day been?' Eric asks, pulling out the stool like a pub customer heading for his favourite seat.

'Good,' Jo says. With a feeling of surprise and a definite feeling of pleasure, she realizes that for once she's not lying. She has got so used to telling her mum on the phone that all is well that it seems strange to be speaking the truth for once.

'How about your day?' Jo asks.

Eric looks thoughtful. 'Interesting case of double vision. Not something you want to see every day as it can mean a brain tumour.'

'Oh, God!' Jo wonders if every time she utters these words she is now going to think of Reverend Ruth. 'Were they okay?'

'Yep. In the end. I managed to get through to the on-call ophthalmologist at the hospital, and when I explained it was sudden-onset diplopia, they fitted him in straight away.' He runs his hands through his hair and Jo thinks he looks tired. 'Sometimes the system works, and when it does it's bloody good.'

'And?'

'The guy's just been back in wearing a patch over one eye. No brain tumour.'

'Do they know what it is?'

'Not yet – they've booked him in for a follow-up appointment.' Eric looks at her for a long moment. 'Don't look so worried, Jo, I saw a couple of girls giving him the once-over as he left wearing his patch. Got a feeling Dwayne will be wearing a patch even when his eye's better. Tell me more about your day.'

Before Jo can answer Eric leans forward, 'Whoa! New pens. Smart. Can I try one?'

Jo takes one of her new pens – bright scarlet, with a chrome clip shaped like a fountain pen nib – and hands it to Eric. Rather than thinking about her day, Eric's comments about Dwayne have made her realize what Eric has to deal with in his work. It wouldn't all be glasses and contact lenses; he would also have to tell some of his patients they were going blind.

Eric turns the words he has written with the tester pen around for her to read:

Stationery Girl has had a good day.

Jo laughs and starts telling Eric that the shop is now attracting the Stationery Lovers. After a while Eric interrupts her, 'Hold on, shall I get us a coffee? I think the café may still be open.'

'No, don't worry, I'll make us one.' Jo glances up at her sliver of sky. It is the colour of graphite, against which the streetlight is glowing pale orange. It is past closing time, but she doesn't want to shut up the shop for fear Eric will notice how late it is and leave. 'Or I could get us a glass of wine?' she suggests, tentatively. 'I've got some red open.'

'Shame I don't drink on days with an "N", in them,' Eric says, sadly.

'Oh . . . well, don't worry. I can make us coffee.'

Eric lets out his walrus-like bark. 'Every time. You make it too easy, Stationery Girl. Wine would be great.'

Jo thumps Eric on the upper arm as she heads towards the back of the shop. Then wishes she hadn't. It is like hitting her fist against rock.

When she returns with two glasses of wine, Eric is flipping through the notebook about William Foyle that she had left on the counter. 'You don't mind?' he says, looking up. Jo shakes her head. 'I just love this guy's handwriting. Who's this one about?' He hands the notebook back to Jo, exchanging it for a glass of wine.

'William Foyle, who started Foyles bookshop.'

'When was that?'

Jo flicks through the book. 'Well, he was born in 1885.'

'Was Lobb, the boot man, around then?' Eric asks.

Jo can't help feeling pleased he remembers their conversation about John Lobb.

'William Foyle would have been ten when John Lobb died, so they wouldn't have met. Maybe William would have walked past Lobb's shop sometimes. I don't know if he ever bought

Lobb shoes or boots though.' As she says this, Jo is distracted by the thought: maybe she could find out. Perhaps there are some lasts in a storage room somewhere, the exact shape of William Foyle's feet.

'Don't go staring off into space – I want to hear more about Will the book man,' Eric prompts, before taking a slug of wine.

Jo takes a sip too, and starts to tell Eric all about how William came to start his bookshop and of his flair for publicity – including creating adverts showing him and his brother Gilbert delivering books on a tandem.

'What was William like?' Eric asks, looking up from doodling a picture on her tester pad.

'It sounds like he was fun. There are loads of stories about him.' She smiles. 'Once he was going to a book sale at an old estate, and on the train there were a load of other book people who also wanted to get their hands on the books in this library that were being sold off. When the train got into the station, these other guys got all the taxis, so William was left standing there. Anyway, he flagged down a passing car, which turned out to be a hearse, and he persuaded the undertaker to give him a lift – and to put his foot down, whilst he was at it. He got to the sale before the others and bought up all the best books. When the other guys found out, they were furious. Especially as they had all stopped in the road and taken their hats off as the hearse shot by.'

Eric laughs. 'This is a great project, Jo,' he says. 'How did you get involved in it?'

'Malcolm's one of my customers. He's interested in local history and is writing a book. Me and another customer, Ruth, offered to help.'

'What's the book about?'

'He hasn't quite decided yet,' Jo says, slowly, 'I think he's just at the research stage.' She is reluctant to talk about Malcolm's idea, as he was so shy about sharing it.

'There you go.' Eric tears the top sheet of paper off the tester pad and hands her his drawing of two men riding a tandem piled high with books. 'One for your collection.'

'Thanks,' Jo says, turning and pinning it to her noticeboard, which is now a colourful mix of words and pictures filling over half the board. These spiral out like paper petals around a central point – Uncle Wilbur's small square calendar.

'What's the most common thing people write?' Eric asks, scanning the collection of words and phrases.

'Most of the time it's their name, and then quite a lot of people scribble it out, saying that they shouldn't leave their signature lying around.' Jo laughs. 'As if I'd ever do anything with them!'

Eric grins. 'You don't have to tell me that.'

For some reason, rather than feeling pleased that Eric the Viking thinks she's honest, she worries that he thinks she's boring. Average Jo.

'What else?'

'What?' Jo replies, momentarily lost.

'What else do people write?' Eric asks, shaking his head at her.

'Oh, all sorts,' she says, hurriedly, 'some write, *the quick brown fox jumps over the lazy dog*, as it has all the letters in the alphabet in it.'

Eric nods and, leaning over, starts a new drawing with the scarlet fountain pen.

Jo studies his hand as he draws.

She finds she just can't help herself.

She forces herself to turn away and look at the board. 'I have no idea what some of my customers write as they scribble away in different languages. I'm pretty certain I have Russian, Gaelic, Arabic and French up there.'

And you also have something in Italian, she thinks, reminded once more of Clare and her Italian pen pal. She rushes on, 'And sometimes people write what they are thinking, and they end up sharing things with me. One woman wrote . . .' She searches the collage to find what she is looking for. She glimpses it hidden under a postcard – it had felt too personal to put on obvious display. '. . . She wrote, *I think I should leave him, though my heart will break.*'

Eric stops drawing and looks up quickly. 'That's really tough. I wonder . . .' he pauses.

'Why she would leave?' Jo offers.

He nods, 'Even though it would . . .' he says, softly.

'. . . break her heart.' Jo finishes.

They stare at each other, and the moment stretches between them until Jo thinks one of them will need to reach out and physically break the silence that holds them. Then – just when she feels she will have to say something, she *will* tell him – he drops his eyes and returns to his drawing. And she wonders what it is she would have said.

After another pause, Jo continues, 'I didn't know what to say to the woman. So I kept quiet.'

Just like now.

Except now, she plunges into more speech, desperate to avoid another silence. 'Some people want to talk, but I got the impression she didn't. I just think she needed to write it down, get it out there.' Jo glances back at the words that the woman had written, wondering what just happened between her and the Viking.

She looks at Eric, head down, still drawing. His hand is tilted towards her, his thumb and forefinger pressed against the body of the pen. She hears herself say, 'There's poetry too.' *Anything to keep talking, to stop herself from feeling so vulnerable.* 'Do you remember the other day there was a flurry of snow? It didn't settle properly, but it was definitely snow.' She can't believe she has sunk to talking about the weather.

Eric looks up, then sits back, watching her, drawing forgotten. 'Yeah, Mrs Patmore got quite excited.'

Jo raises her eyebrows at him, unsure if he is teasing her. For once, she hopes he is. It will feel like a return to normal. Somewhere back there she thinks their conversation got side-tracked into . . . she's not sure what. With thoughts of snow, thin ice comes to mind.

'So what was the poem?' Eric asks, still studying her.

Jo searches for the lines of poetry on the wall. Suddenly she is aware that she has made a mistake. Taken a wrong turn.

This is not a poem about the weather – *oh such a safe subject.* Yes, there were some lines about snow. But that's not why she liked it so much.

She pictures the thin ice cracking under her feet.

'I never really got poetry when we did it at school,' Eric tells her, 'but I read quite a bit now. Don't laugh, but I keep a poetry anthology by my bed.'

Her heart sounds loud in her ears. She knows he will expect her to read these lines of poetry out. Her eyes alight on it, and in the end she reads the words to Eric the Viking, simply because she can't think of a good enough excuse not to.

'*Clouded whispers,*
Breath comes slow.
And outside falls the silent snow.'

The shop is completely still. All Jo can think of is lying in bed with this man, in a cottage, snow falling outside, their breath and whispered words mixing in the dark. His arms around her. His hands against her skin. Her fingers interlaced with his.

'Jo, can I ask you something?' Eric's voice doesn't sound quite like his own.

She doesn't move; she just waits. She has no idea what she is waiting for. But for her, time stands still.

She remembers a line from her dad's favourite poem. *Time was away and somewhere else.*

'I . . . I wanted to say . . .' Another pause. 'You don't mind about Clare, do you?' he finishes.

'No, no. Not at all. No!' It bursts from her, her voice sounding squeakier than normal. She feels caught out, foolish. *Please*

God, would someone just come in the shop. She would even welcome Malcolm staggering through the door, blood dripping from his chin.

'She's really lovely. I think you'd like her if you knew her.'

'Great, great. I'm sure she's great.' Now she seems to be stuck on repeat, anxiety pumping out her words, 'Yes, yes. I'm sure I would. Yes, she seems great.'

When someone taps on the window, Jo whirls around to the sound. Anything to stop this conversation. 'It's Lando!' Jo exclaims, far too loudly.

Lando raises a hand in salute and then beckons to Eric.

'Sorry, Jo. Forgot the time. Lando and I are going to the pub.' He hands her his ink sketch, which is of a fox jumping over a dog. 'Do you fancy coming?'

'No, no, that's fine. Got things to do.' And because she can't seem to stop herself she throws in another, 'No!' for good measure.

'Okay then,' Eric says slowly, getting up from the stool. 'Thanks for the wine.' He tucks the stool back beside the counter. 'Jo . . .'

She is saved by the 'ping' of her phone. She grabs it as if it were a lifeline. It is Ruth asking once more about the idea of them going swimming, and Jo realizes she forgot to reply yesterday to her text about Hampstead swimming ponds.

'Got to get this,' Jo mutters to Eric. She wonders if he can hear the relief in her voice. 'Sorry.'

As the broken doorbell sounds its tinny farewell, Jo texts back: *Yes, I'll give swimming in the pond a go.*

With any luck she'll drown.

26

Some advice from Malcolm Buswell

A date for the swim has been fixed for the following Sunday.
Malcolm was delighted with their suggestion of a commemo-
rative swim in honour of his mother and claimed to be
devastated that he could not join them (the mixed swimming
ponds being closed in the winter). He assured them that
while the water would be freezing, it would be *invigorating*.
Jo gave him a speculative look, but he smiled at her so blandly
that she began to think he really was sorry not to be swimming with them in an outdoor pond in December. It was
only when he scoffed at her suggestion of a wet suit ('As if
Mother would!') and commented that his mother did sometimes wear a bobble hat for warmth, that she began to doubt
the innocence of his smile. There was a glint in his eye that
reminded her too much of Reverend Ruth, and she wonders
if Malcolm is starting to borrow a certain mischievous humour
from his new friend.

In the meantime, Jo has been busy decorating for Christmas and the whole ceiling of the shop is now festooned with twinkling fairy lights. Beside her in the window sits a small Christmas tree, its pine fragrance mixing with the smell of polish that Jo still uses on the oak cabinet. The branches of the tree are decorated with more white lights and are hung with coloured luggage labels on which she encourages customers to write their Christmas wishes. As usual, when picking up a fountain pen, people have surprised her by how personal their wishes are. One of the most moving wishes had been written by a workman who was helping mend the drains at the end of the alleyway. He told Jo that his wife's cancer had come back and he was worried she might have to be in the hospice by Christmas. He wished for one last Christmas at home with his wife and their daughter.

Jo has not heard from Lucy since her last letter. She's worried. Normally she would expect a text reply a few days later. Jo has texted her to ask if she is okay, but all she got back was a terse, *yes, sorry, busy.*

Jo is looking at her phone, wondering whether to try texting again, or even calling, when Malcolm walks in.

'Good morning, Joanne. I have brought you a gift,' he declares happily, and hands her a knitted orange bobble hat with a bright pink pompom.

Jo puts down her phone, and accepts it with a measured look, 'Thank you, Malcolm, that *will* keep me nice and warm.'

He makes a small, smiley humming noise and then stops. He looks at her more closely. 'Joanne, you looked worried.'

'Do I?'

'You really don't have to do this swim if you don't want to,' Malcolm says with concern.

'Oh, it's not the swim,' she assures him.

Malcolm draws up a stool, 'I see.' He pauses as if unsure how to go on. Eventually he says, 'Is there anything I can do? *Anything* at all?'

Jo remembers the last time he asked her this. Then she'd wanted Malcolm to find a way to make James love her. She glances at her phone. Well, she may be worried about Lucy, but there is no doubt about it, there are hours on end now when she doesn't think about James at all.

As if following part of her thoughts, Malcolm asks, 'Is it this past relationship you were telling me about, Joanne? James, I think you said he was called?'

Jo strokes the pink fluffy pompom. 'Not really, Malcolm. I think I *am* getting over him.'

And suddenly she is telling Malcolm all about her time with James. How it had started and how she had turned to him when Lucy left. How she thinks she let her other friends down. It all comes out (well, almost all): how they did everything he wanted to do, how she kept trying, probably a bit too much, but how it had changed when his dad died. 'Then, I think he really needed me. It reminded me of the early days when we used to talk for hours.'

Or had they talked? Hadn't she been the one who listened and gave support as James talked about himself – *endlessly*?

She tells Malcolm about Lucy. Of how close they had been,

how much she had looked forward to her moving back home, and how they never seemed to get back into step. And finally of the vitriol that had poured out of Lucy about James on their last night together.

'Ah, I can see that Lucy is at the heart of what is worrying you. Is that right?' Malcolm asks, delving back into the details of what Jo has been telling him.

'Yes, she is. She's my best friend and we're just not . . . oh, I don't know. I can't seem to . . . it's just all . . .' Jo feels as lost in her speech as she does in understanding what has happened between her and Lucy.

Malcolm sits very upright on his stool and appears to be reviewing the noticeboard behind her. He lowers his eyes to study Jo's face. Slowly, he says, 'Would you mind me saying something to you, Joanne?'

'Of course not,' Jo replies, wondering what is coming next.

'I hesitate because, as you know, I am not a man who makes friends easily . . .'

Jo is about to say, *You have us.*

But Malcolm ploughs on. The words are considered and clearly taking some effort, '. . . I am reluctant to give advice. However, one thing emerges from your recital . . .' he pauses again, nodding to himself. 'Maybe I am recalling my time as an analyst. I was always trying to dig for the truth, in my own way.' He continues, this time with more confidence, 'My observation and conclusion is this, Joanne. James may well have been your lover,' Malcolm colours slightly as he says this, 'but he was *never* your friend.'

Jo sits motionless. She feels like she has jumped (fully clothed) into the swimming pond. The realization is like being doused with ice-cold water.

Of course he was never her friend. Why didn't she see it? It wasn't like she hadn't come across people like James before: those who claimed the designation, 'friend' in the same way they demanded everything else from you – your time, sympathy, attention – while only ever being interested in their own lives, not yours. The truth was she did everything for James, was always there for him. When did he ever put her first or think about what she would like to do? It was always the one-way, James Beckford Street. Why would she think this unacceptable in a so-called 'friend', but accept it in her partner?

'Oh, Malcolm,' is all she can whisper.

She feels physically weak, and slightly sick. But there is also a sense of having discovered something important; a truth – however shocking.

He reaches out and pats her hand. 'The second thing I want to say is of a more personal nature. But I do want to share it with you.' The hand patting hers is stilled. 'I once had a friend who I let go. I did not make the effort I should have done and . . .' he holds Jo's gaze, '. . . it is the biggest regret of my life. Do not make the same mistake I did, with Lucy.'

Jo gets up from her stool and walks around to Malcolm. She enfolds him into a hug and holds him tight to her. At first his body is stiff in her arms, and then, like a sigh, he relaxes into her hug. He stays there for some moments – he does not cry, or hug her back – but Jo can feel the tension easing in him. She thinks back to when she hugged Finn, here in the shop. She wondered then how long it was since anyone had hugged Malcolm. Now she knows that it has been a very, very long time since anyone held Malcolm Buswell.

Dear Lucy,

In the shop I have a Christmas tree. It's covered in fairy lights and I'm tying old-fashioned luggage labels to the branches. People are writing their Christmas wishes on them.

One woman wrote about her longing for a baby. I've tied that one close to the angel on the top. I think you know, Luce, how much I want to have a baby, but you must never think that I won't be able to love your baby or be happy for you. I will be the best Auntie Jo your baby could ever wish for.

This is the wish that I wrote for myself and tied to the Christmas tree:

I wish that I could find my way back to my best friend because I love her and miss her more than I can possibly say.

With all my love,

Jo x

27

The first Sunday in Advent

Today is the day, and Jo and Ruth are making their way across Hampstead Heath. The world around them is grey and fuzzy. A 'dreich' day, Ruth calls it. Soon they are passing women, who are peeling off layers as if it were a balmy summer's day, and, for Jo, doubts are setting in. It may be mild for this time of year, but it is still December. The first Sunday of Advent, Ruth tells her. Jo begins to think Malcolm has the right idea – he is spending the morning with the Sunday papers and meeting them later in La Biblioteca.

When Ruth spots the bulk of a dark wooden changing room out on the decking by the edge of the pond, Jo's spirits lift. At least they don't have to strip naked outside by the benches. As they step inside the warmth of the changing room, they are enveloped in a billow of steam. At the end of the building is a line of showers, one of which is spewing clouds of moist air into the room. Beyond is a large picture window looking over the pond. It is not the view outside that Jo notices, so much as the view all around her. She is surrounded by chattering, naked bodies. Bodies of all shapes and sizes. She is conscious of her clothed state, and despite the devil-may-care attitude that swirls with the steam, she feels suddenly shy.

The sign outside said the water was nine degrees, and much of the chat is about the temperature (*there is a cold snap coming, water could get down to four or five degrees*). And also, wildlife (*has Margery seen that the heron is back?*). Many of the women seem to know each other: a granite-faced, sinewy woman of around fifty (Jo thinks, prison warder?) is greeting a group of three young women, one of whom is pregnant. As they exchange comments about the water temperature and the possibility of snow this weekend, the older woman's face breaks into a smile and the granite becomes a soft landscape.

Jo and Ruth find a space and are soon pulling out their black swimsuits and woolly hats. Ruth's hat is knitted to look like a Christmas pudding. Some of the women around them are putting on bobble hats; the younger women also pull on neoprene gloves and booties. So wet suits are frowned upon, but these are allowed. As she undresses, Jo is tempted to ask if they have any to spare.

Ruth, meanwhile, is standing braless in large, silky, purple knickers, making friends. When Jo glances at the startling colour of her underwear, Ruth tells her in an undertone, 'It's the colour of Advent. I've always loved purple, although I suspect my congregation never knew I had matching underwear under my vestments.'

Apart from keeping this comment between themselves, Ruth seems unfazed by the possibility of being recognized as the Runaway Vicar. But then maybe she thinks people are unlikely to make the connection between an old news article about a vicar and a middle-aged woman undressing in a swimming pond changing room. Nakedness does bring with it a certain anonymity. Instead of feeling exposed, Jo relaxes into the comfort of not caring if these women see the bumps and lumps of her average body. And looking at the variety of female forms around her, she starts to wonder – what is average anyway?

Having struggled into their swimsuits, they follow along behind a group of women to the water's edge. It was starting to feel like quite a good idea in the changing room, chatting to the other women. But now, padding along the freezing boards, Jo thinks she and Ruth are out of their minds. She feels her respect for Malcolm's mother, Eve, increase even more.

Mist is rising from the surface of the pond and the light is dank and dreary. The trees and bushes lining the edge of the pond are vague shapes in the murky distance. The surface of the water is greeny-grey, flecked orange with floating leaves. Jo spots the 'prison warder' by the water's edge. She stretches herself to her full height, although Jo can tell it is costing her something to pull against taut and tired muscles. And then, with a delicate flip, she is an elegant arrow entering the water. She emerges some way out into the misty gloom, and begins a slow and steady crawl away from them. In that moment Jo feels that the woman has left her accumulated worries on the wooden boards at the edge of the pond.

A lifeguard approaches them and asks if this is their first visit. (Is it *that* obvious?) As the woman runs through points about controlling their breathing, not staying in too long; and making sure to warm up quickly afterwards, Jo stares longingly at her fleece.

Duly instructed, they then wait, shivering, as the group of young women descend the metal ladder – their chatter punctuated by squeals as their bodies meet the cold of the water. Then they push off and, as a group, begin to glide across the pond. The pregnant woman flips onto her back and, scissor-kicking, turns her face to the sky, her hands around her bump. Jo is washed with a longing that takes her breath away, far more than the cold water does as it rises up over her thighs.

She is the first in. The cold makes her whole body pant, and she forgets the pregnant woman, Ruth, everything, as she fights the feeling of her body in panic. The cold is stinging, her heart is racing, and she grabs great mouthfuls of cold mist, as she fills her lungs with moist, icy air. Her limbs automatically thrash into some sort of breaststroke. She can hear her mother's voice. *Keep moving, get some feeling into them.*

Out of the corner of her eye, she sees Ruth begin a deep and slow breaststroke across the pond, and hears a startled, 'Holy shiiiiit!' drift back towards her with the ripples of water.

And then her heart stops feeling like it is about to burst, and she is flooded with such elation that she feels like she is young again. And then she remembers that, compared to many, she *is* young, and a laugh erupts from her. What is thirty-nine anyway? It's only a number. The other women have disappeared into the mist and Ruth is just a Christmas pudding bobbing on the water several metres away from her. An, 'Oh my!' is washed back to her and she thinks of Malcolm and his mother, Eve, who flew bombers and who swam here in this pond as the seasons changed around her.

There is a duck drifting through the floating leaves ahead of her. Its beady eyes remind her of Ruth. Ruth, who can so quickly sink into self-critical anxiety. Will Jo ever get to understand what troubles her? Know why she ran away? Will she ever find out about the lost friendship that Malcolm regrets? And the more she thinks about it, the more she is certain there is something behind the purple and orange slippers, rather than simply a love of colour. They looked beautiful but old, so they must be of sentimental value. She wonders how long Malcolm has kept them, and who gave them to him.

She smiles as she swims.

And Eric? She watches her fingers break the mottled surface of the water. Her chocolate-coloured nail varnish an iridescent flash. She shouldn't think about him; they're just friends, and he's clearly with Clare. But just right now, in this water, eye-to-eye with a duck – everything eases. Even the tight kernel of pain that she keeps hidden within her loosens.

'This is amazing!' Ruth appears behind her left shoulder. 'I thought I was going to have a heart attack, but it's incredible.' And with that she strikes out again across the pond, leaving Jo to her slower meandering strokes that are bringing her in a small circle closer to the edge of the pond.

Once in a rhythm with the cold singing rather than stinging, she reviews her week. It has been a good week. The shop has been busy and her mum was cheerful on their weekly Skype (still confident that 'in the spring' Uncle Wilbur would be back). Behind her mum's comfortable face, she saw her dad walk past and lift a finger in affectionate greeting, whilst at the same time shaking his head. So, she is to keep quiet and stay put for a while longer. And that is not so bad. She has experienced the pleasure of finally turning a profit. Maybe this is the beginning of something? A new venture for her? She certainly likes chatting to her Stationery Lovers – feeling she is connecting with her tribe.

She thinks about Ruth and Malcolm and their different ages and how insignificant this feels to their friendship, and she decides James has a lot to answer for. She does a particularly vicious breaststroke kick deep into the water, then gazes up at the leaden sky and thinks of the prospect of lunch with Ruth and Malcolm. With the thought of food and wine, she realizes her whole body is now shaking. The feeling of well-being is seeping away and her muscles are trembling. Her hands and feet are sore with cold.

Ruth reappears out of the gloom. 'Enough of this!' she proclaims. 'I'm going to catch my death if I stay in any longer.'

With that they plough through the water to the metal ladder. Jo reaches it first and hauls herself, scarlet and shaking, onto the side. As she starts the scurry back to the changing room, Jo can hear the splash of the more hardy swimmers, and the gentle buzz of conversation, broken by the occasional burst of laughter.

So, she may not have Eric or James (and does she really want James, anyway?). But she has Ruth and Malcolm.

And now she has this. There is no doubt she will be back here soon. And she sends up a silent . . . she wouldn't call it a prayer (after all, she is still Average Jo, sitting somewhere in the middle when it comes to God) . . . but a thought, a *thank you*, to Malcolm's mother, Eve.

As Ruth pulls herself up the ladder behind her, Jo catches a murmured, 'God bless you, Eve Buswell.'

28

Do seals have ears?

Ruth has already made friends with the waiters and established that it is okay to borrow the old library books. In fact, they encourage it. So, now she is back at the table (still wearing layers and her coat), with a couple of Agatha Christies.

'Are you sure you wouldn't like to take your coat off?' Malcolm is all concern.

And so he should be; Jo has only just stopped shaking. One of the swimmers, who came into the changing room as they were gathering their things to go, suggested that next time she should bring a hot-water bottle with her. 'It's fantastic,' she said.

'What? You swim with it?' Jo asked, and the changing room erupted into laughter. Caught again – she was reminded of Eric.

'No.' The young woman grinned. 'When you're dressed, you shove it down your bra. Works wonders.'

As Jo shrugs off her coat, Malcolm leans forward to help her. Something spills out from under the neck of his crisp grey and white striped shirt. It is a large turquoise medallion shaped like a sun. He hurriedly tucks it away and turns to Ruth.

'No, I'll keep my coat for the time being, *thank you*, Malcolm,' Ruth replies. 'Nice medallion,' she adds, eyebrows raised.

Malcolm stares for some moments at nothing in particular, and then continues as if he hasn't heard the last comment. 'Perhaps I should have suggested you waited for the spring,' he worries.

Jo peers at the neck of Malcolm's shirt (medallion now well hidden) and glances down to check his footwear. Still the black Lobb brogues but, as his trouser hem rides up an inch, she spots startlingly orange socks patterned with large daisies.

Ruth has dropped her pretence at annoyance. 'Nonsense – it was an amazing experience, wasn't it, Jo?'

'I'm thinking of going next week,' Jo tells them.

'You are?' Ruth sounds incredulous, then adds, 'No, no. I can see that it could get quite addictive. How often did your mother swim in the ponds, Malcolm?'

'Oh, Mother went most days. She said that even when she woke up feeling out of sorts, she knew a dip in the ponds would fix her. She was still swimming well into her eighties.'

'Did you ever swim with her?' Jo asks. 'I mean, when the mixed ponds were open?'

'No never,' Malcolm says, briefly, and then repeats the phrase that Jo had wondered about, 'I am not a brave man.'

Pretty brave socks for a retired tax analyst.

Malcolm hurries on. 'Now, let's have a look at these menus, and order you two swimmers some food. You certainly deserve it. My treat. Whatever you like, now. No holding back.'

Jo picks up the menu, but from under her lashes she can see Ruth is still studying Malcolm, a speculative look on her face.

'Hi there, Jo!'

Jo swivels around in her seat to find Lando and a petite, dark-haired woman standing a few feet away. The woman is holding the hand of a dark-haired child who is as neat as Lando (which Jo thinks is pretty amazing for a boy who must be about six). Apart from the hair. His hair looks like he cut it himself. 'Hi Lando, how are you?' Jo replies.

'Good,' he says, slowly. He appears to be studying the pompom hat that she is still wearing. 'Jo, this is my wife, Sacha, and our son, Ferdy. Sacha, Jo,' and the small, elegant woman smiles and holds her hand out to her. 'Yeah, he did cut it himself,' she says, laughing, following Jo's gaze. 'There is quite a lot of glue in there too. He thought it was gel.'

Jo is grinning at Ferdy, who just stares back at her, seemingly deeply unimpressed.

'Do all animals have ears?' Ferdy asks Jo, suddenly.

Jo can hear Malcolm's rumble of laughter. She looks towards him for help, but although he smiles sympathetically, he also raises his shoulders and shrugs.

'I'm not sure . . . umm, I don't know . . .'

Ferdy continues to stare at her.

'Er . . . how about seals?' she suggests.

Ferdy stares a bit longer and then says, 'And what about spiders and worms and crocodiles?' He then adds, solemnly, 'You don't know much, do you?'

Sacha and Lando both jump in. 'Ferdy, that's rude!'

Jo doesn't think it was rude. He was stating the obvious.

She takes the opportunity to introduce her companions, keeping Ruth's introduction as short as possible. The Runaway Vicar may be old news, but she doesn't want to say anything that would reveal Ruth's identity.

Another figure appears beside the table. 'Lando, Sacha, sorry I'm late. Hi, mate,' he directs at Ferdy. Then he spots Jo and smiles. 'Oh, hi! What are you doing here, Jo?'

Looking up at Eric the Viking, Jo wishes she had taken her bobble hat off. She quickly explains their swim and makes introductions, adding in, 'Eric the Optician.'

'Not "the Viking"?' he mutters under his breath in apparent disappointment.

Ruth also mutters under her breath. 'Ah, the Viking is back.'

'You think my hair's noko, don't you, Eric?' Ferdy demands of the Viking, tugging on his hand.

'Course,' Eric responds immediately.

'*See*,' Ferdy says, looking at his parents. Argument won.

Jo looks puzzled, 'Noko?' she queries.

'Oh, Ferdy and Eric make up their own language,' Lando sighs, resignedly. 'I think "noko" means, cool.'

Eric turns to the erect figure seated beside him. 'Are you the Malcolm who is writing a book on Highgate Cemetery?'

Jo is mortified. She doesn't want Malcolm to think she has

been giving his secrets away. She rushes in, 'I've been telling Eric about your research. I explained you didn't know exactly what you were planning on writing yet.'

Malcolm bows his head a fraction in her direction, as if in understanding.

'Yes, it's a fascinating undertaking. Have you been to visit the cemetery, Eric?'

Before Eric can answer, they are interrupted by the arrival of two waiters. The small gathering by the table is clearly very much in the way, and with hurried apologies and half-finished sentences, the two groups separate. Lando, Sacha, Ferdy and Eric are shown to a table at the other end of the restaurant. One of the waiters deposits water and a bottle of red wine on Jo's table, and then proceeds to take their orders.

'So,' Ruth says, reaching for her wine, 'tell us *all* about Eric the Viking, Jo.'

Jo puts her head in her hands, but she finds she is laughing, 'I don't know where to start and I'm not sure there's really anything to say.'

Malcolm begins to pour water for them all. 'I rather think you might tell Reverend Ruth a bit about James, if you didn't mind, Joanne. Set the scene, so to speak.'

The scene for what? Jo thinks, but she does as she's told and fills Ruth in on much of what happened with James and the problems (whatever they may be) with Lucy. She has had no reply yet to her most recent letter about Christmas wishes, and waiting for one is making her feel unsettled and slightly panicky

They are now well into their meal and second glass of wine. Jo's story had taken quite some time in the telling, with both Ruth and Malcolm asking a string of questions, especially about James, before dismissing him as 'Not good enough for our Joanne.' Jo was finding that the more she talked about James, the more she agreed with them. She can feel a growing anger towards him, and also anger directed at herself for having gone along with it all, and for giving up on things and people she liked without a fight. Not that it would have come to a fight. James wore her down by providing endless reasons of why he was right and she was wrong. *A reasonable man*. And if this didn't work, he would sulk. That could go on for days.

'And now to your Viking,' Ruth says, with relish.

'He's not *my* Viking,' she says, then laughs, thinking how ridiculous she sounds..

'I think he likes you,' Ruth declares, with decision.

Malcolm joins in. 'I *know* that young man likes her. I have been watching him and he keeps looking this way. And I am sure it is not you or me that the young man is interested in, Reverend Ruth,' Malcolm says, with a chuckle.

Jo flushes. It may be the wine or the heat after the cold swim. 'But he's with Clare,' she insists, fighting the urge to ask, *do you really think so?* She goes on to explain about Caramel Toffee Clare and how Eric asked if Jo minded about her. 'Like he was seeing her,' Jo explains.

Ruth makes a low humming noise. 'Maybe, but it seems like a bit of a leap to me.'

'I've seen them together quite a bit,' Jo insists. She just can't think of another explanation for his words. And perhaps it's for the best – knowing that Eric is with someone else just protects her from the inevitable. She may be sitting here with friends of very different ages, but she still finds it hard to convince herself that – when it comes to *this* – age wouldn't matter. Her experience with James had taught her that it did.

'My goodness, those tattoos,' Ruth suddenly remarks. 'He looks like some sort of Nordic God.'

'Loki,' Malcolm proclaims. 'Loki with a Birmingham accent.'

Ruth looks at him blankly.

'Loki was a Norse God – very mischievous . . .' Malcolm says.

'You know, like in the superhero films,' Jo says, thinking mischievous is about right for Eric.

'. . . and Loki could turn himself into an animal,' Malcolm adds.

And with that, they are off. Ruth and Malcolm playing verbal table tennis across their pasta.

Malcolm: 'A bull.'

Ruth: 'No, no, too lumbering and angry.' (Swipe)

Malcolm: 'One of those big dogs, then, a Saint Bernard?'

Ruth: 'Too slobbery, Eric the Viking is more of a wolf.' (Swipe)

Malcolm: 'Wolf?! Wolf? He is much too friendly for a wolf.'

At this point Jo interrupts. 'He always makes me think of a walrus.'

Neither Ruth nor Malcolm agree with her (but then, Jo thinks, they have never heard him bark with laughter), and then all chatter stops as the waiter is back to clear the plates and take orders for pudding.

As they wait for these to arrive, Ruth focuses her full and penetrating attention on the question of Lucy.

What had it been like for Lucy with James around?

(Difficult to say – she always thought she was managing it okay, but now . . .)

What had it been like with other boyfriends?

(Okay, apart from Lenny at school, who it turned out was a thief.)

Did Sanjeev like James?

(Not really, but he tried his best.)

How was it when Lucy was in Amsterdam?

(Good, the distance hadn't mattered as much as Jo feared. But she did miss the small things, like having coffee with her.)

Why did she think Lucy was so angry?

(She was really upset James hurt me, but now I think she is really pissed off with me too.)

Why?

(Maybe I wasn't the best friend when she got home to England, and I think she was worried I would go back to James.)

Would you?

Jo smiles at Malcolm. (Not now. *He may have been my lover, but he was never my friend.*)

How do you feel about Lucy's baby?

(Happy.)

At this point Ruth had paused expectantly, but Jo had kept silent.

When is the baby due?

(Early February.)

Ruth says decisively, 'You must go home for a weekend. Malcolm and I will look after the shop.' In the next instance, a shadow of anxiety passes across Ruth's face and Jo wonders why it is Ruth sometimes suffers these mood changes.

'You are right, I suppose,' Jo responds, slowly, 'I do need to go home.' At the same time she wonders: where is home for her now? She had been so sure it was in the North, but with the shop and these friends . . .

As they linger over sticky toffee pudding, Jo finds herself watching the table across the room. From the body language and laughter, Lando and Eric are clearly back to teasing each other. She is reminded of her meal with them when they had interspersed jibes with fulsome praise. In some ways, it is similar to the verbal to-and-fro that Ruth and Malcolm seem to enjoy so much. Eric appears to be drawing Ferdy on to his side, and Jo watches him pull the little boy onto his lap so they can both start pointing at Lando, swaying in unison, heads together. Jo wonders if Eric will get glued there and can't decide if she wants to laugh or cry.

'There's no time like the present,' Ruth suddenly declares, and Jo looks at her, startled.

'I think you should text Lucy now and say you are planning on coming home for the weekend.'

Jo sees Ruth glance towards Eric the Viking and begins to think these are diversionary tactics aimed at helping her. She gets her phone out and composes a text to Lucy. She sends it quickly, before she changes her mind.

Almost as soon as it is sent, Jo's phone pings. She looks down hopefully and then up at Ruth and Malcolm in shock and distress.

'What?' they both say, leaning forward.

Jo holds up her phone so they can see the one-word reply:

Don't

'Oh, my dear,' Malcolm says, reaching out his hand.

'Well . . .' Ruth starts, and then for once seems lost for words.

A second ping makes Jo look down again. This time when she looks up she is beaming, the relief evident on her face. She holds the phone up again, this message reads:

Sorry, sent that without finishing. Don't come home at weekend. I'm coming to see you this week! Sanjeev booked me tickets as a surprise. Will text later, in an antenatal class at mo. Woman's waters just broke. Sanjeev says if it's like this, he's buying a boat. L x

29

William Foyle & John Lobb

Jo feels like a great weight has been lifted; she has no idea what Lucy's visit will bring, but surely they must be able to sort this out? She wouldn't be coming if she didn't want to.

As a waiter arrives with coffee, a thought comes to her. She suddenly knows with complete certainty what the ghosts of William Foyle and John Lobb would talk about on Christmas Eve. She glances towards where Eric and Lando are sitting and then back at Ruth and Malcolm.

'I'd like to tell you about William Foyle and John Lobb,' she says with decision.

'Oh, splendid!' Malcolm declares, pulling his chair up closer to the table.

To start with, Jo tells them all she has learnt about John and William. Their poor backgrounds and the wealth they then accumulated during their lives. 'Not that it was always easy for either of them, even when the businesses were established.'

'So, both self-made men who could duck and dive,' Malcolm suggests.

Jo nods.

'Ah, you think they would have talked business?' Malcolm asks.

'No, that's it. I don't think they would have done. Or not that much.' Her eyes flick once more towards Lando and Eric. 'I think they would have respected each other but probably wouldn't have admitted it. No, I think they would have taken the mick out of each other.'

She looks at Malcolm and Ruth's faces. Ruth is nodding, but Malcolm doesn't look convinced. She continues, 'I think they would have felt easy in each other's company. I'll give you an example of what I mean. When William Foyle came to change his car, he walked into a showroom and picked out a Rolls-Royce he fancied. The salesman apparently was really sniffy, and reminded him that they would insist on a full deposit. William never lost his cockney accent, so the salesman assumed he could never afford such a car. William told the young man not to worry and came back that afternoon with a suitcase of cash for the whole amount, then drove the car away. I could imagine John Lobb doing much the same thing. He was a Cornish boy – I imagine he still had the West Country accent. He would be used to people not taking him seriously. And in a funny way, I think that would draw them together, but also give them something to tease each other about.'

She is glad to see that both Malcolm and Ruth are nodding now.

'John would remind William he's an East Ender, little more than a barrow boy. William could tell John exactly what he thinks of country bumpkins.' She glances again across the room at Lando and Eric. 'But it would be good natured. They might not discuss the similarities and hardships they shared, but they would underpin their friendship.'

She looks expectantly at Malcolm. She so doesn't want to disappoint him.

'This is most helpful, Joanne. Very insightful, if I may say so.'

Jo wants to hug him (again).

'So, what would they do on Christmas Eve?' Ruth asks.

'They would go to the pub. For sure,' Jo answers, with confidence. 'William used to go home each week to the twelfth-century abbey he bought with all his money. He would get his Rolls-Royce to stop at a pub on the way home – I think the pub stayed open just for him.'

'And John Lobb?' Malcolm enquires.

Jo reaches for her phone and shows them both a photograph. It is black and white, and in it four men are grouped together; one is seated, the other three standing. They seem to be in front of a body of water.

'John used to travel quite a lot with friends and colleagues, and that was taken at Niagara Falls.'

'Which one's John Lobb?' Ruth asks, peering at the photo.

'That one there, leaning back on his stick, hat on the back of his head.'

Malcolm laughs. 'Goodness, they all look three sheets to the wind.'

He's right. Their hats are at odd angles and, by their faces, Jo would guess the four old men have been drinking all afternoon.

Ruth is quietly laughing.

'So, come Christmas Eve night, I think William and John would head to the nearest pub. I don't know how much further they would get than that. I don't think they would need a pub crawl. Just each other's company, a few drinks, and the chance to insult one another. And, on the very odd occasion, I think they might sneak in the odd, heartfelt compliment. Neither would have any illusions about how hard their paths had been. But I don't think either would boast to the other about their achievements. They wouldn't need to. And that is why I think they would have such a good time.'

Malcolm has drawn out a small book and is now scribbling down notes. He glances up. 'I can already see these two deciding to meet up again next Christmas Eve,' Malcolm says, contentedly.

Jo sits back. It isn't that she has experienced a friendship like the one she is envisaging for John and William, but she knows she has had friends (beyond Lucy and Sanjeev) in whose company she has felt at ease, and whose friendships have meant a lot to her. And she is also aware she has not looked after those friendships as she should have done. It was one thing to wake up to the fact James got things very much his own way, but she cannot blame him for all of it.

She smiles to herself; the ghosts of William Foyle and John Lobb have reminded her how precious friendship is. The ghosts, plus a Runaway Vicar and a man called Malcolm. Jo lets out a small, contented sigh.

As Malcolm writes, Ruth and Jo finish their coffees in silence. Jo is suddenly feeling very sleepy. She studies the wall of old library books and thinks she might take one home with her.

Something flutters onto the table in front of her. She looks up quickly. Eric is standing beside her, Lando and Sacha just behind him. Ferdy is draped over Eric's shoulder, fast asleep. He looks very much at home there, and Jo rather envies him.

'Sorry, Jo,' he says, nodding towards the piece of paper that had landed in her place. 'Ferdy drew that for you.'

Jo picks it up and turns it over. It is a drawing of a seal (or maybe a worm) with very large ears. And a bobble hat. She grins up at Eric. 'When he wakes up, will you thank him and tell him it will have pride of place on my board in the shop.'

'Will do,' Eric says, adjusting the hold he has on the comatose little body, and he and the others move on.

Jo watches Eric navigate the restaurant door, carefully covering Ferdy's head with his hand so he doesn't get bumped by the doorframe.

'No, definitely not a bull or a wolf,' Ruth mutters.

Jo lets out another sigh, sadder this time. Eventually Ruth asks, 'What are you doing with the rest of the afternoon and evening?'

'Oh, I think a nap,' Jo says, suddenly feeling exhausted, 'and then I need to get the flat ready for Lucy's visit.'

'Will it take long?'

'No, I don't think so.' And something in Ruth's tone makes Jo enquire, 'Why?'

'Just that I thought I would go along to St Michael's on the edge of the heath for their Advent service.'

Jo tries to rid her mind of purple underwear.

'I wondered if you'd like to come?'

'I'm not sure, Ruth,' Jo says, hesitatingly. She wants to go to please Ruth, to do right by her friend, but knows she doesn't believe in God, so it seems hypocritical. But mainly she knows that once inside in the warm flat, it would take a crowbar to get her out again. 'Do you mind?' she adds. 'Maybe Malcolm?' Jo suggests, tentatively, looking at the scribbling figure.

Ruth lets out a snort. 'I don't think so, do you?'

'Think what?' Malcolm says pleasantly, looking up.

'Ruth was talking about an Advent service—' Jo begins.

'I hardly think so,' Malcolm scoffs, then his face softens. 'I do apologize, Reverend Ruth. Have you found an agreeable church nearby?'

'Oh, I tried a few out. Sat at the back and gave them marks out of ten on a number of criteria. Only got caught once,' she says, meditatively, 'and then they thought the bishop had sent me,' she adds, with a grin. 'I came across Reverend Abayomrunkoje . . .' As an aside, Ruth says, 'He was such fun and very engaging. So that's where I go now.'

'Whereabouts is the church?' Malcolm asks, politely.

Ruth tells him, then adds, 'It's all right, Malcolm – you don't have to keep on being polite. I'm quite happy to go on my own. The Advent service is quite lovely – one of my favourites.

From darkness into light. Reverend Abayomrunkoje is of my mind: start with the church in complete darkness and then process in with candles. I shall be helping him with the lighting of the church. The whole service is then held in candlelight.'

Ruth starts to reach for her coat and hat, 'Although,' she continues, thoughtfully, 'I think to assume that light is the be-all and end-all is a bit short-sighted . . . as your optician might say,' Ruth adds, with a crafty look at Jo.

'He's not my—'

'Darkness,' Ruth interrupts, 'can have a unique kind of comfort, don't you think?'

Jo's not sure what she thinks; she is too sleepy and full of good wine and food. She starts to gather her things and to thank Malcolm for their lunch.

'Not at all. It is I who must thank you. My mother would have much appreciated your efforts on her behalf.'

Before they go their separate ways, Jo tells Reverend Ruth about the Christmas wishes tied to the tree in her shop and asks if she might say a prayer for a man who wants his wife to be able to spend her last Christmas at home with her family.

'Of course. I will light a candle for them,' Ruth replies, composedly.

Later that evening, Jo is standing on the footpath opposite St Michael's, keeping a watch on the darkened windows. She intended to stay in, but she couldn't help feeling she was letting Ruth down and should have said, 'Yes', when asked to the Advent service. She thought back to William Foyle and John Lobb, and of her resolve to now make more of an effort with her friends. So she layered up once more and set off.

When she got to the church, the doors were closed. Worried about interrupting the service, she took up her vigil in a bus shelter opposite.

The flicker starts just a few moments before the singing. Little by little the glow fills the windows, and the organ music and sound of voices filter out into the cold winter air. Jo thinks of Ruth's comment about darkness not necessarily being a bad thing. Here she is in the darkness, watching the warm glimmer within, and she feels content to be an observer. She watches until the church is aglow with light and then she turns and heads for home.

30

One of those days

Jo is trying to focus on the good things in her day, but it is hard. Over the past couple of days, her excitement about Lucy's visit has transformed into apprehension, and she feels like a woman who is preparing to face a great storm.

Then there have been today's customers. First was the extremely posh woman with the enormous handbag. She dumped this on the counter and Jo could hear the metal studs on the bottom of the bag scratching the glass. She tried a gentle, 'Would you mind . . .' but to no avail. The woman was off, demanding to try every fountain pen that Jo had, decrying the fact she did not stock Mont Blanc. She flung each pen aside when she had finished with it, without bothering to refasten the cap. The woman left the shop without buying anything, smiling vaguely at Jo and finally declaring, 'Well, that was fun.'

Jo only had a few moments to shut her gaping mouth (and clear up the carnage) before two children came in with their mother. Normally Jo liked children trying the fountain pens, and enjoyed showing them how to hold them and explaining how they were filled with ink. Usually it was the parents who were reluctant for their offspring to handle the pens, and it was Jo who coaxed them into letting the children have a go. Another nudge in the direction of getting more people to write. And maybe, she hoped, thinking of 'Sacha the magpie', she would be passing on snippets of information that people would remember.

These children didn't wait for any assistance from Jo, or even ask if they could try the pens. They fell on them, tore the tops off, and chiselled their names in the pad of paper, pens held tight in fists like daggers. Their mother completely ignored them. And the children completely ignored Jo when she tried to show them how to hold the pens. After several minutes, the woman abruptly left the shop with Sholto and Allegra in tow. As Jo cleared up, it gave her a certain twisted pleasure to see that Allegra couldn't spell her own name. She took a perverse delight in pinning this to her board.

The shop is now quiet and Jo is just beginning to feel the day might get better when she discovers someone has stolen one of her tester pens. It is the scarlet one that Eric liked so much.

She is on her knees, dungareed bottom in the air, poking under the cabinet with a wooden ruler when Eric comes in.

'Lost something?'

Jo quickly sits back on her heels. She already feels at a disadvantage with Eric the Viking; being found scrabbling around on the floor isn't helping. 'Someone's nicked one of my pens,' she tells him, sighing and hauling herself to her feet. 'It's been a horrible day.'

'It'll bring them no luck,' Eric says philosophically, planting himself on the stool beside the counter.

'You think that?' Jo asks, wondering if this is more of it. Not religion but something spiritual – like her sending good thoughts to people. A type of karma? 'Do you really think bad things happen to bad people – and vice versa?' she asks.

'Not really sure. It was just something my grandmother used to say. "They'll get no luck of it."'

'An Icelandic saying?'

'No,' Eric grins, 'she was Scottish. Do you know who stole it?'

Jo tries to remember all the people who have been in the shop since she last saw it. 'Not a clue,' she tells him.

Thinking about it only makes her feel worse. Someone she was chatting away to was quietly stealing from her.

'It happens sometimes with me. Although why anyone would want to nick the glasses we've got on display beats me. They've all got clear lenses in them.'

'Perhaps the thieves just want to look more intelligent,' Jo suggests, sitting down on her side of the counter.

'Ah, that's where I've been going wrong,' Eric says, rubbing his chin. 'Hey, you look done in. Shall I get us some coffee and cake – the café is doing great Christmas cake at the moment.'

'Go on then,' Jo says. 'And thank you.'

As he goes out through the door, Jo puts her head onto the glass of the counter. It is cool against her forehead. Her head aches and she feels abnormally despondent. A thought wheedles in: he's *so* nice. She knows people who despise the word 'nice' (James, for example); Jo decides she's not one of them. She lets out a low groan. Why did she spend all those weeks obsessing about that bollox James (Uncle Wilbur was quite right) when this man was walking past her window each day? And now he's with someone else. And unlike Nickeeey, this 'someone else' seems really nice. *That word again.*

When Eric comes back through the door carrying a cardboard tray containing coffee and cake, he catches her staring off into space. 'What are you thinking about?' he asks.

She can't say, *You*, so instead tries, 'Just some of the customers who have been in today. Do people ask you really stupid questions in the optician's?'

Eric manoeuvres the tray onto the counter. 'What do you mean?'

'Oh, it's just I've had quite a few today. Like, "How long will my ink cartridge last?" I guess I can see why they ask, but I get tired of saying, "It really depends on how much you write."'

Eric grins, 'It's a bit like asking someone, "How many days before I need more petrol?"'

'Exactly!' Jo says, pleased to find someone who understands.

'I get patients asking if they can clean their contact lenses with spit.'

'Yuck!'

It is Eric's turn to say, 'Exactly!'

Eric appears to be warming to the theme, 'Now I think about it, it isn't so much the questions as the comments we get. Like the number of people who tell me that their glasses were broken when they opened up the case. When it is obvious they have sat on them or the dog has chewed them. Sometimes you can even see the teeth marks.'

'I have people who look at our fountain pen covers and ask me, "Will my pen fit in that?" Again, I kind of know what they mean, but I want to say, "How the hell should I know?"'

'That, I'd like to hear.'

'I did say to one woman, "If your pen is smaller than the cover, then yes it will. If it is bigger, then no",' Jo confesses, a little guiltily.

Eric laughs. 'I had a woman in this morning who told me with a completely straight face that when she doesn't have her glasses on, she can't see as well.'

'Thanks for this, Eric,' Jo says, gesturing to the tray. 'It's just what I needed.' And she means more than the coffee and cake. She begins to wonder if Reverend Ruth was right, maybe she had read too much into the question, 'Do you mind about Clare?'

Just then, there is a gentle knocking on the window and, without looking up, Jo knows who it will be. It was going far too well, and this, after all, is one of those days.

Clare is smiling at them both, face rosy, looking Christmassy in a scarlet coat and dark green scarf. Eric beckons to her, but Clare shakes her head, caramel toffee curls bouncing. Eric heads for the door, coffee and cake forgotten.

Jo takes a sip of her coffee and a bite of cake, all the time trying not to look like she is watching the pantomime going on outside. She reminds herself that Eric the Optician, of all people, will know that women have good peripheral vision, so he will know she is studying them from the edge of her eye. Not that he seems interested in Jo; he is concentrating on Clare. At first it looks like an argument, and she finds herself hoping it is. Then she sees Eric shake his head, as if he is giving in to Clare (well you do that, don't you, when you're in love) and she sees him lean in and give her a long, warm hug. She was right: it really is a bloody awful day.

Eric is suddenly back in the shop, grinning at her. 'Got to go, but I . . . well, we . . . wondered . . . and no rush, next time . . .'

Jo wants to shout at him – at them – *For God's sake, spit it out!* Instead she sits there, trying to look completely unfazed.

'Next time Finn's down, I was wondering if the four of us could go out?'

'What? Christ, no!'

Two things strike Jo as she all but bellows this. That Eric looks confused and upset, and that now she is going to think of Ruth each time she says *Christ*. This is followed by the realization that she just can't bring herself to add: *He's not actually my boyfriend. He will not be coming down to see me. He's got a new girlfriend keeping him warm in Northumberland.*

'Oh, okay. Right, sorry. Just a thought,' Eric says, looking at her as if he is seeing her for the first time, the new Jo, who is neither average nor honest. Just rude.

And still she can't say anything. If she says she's not with Finn, Eric and Clare might feel sorry for her. And that she couldn't bear. They might even say, come out with us on your own anyway. And she would rather throw herself naked into Hampstead Ladies' Pond with a rock tied around her than do that.

'Nice thought though,' she says, meaning it to sound conciliatory – a type of apology. But it comes out just as she was thinking it – dripping with sarcasm.

Eric turns on his heel and the door closes with a bang. There follows a tinny clink from the broken bell, and finally the rattle of glass. She feels the loss of him like a physical force, like his leaving has created a vacuum and something of herself has been sucked out of the shop after him.

Next time she looks towards the window, Eric and Clare have disappeared.

Jo leans her elbows on the counter and puts her forehead in her hands. She was beginning to think that maybe, just maybe, she did read too much into Eric and Clare's meeting. She allowed in a glimmer of hope, let her guard down, and now she feels the pain of disappointment and loss slicing between her ribs.

And it feels like a double loss. She stares, unseeing, at the glass top of the counter. She thinks of a woman she once met on a bus in Greece. They talked for two hours non-stop. Then in Athens they went their separate ways, never to meet again. At the time Jo thought the woman could have been a close friend, if things had been different. Like Caramel Toffee Clare, the what-might-have-been friend.

Jo looks up at the twinkling lights. What is she doing here? Running this shop. Her life on hold. She thought she'd discovered something special through her love of stationery, but after a day like today – who's she kidding? She may feel close to Uncle Wilbur here, have found a precious and unexpected friendship with Malcolm and Ruth, but London isn't her home. Had she really thought it could be?

Her phone pings. Malcolm. His texts always make her smile (which is just what she needs right now). They are long, polite, and the punctuation is always correct.

Dear Joanne, I would like to discuss George Eliot and Issachar Zacharie with you and the Reverend Ruth. Our conversation the other day has spurred me on to reach certain conclusions, which I would like to share with you. The Reverend Ruth can make Friday. I hope you will be available too. Perhaps we could meet in the lounge bar of the public house near to Highgate Cemetery? Kind regards, Malcolm.

Jo texts straight back, inviting them to come to her flat for supper instead. She feels the need to submerse herself in her friendship with Ruth and Malcolm (and the ghosts), and she wants to do something nice for them. For all the mysteries and complexities surrounding Ruth and Malcolm, things seem easier when the three of them are together.

Besides, Friday is just after Lucy's visit and Jo is pretty certain she will have a lot to discuss with them by then.

31

Lucy

Jo looks up and there she is, radiant (and very pregnant) in a burnt-orange dress, purple tights, cherry suede boots and a black-and-white checked swing coat. Her dark hair is piled on her head and Lucy is wearing her signature scarlet lipstick. Beside her is Lando, holding tight to a straining Ferdy, who is trying to pull him towards the door.

Jo was in the kitchen at the back of the shop, and the unexpectedness of the trio now standing by her counter momentarily throws her off balance. And then she is propelled as if by a force towards her best friend. She reaches her and hugs her, having to sidestep her belly to get as much of her in her arms as possible. Jo feels the power of Lucy's returning embrace and she thinks, whatever follows, they will be okay. Their friendship has grown and been shaped over years and, despite losing their way, this counts for something. It is part of the two of them; it flows through them both and it is precious.

Lucy is now laughing and Ferdy is moaning.

'I want to see Eric. This is the *wrong* shop.'

Jo is drawn back to the unusual sight of Lando in her shop (a Lando who is looking abnormally harassed), and she asks, 'You okay, Lando? Can I help?' while still holding tight to Lucy's hand. 'Oh, by the way, this is my best friend, Lucy,' she adds. She says the 'best friend' with pride, and she hopes that Lucy hears it.

Lucy gives her hand a squeeze before releasing it. 'Good to meet you, Lando. Now, Jo, where's the loo? This baby has been tap-dancing on my bladder for the last half an hour.'

Jo points the way, and takes Lucy's bag from her, storing it behind the counter. She knows she is beaming at Lando – a complete contrast to his expression.

'Sorry Jo, Sacha's got a stomach bug and so Ferdy's had to come in with me. I don't like to have him in the shop . . . needles . . . health and safety . . .'

'Oh, I'm sorry, Lando . . .' Jo starts. She wants to help but she only has a short time with Lucy – just the one night – and is planning on shutting the shop early.

'. . . Oh, don't worry, I wasn't going to ask you to look after him . . . Ferdy! Will you stop pulling! We'll go there in a minute . . . No, Eric has said he can hang out with him. I just wondered if you've got any colouring stuff, pads of paper, that sort of thing?'

'Of course!' Jo exclaims. She does a quick tour of the shelves, selecting coloured paper, crayons and gel pens. She then rummages in the box of old stock and pulls out a carbon receipt book and a stamp with an accompanying pad of ink. She puts them all in a brown paper bag and presents this interesting bundle to Ferdy, who momentarily stops struggling. He looks at the bag, half doubtful, half hopeful. 'Is that for me?'

'It certainly is. All yours,' she says, handing it to him.

For an instant she feels her uncle at her side. The sensation is so strong that she turns around, but all she sees is the noticeboard, now three-quarters full of her precious magpie collection.

'Noko,' Ferdy says, taking it from her.

'Thanks, Jo,' his father adds, 'how much do I owe you?'

'No, it's a gift,' Jo insists.

'Really? Thank you so much.'

'Hope you have a good day,' she calls after Ferdy as they head for the door.

Lucy is soon back carrying two mugs of tea; she hitches herself onto one of the stools in front of the counter, resting her feet on the rung of the other. Now it is just the two of them, Jo senses a nervousness in Lucy that echoes within herself.

'So, was that the tattoo artist, or the optician?' Lucy asks, her voice sounding light and overly breezy.

'That's Lando the tattoo artist. Eric the Viking is the optician,' Jo explains, knowing her tone is a replica of Lucy's.

'The Viking who is doing a spot of child-minding. Gotta love a man who likes kids. So, when do I get to see the Viking?' Lucy sips her tea, starting to sound more like herself.

For once Jo doesn't want to think about Eric; she has so much she wants to say to Lucy.

Before she has a chance to start, Lucy pulls back slightly on her stool, and looks Jo up and down. 'Are those my dungarees?!'

'Ah, yes. Should have said. You left them at my cottage and I brought them with me . . .' Jo isn't sure how to finish.

But Lucy just gives a small grunt and a smile. Finally she says, 'They suit you.'

'I'll give them back to you, you know, once the baby comes,' Jo assures her, for the first time properly considering Lucy's bulging belly. Has she been avoiding looking at it?

Her best friend strokes the side of her bump. 'No, that's all right. You should keep them.' There is a pause and Lucy adds, 'I'd really like you to have them.'

Jo slips down from her stool and goes to the door, turning the sign to 'Closed'. Whatever is coming next is too important to be interrupted.

Before she is even back at the counter, she has rushed into speech, the words tumbling out of her, 'I'm so sorry, Luce. I've been . . . I don't even . . . I can't bear to think about it all. I do know I've been a useless friend and you deserve *so* much better. I really thought I was making time for you when you came home, but now when I look back there were so many times I should have been there and wasn't.' She is standing in front of her friend, staring intently at her, trying to read the expression on her downturned face. 'You've never let me down, Luce, *ever*. But I got used to always being with James, doing what he wanted, and, you know, with all his friends it felt like I was being part of the latest thing and, I thought, sort of cool—'

'It wasn't,' Lucy interrupts, looking up, 'it was twattish.'

Jo can feel the humour twisted in with the hurt, and she breathes out a little. 'I did think I was trying.' Jo wants so hard to explain, 'I knew you didn't like him. But I really did, Luce – he really mattered to me. I thought I loved him. Now when I think about him, I don't know why I fell for him. I can't explain it . . . but back then . . . I just . . .' Jo shakes her head. What was it? Chemistry, infatuation; some need in her? She knows she had labelled it as 'love'. Malcolm's words come back to her: *He may have been your lover, Joanne, but he was never your friend.*

Jo looks at the woman in front of her and cannot believe she weighed friendship so lightly. When it came to loving a man (a man she thought she wanted to have a baby with), how could she believe there could be love when there was no friendship?

Lucy has gone back to staring into her tea; she looks up now. 'Jo, I know I didn't always make it easy. I know I speak before I think sometimes.' She takes a deep breath. 'I could cope with not really liking him. We all know some fuckwit people.' Jo wonders if she is thinking of her mother. 'But I didn't want you to "*make time*" for me. How do you think that made me feel? It shouldn't be like that. I was *so* looking forward to being back with you.' She says more softly, her brows furrowed, 'It never used to be like that.'

'I know. I'm so sorry, Luce,' is all she can whisper.

Lucy sighs. 'Look, I do get it. I really do. Things move on. You were stuck. And you weren't that shit a friend. Really.

And you were great when I was in Amsterdam. Brilliant, in fact. It's just, you were different when I got back. And I missed you . . . us.' She grins sheepishly at Jo. 'Anyway, I always thought you would come back to me. Jemima thought so too.'

Jo stares at her, startled. '*Jemima?* What, Jemima from work?' *Jemima who rescued her in that awful meeting.*

'Ah, yes,' Lucy shifts on her seat, 'forgot to mention that.'

'How the hell do you know Jemima?' Jo demands, distracted.

'She's part of that monthly Sunday market that I started doing when I came home. I do the vintage stuff, and she has a stall next to mine. You know the sort of thing: tea towels and mugs with Labradors on. We got talking.'

That would be Lucy all over: she took an interest and she talked. Had Jo ever really talked to Jemima? No, she had just followed James around . . . well . . . like a Labrador. 'What did you talk about?'

'Mainly James. Boy, she really doesn't like him,' Lucy says, a little guiltily. 'I might as well be honest,' she says, grinning, 'we bitched about him non-stop. He really was a self-satisfied tosser, Jo,' Lucy says, almost pleadingly.

'Was he?' Jo says, but there is no conviction in her question. Once more she sees Wilbur, Finn, Lucy and Jemima in a line – this time tutting at her, eyes raised to heaven. Lucy and Jemima are now standing arm-in-arm in her imagination.

'Jemima really likes you, though,' Lucy adds, encouragingly.

'Does she? I don't know why,' Jo says, and now with the cosy image of Lucy and Jemima fresh in her mind, she's not sure if she wants Jemima to like her.

'You just don't get it, do you?' Lucy says in a rush. 'It's why I was so angry. You're such a great person, Jo, and he made you feel like shit. You're kind and fun – and you give people space to be themselves; you don't overwhelm them, like some people do,' Lucy grimaces, pointing at herself. She pauses, 'Then James came along and it was like all the good stuff was sucked out of you.' She continues, quickly, 'Well, not all the good, but it was like when you were with him you were a washed-out version of you and you just went along with what he said. I mean you were *always* the one who came up with the best ideas, and yet he used to just overrule you and talk over you.'

Jo can see the distress on her friend's face.

'I couldn't bear it, Jo.'

'Why were you so angry when we split up then?' Jo asks her.

'Well, I was bloody furious with him, 'cos I could see you were hurt, and you didn't deserve it. Not from *him*. I know he's good-looking and all that, but he was a shit, Jo, and you are worth a million of him.'

Jo puts her hand on Lucy's arm, but a small part of her senses there is more to it than Lucy is saying. She feels Lucy shift on the tall stool and is suddenly conscious of how pregnant her friend is.

'Look, let's talk upstairs – you can sit down properly with your feet up.'

Lucy looks around, 'What about the shop?' she asks.

'Oh, I've decided to give myself a half-day,' she says, reaching down to pull out Lucy's bag from behind the counter.

'You don't have anyone who could help you?' Lucy enquires.

Jo shakes her head. 'It doesn't matter just for half a day,' she assures Lucy.

'Couldn't you get your new friends to look after it for you? Couldn't they help out?'

'What?' Jo is disconcerted by the edge in Lucy's voice.

'Oh, never mind,' Lucy mumbles, struggling to get her bulk off the stool.

Jo is going to say something more, but Lucy pipes up, 'Oh, are those the wishes you wrote to me about?' and she squeezes past Jo to read the luggage labels tied to the Christmas tree. She does this with a studious intensity that bars any interruption.

Jo watches her for a moment, then goes to the door. Just before turning off the lights and locking up, she slips outside. She takes a few steps towards Eric's shop and peers in at the corner of his window. Eric and Ferdy are on the floor, surrounded by three large cardboard boxes that they appear to be cutting up. Well, Eric is doing the cutting, Ferdy is trying to get into one of them.

'Hold on mate, give us a chance,' Jo hears Eric tell him. 'Look, put this string through that hole there,' he instructs his helper.

Eric looks up and Jo quickly dodges out of sight.

32

Stormy weather

They are upstairs in the sitting room. Lucy is lounging in Uncle Wilbur's chair, feet up on a cushion on his coffee table. She has discarded her orange dress and is plumply filling a pink onesie covered in cherries.

They have been catching up on family news, although Jo has avoided asking about Finn, worried she might give something away. As Finn said, it's 'his stuff' too. As they chat, Jo cancels the online booking she had made for lunch at a nearby tapas bar – Lucy looks tired – and Jo suggests that instead she go out and get them a selection of food from the local deli. She persuades Lucy to have a nap whilst she pops out, and she makes up Uncle Wilbur's bed for her. She's retreating back to the spare room for the night, so Lucy can have more space.

'I'm sorry about the Jemima stuff,' Lucy says, as she starts to haul herself up from the chair.

'Yeah, that was a bit of a bolt from the blue,' Jo agrees. 'Do you see much of her?' She experiences a slight twinge of something she recognizes as jealousy. She wonders just how long the two of them have spent talking about her and James.

'A bit.' Lucy sounds cagey.

'She's still at the bank, though?'

'Oh, yes. She only does the market stuff as a hobby.'

'Does she ever mention James?' Jo doesn't know why she asks. Some sense of being left out of things?

'Yes . . .' Lucy says, slowly. 'He's split up from Nicky,' she continues, watching her friend warily.

So it didn't last with Nickeeey . . . Jo is not sure how she feels about that. A big part of her is pleased it didn't work out. James certainly didn't deserve 'happy ever after'. A few weeks ago, she knows she'd have seen this as a splinter of hope, a sign that James had come to his senses, would want her back. And now? She thinks of Malcolm's words: *He was never your friend*.

'Say something, Jo.' Lucy is now on her feet facing her. 'Oh, please tell me you wouldn't . . .' she doesn't finish.

'No. I don't think I would.'

'Well, try and sound a bit more convincing,' Lucy says, and the edge is back.

What did make her hesitate for the tiniest of a split second? That getting back together would prove he was wrong and that she was worth having?

It seems all Lucy hears is the hesitation; the rise in the pitch of her voice is a measure of her exasperation. 'God, Jo, he's not worth it. Open your eyes. He was *never* worth it.

He isn't the man you thought he was.' Lucy takes a deep breath, 'Please tell me you don't still believe the "at least he was faithful" crap?'

Jo feels like she has been slapped. She'd had doubts, it's true, but then she'd checked his phone and email records – and more (it wasn't as if James ever changed his password).

'But I looked,' is all she can think to say. Followed quickly by, 'You know something.' It isn't a question.

Lucy stands, feet slightly apart, and is glaring at Jo. Despite the pink onesie, she is an imposing figure. '*Everybody* knew, Jo! Well, that's what Jemima told me. He made a point of looking after the graduate trainees and used it as an excuse to chase after Nicky. Why would he need to email her? Jemima said he saw her every day. And I'll give him this, he was a piece of work, Jo, but he wasn't stupid. He didn't start splashing it around on Instagram until months later, and while you were together he probably knew you'd look at his phone and emails. You always knew more about IT than he did. For God's sake, he even got you sorting out his mum's computer. Rushing round there every hour of the day, after his dad died.'

Jo can't assimilate the barrage of information. Yes, she'd helped his mum. Done so much for her and for James. Wasn't that what a partner did? How could Lucy give her a hard time when she was only trying to be kind? The voice that says, *but what did he do for you, Jo?* is washed away in the next thought that sweeps everything else before it.

'You knew and you didn't tell me?' Jo is surprised to hear that she shouts this.

In her mind she replays the scene with James, like old film footage: *There is no one else.*

She hadn't even asked.

Lucy blanches, but shifts on her feet as if getting purchase. 'Bloody hell, Jo, loads of people knew. It wasn't just me.'

Hurt and humiliation swamp Jo and then, erupting out of this, fury.

'But you're my best friend! Why didn't you tell me?'

Lucy blows out a breath that is so long Jo half expects her to deflate. 'I wanted to, Jo. But how could I? We weren't . . . it wasn't like it has been . . . I wasn't sure you would believe me.'

'So you and Jemima had a good laugh about poor old Jo.' She spits this.

Lucy puts her hand to her eyes. 'No, it wasn't like that.'

'Well, what was it like? I was trying to do the right thing by that fucker James, by you, by his family . . . and you're sitting round having a nice cosy bitch about me?'

'No!' Lucy's voice is almost as loud as Jo's now. 'I went to see the shitbag.'

'Nice chat?' Jo rips back with sarcasm.

Lucy's voice lowers. 'Oh Jo, it was awful. I said if he didn't tell you, then I would.'

'But he didn't tell me, Luce,' Jo checks the sob, 'and you let me go on, talking about maybe getting married one day. Talking about babies . . .' Her voice breaks. 'How *could* you?'

Suddenly it is as if Jo has lit the Lucy touchpaper. She turns on Jo. 'How could I?! Fuck it Jo, you hardly saw me. You *fitted me in* like I was a meeting you didn't want to go to.'

Jo fleetingly thinks, now it's coming . . . now, maybe the storm will break.

'I said you weren't a bad friend. But I lied. You were a shit friend. I so wanted to just do some normal stuff with you when I got back. I knew things might have changed, I did get that. But all you could think about were the wanky-swanky places you were going to. You might have asked me along, but you knew I couldn't afford it. And then what did you do? You offered to pay for me. How do you think that made me feel, Jo? Bloody crap. That's how!' Lucy bellows this and her belly shakes with her rage.

For an instant Jo worries about the baby and she is filled with shame. James kept saying *don't ask Lucy, Lucy doesn't fit in*, and she wanted to prove him wrong. But why did she think Lucy needed to be friends with people she no longer hears from and never cared for?

She wants to say how sorry she is, but a single thought stoppers her mouth. *You knew James was cheating and you didn't tell me.*

They stare at each other in horror.

Lucy sweeps past her to the door to Uncle Wilbur's room. 'I can't do this. I need to sleep,' she mutters. Then the muttering forms into words. These she throws at Jo. 'You could have come home. You could have come to see me, but you didn't. I kept telling myself I shouldn't mind, I'd gone away for four years. But you could have come, Jo.' There is deep regret in her words, and then the bitterness creeps in, 'But why would you want to? Got your new friends, and it's all about the

251

bloody vicar and a sodding man called Malcolm. Well, have a great life, Jo!' and with this she slams the door.

Jo instinctively steps towards the closed door, but it feels as impenetrable as Fort Knox. Her second instinct, she acts on – with shaking hands she texts the bloody vicar and a sodding man called Malcolm.

Five minutes later, Jo leaves the flat, having first stood irresolute in front of Uncle Wilbur's bedroom door. In the end she posts a note under the door saying she is going to the deli to get food. She wants to add something conciliatory, but for once her fountain pen is lost for words.

Jo slips out of the shop door, feeling like a villain leaving a crime scene; she turns left and walks quickly down the alleyway towards the High Street.

Ten minutes later, Eric and Ferdy are ready. The boxes are now joined together and from the centre of the main box sticks a broom handle. A sheet-like sail is attached to this. Ferdy is sitting in the box. He is wearing an overlarge helmet with horns. Draped around his shoulders, completely enveloping him, is a sheepskin rug held together at the front by a yellow bulldog clip.

'Good to go?' Eric asks.

Ferdy nods, holding tight to the cardboard sword in his hand.

Eric starts to push the 'ship' down the alleyway in front of Jo's window. Both man and boy are giggling.

As they pass the wooden counter that sits in the window, Ferdy says, 'Where is she? She's not there.'

Eric stops pushing and stands up.

The shop is in darkness.

'Where is she?' Ferdy asks again, his voice wavering with his disappointment. Just before the sob breaks, Eric scoops him up out of the 'ship'. He holds him on his hip and points into the window.

'What a shame, mate. She's had to go out, I expect. But, hey, look, there's your picture of the seal. She's put it in the best spot on her board. She must really like it. Well, who wouldn't?' he says, giving Ferdy a hug. 'And hey, we can do it another day. This ship is built to last,' he says, encouragingly.

Ferdy mutters something.

'What's that?' Eric bends his head low over the child's.

'It's not a seal – it's a salamander.'

'Of course it is, mate!' Eric then whispers conspiratorially, 'Shall we sail into your dad's place and give him a fright?'

'Yeah,' Ferdy says, perking up, 'noko.'

33

Some advice from Reverend Ruth Hamilton

'Oh, Jo.' This from Ruth.

'Oh, Joanne,' from Malcolm.

This is what Jo had hoped for. They are sitting at a small table in a café that is set into the bay window of the deli.

'Oh poor Lucy,' Reverend Ruth says with feeling.

'Yes, indeed, poor, poor Lucy,' Malcolm echoes.

Jo thinks, *Not* poor Lucy. *What about* me? *You're supposed to be on my side.*

Ruth seems to catch some of what Jo is feeling and bumps her shoulder up against Jo's. 'Yes, *and* poor Jo.'

Jo feels as if she has been caught out like a spoilt child looking for attention.

'She should have told me' is all she can think of to say.

'I expect she tried,' Ruth suggests.

'And she did go to see that rotter James, and I am sure that took a lot of courage,' Malcolm insists.

Jo gives up, and continues with a shaky laugh. 'You're on her side, aren't you?'

'I don't think it is a matter of sides, Joanne,' Malcolm says, soothingly.

'What would you have done in her position?' Ruth cuts in.

'Sanjeev would never cheat on Lucy,' Jo tells them categorically.

'But if he did?' Ruth presses.

'Well, I suppose I would go and talk to him . . .'

'And if he didn't have the courage to tell her himself . . .' Ruth leaves it hanging.

Would she have told Lucy? She thinks so. She hopes so. But would Lucy have believed her, and if she did, wouldn't it have ruined their friendship?

'Oh, I've got it all wrong,' Jo groans, looking from one to the other. 'It was just the thought of the two of them, Lucy and Jemima, talking about me. I couldn't bear it.' She knows she is trying to excuse herself.

'Oh, don't make too much of it,' Ruth says, bracingly. 'You've just been bitten by the green-eyed monster.'

'I thought I'd outgrown all of that,' Jo replies.

Ruth laughs out loud at this. 'You think!' She shakes her head at Jo, and Malcolm joins in. It reminds her of her vision of Lucy, Wilbur, Jemima and Finn, pursing their lips, crossing their arms and shaking their heads at her over James. At least with this image comes the clear thought: I will *never* go back to that man. She thinks again of Malcolm's words . . . *Joanne, he was never your friend.*

'Okay,' she demands, turning to her friends, 'tell me what to do.'

'I think, to start with,' Ruth suggests, 'you need to see it from Lucy's point of view. *You're* jealous? How do you think *she* feels?'

'Indeed, my very thoughts,' Malcolm says, taking over. 'It seems to me she will have been jealous of you spending time with James's friends,' as an aside, he adds, 'quite frankly I struggle to call them "friends", let's say his posse . . .'

'Oh no, please let's not, Malcolm,' Ruth says, grinning, 'but you're quite right, Lucy lost you to them. Then she lost you to London. And now she's frightened you're going to stay here and she will lose you to us.'

'She probably felt she couldn't make a fuss, having herself spent time abroad with her husband,' Malcolm adds, perceptively.

'But I was always going home,' Jo says, in surprise.

'Were you?' Malcolm asks, and Jo can hear the regret in his voice.

'Well, at some point,' she replies, thinking of the times she wondered if her future was in Uncle Wilbur's shop. There had been doubts, but now? She knew home was not London.

'Does Lucy know that?' Ruth asks, simply.

'Oh.' Jo lets out a breath that is almost as long as the one that Lucy exhaled in Wilbur's flat. She now understands Lucy not replying to her letter that mentioned Ruth, Malcolm and the shop. Her barbed comments about her friends. Jo's, 'Oh,' turns into an, 'Aah.'

Jo declares, 'I need to get back to her.'

Ruth puts out a restraining hand. 'Before you do, I'd like to tell you something.'

Jo pauses, and looks into Ruth's face, which for once is solemn, all trace of humour gone. She wonders, *is this it?* Are they going to learn the secret of the Runaway Vicar?

'My best friend, Julie, died when we were both in our early forties. She had breast cancer.'

Jo and Malcolm instinctively move closer.

Jo has not been expecting this.

'It was devastating for her husband and family, of course, but very few people understood how I felt as her best friend. I don't think we realize what that kind of friendship can mean to someone. It doesn't have a place in how society proportions grief.' She smiles sadly at Jo. 'Julie's death was well over fifteen years ago, but I still think of her most days. I have often thought we spend too much time obsessing about finding, "the one", and we forget that a best friend can be a lifelong love. There is a fundamental truth, comfort and joy in having a best friend.' Ruth smiles, a little mistily. 'I think of it sometimes; all over the earth there are these unacknowledged love stories, making the world a better place. I personally think it is one of humanity's best-kept secrets.' Ruth looks at Jo, 'You need to put things right with Lucy.'

Jo does not reply. She doesn't have to.

By now the three of them are sitting so close, they are almost touching, and Jo remembers the pub. That was the first time they broached the subject of Ruth running away. Jo doesn't think this will be the reason behind it, but more than ever she wants to understand what troubles the vicar.

'You must never give up on your friend,' Malcolm urges, and Jo recalls the time he also gave her advice and hinted about the *greatest regret of his life*. She realizes how much she still has to discover about these friends, and she just hopes that she has the time. She feels a decision about her future is looming.

Before they say goodbye, they confirm what time they will be meeting at Jo's for supper on Friday, Malcolm trying to suppress his eagerness to share with them what George Eliot and Abraham Lincoln's chiropodist, Issachar, might talk about. Jo wonders if this will give them any insight into Malcolm's life and his regrets. She certainly found that William Foyle and John Lobb pointed her very clearly towards appreciating the importance of friendship. And with this thought, she knows she needs to get back to Lucy.

As she walks away from the deli (carrying a bag full of food she thinks Lucy will like), she wonders why neither she nor Ruth had thought to comment on Malcolm's apparel. He had been sporting a knitted tank top in a glorious shade of tangerine with lime green tassels around the bottom edge.

Too busy unravelling Jo's problems?

Just too startled?

Or maybe, she thinks, they are getting used to the transformation of Malcolm Buswell.

This time, Jo doesn't let the closed door stop her. She knocks softly then pushes her way into Uncle Wilbur's bedroom, manoeuvring the door with her foot, her hands grasping mugs of hot chocolate – Lucy's favourite.

Lucy is half sitting, half lying on the bed and is looking at her phone.

'Don't worry, I can get an earlier train. I'll get out of your way soon.'

Jo ignores this and puts one of the mugs down on the bedside cupboard. 'Budge up,' she says, settling herself on the other side of the bed to Lucy. 'I've brought you some hot chocolate.'

Lucy reluctantly accepts the proffered mug.

Before Lucy can say anything, and before Jo can lose her nerve, she starts.

'Luce, you are my best friend. You always have been and always will be.' Jo hears her voice waver but she keeps going, 'The thing is, you can only ever have one best friend. I guess the clue's in the name, really, but it does mean that we're linked together; you are mine and I am yours. Someone told me today that they thought the joy of having a best friend was one of humanity's best-kept secrets.' Then Jo repeats what Reverend Ruth had said, 'All over the earth there are these unacknowledged love stories, making the world a better place.'

Jo says all of this not looking at her best friend. She hears Lucy put down her mug of hot chocolate.

'And I need to tell you something.' Jo draws in a trembling breath.

'Just before James left me, I thought I was pregnant.' Jo can feel the body stiffen beside her. Jo still cannot look at Lucy and so she talks to the opposite wall, on which hangs a water-colour of Ullswater. 'I was only a week late; after ten days I took a test. I was, it was . . .' Jo can't finish, and she thinks if

259

she lets the tears come now they might wash her away. 'Three days later, my period started and well . . . that was that.' Jo feels Lucy's hand slip into hers. 'I told myself it was a mistake, maybe I had misread it and that I hadn't really been pregnant.'

Now she holds tight to her best friend's hand, focusing on the warmth of it, trying to make it all that she can feel. 'But I *was* pregnant, Luce, and when . . . well, after that, all I could think about was a baby. The desperate ache of wanting to be a mum became part of me. I thought about talking to James, but I couldn't.'

'Oh Jo.'

'I should have known then. I was worried about telling him. Wasn't sure if he'd be pleased.' Now she looks at Lucy. 'I think I knew, he wouldn't have been. But I told myself, he will be one day. When the time is right.' Jo's twisted smile turns to a small shudder. 'So, I kept telling myself that I hadn't really been pregnant, that it didn't count, had been nothing. Nothing to make a fuss about.'

For a moment Jo thinks of a storm breaking and she thinks, ah, *this* is the storm, and she leans forward over her belly, which once held the promise of a baby, and she rocks on the bed. The tears come in earnest now and the sobs break from her, and she feels them as part of a rhythmical anguish, which rocks along with her. And then Lucy has her arms around her – and she is part of it – and Jo feels the comfort of her, the movement of the two of them, soothing her, even as their tears flow.

34

Mindy from Hot Springs

They are back in Uncle Wilbur's sitting room. Lucy in his chair, Jo on the floor with her back resting against it. On the coffee table are the remnants of their impromptu picnic.

'Will you be home for Christmas?' Lucy asks.

'Of course I will. You know I was always coming home, Luce. I was never going to stay in London.' Jo means what she says, but she realizes it costs her something to say it.

'And when the baby comes in February . . . ?'

Jo swivels on the cushion she is sitting on and looks up at her best friend. 'I meant what I said: I will be the best Auntie Jo your baby could wish for.'

'But will it be . . . I don't know. Jo, will you be okay?'

Jo thinks of the conversation they had earlier, hugging, toes tucked under the tulip-covered duvet. 'Of course. That baby will be sick of the sight of me.' As she says this, Jo knows her commitment is unfailing, but she is left wondering about the rest of her life. Who will she be, apart from Auntie Jo? She wouldn't want to work in a bank again, she knows that. She thinks of Eric the Viking calling her Stationery Girl? What will happen to her?

As if reading her mind (well, Jo thinks happily, best friends do that), Lucy asks, 'What about this Eric – you texted quite a lot about him. I haven't got to see the Viking.'

Jo is about to launch into an explanation about how Eric is with someone else and all about Caramel Toffee Clare. Then she realizes that if she mentions the double date it will bring up Finn, and she doesn't want to go there. So, instead she says, 'He's not into me, well, only as a friend. It was never going to work. He's too young for me.'

'What is it with you and age? You're always banging on about it.'

'Well, James . . .'

'Not all men are like James. Thank God.'

Jo thinks about all that she has kept from Lucy. There is one final thing she knows she needs to share with her.

'Look, when I was getting suspicious about James, I did check his phone records and stuff, but I also looked at his social media. And what made me feel really, really crap about myself, apart from all his snidey comments, was his thing on social media for younger women.'

'How young?' Lucy demands.

'Oh, early twenties, nothing sick, Luce, just – well – definitely a lot younger than me.'

'Sounds pretty sick to me,' Lucy declares. 'You know

Jemima says he's going bald,' she adds with relish, 'Definitely thin on top.'

This does make Jo smile.

'So what did you find out?' Lucy continues.

'It was his Instagram,' Jo says, and she feels cold and clammy, as she did the first time she scrolled through all the women that James was following.

'What? Weird stuff?' Lucy queries – Jo thinks, hopefully.

'Well, not really. They were women who were professing to be financial experts or stuff like that. All blonde, all about twenty. And from all over the world. They were called things like Brandi, and there was one he was really into, Mindy from Hot Springs, Arkansas. They kept posting stuff that was so cheesy. You and I would have laughed.' But back then Jo certainly did not feel like laughing.

'What sort of stuff?' Lucy sounds intrigued.

'Oh, things like, "Brand Me is rockin' it. And you can take that to the bank", and there was a hell of a lot about loving themselves.'

Lucy is snorting in derision, 'What a load of crap!' she declares. 'And James was into this stuff?' She doesn't sound surprised.

'Seems like. And it was the images they were posting. They were all pouting at the camera. You know the sort of thing, shirts unbuttoned a bit too low. Sitting on a desk, leaning back. And that did it for him. Well, going by his comments.'

'What sort of thing?'

'Oh, just that they were gorgeous, inspiring, really got him thinking . . .'

'Why the hell didn't you say something to him?'

'I kept thinking, I shouldn't have been looking. I felt I would be making a fuss. It was *only* Instagram.'

'Baldy bastard!' Lucy cries. 'Why didn't you tell me?'

'It was really hard, Luce, I guess it was easier to pretend it wasn't happening. Not take it seriously.' She pauses. 'Once you say it, it's real.'

'Yeah, I can see that.'

'I also knew he would laugh it off and I would end up feeling like I was in the wrong.'

'Oh, Jo,' Lucy says, much more softly.

Jo is now huddled on the cushion on the floor. Arms wrapped tight around her knees. 'I just thought, these women are not me. I'm too old for him. I am going to lose him.' Jo feels her best friend's hand on her shoulder.

'You are worth so much more, you do know that?'

Jo thinks back to Malcolm's story of the fox in the graveyard. And the words. *You, Jo Sorsby, are enough*, come to her. 'Yes,' she tells Lucy with perfect truth. 'Now, I do believe I am.'

It is an hour later, over coffee (peppermint tea for Lucy), that Lucy reaches for her phone. 'Gotta have a look at what my man is following.'

Jo turns quickly. Why does she feel worried? She *knows* Sanjeev.

Lucy stays silent for some moments, then laughs.

'What?'

'Normal, I guess. Friends, too much football, cats doing stupid stuff, surprising interest in gardens and birds – who'd have thought? But look at this.' She turns her phone towards Jo. Sanjeev has clearly been following some posts about how to decorate a baby's nursery.

Jo relaxes.

Lucy glances down at her, 'You weren't really worried, were you?'

'No, of course not. But it throws you when you find you don't know someone like you thought you did. That you have wasted six years of your life on a total wanker. A manipulative wanker,' she adds, for Lucy's benefit.

Lucy is uncharacteristically quiet for some moments.

'Jo, look, I know I didn't like the man, but it wasn't all bad. I can see that. When you guys met – blimey, you set a room alight, the two of you. I was a bit jealous. I'd never seen chemistry like it. I think you were bound to get together, and you had to see it through.'

Jo is shocked. She knows it will have cost Lucy a lot to say this. She turns to Lucy. 'Do you believe in chemistry that lasts for ever?'

'You mean love?'

'No, I'm not really thinking about that. I guess I mean when you feel so drawn to someone, like you have a powerful connection with them.' The image of Eric the Viking's hand smoothing out a page with the words *Dear Lucy* on it flits across Jo's mind.

'Yes, of course,' her friend says, simply. 'I know my man farts, eats too many sweets in his car, which he thinks I don't know about. But still, when he comes through that door . . .'

'But how do you know it will last?' Jo insists.

Lucy smiles. 'Well, I guess it's a bit like God – you don't make a conscious decision about it. You either believe in it or you don't.'

35

Supper at Average Jo's

The first thing Jo notices is Malcolm's cravat. Well, it would be hard to miss. It is covered in a series of psychedelic circles. A swirling splatter of purple, lime-green and orange, in an otherwise grey landscape (apart from his turquoise suede desert boots). 'You look nice,' Jo offers as she takes his coat. Malcolm touches his cravat nervously.

Jo thinks that Lucy was right. Before they said goodbye this morning, Jo told her about Malcolm. Lucy asked detailed questions about his colourful fashion choices, and concluded: 'Those are vintage pieces. We're talking Sixties and Seventies. There is more to this than a man simply introducing a spot of colour into his wardrobe.'

'Groovy Baby!' exclaims the Runaway Vicar, giving the tall, awkward, angular man a hug. She then swings around to Jo and repeats the manoeuvre, enveloping her in a wave of cashmere and gardenia. 'Nice dress,' she adds, approvingly. Jo has once more ditched the dungarees and worn her emerald green wrap-around dress.

As soon as Ruth has finished hugging and Malcolm has finished blushing, the conversation turns to Lucy. 'And?' Ruth asks.

'All good, all sorted,' Jo assures them, and she feels content leaving it at that. Some things are part of another era, another life. Her London friends nod approvingly but do not push her for more information.

They are seated in Uncle Wilbur's sitting room, each with a glass of champagne in their hand. Jo wanted to make the evening special and has invested in good wine, food she knows she can cook, and some Christmassy serviettes and candles for Uncle Wilbur's table. Now, with everyone here, she is flushed and hot, but she thinks she has everything ready.

Ruth has been telling them about a visit she has had from an estate agent. It seems that the lease is coming to an end on her small studio apartment. 'Oh, well,' Ruth says, slowly, 'perhaps it's time to move on.'

'No!' Jo is surprised at her own shock. She sees Malcolm lean towards Ruth, a look of distress on his face.

Ruth glances from one to the other. 'I have to go at some point.' Then she sighs. 'Jo, you won't be here for ever, will you?'

Jo feels the truth of this in her bones, but before she can answer, Malcolm says, 'And me? Must I move on too?'

The three of them stare at each other – their easy camaraderie showing the first faint signs of cracking. This can't last for ever. Looking out of the window at the darkness beyond the city lights, Jo senses a great loss lurking.

Malcolm is the first to recover. 'We are getting ahead of ourselves. We have the here and now, in this very pleasant room . . . and I must say, Joanne, this is the most comfortable chair . . .' Jo has given him Uncle Wilbur's chair by the fire. '. . . there are very enticing smells coming from the kitchen. And we have the three of us.' He turns to Ruth. 'I may not have your belief, Reverend Ruth, but wouldn't your God tell us to be grateful for these many gifts?'

'He would indeed, Malcolm. And he would also kick me up the backside for being a tactless fool.'

They settle back in their chairs, and sip their drinks, but Jo knows something has shifted. She thinks of her mum, holding on to the belief that Uncle Wilbur will get better. Is it so wrong to want to keep things the way they are?

She resolves to make a decision about her future in the New Year. She is pretty certain she knows *where* she will be, but as yet she doesn't have the first idea of what she will be doing (or quite who she will be, beyond being Auntie Jo). But for now she might as well enjoy the run-up to Christmas (it is only two weeks away) and put everything else from her mind. She is about to share something of this with Ruth and Malcolm, when Malcolm puts his glass down.

'I have to say I have been so looking forward to this evening,' he says, and turning to Jo, adds, 'and the icing on the cake is that you have made your peace with poor Lucy.'

'Yes, poor, *poor* Lucy,' Ruth echoes.

When Jo glances at her in consternation, Ruth winks, and Jo is reminded of their first meeting, and the *No one believes in God any more*. It seems so long ago now. 'Well, enough of *poor* Lucy,' Jo says, pointedly. 'You were saying, Malcolm?'

'Well, I would like to tell you over supper about George Eliot and Issachar. I really do believe that if I took those two as my role models, I would learn to be a different man. My goodness, when I think of the courage of George Eliot and, well . . .' he holds his hands up, '. . . the just go heck of it, of Issachar. I do think that combination really could inspire me to be braver.'

Ruth smiles, eyeing the cravat. 'I can't wait.'

Before Malcolm or Ruth can say more, Jo suddenly claps, 'I've got it!' It has come to her in a flash.

Ruth and Malcolm start, Ruth spilling some of her drink. Both of them stare at Jo.

Maybe it was the mention of Lucy, but something has suddenly fallen into place. Jo leans forward, smiling, 'Can I ask you something, Malcolm?'

He nods, but his eyes are wary.

'Have you by any chance ever been a hippy?' It seems so clear to her now: the man in grey is hankering after a more psychedelic era. Now she can see that over the weeks Malcolm has been transforming into a hippy before their very eyes. Flickers of it at first, but now the fashion choices becoming more overt statements.

'Ah, ha!' Ruth declares in obvious agreement, then she repeats her earlier comment, 'Groovy baby.'

Malcolm puts his head down and shakes his head. 'No,' he says, followed by a much more drawn out, 'oh, no.'

Jo and Ruth look at each other in concern.

Jo tries another tack; she instinctively feels she is on the right line. She says, less brightly, but still with assurance, 'Well, have you ever fancied being a hippy?'

To their horror, Malcolm Buswell puts his head in his hands and he gives a long, guttural groan. He sits like this for some moments, then from deep within him rises up a sob that racks his body. This is followed by another and yet another. Jo is painfully reminded of sitting on Uncle Wilbur's bed with Lucy. Like Lucy she leans forward and wraps her arms around Malcolm; her hands meet Ruth's arms, which are simultaneously enveloping him from the other side.

'I am so sorry, Malcolm, I am so, so sorry,' Jo almost pleads, without having the least idea of what she is sorry for.

It is a while before Malcolm stops crying, Ruth handing him tissue after tissue, Jo sitting on the arm of his chair, rubbing his back. After a while he appears more composed and then the apologies start:

'I really shouldn't have . . .

'Spoiling this lovely evening . . .

'A sentimental old fool . . .'

Reverend Ruth brings him up short, 'Enough to that, Malcolm Buswell. You are amongst friends. And now, I do believe there is something that you want to tell us.'

Malcolm turns to Ruth and a look passes between them. It reminds Jo of their silent exchange in Highgate Cemetery. It comes to her that Ruth has been waiting for this moment. The good reverend knows that Malcolm has a story that one day he would want to share with them.

'You are quite . . .'

Jo thinks he is going to say 'right', but Malcolm clearly can't find even this simple word; whatever he might want to tell them, it is beyond him. Instead he sits in silence, head bowed.

Jo suddenly remembers the supper that will be ready by now, and an idea comes to her. 'Malcolm,' she says, starting to rub his back again, 'would you mind terribly if you told us about this after we eat? I think everything is ready and I'd hate the food to spoil.'

It works.

Malcolm looks up. 'Of course, of course, Joanne.' He draws his shoulders back and is, once more, his old solicitous self. 'You have gone to so much effort.'

Ruth looks at Jo and nods her understanding.

Jo then continues, 'Do you think over supper you would be able to tell Ruth and me about George Eliot and Issachar?' It strikes Jo that in telling their tale, Malcolm will be walking side by side with his ghosts, and that they might provide him with the courage he needs to tell his own story.

Malcolm sits up straighter in his chair. 'I could certainly do that, Joanne.' And Jo thinks she can hear a measure of relief in his voice.

She hands Malcolm a bottle of red wine to open, directing him to the glasses on the table, and heads to the kitchen. Reverend Ruth follows close on her heels.

Once there, they stare at each other in silence. Jo is just about to say something when Reverend Ruth tilts her head on one side. 'Good idea to bring him back to his ghosts.'

Jo smiles and remembers something that Lucy told her during their conversation the previous evening. It seemed that just as Jo borrows from her best friend, so Lucy borrows from her. Lucy confessed: 'When I get stuck and need an idea to get stuff done or to solve a problem, I always think – what would Jo do?'

'Smells wonderful,' Ruth comments, as Jo starts to pull a large earthenware casserole from the small oven. She opens the lid and looks at it anxiously. All is well. She has cooked an old favourite: slow roasted lamb with ginger and apricot, and roasted vegetables. She puts some plates in the oven along with a dish of flat breads. 'I'll just warm these through.'

She looks up at Ruth. 'By the way, how was the Advent service?'

'It was wonderful. I think you would have enjoyed Reverend Abayomrunkoje's sermon – it was all about the colour purple.' Ruth opens her eyes wide.

Jo decides to confess. 'I did come actually.'

'You did?! I didn't see you there.'

'Well, the service had started, so I didn't like to come in.'

'Oh, Jo, you should have done.'

'I watched and listened from outside; it sounded beautiful and looked amazing with the lights flickering across the windows.'

'I lit a candle for your customer whose wife is dying,' Ruth tells her. 'And for your uncle.'

'Thank you.'

Jo doesn't believe in God, but she thinks there is no harm at all in having the Reverend Ruth Hamilton on your side.

36

George Eliot and Issachar Zacharie

Malcolm puts his knife and fork down and, with a contented sigh, settles back into his chair. Jo and Ruth wait expectantly.

'I think with George Eliot we need to go back to the start. She was from a comfortable, but by no means wealthy background. Her childhood, I think, was a sad one.' He nods slowly, 'She was sent away to boarding school at five. Her mother was a distant woman and died young. I believe George Eliot then fixated on her father and strived, in her mind, to make him the good and loving parent she so dearly needed.' Malcolm pauses. 'But he was sadly wanting. And I do not believe the rest of her family were much better.'

'In what way?' Jo asks, pushing her empty plate away and reaching for her wine glass.

'Well, certainly in their reaction to her choices.'

'Living with a married man,' Jo remembers.

'Yes, and her questioning of God,' Malcolm says, half smiling and raising his glass in ironic salute to the Reverend Ruth. 'Also, her refusal to come back to the family home when her father died, and live out her life like a good spinster should – nursing the family and being an unpaid housekeeper.'

'So neither a dogsbody or a godsbody,' Ruth comments wryly, her eyes gleaming. She is sitting with her chin in her hand, one elbow on the table, her face flushed.

'Precisely,' Malcolm says, appreciatively.

'As a young woman, George Eliot had the worst possible taste in men. She had a series of undignified, misguided crushes on mainly older men, often married. I suppose she was searching for a figure to replace her mother, her father . . . oh, when I think of that poor child sent away at five.' Malcolm shakes his head. (Jo notices Ruth's eyes are following Malcolm's cravat.) 'No wonder she felt in want of a protector, a mentor and, above all, unconditional love.'

'And did she find it?' Jo asks, wistfully.

'She most certainly did – a bit later on in life, it is true, but she and George Lewes were very happy together. There was no doubt it was a meeting of the hearts as well as the minds. And George protected her, giving her the mental space and confidence to write. She was always a brave woman, but I believe he made her braver, enabling her to fulfil her potential.'

Malcolm concludes, 'So, yes, George Eliot: a damaged woman, a tricky character, a woman of astounding talent and, oh my goodness, what a courageous woman, battling her demons and her society to live her life the way she wanted.'

'A woman who would inspire bravery in others,' Ruth suggests, giving Malcolm a long look.

'Hmm,' he replies, returning the look. 'I *will* get there, Reverend Ruth,' he says, 'but first Issachar.'

'Oh, yes,' Ruth responds, sitting up a bit straighter, 'Abraham Lincoln's chiropodist. I want to hear all about him.'

Malcolm smiles slowly. 'Oh, not just a chiropodist, Reverend Ruth, but also a spy.'

'What!' Ruth cries.

'Now you have to tell us,' Jo insists.

Malcolm pours them all another glass of wine and begins, 'Issachar started his days in Kent. He would have been six years younger than George Eliot.'

Jo and Ruth settle back to listen.

'His father, who was a Polish Jew, ran a store near the docks, but the family emigrated to America when Issachar was seven. By the time Issachar was sixteen, he had taken out an advert describing himself as a "Chiropodist". I can't imagine he had much training, but this didn't deter him. Chiropody was looked down on by doctors, yet Issachar could see its potential. People were on their feet all day, often in ill-fitting boots—'

'Ah, they needed John Lobb,' Jo throws in.

'Indeed they did,' Malcolm agrees. 'In those days, poor foot-wear often made people's lives a misery. Two months after setting up as a chiropodist, Issachar started calling himself "Doctor".'

'I expect he'll soon be asking Bertie for a Royal Warrant,' Ruth jokes.

'Reverend Ruth, you are not far off the mark. Indeed, Issachar put a testimonial up in his "surgery" from Queen Victoria's personal physician, saying what a grand chap Dr Issachar was. All false, of course. Anyway, that was how his life went. He moved from city to city; each time he moved, his testimonials got better and better. He also published a book about chiropody, which he blatantly copied from another practitioner.'

'Did no one catch him out?' Jo asks.

'Well, no. As it happened, Issachar really was a good chiropodist. So some of his testimonials were true. And, rather like John Lobb, he was never afraid to ask for them. He was a man with the gift of the gab. A flamboyant man who could carry it off.'

'How did he meet Lincoln?' Ruth asks.

'Oh, through some politicians who had given him references. I believe he just turned up. Now Abraham Lincoln had large feet, size fourteen, and he suffered awfully from corns – and I think it is safe to say that Issachar did make a difference. Lincoln found he enjoyed talking to his chiropodist, and so a friendship of sorts sprang up. I would rather like to have seen them together: Lincoln a rangy six foot four; Issachar a cherubic five foot seven. Oh, yes, indeed.' Malcolm puts the wine glass he has been holding down, untasted. He continues with enthusiasm. 'And Issachar was no fool; he included Lincoln's wife in his expansive charm. Some referred to Lincoln's wife as "Her Satanic Majesty"—'

'Presumably not to her face,' Ruth suggests.

'No, indeed,' Malcolm laughs. And Jo is warmed by the sound of it.

'Soon Issachar was sending her gifts of pineapples and including her in his best wishes to the president.' Malcolm pauses for dramatic effect. 'However, during the Civil War, Issachar made the transition from Lincoln's chiropodist to the president's personal spy.'

'Goodness!' Ruth responds.

'Lincoln saw that Issachar could get himself anywhere and talk to anyone. So the president used these skills for his own ends. He sent him to see one of his key soldiers, General Banks, purporting to have messages for him. But in reality he was asking Issachar to check up on the general and to test his loyalty. After a while, Issachar was being paid by Secret Service funds.'

'This is amazing,' Jo says, shaking her head. For a moment she thinks how much she would like to tell Eric about Issachar. Then, in her mind, she hears the sound of her shop door slamming.

'So how on earth did he end up in Highgate Cemetery?' Ruth asks, in astonishment.

'Well, in 1874 Issachar decided to move back to England and settle in London. He bought a large house on Brook Street and set up a surgery, now proclaiming he was Dr Zacharie, Chiropodist General to the US Army,' Malcolm declares, with suppressed delight.

'In 1874? Could he have bought his boots from Lobb?' Jo wonders aloud.

'Possibly,' Malcolm reflects. 'I myself have wondered if he ever met George Eliot. He was a man who enjoyed the high life; he threw lavish dinner parties and liked to go about in society.

He also had an interest in literature. I forgot to tell you he plagiarized yet another book about chiropody, but in this one also included extracts from Shakespeare. The reviewers called it, "The Poetry of the Foot".'

Jo laughs, then wonders why she is surprised. After all, she knows an optician who likes poetry.

'And why Highgate Cemetery?' Ruth repeats.

'I have a theory as to why Highgate Cemetery, and I will come to that.' He turns to Jo. 'But first let us help you take the plates to the kitchen, Joanne,' and with this, he rises to his feet. 'That was a marvellous meal, Joanne,' he says, bowing his head slightly towards her, his chin nestling into the folds of his psychedelic cravat.

37

The dear friend of Malcolm Buswell

Jo has put a plate of mini mince pies on the coffee table and refilled the champagne glasses. They have settled themselves in Uncle Wilbur's armchairs around the gas fire.

Jo raises her champagne glass to Malcolm. 'To bravery.'

Ruth follows suit.

Then they wait.

Malcolm takes a deep breath, and although his shoulders sag, he looks determined. 'Well,' he begins, 'I was given this cravat many, many years ago by my very dear friend Rupert. I met him when I was eighteen.' He looks at each of them, nodding. 'He had chained himself to the railings in Berkeley Square, where I often ate my lunch. I ended up sharing my sandwiches with him.'

Jo can't help it; she smiles.

'Oh, please don't laugh,' Malcolm begs, and Jo instinctively puts her hand to her mouth.

'Oh Malcolm, I wasn't meaning to make light of this.'

Malcolm sighs, and pats her arm. 'Oh, indeed I know you weren't, Joanne. It is just that it reminded me that I *did* laugh. I mocked what he was trying to do. I wish now that I had ripped my tongue from my mouth.'

'What *was* Rupert trying to do?' Ruth asks.

'He was trying to change his life, and also the world we lived in. He wanted a fairer world, a world without prejudice. This was towards the end of the Sixties. Rupert rather took to the Sixties, whereas I'm afraid I was a boy forged in the Fifties, and sometimes I think that is where I remain.' Malcolm stops, apparently lost in thought. 'Anyway,' he refocuses on his companions, 'Rupert, now, he took part in many demonstrations in London. There was always some cause he was fighting for. We became close friends, even if I did tease him about all his "lame ducks".'

'How long were you friends?' Jo asks.

'For around two years,' Malcolm replies. 'Yes, during those months we were very much in each other's company. But in the end he thought going to America would be the answer. It was the time of the Vietnam War and he wanted to join the peace movement.'

'You weren't tempted to go with him?' Ruth asks.

Malcolm's face is a mask of sorrow; there are no tears, but maybe, Jo thinks, he has shed so many for Rupert there are none left.

'He held his hand out to me. I can picture it still. He wanted me to go with him. But I was young and afraid and weighed down by the thought of what people might say. Oh, what a fool I was.' He shakes his head, a gesture of incredulity. 'So, I turned away. My mother, that brave woman, urged me to go. She understood what Rupert really meant to me.'

Jo thinks of what Malcolm said, about a lover who is also a friend. No wonder Malcolm understood so well about James.

'*She* would have gone,' Malcolm tells them. 'A woman who took a bomber up beyond the clouds and flew it blind. She wasn't afraid. Oh, what a disappointment I must have been to her.'

Jo wants to interrupt him, to contradict him, but in amongst the sorrow she can sense the relief that Malcolm feels in telling his story.

'So, when I read about George Eliot, another unconventional but brave soul, I was drawn to her strength like a moth to the flame.' Malcolm looks towards the Christmas candle Jo has lit on the coffee table. 'Yet even now I fear the fire, fear I will be burnt. Even now as a dull and decrepit old man, I am afraid.' He looks up at them. 'Back then I was so frightened of trying for a different life. I spent so much of my time being terrified of failing that I never thought – what if I made it?'

He looks around the room, as if uncertain where he is, lost in remembering a very different time. 'With Rupert holding my hand I might have made that leap.' He looks at the two women seated either side of him. 'Oh, my dears, I have wasted so much of my life.'

Jo thinks she has never heard such desolation in a voice.

'What happened to Rupert?' Ruth asks, gently.

'He went to America. Without me. He did what he could. The world didn't change, or not immediately, but I genuinely believe he was part of history.'

Jo notices the use of the past tense.

'And Rupert?' Ruth repeats, softly.

'We were not in touch. I think I had hurt him too much for that.' He turns to Jo. 'You see, I let him go.'

His next words are hard to hear, and Jo knows they will have cost Malcolm a great deal to say them. 'I heard that Rupert died in 1984 in New York. His friends contacted me after he died. He still had my address and a poetry book I had given him.'

Malcolm tries to smile and Jo thinks her heart is going to break.

He pulls her closer to him. 'Oh, Joanne, no tears. It was a long time ago.'

Malcolm tugs at his cravat with his other hand, trying ineffectually to pull it from his neck. His sorrow has turned to frustration and anger. 'And here I am trying to recapture something, go back in time and be the hippy I always wished in my heart to be.' He leaves off the tugging, his hand falling into his lap. 'Rupert – he knew what I really wanted. He always said if he could ever peel away the grey, he would find I had a psychedelic soul.'

Ruth has been unusually quiet. Jo sees that both she and Malcolm are watching her. They sit in silence for some minutes. Ruth picks up a glass of wine and swirls it in her hand, apparently lost in thought. The silence stretches on.

Eventually she speaks. Her words are slow and measured. 'The thing is Malcolm, maybe it is not enough to dress like a hippy. To really follow in Rupert's footsteps, I think you need to find something to fight for.'

Malcolm doesn't reply but Jo is startled by the look on his face. She wonders if her face held the same expression when Malcolm had said, . . . *he was never your friend, Joanne.* It is a look of incredulous realization.

When Jo looks at Reverend Ruth, she can see a shadow of sadness in her expression, then she gives the ghost of a smile and winks. Meanwhile Malcolm stares at the Christmas candle that burns on the coffee table like a man in a trance.

After a while, Ruth nudges him, 'So, Malcolm, are you up to telling us what you think your ghosts would talk about?'

'What? Oh, I beg your pardon.' Malcolm rouses himself. 'Well, yes, I think so. If you are still interested?'

'Are you kidding?' Jo says. 'Of course we are.'

Malcolm smiles at them both. 'Now let me see . . . I need to get my thoughts in order. The truth is, I think George Eliot would have loved meeting Issachar. He would have been just her cup of tea – George Lewes was himself a flamboyant man.' Malcolm rubs his hands together, and Jo is pleased to see a gleam in his eye. 'And George Eliot had what Issachar wanted above all things.'

'Which was?' Ruth asks.

'He desperately wanted to be famous. And *that* is the reason I believe he wanted to be buried in Highgate Cemetery. It was a resting place of great prestige.' He nods as if to accentuate the point.

'What do you think they would talk about?' Jo asks.

'We are speaking of a man who included Shakespeare in a textbook about feet. They would most certainly talk about literature. I can see Issachar escorting George Eliot down Highgate High Street, making a great fuss of finding her books in the bookshops there. Showing her that she is *still* famous.

'Above all I think he would ensure she had a jolly time. Apparently he had a good sense of humour and never minded people teasing him. And, as he escorts her and fusses over her, I feel confident he would ensure that as many people as possible see them together; Dr Issachar Zacharie, strolling along, with the famous George Eliot on his arm.' Malcolm sits back, flushed from his efforts.

'And you told us, Malcolm Buswell, that you were a dull dog when it came to conversation. I think this is brilliant,' Ruth says, thumping him playfully on the knee.

'It *is*, you know – it's wonderful. I can just picture them.' As Jo says this, she feels that Malcolm's ghosts really have given him courage, and in some way have comforted him. She knows that tonight hasn't washed away years of sorrow and regret, but she believes that by walking with his ghosts, something has changed for Rupert's old friend.

Malcolm interrupts her thoughts. 'I am also reminded of something else. Some words written by George Eliot that resonate with me.'

Ruth and Jo look at him expectantly.

'George Eliot once wrote these words: "It is never too late to be what you might have been."'

38

The mashed potato

The clearing up isn't going quite to plan.

What started as some background music for washing up (Ruth and Malcolm insisting they help, rather than leaving it all to Jo) has become a shuffle through songs of the Sixties and Seventies, until they are now playing (loudly) all their favourite dance tracks.

Plates are washed and dried as they shimmy to The Supremes and The Kinks. Then tea towels are put aside as Malcolm demonstrates the mashed potato and Reverend Ruth does the twist. After that it is but a short step to Jo teaching them her Beyoncé moves. When Jo catches the reflection in the window of the three of them strutting in a line, heads down, fists pumping, she thinks she might choke from laughing.

Half an hour later, they are sitting, exhausted, with their feet up on the coffee table, coffee and chocolates set out in front of them. Conversation has turned to causes dear to Malcolm's heart that Ruth is encouraging him to embrace and fight for. It is not going well.

'Campaigning for the preservation of ancient choral music is not going to cut it, Malcolm.' (Swipe)

'But it really is most important that . . .'

'No Malcolm! Think again.' (Swipe)

'Now wildlife conservation is something I could certainly campaign for. The nightingale is just one of many British birds that are now endangered.'

Ruth pauses. 'Maybe . . .' but she doesn't sound convinced and Jo thinks she has images of Malcolm the Hippy marching on Number Ten for a much more radical cause. Ruth's next words convince her that she is right.

'But would you really chain yourself to the railings outside Number Ten for a nightingale?' (Smaller swipe)

'Maybe not, but perhaps the railings of Berkeley Square?' Jo suggests.

'Oh, indeed, Joanne,' Malcolm says, apparently struck by this idea, and a faraway look comes into his eyes.

Jo notices that even Ruth is nodding.

They fall silent as they sip their coffees and pass around the chocolates. Jo wonders what is going to happen to the three of them. Ruth's words about leaving come back to her. She feels an ache within her.

'Do you think friendships can last for ever?' she asks of no one in particular. Maybe the drink is making her melancholy.

'Oh, I think some can,' Ruth replies, 'but others . . . no.'

Jo wonders if she is thinking of her best friend, Julie.

Over the past week or so, Jo has started reaching out to old friends on social media. Many of the responses have been friendly (much more friendly than she thinks she deserves) but there have been silences from two or three people and she has felt her guilt pierce her anew.

Ruth continues, her voice low and reflective, 'Sometimes we try to hold on to friendships when really they were there for that particular part of our lives.'

Jo wonders if Ruth is thinking of the three of them.

'I have come to think of it as being on a stage. Sometimes other people are on that stage with you, and sometimes they leave. And like in a play, I suppose, that feels right. They were there for that act or scene in your life. Trying to pull them back on stage would be wrong.' She looks at Jo. 'Better to let them go and recall the joy of being on the stage with them for that glorious scene.'

Jo will never forget tonight: the three of them dancing around her Uncle Wilbur's kitchen. Is she wrong to want to make these people a permanent part of her life? Another thought comes to her. With the friends she is contacting again, those who are not replying to her, maybe it is better to let them go and just remember what they did have. She thinks of the database crowd at the bank. An odd assortment of characters, good friends who'd been fun to work with. At that time.

'*A place for everything and everything in its place*,' she says, softly, something easing within her.

Ruth leans closer as if to hear better.

From Malcolm comes the sound of a gentle snore.

* * *

Jo lets Ruth and Malcolm out of the front door of the shop. She watches them wander down the alleyway arm in arm, Malcolm's head bent to listen to Ruth, and again she is flooded with a feeling of melancholy.

She closes the door and stands still in the silence, the lights from the little Christmas tree (the only illumination) casting a ghostly glow over the shelves of stationery and the old oak cabinet. She moves over to the window and breathes in the smell of polish, which is now mixing with the scent of pine needles. She rubs a hand over the smooth curved edge of the cabinet, then picks up a Christmas card from her mum that is lying on the counter. She pins it up.

It fills the final gap on her noticeboard.

Does that mark the end of filling her time here, or has she created something of worth during these months? She thinks maybe she has, but she knows this is not where her heart lies. So, what about the future? She could go back home and easily get a job in a company working on databases. But so what? Her fingertips trace the outline of some of her precious collection: the words, the drawings, the cards. She then places her hands flat on the wall of the shop, as if she will be able to feel something of the person who works on the other side of that wall.

But she can get no sense of Eric the Viking, just the feel of cold plaster beneath her palms.

The ping of her phone from her dress pocket makes her jump. Malcolm or Ruth? Or – she brightens – maybe it will be a text from Lucy?

She pulls out her phone and it takes her a few seconds to assimilate the words.

She just stares at the screen, her mind blank.

It is nearly Xmas (and at Xmas it's the time you tell the truth). And the truth is I miss you Babe and I want you back. Come home where you belong. James x

Her brain seems to go from completely empty to full in less than a second, like a thunder of thoughts are all arriving at once:

Isn't that a quote from the film, *Love Actually?*

James hates that film.

Come *home?* She has no idea where home is.

He wants her back.

He wants her back.

Isn't this the text she dreamt of for all those weeks?

Babe?

He never called her Babe.

Has he sent it to the wrong person?

But she knows he hasn't. This is meant for her, Jo Sorsby.

Then come the slower thoughts. She drops onto the shop stool, unsure if her legs are going to hold her. It is as if they are unable to carry the weight of all that she is thinking.

Wouldn't this be a way out – a way back?

A way to a family?

This catches her for as much as thirty seconds.

But James?

James?

When she thinks back to how she was with him, she is not sure she recognizes that woman. Or wants to acknowledge her.

Words come into her head, words written by George Eliot and spoken by the kind and gentle Malcolm Buswell: *It is never too late to be what you might have been.*

She isn't sure what she might have been, or what she wants to be. But one thing she is absolutely sure of: she does not want to be the woman that she was when she was with James.

And *Babe?*

Who the hell does he think he is?

No apology. No, *sorry Jo, I dumped you.* No *sorry about Nickeeey (who by the way I was shagging on the side).*

She picks up her phone.

There is only one possible reply.

No thanks, James. I don't want you back. It's not me, it's you.

She is about to press send when she thinks of something to add.

By the way, Mindy from Hot Springs is really a 52-year-old security guard from Scunthorpe called Dave.

She thinks her friend the vicar would forgive her this lie. She is pretty sure James will believe it. After all, she is the one who knows about IT. He is the man who never changes his password.

As Jo heads back upstairs to the flat, an image comes into her mind: Lucy, Finn, Uncle Wilbur and Jemima are standing in a line high-fiving each other. They are joined in her imagination by Malcolm and Ruth. All of them are beaming at her.

39

My friend the vicar

There is a vicar standing in front of her, studying the row of tester fountain pens and she wants to say to him, 'My friend's a vicar, too.' The urge is almost overwhelming.

Jo watches as the vicar, who looks about forty, with a mop of chestnut hair and a pale round face, picks up two of the black tester pens and examines each in turn. He holds the nibs up to the light, and then unscrews each of the pens and gazes at the ink cartridges and examines the barrels, trying to peer inside them. In that moment it comes to Jo that he is not a vicar, he is a man. This is what many men do. Some women too, but more often than not it is certain men who pull the pens apart. They are keen to know about the inner workings, the mechanisms, and the nibs.

'What are the nibs made of?' he asks, pleasantly, as he holds them up to the light once more.

'The one on your right is stainless steel, the other is gold-plated.'

'Aaah,' he says slowly, continuing to study them. 'Thank you – I think I'll take this one. My partner will love it. He's just bought himself a new desk and this will look great on it.'

The vicar leaves the shop, and Jo is left with her thoughts.

He doesn't know it, but she knows it – she has been found guilty. She looked at this customer as a vicar, rather than a person. She of all people should have known better.

Ruth has done so much for Malcolm and for her, but have they been treating her like a vicar – assuming their problems take precedence? Jo is washed with a sense of shame; they still have no idea why Reverend Ruth became the Runaway Vicar. They did ask her about it in the pub, but since then have they tried to help her? And now it looks as though Ruth may be leaving.

Jo reaches for her phone and starts typing a message. Well, two messages.

A moment later, looking up from her screen, she sees Eric walk past the window. He neither waves nor smiles at her. As he progresses towards Highgate High Street, she can't help noticing he has lost some of his usual Viking bounce.

Jo looks at the patch of wall next to the now overflowing noticeboard and can almost feel the sensation of cold plaster against her palms.

The following day, Jo is the first to arrive at Highgate Cemetery. It is early and she has put a notice on the shop door saying she will be opening later than normal.

She waits on a bench near Karl Marx's tomb.

The graveyard is quiet, apart from the rustle of birds as they emerge from the contortion of leafless branches above her. Below this skeletal canopy, shrubs and ivy are shrouded in a blanket of white, only the larger leaves showing dark green, outlined with a fuzzy edging of frost. A crackle on the path announces the arrival of Malcolm. He is wrapped in a dark grey coat, rather like the one Jo is wearing (she has borrowed Uncle Wilbur's long winter overcoat). However, to keep his head warm, Malcolm is wearing a floppy woollen beany, striped in green, orange and gold.

Before she can say anything, another figure bundles along the path behind him, half running, her face flushed. 'Sorry I'm late,' Reverend Ruth pants.

'Take a seat, Reverend Ruth,' Malcolm says, solicitously.

'No, no, you take it, Malcolm. I'd rather stand.'

'But you seem flustered. Do take the seat,' Malcolm insists.

Reverend Ruth takes Malcolm by both arms and manoeuvres him onto the bench beside Jo. 'Well, no, Malcolm, that's where you're wrong.'

Jo and Malcolm look up at her.

'On the way here, I walked behind a young man smoking a really powerful spliff. I was *so* annoyed,' she says. 'He went so quickly that I had to walk really, really fast to keep up with him.' She breathes in deeply, smiling, 'And now,' she concludes, with a sway from one foot to the other, 'I'm feeling rather mellow.' Ruth turns to the laughing Jo. 'So lay it on me, Jo. Why did you want us to meet up?'

Now they are here, Jo finds it difficult to start. Malcolm

pulls her arm through his and pats it encouragingly. He already has some idea of what is coming next from the texts that he and Jo have exchanged.

'Well, I suppose it's about you, Ruth,' she starts.

Ruth stops swaying and studies her.

'It's just that you have done so much for us, and Malcolm and I wondered if there was anything we could do to help you?' When Ruth doesn't say anything, she adds, 'I mean, what about your ghosts? Do you want to tell us about them?'

Jo isn't sure why she is putting so much faith in the ghosts of Highgate Cemetery but now, sitting surrounded by the frost-covered tombs, it feels right to trust in them. They haven't let Malcolm and her down. And, she reasons, didn't vicars and cemeteries go together, like . . . well, like blood, poo and vomit?

Ruth starts to pace up and down in front of them. 'I *do* want to tell you about Karl Marx and Hutch. And I have found some inspiration for what they might chat about on Christmas Eve. I think mine came because I've been thinking about my own life rather a lot recently.' She turns to face them. 'In particular, my family.'

Jo can feel Malcolm squeeze her arm.

'But, oh . . .' Ruth pauses, and twists her foot into the gravel. 'I feel like I've been keeping a secret from you,' she eventually declares.

You and me both, Jo thinks.

But it seems Ruth is not following the same line of thought as Jo. 'The thing is, it has been so much fun investigating these people.' Ruth turns abruptly towards Malcolm. 'It really has, Malcolm. It has been a Godsend.' She smiles, and Jo is glad to see her anxiety lift a little. 'I might as well make a clean breast of it,' she proclaims. 'I didn't like Karl or Hutch. In fact, I grew to really dislike them.'

Jo laughs with relief, and Malcolm cries, 'Now, why would that trouble you so? We cannot like everyone we meet.'

'I wanted it to be enjoyable, in the way it was when you spoke about your ghosts,' Ruth says, a little wistfully, 'I know it was hard to get there, but when you talked of Issachar and George Eliot strolling through London, it sounded such fun.' She half smiles. 'But you get what you're given. And, in the end, I believe I was given what I needed.'

Is that how it works? Jo wonders. Is she being given what she needs? Right here and now?

She almost misses it when Malcolm repeats, 'But, Reverend Ruth, we can't like everyone.'

'I know that, but I have a different perspective to you. If I mention it, I know what you're going to say, Malcolm,' Ruth says, ruefully.

'Go on,' Malcolm responds.

'It is important to me to find the good in them because I try and see the face of Christ in everyone I meet.'

Malcolm stays quiet, which Jo thinks is taking some effort on his part. But he cannot stop himself from shaking his head.

'You see,' Ruth says, almost cheerfully.

'We are never going to agree on this, Reverend Ruth. I see what goes on in the world and it convinces me there is no God.' He opens his palms outwards in mute appeal. 'I read history and it is plain to me where religion has emerged from: circumstance, need, and the desire of the powerful to keep the weak where they are.' Malcolm glances towards Karl Marx's tomb.

'I think there is a lot we might agree on,' Ruth says thoughtfully, 'but I don't want to talk about it now. And, Malcolm, I probably never will.'

Malcolm looks taken aback, and Jo is reminded that Ruth is not the one who usually starts talking about religion. She certainly has never tried to convert them. But at the same time Ruth does not shy away from saying what she believes. Jo is torn – Average Jo – caught in the middle. She agrees with what Malcolm says, but there is also something alluring about Ruth's faith and her belief in people.

Ruth goes to speak, but Malcolm interrupts, 'I do think we should look for the best in everyone.'

There is silence. In the distance Jo hears a cracking sound. A stone contracting with the cold? Someone stepping on a fallen branch, deep within the cemetery?

Ruth's smile is slow and warm. 'You see, we're agreeing already,' she says, and then swings around to continue her pacing.

'Do unto others?' Malcolm muses.

'Exactly. I have two things I try and live my life by. That is one of them,' Ruth says, over her shoulder.

'What is the second?' Malcolm asks.

Ruth once more stops her pacing. 'Oh, we don't have time for that. And I have no desire for a fight, which I know is what I would get from you, Malcolm Buswell.' Before Malcolm can respond, Ruth steps towards them. 'Okay. Budge up then,' and she pushes in between Malcolm and Jo. Ruth grabs Malcolm's arm, linking her other arm with Jo's, pulling them both close. 'Now this is cosier. My goodness,' she says, looking around, 'it is beautiful here. And to think London is going on all around us.'

They sit in companionable silence for a moment. Jo catches a wisp of gardenia scent in the still, cold air (Ruth's fragrance); she thinks of being on a stage and of friends coming and going. Instinctively, she holds Ruth's arm a little snugger. She doesn't want to lose this. But what is the alternative? Jo knows she will soon be going home; she is only a visitor in London, in this borrowed life of hers. Perhaps they will write letters to each other after she leaves – but it won't be quite the same.

She catches once more the sweet smell of gardenia. Whatever happens next, she knows that meeting Ruth and Malcolm has changed her, and maybe experiencing their friendship is like imbibing a bit of their fragrance – you breathe it in and then they become part of you.

Ruth lets out a long sigh. 'I would like to tell you about Karl and Hutch and what I think they would talk about, but I have something I need to do now. Maybe this evening?'

'In which case, may I invite you ladies to come to my house for drinks and nibbles later,' Malcolm suggests. 'My goodness, it has been a long time since I did Christmas drinks for anyone. I would very much like it if you would both join me.'

'Of course,' Jo replies. This is followed by, 'That would be lovely,' from Ruth.

As they rise from the bench, Malcolm turns to Ruth, 'I am so sorry that you did not enjoy your ghosts, Reverend Ruth, and I am sad that they did not bring you comfort.' He bows his head slightly towards her.

'Oh, Malcolm, I didn't warm to them, that's certainly true, but wasn't I the one who said that who we meet is often random? So you mustn't think it's your fault. And in the end, I do think they challenged me, and who knows . . .' She stares around her. '. . . maybe that's what I needed.'

Jo feels as if Reverend Ruth's anxiety is back, and this time it is mixed with sadness.

'Oh, dear,' Malcolm cannot help muttering.

They are about to turn to leave, when Malcolm plucks at Reverend Ruth's sleeve. 'One moment – there is something I need to show you.' In response to her hesitation he adds, 'Really, it will be worth it. It's only over here.' He nods in the direction of Karl Marx's tomb.

They follow him to a plain rectangular plaque, set in the ground to the left of Karl Marx's monument. On it is inscribed:

Claudia Vera Jones
Born Trinidad 1915
Died London 1964

'Who is she?' Jo asks, realizing she now often refers to those in the cemetery in the present tense.

'I give you Claudia Jones,' he turns to Ruth, 'I know perhaps Karl and Hutch were not people with whom you had a natural affinity, but please let me at least introduce you to Claudia. And now let me tell you about this astonishing woman . . .'

With this he links arms with Ruth and Jo, and on the way back to the cemetery gates he tells them the story of Claudia Jones – the woman who helped start the Notting Hill Carnival and who fought for justice for so many people.

As they part, Ruth thanks him and he smiles at her, saying formally, 'Please consider Claudia a Christmas gift.'

Jo cannot help wondering if it is also a parting gift.

Back in the shop, Jo is kept busy, and it is mid-afternoon before there is a lull. Over a cup of tea she reaches for her phone and starts to look up more about Claudia Jones. During their walk through the cemetery, Malcolm explained that it was very fitting that Claudia was laid to rest to the *left* of Karl Marx. Claudia was a writer, journalist and protester (she was sent to prison several times). She was an inspirational leader, a Communist and a black woman. Jo is certain that she terrified those in authority. She wonders if she would have scared Karl Marx too.

Scrolling through her screen, Jo reads snippets from her writing. One particular passage catches her eye. It is from one of her last letters. It is melancholy in tone, and in it Claudia reflects that, with her constant campaigning, she fears she is boring – and confesses that she even bores herself. She died not long after writing this, and Jo is saddened that at the end of her days this magnificent woman was filled with such self-doubt.

Her thoughts turn to her friend, the vicar, who also displays moments of anxiety and self-doubt, and she wonders whether she will ever know the reason the Runaway Vicar ran away.

40

Karl Marx and Hutch

They are back in the woodland sitting room, but this time it is a woodland lit by fairy lights and candles. These add to the soft glow from the pale green table lamps and Jo feels like she has wandered into an enchanted forest. They are sitting in their normal seats around the fire and a tray of drinks is resting, ready, on the ottoman.

Malcolm watches as Jo and Ruth survey the room. There are candles in mini-lanterns arranged on each shelf of the bookcases, and fairy lights strung over the fireplace. In the bay window to the left of the front door is a Christmas tree, also decorated in twinkling lights. On the branches are hung clear glass baubles etched with winter scenes. These seem to draw the light into them, and then in turn send it out into the room in a sprinkling of tiny stars that dance around the walls.

'This is so beautiful, Malcolm,' Jo says, feeling for the first time the anticipatory tingle of Christmas.

'I must admit it has been very pleasant to think about Christmas. Mother and I used to love decorating this room, and yet since her death I have made very little effort.'

Jo notices Malcolm has also made an effort with his appearance. He is wearing a pair of aubergine velvet trousers (flared), his Moroccan slippers, and a raspberry pink jumper covered in white reindeers.

'Nice jumper,' Ruth comments from her place by the fire.

Malcolm pulls a little nervously at the cuffs. 'You don't think it's a bit much?'

'Not at all, very elegant and understated,' and with this Ruth starts fiddling with the cuff of her own jumper – a dark green affair with the faint outline of a robin on the front. Before Jo can say anything, the robin appears to spring into life, red and green lights flashing across Reverend Ruth's ample bosom, and a squeaky rendition of 'Jingle Bells' fills the room. Ruth stands up to enable them to enjoy the full effect of her Christmas jumper. She twirls around so they can see the emblem of a flashing Christmas tree on her back.

'Nice. Subtle,' Jo says, above the screeching of the jingle.

Malcolm does not seem able to speak for laughing.

'Now, enough of that,' Ruth says, and she fiddles with her cuff until she finds the switch, and all is quiet. 'And this is far too hot.' She peels off her jumper, revealing a simple navy shirt. With a shock Jo sees she is also wearing a white clerical collar.

'You really are a vicar,' Jo says. She wonders why she sounds so surprised.

'Yes, I am,' Ruth replies, softly. Jo gets the impression she is speaking more to herself than to them. Ruth sits back down in the chair and studies them. 'I have written to my bishop and in the New Year I hope to . . .' She doesn't finish.

Jo wants to ask – go back? Move on?

Malcolm looks like someone has punctured him and he sits, deflated, in his armchair. His eyes are fixed on Ruth's dog collar.

Ruth turns to him. 'Malcolm, you once said to me that we have the here and now.' She looks around the room, 'And this seems like a pretty special here and now to me.' She reaches over and taps him on the knee, demanding, 'Now what about those drinks.' Jo notices her voice is not quite steady.

Malcolm takes a deep breath, and smiles a little sadly at her. Then he rises to his feet, 'You are quite right, Ruth . . .' It strikes Jo that this is one of the few times she has heard Malcolm drop the 'Reverend'. '. . . I thought I would mix us the Christmas cocktail my mother and I used to drink.' He smiles crookedly at them and then rubs his hands together briskly. 'And then we must talk about getting a Christmas jumper for Joanne.'

His attempt at heartiness and humour tears at something within Jo and she wonders what life will be like for Malcolm when she and Ruth have left.

And she does want to leave. The anticipatory thrill of Christmas is like a keening cry from her other home. A clarion call from her family. She wants to hold them close, to sit by their firesides. Be wrapped in her mum's huge hug. She yearns to walk out onto the fells and raise her face to an ink-black sky, studded with the pinpoints of a thousand stars; feel a wind like iced water on her cheeks.

But what about this? What about Malcolm? Will they leave any impression on his life? Will Malcolm go back to his old routines, researching a book he will never write? Or will he find something to fight for?

And Ruth? She tries to think of the three of them on a stage, just before the scene changes. There is little comfort there.

'No! This can't just be it!' She is on her feet, and Ruth and Malcolm are staring at her. She sits down as suddenly as she stood.

'What is it, Joanne?' Malcolm is back to his solicitous self.

She cannot voice all she is thinking, but manages, 'We will stay in touch, won't we?' She knows she sounds like she is pleading.

'We will find a way.'

It is Ruth that says this. And in that instance, Jo knows what it is that Ruth brings to people. What she carries as a precious gift, along with her bottle of wine, to the sick, the dying, the bereaved, the frightened. It is not her belief in God. It is *hope*. And in the next blink of a second Jo understands that, for Ruth, these are the same thing.

'It will be all right, Joanne.' Malcolm sits on the arm of the sofa and rubs her arm. He sounds as though he is reassuring himself as much as her.

'It has made a difference, hasn't it?' She knows she is not making much sense. She's not even sure what has happened to her over the past few weeks with these people; maybe that will come to her in time. But something has changed.

'Oh, yes,' Ruth says, quietly.

The only sound is the gentle crackle and hiss from the fire. Then Malcolm rises to his feet once more. 'Now how about that cocktail?' he says, a little too heartily, as he moves towards the tray of bottles and glasses.

Malcolm and Eve's Christmas cocktail really is excellent, and Jo is on her third. She likes it so much that Malcolm has written the recipe out for her. Over the first cocktail she told them about James's text and was warmed by their shared outrage and laughter. 'Dave from Scunthorpe, oh very good,' Malcolm chuckled.

As Jo sips her third drink, she can feel a pleasant heat spreading all the way through her body to her fingertips. Malcolm has also provided a startling array of nibbles, all homemade, all delicious.

'Oh, enough of this chitchat,' Ruth says, suddenly. 'I want to bitch about Karl and Hutch.'

Jo looks at her rosy cheeks above her dog collar and wants to laugh.

Malcolm settles himself back in his chair, legs stretched out. 'Off you go then. Joanne and I are all ears.'

'I'm going to tell you all their good points first,' Ruth begins, virtuously. 'Now Karl Marx . . . There was no doubt he was a man dedicated to his cause; he spent many hours ensconced in the British Library, warm and cosy, writing all about Communism, whilst his family went cold and hungry—'

'Reverend Ruth,' Malcolm interrupts, '. . . ah, good points?'

'Oh, all right,' she says, kicking off her shoes and putting her feet up on the ottoman. 'Karl clearly influenced many and changed political thinking,' she says baldly.

'And Hutch?' Jo asks.

'Now, he certainly had his share of talent; he was a great pianist and singer. We might find his style very dated today, but in the Thirties and Forties he was a world-famous cabaret star.' She pauses, as if considering. 'Yes, I would say he was dedicated to his art and worked hard at it. A poor boy come good. Oh, and he was a good linguist too. He may have started life in Grenada, but he moved to America, France and then England, mixing with the rich and with royalty. Yes, Hutch could be charming, excellent company, and – on occasion – generous,' Ruth lists, counting these qualities off on her fingers. 'He was brave, too – I think it must have taken a lot to overcome the prejudice he encountered.'

'Any other good points?' Jo asks.

'Well, he had an enormous member that he was always getting out and showing people. I don't know if that counts.'

Malcolm chokes on his drink and it takes a considerable amount of slapping on the back by Jo for him to stop coughing.

'Well, you did ask,' Ruth says, with a glint in her eye. She continues, thoughtfully, 'He had *hundreds* of lovers, both men and women. Cole Porter wrote "I'm a Gigolo" about him.'

Jo picks up a plate of canapés and hands them around. She is enjoying this, and she can see the good vicar is too. 'Now for the bad points,' Jo says, encouragingly.

The gleam in Ruth's eye becomes even more pronounced and she holds out her cocktail glass for a refill.

Malcolm dutifully tops up her glass. As an aside to Jo he adds, quietly, 'I've watered this one down a bit, I hope you don't mind.' Jo doesn't. In fact she thinks it is a very good idea.

'Now, Karl,' Ruth begins with relish, 'he was a bombastic, overbearing man who fell out with just about everyone he met. A bully and, oh, as for his double standards, don't get me started.' With this she starts anyway. 'He claimed it wasn't right that he should lead a proletariat life, and so he scrounged off everyone he knew. He slept with his maid and then, when she had a baby, Karl completely disowned his son because of what it might do to his reputation.' Ruth looks around at them gleefully. 'He was a shocker.'

Jo wants to laugh.

'And Hutch?' Malcolm asks. Although as he says this, it occurs to Jo that he will already know. After all, this is his research.

'Now Hutch.' Ruth actually rubs her hands together. 'He could be mean, suspicious, arrogant, extravagant, selfish, and he had a very short temper.'

Malcolm goes to speak, but Ruth hasn't finished.

'He could be nastily homophobic when he was with his heterosexual friends, despite being bisexual himself. He held grudges and could be extremely callous. He fathered goodness knows how many illegitimate children, and all he had to say about them was that their mothers should consider them-selves lucky.'

'Did he—' Jo begins.

However, Ruth still hasn't come to the end of her list of Hutch's faults.

'When some school friends came from Grenada to England and wanted to hear him perform at the Palladium, they found they couldn't afford even the cheapest standing space. Did Hutch help them? Did he find a spot for them in the wings? Pay for their tickets? Treat his old mates to a box? Meet them for a drink?'

Jo and Malcolm know the answer without being told.

'No, of course not,' Ruth proclaims.

Jo sips her drink, and waits to make sure Ruth has finished. 'And so those are the reasons you didn't like hanging out with your ghosts. Yep, I can see why,' she reflects.

'Oh, I haven't even got started on why I really don't like them,' Ruth says, happily. Unconsciously she touches her clerical collar. 'I must say it feels good not to hold back for once.'

Jo notes the glee in her voice. She just hopes her ghosts haven't turned the good reverend.

'Top them up, Malcolm,' Ruth instructs, gesturing to her glass, her nose quite pink, 'then I'll tell you what I *really* think.'

41

What Reverend Ruth really thinks

Reverend Ruth leans back in her chair. 'The real reason I dislike Karl and Hutch so much is because of the way they treated their families,' she declares, looking from Jo to Malcolm.

'First, let's take Hutch. No one seems to know much about his wife, Ella, but there are photos of her in Paris with him – a pretty, shy-looking black girl. A complete innocent abroad. When they moved to London, he bought a house not far from here, south of Hampstead Heath. Here she cleaned and cooked for him and laundered all his many shirts. Here she brought up their daughter, Leslie – named after him. Here Hutch entertained his lovers, some of them staying over with no thought for his wife and child. He even moved one of his lovers in next door. If anyone met Ella, he often told them she was his housekeeper.' Ruth looks at them to check how her story is going down.

'Shocking,' Malcolm says, encouragingly.

'Ella died on her own in their Hampstead house at the age of sixty-three. After finding her body, Hutch went out that evening to perform as usual. He had her buried in an unmarked grave in a large corporation cemetery. There were three other bodies buried in the grave with her.'

Jo thinks of Highgate Cemetery. Of the splendour of the tombs and the sense of hushed, ornate serenity, and she is not surprised that Ruth dislikes Hutch so much. She is almost frightened to hear about Karl Marx, but she asks anyway. 'And Karl?'

'Ah, Karl Marx,' Ruth says, sounding at once sadder. 'He was a man who could earn a reasonable income from his writing, but he spent all of that – and what he borrowed – on himself and on creating the illusion of a lifestyle that was beyond his means.' She sighs. 'Two of his children died; one was a little boy named after Guy Fawkes, as he was born on the fifth of November. Just like Karl to name his son after the man who tried to blow up Parliament. Despite having money coming in, he let his family go hungry, didn't save for a doctor, was thrown out of numerous houses, often living in a couple of squalid rooms. He let the bailiffs come and take all they owned, including this little boy's bed and toys. Meanwhile, he was writing in the warmth of the British Library; he insisted on keeping a secretary and he always had enough money for his drinking.' Ruth declares, in disgust. 'His son's nickname was Fawksy,' she adds sadly. 'What sort of father would allow that to happen?'

It is Malcolm who breaks the silence. 'So what would Karl and Hutch ever find to talk about?' he asks.

Jo isn't sure if it's the effect of the drink, but the meeting of these two brilliant but flawed characters has become real to her, and she finds it really matters that Ruth hits on something they might share.

Ruth's answer surprises her.

'I think they would talk about the importance of family.'

Malcolm voices Jo's thoughts. 'You *cannot* be serious, Reverend Ruth! After everything you've told us.'

Ruth smiles at him sleepily. 'You may not have noticed, Malcolm, but I am a vicar.' She wags a finger at him, then briefly touches her dog collar.

Malcolm looks at her under his eyebrows. 'I had noticed that,' he says pointedly.

'The thing is, we vicars believe in redemption.'

His frown intensifies.

'It goes with the job,' she adds, 'along with the blood, poo and vomit.'

It seems her ghosts are having quite an impact on the Reverend Hamilton. Not only is she 'saying what she really thinks', but now she is also gambling. Ruth has bet Malcolm that she will convince him that Karl Marx and Hutch will talk about their families. And, she assures him, not with hypocrisy, but with sincerity. Malcolm has said he will require some evidence, it can't just be something based on her religious beliefs. (Jo thought he was going to say 'make-believe', but he stopped himself in time.) Ruth has agreed and Malcolm has assuaged his mounting frustration at her smug imperturbability by noisily clearing away the remains of the drinks and nibbles and preparing coffee for them all.

Now, filled with caffeine, Ruth is perking up. 'So, for my evidence, I'm going to start with the general and then I'll hit you with the specifics,' she declares.

Jo's father taught her to play cards when she was a little girl and they spent many a wet, Sunday afternoon (before he went out to check on the sheep) playing for buttons. He always told her, *Play your trump card first*. And this is what Ruth does now.

'I have watched men die.'

Jo knows that Ruth need say no more. The small figure in front of them has experienced death in a way she and Malcolm will never have done. Up until this point, she has not thought of Ruth as the figure by a bedside, many bedsides, holding the hands of those whose days are ending. She will know better than anyone what thoughts fill their final moments.

Ruth lets the words sit, and then quietly moves on to the specifics. The reasons that make her believe that in the time between their deaths and their meeting on Christmas Eve night, Karl Marx, philosopher, and Leslie Hutchinson, cabaret artist, will both have been dwelling on their families with a deep sense of regret.

'I'm going to start with Karl,' she says. 'I think he genuinely loved his family. He wrote his wife, Jenny, many love letters, and his grief at the loss of their children was very real. So, despite his shortcomings and his preoccupation with himself and Communism, his family were very much part of him.

He was constantly watched by the secret police, and even their reports relayed how gentle he was when he was with his children, spending hours telling them stories.'

Malcolm is nodding along. 'Tell Joanne about his father,' Malcolm encourages. It seems he is now content to help Ruth win her bet.

'That *is* interesting,' Ruth says, smiling warmly at him. She turns to Jo, 'He had a pretty awful relationship with his dad and wouldn't even go to his funeral . . .'

Malcolm cannot help himself. 'But when Karl Marx died, they discovered that he carried an image of his father around with him in his breast pocket.'

'It was interred with him,' Ruth finishes.

'And Hutch?' Jo asks, now convinced that Karl Marx might indeed wander the cemetery – maybe sit on the bench they had sat on – and think about his family.

'Some of Hutch's friends noticed a very peculiar thing. Wherever he was staying, he would ring his wife Ella, often daily, and be on the phone to her for hours. Maybe with her he could relax and he didn't have to put on all his airs and graces,' Ruth reflects. 'It was said he had at least four different accents he would use, depending on who he was with. Maybe it was only with Ella that he could drop the façade.'

Ruth falls silent for some moments and then holds her palms out to them. 'I rest my case,' she says.

'So, Karl and Hutch, together on Christmas Eve night, talking about their families and their regrets,' Jo concludes. 'Ruth . . .' she continues, slowly, 'you said that Karl and Hutch had made you think about your own life. Do you mind me asking about your family?'

'Well, there is only me and my brother Don now. He's a couple of years older than me. But, yes, you're right, I've been thinking about family. My parents were strict Scottish Presbyterians. Nothing wrong with that, of course. But it wasn't a whole heap of fun growing up.' Ruth gazes into the fire.

'What were they like?' Jo asks, trying to imagine Ruth as a young girl.

'Strident and strict . . . oh, how they loved their rules. And what made it tricky was these rules changed. So one day I was too noisy, and another day I'd be told I wasn't joining in enough. Either way the fault was always the same: I thought too much of myself.' Ruth's voice takes on a reflective tone, 'My brother, now, he seemed to get it right. Perhaps he was more sensitive than me.' Ruth then lets out a small bark of a laugh and shakes her head. 'No, it's no good, when I think of Don, no, definitely not. I shouldn't say he has a sensitive bone in his body.'

'Maybe he had a copy of the rule book,' Malcolm suggests with a slight smile.

Ruth sighs. 'Who knows? But there we were: one getting it right, one getting it wrong. I left as soon as I could.'

'Did you ever go back?' Malcolm asks.

'Yes, I did. I tried to see them a few times a year, but it got a whole lot more difficult once I decided to train as a priest. And within the Church of England too. You can imagine how that went down with Scottish Presbyterians. Plus they had very strong views about women in the church. Basically, they believed there was no place for them, unless they were polishing something. After my dad died, I thought it might get easier, and I did move in to help my mum when she was diagnosed with dementia, but . . .'

'What happened?' Jo prompts, thinking of Uncle Wilbur.

'Don put her in a home, and that was that. No discussion. What he said went. A chip off the old block is Don.'

'And you've been thinking about your family recently?' Malcolm prompts, gently.

'I have,' Ruth says. 'To be honest, reading about Karl and Hutch, it made me feel like my childhood really wasn't all that bad. A breeze compared with what Fawksy had to put up with.'

'Are you still in touch with Don?' Jo asks.

'Now and again. But not often. And that's why I've decided to go to Glasgow. I really think I should see him and try and find . . . oh, I don't know . . . some resolution for the two of us.'

'Redemption?' Malcolm suggests, and Ruth glances quickly at him. 'Yes,' she says slowly. 'The thing is, I can't help feeling I've been at fault too. I could have made more of an effort, tried to fit in more, who knows?' She rubs her forefinger up and down her forehead, and she looks tired. 'It's difficult to untangle. The more I think about the past, the more I can hear all the old criticisms: too difficult, too nosy, too pushy, too self-important—'

'That's rubbish,' Jo can't help saying, at the same time thinking this journey into the past explains Ruth's sudden plunges into anxiety.

'Thank you, Jo, but what I need to work out is what I do need forgiveness for and what I should let go of. And thinking about Karl and Hutch makes me realize you shouldn't leave it until it's too late. It might not work, but at least I should try.'

'When are you leaving?' Malcolm asks, and Jo thinks he looks tired too.

'Tomorrow.'

'So soon?' Jo says, in shock.

Ruth nods.

'Oh,' is all Jo can think of to say, but a great weariness sweeps over her. It is tinged with regret and loss.

They are a subdued trio as Malcolm helps them into their coats. Ruth gives them both a Christmas card and this seems to underpin their parting. Jo wonders when the three of them will next be together.

Maybe it is this sense of time slipping away that makes her ask. It seems like it might be now or never.

'What was it that made you run away, Ruth?'

'She didn't run away, she just didn't—' Malcolm begins.

Ruth holds out a mittened hand. 'It's okay, Malcolm.' She smiles at him. 'And kind of you. But I think we all know I did run away.' She looks at Jo. 'And you want a reason?'

Jo drops her eyes to pull on her own gloves; she should say something, stop this. But curiosity gets the better of her.

'I can give you plenty to choose from,' Ruth says, her voice tinged with something that Jo thinks might be disappointment.

'We could start with the never-ending worry about the state of the buildings.'

Jo looks up. She hadn't been expecting that.

Ruth half laughs, in recognition of her surprise. 'So, you have endless fundraising to keep the buildings from falling down, and in the meantime you have to become an expert on boilers, insulation, pointing, guttering and fuse boards. There are the piles of admin, from the diocese and the PCC – paperwork that I could have papered the entire church with. Then come the weddings, the christenings and funerals – all of which you want to make personal and special. And when that's done, there are more letters, more sermons . . . oh, and the plays. I can't think how many nativities I've written over the years, and each one has to be different from the last, otherwise it will be commented upon. A bit tricky when you're talking about the same story each year.' Ruth snorts. 'One time I made the kings three chefs in tall hats. I rather liked that, but apparently Colin Will-kill-soon didn't.' Ruth presses on. 'And so we come on to the complaints: why didn't I include Ethiopia in my prayers, it's a disgrace?; why am I not using the ancient text but at the same time why am I not getting young people into church?; why can't I be more like the last vicar and his wife? Alan played the bassoon so well, and Trish was so good on the guitar . . .'

Ruth sees the look on Malcolm's face. 'You think I'm joking, but I'm not. You have to be a musician, oh, and counsellor, when the organist has his weekly crisis of confidence. That's before juggling all the personalities on the PCC, and the churchwardens and your curates. One curate who used to be in the City and thinks he knows it all, while the other one knows a lot but she's too shy to say anything. So there is the cajoling, the listening, the encouraging, the pacifying. And that's without thinking of all the people you are trying to help in the parish, who are the reason you're there in the first place. And that's not just your congregation – your parish includes *everyone*. So you spend your time loitering in the village shop and listening in the pub, casually walking by the school at home time, because that is when you get to hear about who is in trouble and having an utterly wretched time. Then when these poor people *do* open up to you, you try your utmost to get them the right help.'

Ruth pulls her coat tightly around herself, hugging it to her. 'I never minded that,' she says, 'even if it could be a battle . . . more letters, emails, phone calls . . . more bureaucracy. I always felt that was what I was there for. But the rest? The rest!' Jo sees Ruth is trembling. 'And you know what the worst was?' She doesn't wait for an answer, the words are pouring out of her now. 'All those personal comments that you are just supposed to take, because you're a bloody vicar!' She looks at Jo. 'You've put on weight; your earrings are too showy; that new haircut is awful; you shouldn't spend so much time in the pub talking to people. And so it goes on. So what made me run away? You want one reason? Jo, you can take your pick.'

Her agitation is now shaking Ruth's whole body. Jo remembers a spaniel they once had on the farm that was terrified of storms. Like Ruth, its whole body shook with suppressed emotion.

Jo holds both of Ruth's arms as if to steady her. Malcolm takes a step closer. 'I'm so sorry, Ruth,' Jo says. 'I'm so, so sorry. I should never have asked.'

Ruth takes a deep, shuddering breath.

Jo says, again, 'Ruth, I am really sorry, I feel terrible, I shouldn't have asked you that.'

Ruth shakes her head, breathing more slowly now. 'No, I think I needed to get that off my chest.' She sniffs and gives Jo a watery grin. 'Don't worry. If it had been me, I would have asked that weeks ago.'

It is only as Jo is curled up in bed later that night that a doubt solidifies within her brain, and she wonders what the *real* reason was that the Reverend Ruth Hamilton ran away. For she is now certain, Ruth did not tell them.

42

Meeting point

The following days pass slowly for Jo, and increasingly she dwells on the life of Hutch, the ultimate performer. She feels that her life is divided into her public face and her private face. In the shop, in front of her customers, she is chatty and friendly. At times, this does not feel like a performance; there are moments when she forgets about Ruth and Malcolm, and her worries about her future.

At other times she is swamped with a great lethargy. She would like to call in next door to try and put things right with Eric, but she can't find a face brave enough; she thinks of going swimming but she would be there without Ruth and her, 'Holy shiiiit!' She tells herself there might be others she could talk to. She reminds herself of the naked friendliness of the changing room. But why would she bother to try and make friends? She is leaving soon. She has given herself until the New Year, and Christmas is just over a week away.

One afternoon, she closes the shop early and walks to Highgate Cemetery. She wanders deep into the graveyard, exploring parts she has not seen before, not wanting to re-tread the paths she has walked with Malcolm and Ruth. In the tangle of growth she finds new names and new stories, which for a while distract her, until she remembers Malcolm's research and then she is back to missing Ruth and to missing him. She even misses the ghosts. She has heard nothing from either Malcolm or Ruth, which means she is held in a perpetual suspension of waiting. A new kind of limbo.

Sitting on a wall at the side of the cemetery, Jo contemplates what she is going to do with her life. She digs her fingertips into the moss that fills the cracks between the stones, but finds no answers there. She stares at the different-shaped stones, the large, the small and the average-sized stones. She wonders why she has spent so much time dwelling on what it is to be average. Is anyone ever really 'average'? Perhaps it is feeling not quite one thing or the other, feeling out of place? (*A place for everything and everything in its place.*)

And then she is back to thinking of 'home' and where that might be. She remembers talking to Eric in the shop, telling him about the very people who lie buried around her here. That felt like home. She did not feel average or dull during those times.

Well, it's nearly Christmas, and New Year is fast approaching, her deadline. What then? She is swept by a feeling of overwhelming loss. She has lost something with Eric; she is conscious of that. She thinks of Lucy and her family, who she wants to return to, and the small shop in London that she has come to love and doesn't want to leave.

And Ruth? Where was she now? With her brother, Don? She cannot help feeling that she has let Ruth down. She believes now that she did not confide in them about all that troubled her, the real reason she left. She wonders if she could have pressed harder, if she could have helped.

Jo looks around her and it dawns on her – there is someone else who is left behind. She is not completely alone. Jo jumps down from the wall and starts walking.

Malcolm answers the door before her hand has left the knocker.

'Oh, Joanne, it's you!' He looks over her shoulder.

'Were you expecting someone?' Jo asks, looking back down the path. For a second, she wonders if it might be Ruth.

'No. Well, yes. But not for ten minutes. I thought it might be early. Do come in.'

Confused, Jo steps inside. The room is very different from her last visit. None of the lights or candles are lit; the fire hearth has been swept clean and the Christmas cards have been cleared away. By the side of the Christmas tree is a small wheelie suitcase.

'I thought you might be the taxi,' Malcolm explains, seeing Jo looking at the case.

'You're going away?' Jo says, stating the obvious. But feeling, *you too*. It seems a sad irony that she will be the only one left here in London – along with the ghosts.

'Yes, but we have ten minutes.' He ushers her to a seat but does not offer to take her coat.

Malcolm is wearing grey trousers and a grey overcoat. Jo's heart sinks. For a moment she falters. She was debating if she should ask Malcolm to come home with her for Christmas, and now it dawns on her that she knows nothing of his other friends and possible family. She hardly knows the man.

Then he smiles at her and he is still Malcolm: the man who buys notebooks; the customer who strides up the alleyway to her shop; the host who mixes fantastic Christmas cocktails; the gentle man who has carried a secret loss within his heart; the man who does battle with a vicar.

The words spill out. 'I know it hasn't been long, but I miss her, Malcolm. Have you heard from her?'

Malcolm looks troubled. 'Only a short text. I don't think the meeting with her brother, Donald, went well.'

'Are you . . . going to see her?' Jo asks, glancing again at the case.

'No. Not exactly.'

Which Jo thinks makes no sense at all.

Instead of asking Malcolm about this, a completely different thought comes into her mind. 'Do you think we miss out because we don't have so many vicars around these days? I'm not discounting other religions, but there was a time when every community had a vicar, and it struck me, Ruth did *so* much.'

'Oh, Joanne, it's difficult for me to answer that. My view is coloured by the harm religion has inflicted on society over the years.' He smiles slightly. 'And by some of the vicars I have met. But I concede, society does need people like Reverend Ruth.'

Jo smiles back. 'Are there many like Ruth?'

Malcolm sits on the arm of the sofa. 'Perhaps not quite in her mould – she may well be a one-off – but there are always people who are keen to help others. I strongly contend you don't have to believe in God to have a moral code or a sense of community.'

'But how many people actually do anything?' Jo muses, thinking specifically of herself. Could she do more? Of course she could.

'So, what are your plans, Joanne?' Malcolm asks.

'I'll go home for Christmas, and then . . .' She shrugs. 'This has been the strangest time.' She smiles at him, 'Good, in so many ways.' She looks towards his bookshelves. 'I keep thinking of a poem. It's my dad's favourite. I can't remember who wrote it but there's a line in it: *Time was away and somewhere else.* I feel like everything has been on hold. But now I don't think I know how to restart my life.'

'Louis MacNeice.' Malcolm nods.

'You know it?'

'Yes, indeed. "Meeting Point".'

Jo thinks of the poem's title. Has their time together, her, Malcolm and Ruth, been a meeting point in their lives?

Malcolm gets up and walks over to his bookcase. 'I believe I have it here somewhere.'

Jo's phone starts to ring and, pulling it from her pocket, she is about to mute it when she sees the name. Her stomach lurches. Her dad never calls her.

'Sorry, Malcolm,' she mutters, 'I've got to get this.'

'Dad?'

'Sorry, JoJo . . .' The use of her childhood name is a warning. '. . . It's your Uncle Wilbur. I'm afraid he died this morning. He had a stroke.'

She is holding tight to her phone, nodding. She looks up and sees Malcolm watching her intently.

'We gave her time, Jo, but now I think your mum needs you.'

43

Lighting candles

Jo cannot think of anything except getting to her family. The place for her now is at home. (*A place for everything and everything in its place.*) She wants to leave for the station straight away and catch the first train, but her father persuades her to take the rest of the day and evening to sort out the flat and the shop, and to get an early train the following morning.

Then her dad passes the phone over to her mum. Jo fights the tears, not wanting to distress her mum further, but when she comes off the phone, Jo breaks down completely. Malcolm sits beside her, murmuring soothing nonsense, and she is glad that it is an old man by her side. She thinks of her craving for a baby and it comes to her that there are other relationships that are precious and that shape people. She remembers an uncle and a favourite niece. Nothing was ever said, but she always knew she was Uncle Wilbur's favourite. This makes her cry even more.

Malcolm suggests that he puts off his trip and helps her, but Jo is adamant. There is very little she has to do. So in the end he delays his taxi for an hour and then makes them tea, hot and sweet. He also insists they let Reverend Ruth know, and texts her. Though why he feels this need – echoed in her – she isn't sure. Ruth replies immediately and writes that she will light a candle for Uncle Wilbur and also for Jo and her family. Jo experiences a glimmer of comfort, and thinks of the times she has lit candles in churches in foreign lands, not believing in a God, but feeling she is illuminating the love she is sending to those at home – including for her Uncle Wilbur. After reading Ruth's text, Malcolm nods several times and says, 'Now, that's nice. That's good.'

Jo cannot resist saying, 'But Malcolm, you don't believe in God.'

He replies, defensively, 'Neither do you.'

Has she ever told him this? Maybe he has interpreted her silence for what it is. At best ambivalence, at most a clear denial.

The taxi arrives at this point and there is a flurry of locking up and goodbyes. As he is lowering his tall frame into the car, he returns to their earlier conversation and says, 'Joanne, I may not believe in God. But I do believe in the Reverend Ruth Hamilton.'

The rest of the afternoon and early evening are spent packing and cleaning. Jo is just hanging a notice in the shop window telling her customers she has had to go away, when a large figure appears in the alcove leading to the front door. She turns quickly, searching the gloom for a shaggy blond head and an arm decorated with tattoos. It is the young police officer. He nods towards her notice and shakes his head. Jo unlocks the door and the young man instead gives her very good advice about keeping thieves out while she is away.

After this he helps her take the large sheets of paper that are stored in the drawers of the oak cabinet and stick these across the window. Rummaging in what remains of the hardware products, he finds a plug that works on a timer and sets this up in the hallway to Uncle Wilbur's flat, along with a lamp, so it will look like someone is still living there. Next he carefully words a notice that states the shop is closed, but also implies someone is still around. After this he produces his trump card by telling her he will get the lads at the station to keep an eye on the shop. It is then Jo discovers he is twenty-eight (not twelve) and an inspector, called Kendrick.

Following Kendrick's visit, Jo wanders off down Highgate High Street, hoping to find some gifts for Christmas. She doesn't know how much time she will have for shopping once she gets home. Many of the shops are still open, and the streets are busy with late-night shoppers. The air is crisp and cold with occasional wafts of spices and coffee. The windows of the shops shine rosy against the darkness of the buildings above. Jo has to step around a crowd gathered outside a flower shop, couples choosing Christmas wreaths bursting with clumps of pine cones, berries, roses and glistening ribbons. These are glorious, sophisticated confections. A far cry from the wreath her mum will hang on their door; foliage cut from hedgerows and the garden.

Jo escapes into the open doorway of the shop next door, stepping away from thoughts of her mum's grief and wanting to distance herself from the companionable couples. It is a greengrocer's, and she decides to buy some clementines for the train journey home.

It is when the girl who is serving her hands over a brown paper bag bulging with oranges that she starts to cry. She leaves the shop without the fruit, unable to explain to the young girl that she has just realized she will never see Uncle Wilbur again.

Jo retraces her steps back up the High Street, only pausing once to visit a bookshop. She heads straight to the 'Classics' section and draws a George Eliot novel from the shelves. With the substance of the book in her hands, she feels her breathing ease.

In the end she returns to Uncle Wilbur's shop carrying a parcel of three books. One of these, *Middlemarch* by George Eliot, she puts into her suitcase along with a selection of fountain pens and stationery from the shop (she will sort out who will get what for Christmas later), then she gift-wraps the other two books. The first of these is about the artist, Banksy. She posts it through Lando's shop door with a Christmas card explaining about Uncle Wilbur. She signs off saying she hopes to see him in the New Year when she will be down to help sort out the shop. The second book, a slim volume of Louis MacNeice's poetry, she puts through Eric's door, along with her spare key (Kendrick having said it was best to leave one with a neighbour). Her note to Eric the Viking is short and to the point. Her desire to write more robbing her of words.

Before wrapping the poetry book, she finds the poem she talked to Malcolm about and places the ribbon bookmark next to it.

Wrapping Christmas gifts makes her think of Malcolm and Ruth. She has nothing to give them, and no way to contact them, apart from texts – their replies spasmodic and short. Malcolm has admitted he doesn't like texting and has taken her parents' address, telling her he will write to her soon.

It is just before the cold in the shop drives her upstairs to spend her last night in Uncle Wilbur's flat that inspiration comes to her. She knows what she would like to give Malcolm and she plucks a large green notebook from the shelves in preparation. Ruth? Well, Ruth will take more thinking about.

Jo has everything packed ready and it is time to leave for the station. She is sitting on the stool by the counter, her wheelie suitcase at her feet. How many hours has she sat here watching the world go by? It feels right that the window is now blank, shrouded in white paper, giving no indication of what is outside – or clue to what the future brings.

Jo studies the floor tiles that mark the entrance to Uncle Wilbur's shop. On sunnier days, when shafts of light penetrate the front half of the shop, casting ripples over these indigo and bronze floor tiles, Jo could believe she is looking at mosaics stolen from an Indian palace. At other times, when the sky outside is grey or, like now, when the light is muted, the colours of the tiles merge together and she cannot see where the tiles end and the wooden floorboards begin. As her uncle's life faded, so she feels the life she has led here is now receding. Yet the memory of the people she has met over the past months still remain in sharp focus.

As Jo is closing the door of the shop, she catches sight of the noticeboard, now completely covered in a record of her past few months. She wonders when she will see it again.

44

The gods

Her dad is waiting for her at the station. He carries her bags to the car, disdaining the use of the wheels on her cases. He is a small man, with trousers bagging at the knees, giving the impression of a loose softness at odds with the strong, taut arm that hurls her bags effortlessly into the car boot.

It is as he is reversing out of the parking space, fists gripping the wheel, that Jo focuses on the liver spots on his hands. She looks at her dad's profile, his eyes concentrating on the rear-view mirror, and she thinks it won't be long before it is her brother, Chris, who is the Sorsby running the farm, and her dad will be driving her back to the cottage rather than the farmhouse. It is the way of things. Things are moving on.

Then why can't she?

'How was London?' her dad asks.

'Fine. How are things on the farm?'

'Fine.'

It is not that they aren't interested in each other's lives. But this stuff isn't the substance of what they hold between them. The precious stuff. That is contained in a dozen small actions: the cups of tea that Jo makes; the things she finds for him online; the World War II videos she rescues from her mum's charity box, knowing her dad still has an old video player in the farm office. In turn, he has given her old horse a retirement other OAPs would envy, he makes sure she has a car that will never break down, and when she comes to sit with him in the farm office, he pours her sherry from the supply he keeps for himself and his ancient secretary, Miss Jennings.

They wind their way through the familiar roads, heading away from Northallerton towards the North York Moors. Her parents' farm is set on the edge of these moors.

'How's Mum doing?'

'Oh, you know,' he says, and Jo thinks she does. Her mum will be upset but coping.

'She'll be glad to see you.' Then, squinting into the low winter sunshine, her father adds, 'being the last one left in her family is tough. And she was very fond of Wilbur. It's hit her hard. Still, she's been better today, knowing you're on your way.'

This is a long speech for her dad. Maybe her mum isn't coping so well, after all. The car falls silent again.

'Dad, do you believe in God?'

'Nope.'

Her father is back to his normal self.

'What is it that you do when you go out and thank the gods, then?'

This has been a recurring memory from her childhood. A family joke. Her father would pick up his glass of wine (always red) and go outside with it, telling them he was going to thank the gods. He usually walked across the garden to the stone wall that marked the border to his first field. Sometimes he would climb over the wall and head up to the large oak tree that grew between the field and a small brook.

As she grew older, Jo began to think this act was a signal that he wanted some time on his own; perhaps a bit of peace from her mum who could, and would, talk for the both of them.

Her father keeps driving, like he hasn't heard her.

'I used to think it was to get away from Mum,' she prompts.

'Could be,' he says, briefly.

'But then I saw that you tip wine onto the earth. What's that about, Dad?'

'Aah,' is all he says.

They are now turning into the farm track that leads to the house. 'Why the wine?'

Her father slows the car, bringing it to a halt just before the open gateway that is the entrance to the yard in front of the house. The farmhouse that both Jo and her father grew up in.

'I don't believe in Almighty God. And when you're dead, you're dead. Seen too much death to think different. But you can't spend as long as I have out on the hills without thinking there's more to it. From sunrise to sunset.' His voice drops. 'Still takes my breath away, JoJo.' He falls silent, then turns to look at her. 'So, call me an old fool if you like, but I thank whatever's out there by pouring good wine on the earth.' He nods towards the house. 'And when one of you is in trouble' – Jo knows he is thinking of his wife – 'I ask the gods for a bit of help.'

He doesn't wait for a response but puts the car in gear and accelerates towards the house. He pulls up abruptly, leaping out to get her bags. Her father has said all that he intends to. And for him, it was a lot.

The door to the house is open before she has undone her seatbelt. In a rush Jo heads for the tall bulk of her mother. She grabs as much of her as she can, and her mother folds her large arms about her and pulls her close.

It is the smell of her that makes Jo cry. She remembers when she caught the whiff of her mother's perfume in the air when she was in London, and followed a perfect stranger into a shoe shop.

Jo had every intention of comforting her mum, of being the one helping her. But she finds herself crying like a little girl, her mother murmuring into her hair, 'Oh, my Jo, it's all right.'

She thinks of her family nickname, 'Average Jo'. She whispers, 'I'm not just Average Jo, am I, Mum?'

Her mother catches her words, and pushes her daughter away slightly, so she can see her face. 'Now whoever told you that?'

Jo wants to say *you all did*, but she thinks, the truth is – *I did*.

*   *   *

Jo is doing everything she can think of to help her mother. She feels guilty that on arriving at the farm, she broke down, rather than being the one comforting her mum. It is clear that her mum is shaken by her brother's death. So Jo has helped with the cooking, phoned family members, spoken to the undertaker, the florist and the printers. As it is only a few days until Christmas, the funeral is set to take place after the New Year. Uncle Wilbur is going to be cremated, and her mum will travel to the Lake District in the spring to scatter his ashes by the edge of Ullswater. Jo has promised to join her. In the evenings, her mum talks about her childhood with Wilbur, and as she unfolds and smooths out these old memories in front of them, Jo sees her settle back into her old self. Sad, but coping.

A day after her arrival, her father drags a Christmas tree he has cut into the sitting room, and her mum and she spend the evening decorating it. Her brothers call in, but they are awkward guests, having clearly decided to put their usual one-upmanship on hold for their mother. The falsely grating bonhomie is worse than the bickering.

More than anything, Jo wants to see Lucy, but her best friend is visiting some of Sanjeev's family in Hertfordshire. Still, she will see her on Christmas Eve. She is due to meet Lucy and Sanjeev in one of their favourite pubs for lunch, and she will stay with them over Christmas. Her parents are spending time with her brothers (on separate days) and Jo will pop in, but her mother has assured her she doesn't need to be there for the whole time. Her dad has her old car filled with fuel, oil and screen-wash, ready and waiting in the barn nearest the house.

Of Ruth and Malcolm, she has heard very little. She is the one who texts more often than not. Their replies communicate little beyond that they are okay and thinking of her.

It is now three days before Christmas, and Jo is lying on her childhood bed, looking up at the window. The curtains are drawn back and she is staring up at grey sky, mottled purple in places, like a great bruise. Her thoughts are of Ruth and Malcolm and of the ghosts whose stories and conversations they wove together.

She glances at the notebook by her bed. It is almost full, and she will send it to Malcolm soon. Well, as soon as she knows where he is. So far, the promised letter has not materialized.

The idea was a result of her last visit to Highgate Cemetery. Hidden behind the more ornate tombs she discovered gravestones that clearly dated from the First and Second World Wars. She looked them up online to discover that there were hundreds of servicemen and -women buried in the cemetery. Their graves were often obscured from view as many families wanted the plots to be in the more private spots. These men and women had not perished when fighting abroad, but had often died months and sometimes years later of their wounds. Jo searched for evidence of someone, preferably a woman, from the ATA who was buried there – but with no luck. So in the end she researched airmen who would have flown the planes that Malcolm's mother and her friends would have delivered.

She has been writing these stories for Malcolm in one of

the notebooks from Uncle Wilbur's shop. She will send this to him for Christmas.

Underneath her notebook for Malcolm is a poetry book that she has borrowed from her dad. She thinks it is the only poetry book in the house, and it fell open at the Louis MacNeice poem, "Meeting Point". Flicking through the rest of the pristine book, she doubts her dad has read any of the other poems.

It is the fifth verse that makes her think of her parents, who had met in Skegness, out of season, in the late autumn. Two farming families, taking a break when the farms were quiet. Her mother has often told her that, after bumping into each other in the bed and breakfast's dining room, they spent their days in a coffee shop looking out over a rainswept seafront, drinking tea and talking. So her father did once find the right words. She thinks her mother must have made quite an impression on him.

She rereads the verse, picturing them holding hands across the table.

> *Time was away and somewhere else,*
> *The waiter did not come, the clock*
> *Forgot them and the radio waltz*
> *Came out like water from a rock:*
> *Time was away and somewhere else.*

Would she ever have a meeting point like that? Isn't that what she really wants? A partner, a family. The yearning for a baby stirs within her, asleep at present, but never gone. She thinks of Eric, sitting on the stool in Uncle Wilbur's shop, and of their conversations about ghosts. Of course, he didn't know that they were ghosts – she wishes now she had told him that. Explained that these ghosts would meet and speak to each other.

She kneels up on her bed and pulls open the window, breathing in great gulps of air rich with the scent of moss and the tang of heather. The cold makes her eyes water, but she keeps the window open, staring up at the great, bold sky above her. This is what she has missed. And yet, part of her is still hanging her head out of her London home, searching for the scent of tobacco and spices, and the smell of tarmac after the rain. She closes the window with a shuddering bang.

The truth is, she doesn't know what she wants.

She grabs the clothes she left on her bedroom chair and dresses in a rush, keen to get out onto the hills. She has promised her mum she will collect foliage to make a door wreath for her, and she needs some space and time to think.

By the time she comes back off the moors, tired and muddy, carrying great swathes of ivy, holly, snowberries and hawthorn, Jo has made a decision.

In a small stationery shop in North London, a pen-and-ink drawing of a Viking wearing overlarge glasses slips free of its pin and flutters to the floor, where it comes to rest in the dust underneath an oak cabinet.

45

Dear Joanne

Dear Joanne,

As you will see from the address at the top of this letter, I am back home in Hampstead. They say there is no place like home, but I am not sure I agree with this sentiment any more. However, enough of that. I wanted to send you my best wishes and say that I am glad that the funeral plans are progressing well. I do believe your uncle was a good man and no doubt will be missed. It is a shame I did not get to know him better.

I am sitting here now, pen in hand, wondering how best to describe the last few days to you. When I left you, I really had no idea what I hoped to achieve and so remained silent on the subject. I also felt I was not completely honest with you when I mentioned Reverend Ruth's state of mind. After her text I called her, and she really was very distressed.

The reason for her descent into such darkness was not

difficult to surmise: her brother, Donald. She has not described his physical attributes to me, but I find myself imagining a large man with a thick neck and flat forehead. Mere fantasy, I am sure, he may well be a small, pipsqueak of a man, but you will see in my mind I am thinking of a bully; and that is what Donald undoubtedly is. After her visit to him, which as you know was embarked upon in the spirit of reconciliation, the poor woman was crushed. It seems brother Donald dug up every childhood fault her parents had ever thrown at her and added in a few of his own for good measure. I think what hurt her most was his accusation that she was by nature a selfish and un-Christian woman. In short, she was not worthy of her calling. I do believe she might, in time, have dismissed his criticisms; however, I felt something of a personal nature was worrying her and was lending weight, in her mind, to his point of view.

The conversation led us to no clear conclusion, but I hope in a small way I helped her. However, it left me uneasy, which is why I resolved on my little trip. You see, Joanne, I decided to visit her parish and find out for myself if there was more behind her decision to run away. I could not help but feel she had not told us everything. Whilst I had no wish to invade Reverend Ruth's privacy, I felt a strong inclination to help her if I could. For this I would need all the facts.

Consequently, I have spent the last few days in Warwickshire, talking to her parishioners, members of her congregation and to her team. I even attended a church service. I tell you this because I know it will make you smile.

Below I have outlined my findings. Ever the bureaucratic analyst, I have listed them by topic.

1. Setting.

The parish is situated in undulating countryside and has many pleasant aspects. The sense is of a quaint hamlet that over the years has expanded to form what today is somewhere between a village and a town. There are a number of small shops and two pubs. I stayed in one of these, the Fox and Hounds, and was made most welcome by the publicans, Mr and Mrs Barton. Reverend Ruth's church is in the centre of the village, parts of it dating back to Norman times.

2. The Church Community.

I was welcomed into the church by a curate named Gordon. I believe him to be the ex-City gent that Ruth spoke about. He had a lot to say for himself, but in the course of this he did introduce me to others. The congregation was mainly made up of older residents and, judging by some comments made over coffee, it appears that the numbers have dwindled considerably in the months since Reverend Ruth's departure. While this may not be the place in my notes for personal reflections, I have to admit to you, Joanne, behind my nodding concern, I hid a big smile for our friend.

The members of the church and congregation were friendly, apart from, I am sad to say, the new vicar, and Colin Wilkinson, the churchwarden. First I shall describe the vicar. He was a small, nervous man, and my conclusion was that his apparent disinterest in those around him sprang from shyness. It seemed that Colin Wilkinson, in particular, made him extremely uneasy.

As I pause to write about Colin (you see how I am wandering from a clear, concise style), Reverend Ruth's words come to mind regarding 'Mr Will-kill-soon', and I also recalled her saying of Hutch and Karl, 'I really disliked them'. I would say the same of Colin Will-kill-soon. He is a man whose imperious bossiness crosses the line of what is acceptable, and yet when called up on it, as he was, very bravely, by the curate, Angela (more of her later), his fall-back position is to claim that his comments were all part of a joke. This leaves those, like Angela, feeling foolish, and I would suggest reluctant to challenge him again. As an aside, I had to deal with such a character at work once, a Mr Waddington. Suffice to say I relocated him to a small office in Henorsford. (Where the hell, you may well ask, is Henorsford? Which I believe is exactly what Mrs Waddington asked him.)

I am afraid, Joanne, this is getting less and less like a properly structured report. I confess, I write it with my feet up on the ottoman, and a glass of the excellent whisky you were so kind as to bring me, by my side.

My final word in this section is about Angela Green, the second curate. She is a shy but charming woman, who holds our friend Ruth in very high regard. I have included her email address at the end of this letter as I believe we may wish to contact her again.

3. The Nub of the Matter.

First, I should write that, in my general interactions around the village, it is clear that Reverend Ruth is very well thought of, and is missed by many. However, it is apparent there are also rumours circulating about her sudden disappearance. There seems to be a suggestion of some sort of scandal, but I am afraid to say no one I spoke to was prepared to say more. It was rather in the nature of hints and veiled references. I know no more than that, Joanne, but it appears that some kind of slip, an indiscretion, may have contributed to Reverend Ruth doubting herself and her fitness for her calling.

It certainly seems from the feedback I have had of her work in the parish that she has nothing to feel guilty about there. In fact, the complete opposite is true: she seems to have done a great deal of good. I therefore believe a catalyst – something she would view as a serious failing – is at the root of it all.

My dilemma is this: what do we do? I shy away from raising this issue with Ruth directly. Hence my letter, dear Joanne; I felt the need to consult with another who cares for her.

And on that rather inconclusive note, I leave you. Christmas will soon be upon us, and you will be tied up with family matters. However, I hope very much that we can consult with each other in the New Year.

In the meantime, I am your obedient servant and friend.
Malcolm Buswell

46

A hidden life

Jo rereads Malcolm's letter for the third time. Parts of it make her smile, while other passages worry her. How on earth can they help Reverend Ruth? Especially as she hasn't confided in them.

She rereads the letter for the fourth time, then stares out of her bedroom window at the skyline – an angular edge of moorland dusted with snow. It is an hour later, when the afternoon light is fading and the ridge of snow has finally merged into the creeping darkness, when she eventually comes up with a plan. She thinks of Lucy briefly. Hadn't she said that Jo was the one who came up with ideas?

Well, she has had an idea.

She reaches for her laptop and sends an email to the shy but charming curate, Angela Green.

* * *

Jo has decided to go to the carol service with her mum. There are three reasons for this. Firstly her mum asked her to; secondly she feels in some way it may help her connect with Ruth (she even wonders if there might be a candle she could light for her), and thirdly it will stop her checking her email every few minutes in the hope of seeing what Angela thinks of her idea.

The service is beautiful and the church packed. Jo knows many of the faces and is warmed by the smattering of friendly greetings. The glow from the candlelight brings back memories of standing in the bus shelter watching the windows of another church slowly fill with light. The children sing a special carol that makes her smile, and the soaring descant of the church choir brings her close to tears, as she thinks of her favourite uncle. Watching the children dressed in tea towels and dressing gowns act out a scene from the Nativity, she knows more than ever she wants her own family. But it comes to her that Uncle Wilbur didn't have children and yet he still forged a special relationship with his niece. He still had family. And soon she will be 'Auntie Jo' to Lucy and Sanjeev's baby. Maybe this could be enough? As the service comes to a close, she finds comfort in the retelling of the Christmas tale and happily breathes in the scent of pine needles and polish, reliving her time in a small shop in North London.

But despite all this, she still cannot shake off the feeling that she is a fraud. However much she admires Ruth's calling, the truth is that she can't persuade herself to believe. Faith is more elusive than that – not simply a judgement a person can choose to make.

As she leaves the church, with her arm tucked comfortably in her mother's, she acknowledges that the Highgate Cemetery ghosts are more real to her than an all-seeing, all-knowing God.

Now, back home, she helps her mum with supper. They are going to have local cheeses, with her mum's homemade bread, sitting by the fire. Her dad has already poured the red wine.

Supper ready, her parents settle down to watch *It's a Wonderful Life*, one of the few Christmas films that her mum can persuade her father to watch. Jo checks her phone for the tenth time. This time there *is* an email from Angela. It is a long one.

She rushes upstairs to collect her laptop and spends the rest of the evening, curled up on the sofa, typing and scrolling through various sites. At intervals she reaches for another chocolate from the china bowl on the coffee table, and sends links to Angela, who she gathers is already in bed, her dog, Betty, resting on her feet.

It is past midnight when she finishes and shuts her laptop. Her parents have disappeared upstairs long ago, and the sitting room is now lit solely by firelight and Christmas tree lights. Standing up and stretching, Jo picks up her half-empty glass of red wine and walks over to the French windows. She pulls back the long moss-green curtains and stares out through the glass.

She can see a crescent moon, bright in a pitch sky. The lawn is glistening with frost, and the cold flowing through the glass turns her breath to mist. Unlocking the door, she steps outside. Hugging her jumper closely to her, she steps onto the lawn.

Her footprints dot the grass as she picks her way towards the flowerbed where her mother's roses grow. The plants are sharp spikes in the moonlight, the earth underneath like charcoal and ash. Looking up at the moon, she tips some wine onto the soil, and silently asks the gods for their help.

The gods have been busy. The forum that Jo and Angela have set up for people to leave their Christmas wishes for Reverend Ruth is already full of posts. And as Jo hoped, people haven't just sent Seasons Greetings; it is clear they want to thank Ruth for all she has done for them.

Jo does a quick scan. She and Angela agreed on strict moderation, and should Colin Will-kill-soon feel the need to post anything, they have decided that he will very quickly be deleted. She and Angela didn't need to worry. There are nothing but positive comments. It seems the inhabitants of her parish are welcoming the chance to tell Ruth what a difference she made. As Jo scrolls down, more and more comments are added.

An email pops into her inbox from Angela with the title: *Have you seen this?!*

There is nothing in the content except for exclamation marks and smiley faces. Jo really hopes she gets to meet Angela Green one day. And her dog, Betty.

So many stories of kindness emerge from the various posts. There are good wishes from people that Ruth visited when they were sick or bereaved. There is a note from Josh's parents: since a baby, their son has been seriously ill and in and out of hospital, 'Like a yoyo.' All through this, Ruth visited them, bottle in hand.

Drink is mentioned quite a lot: George recalls sharing a nip of whisky with her on his allotment when his wife June died; Gina, a teaching assistant who was made redundant, remembers Prosecco; and Joyce and Martin, whose dog was run over, recalled the three of them toasting 'Archie' with a nice Amontillado (Ruth had also said a prayer over his grave by the weeping willow).

A builder from an outlying hamlet thanks Ruth for conducting such a special wedding service for his daughter (and then adds a note to say he is available for extensions and conservatories). This seems to stimulate a rush of good wishes and thanks for weddings, christenings and funerals. Jo finds the funeral posts the most touching, as it is clear that Reverend Ruth spent a lot of time with the dying and their families. And also that she remembers anniversaries of deaths as well. Bottles of wine are mentioned here too.

A former asylum seeker, now a pharmacist working in Birmingham (Jo sends silent thanks to Angela for having spread the word so successfully), writes about how, when he arrived here from Afghanistan and had poor English, no one would believe he was an educated man. But Ruth took him in and let him stay in the vicarage for several weeks. Jo wonders what Churchwarden Colin had to say about that – she suspects quite a lot.

Soon it becomes obvious that word is out in the local school. There is a flurry of posts wishing Reverend Ruth a Happy Christmas (with lots of emojis). Quite a few mention her 'noisy prayer' which, if the emojis are anything to go by, involved thanking God by bouncing up and down and shouting the words out very loudly. Jenny thanks Ruth for presenting her with first prize in the school's poetry competition, and Amir thanks her for telling him, when he didn't win, that footballers earn more money anyway.

A screenwriter posts very movingly of his wife's suicide, and an anonymous couple of their son's battle with drugs and eventual overdose. Jo wonders if this is the couple that Ruth had told her about, whose son, Paul, had been found dead in their garden. In both these messages, Ruth is thanked for talking about the wife, the son when others wouldn't, for fear of upsetting them. Jo recalls Ruth's directness and, not for the first time, thinks how her openness offers a form of relief.

There are also smaller kindnesses mentioned, acts that would not cause so much as a ripple in the local news. Ruth putting her neighbour's bins out when he had broken an ankle; helping a woman called Jill deal with scam phone calls (Jo smiles at the memory of Ruth dealing with just such a call in her shop), and walking Brendan's Alsatian, Maximillian, when Brendan was recovering from his hernia operation. The captain of a local hockey team posts about how Ruth often came along to cheer them on (and on one occasion took one of their midfielders to A&E). All these people want to send their love to the Reverend Ruth Hamilton at Christmas. And more posts keep popping up on Jo's screen.

Jo sends a quick email to Angela asking her if she wants to let Ruth know what they have done. Then she texts Malcolm with a link to the forum.

As she is waiting for their responses, a new post flashes onto her screen. It is from Colin Wilkinson, Churchwarden (in bold) stating that this website does not have the official sanction of the Parochial Church Council (in bold, and italics). Jo doesn't get a chance to read the rest of the message as a new box comes up obscuring it.

Moderators of this site are opposed to online abuse and misrepresentation in all its forms. Comments that we deem to be inappropriate, bullying or offensive will be removed immediately.

Jo grins. Oh, how Angela must have enjoyed posting that. She imagines it is payback for years of patronizing put-downs.

A text from Malcolm pings on her phone at the same time as an email arrives from Angela.

Angela's message is just a line of air-punching female vicars (where the hell did she get that emoji from?), and a short message: *your idea, you tell her, but send her my love.*

Malcolm's message is equally brief: *Inspired, dear Joanne. Happy Christmas.*

Jo just hopes that it makes a difference to how Ruth feels. She felt that if they could balance the scales in some way, remind her of what she had achieved during her time in Warwickshire, it might ease her doubts about herself. Jo decided, above all things, that this is what she wanted to give Reverend Ruth for Christmas. So she copies the link, types a text message from her and Angela to Ruth, and presses send.

As she looks out of the window, she feels the need to get back out on the moors. She won't go far; more snow has fallen in the night, and it is now lying on the lower ground. She can see that a stiff wind is blowing. But she would like to be out there under that huge, grey sky and fill her lungs with raw, clean air.

She will take a small flask with her, to pour a small amount of red wine onto the rough patchy earth where the greener grass gives way to moorland.

She knows without her dad having to tell her that, when the gods help you, it is important to thank them. In this, she now knows she is her father's daughter.

It is a while before she looks at her computer again. After her walk, she rushed to the post office to send Malcolm his note-book. It is Christmas Eve tomorrow, but with a special delivery she can get it to him in time for Christmas Day.

When she does open up her laptop, she sees that even more messages have been posted. It seems Ruth helped with the village fete cake stall, made pickles to raise funds for the OAPs' Christmas lunch, and entered a fun run against the advice of 'certain busybodies' – Mr 'Will-kill-soon', Jo thinks.

Just as she is about to close her laptop, another message appears. It is simply a quote from George Eliot's book, *Middlemarch*:

For the growing good of the world is partly dependent on unhistoric acts; and that things are not so ill with you and me as they might have been, is half owing to the number who lived faithfully a hidden life, and rest in unvisited tombs.

It is signed,

With very best wishes for Christmas, from your friend, Malcolm Buswell, and from the ghosts who rest in Highgate Cemetery.

47

Advice from Lucy

It is Christmas Eve and Lucy is back – and still married to Sanjeev, which she claims is quite an achievement after a prolonged stay with his family. They are meeting at the pub for lunch, and Jo cannot wait. Sanjeev is going to see Jo later at home, giving Lucy and her the chance to catch up properly. It also allows time for his wife's best friend to remind her of all his good points, which he knows he can rely on Jo to do.

The pub is glowing amber with warmth and light, and buzzing with conversation. Holly and ivy are strung from the beams, and in the inglenook fireplace huge logs are crackling and smouldering. Jo spots Lucy at a small table in an alcove near to the fire. A bright spot of crimson, in dungarees, with a green scarf in her hair. As always she is wearing her signature scarlet lipstick. Jo pushes towards her and hugs Lucy to her. She is swept with a feeling of great contentment for her best friend. How can she ever have thought she would run away from this? They hang, limpet-like, to each other for a few moments.

'Ah, so good to see you, BF,' Lucy says in her ear.

'What the hell!' The words are catapulted from Jo, and Lucy steps back, startled.

Over Lucy's shoulder, Jo can see a back she recognizes, a cycling jacket she knows. 'It's Finn,' is all she can say.

Lucy glances towards the bar, 'Yeah, and so?' She looks at Jo in bemusement. 'Oh, the girlfriend . . .' Lucy adds, still staring at Jo in wonder.

Finn has his arm around the waist of a woman. Her caramel toffee curls cascade over the sleeve of his jacket.

'What the . . .' is all Jo can manage.

'I'm not with you?' Lucy says, slowly. 'Oh, that's Finn's new girlfriend.'

Words tumble from Jo. 'But she's with Eric the Optician. What the fu—'

'No more! What are you on about?' Lucy says, starting to laugh. 'Do you know her? I thought he'd hooked up with someone up here, but apparently he met her in London.'

Caramel Toffee Clare turns round and – seeing Jo – gives a small wave, nudging Finn. She has the same look on her face as she had when she walked past Jo's shop window. Embarrassed.

'Oh, my God!' and Jo grabs the back of the chair, turning it so she can sit down. Or rather fall down.

Lucy takes the other chair. 'Out with it. And this had better be good.'

'I thought . . . but how on earth did they meet? . . . Oh, my God . . . the key . . . Mrs Patmore.'

'Nope, not getting it so far,' Lucy says, laughing, pouring a glass of wine for Jo and a mineral water for herself.

Jo tries again. 'The thing is, I thought—'

But she gets no further. Clare is at their table with Finn in tow.

'Hi there, Jo. Good to see you, sis,' Finn says, cheerfully. A man oblivious to undercurrents. A man in love. And who wouldn't be in love with this woman, Jo thinks, looking at Clare.

All she can manage is, 'But I thought . . . What about Eric the Viking?'

Now everyone is laughing and she wants it to stop; she wants someone to explain.

It is friendly, freckle-faced Clare who speaks first. And Jo thinks, after Lucy (of course), this girl may soon be her deputy best friend. 'Eric?' she says, with a frown of confusion. 'Have you spoken to him since you left London? Oh, he really, *really* likes you, Jo. He thought he'd blown it when he asked you out, but I hoped . . . I was worried I might be to blame there – he was going to ask just the two of you . . .' She continues in a quieter voice, turning away from the others, '. . . but I knew you were Lucy's best friend, and she is *so* important to Finn, I thought if I got to know you, it wouldn't be so daunting meeting her over Christmas.' She pauses. 'It was so obvious that Eric and you . . . well, I could see it, but he wasn't so sure and when you said, no . . .'

Jo relives the *Christ! No!* in her mind. The sarcastic, *Nice thought though*, that followed quickly behind.

Oh God. What has she done?

'He thought that was it,' Clare finishes.

All Jo can think about is the question Eric asked about her minding about Clare – what was that about? 'But why . . .' she begins, but gets no further.

'Why didn't he ask you out sooner?' Clare says, trying to help her out. She lowers her voice, looking a little shamefaced. 'He thought you liked *Finn*, to be honest. He walked past the shop when you were hugging and . . . He was worried I might be muscling in on that, at first. Until I told him that Finn was your best friend's brother.' She continues, in less of an undertone, 'Eric was there when we met. I'd just had an eye test when Finn came in for your key . . . and well.' She looks up at Finn, smiling.

'Love at first sight. Blew me away,' Finn offers. Which Jo thinks would be tactless if it wasn't music to her ears. 'It was like one of those sliding doors moments. She's heading to the door. I'm standing there, mouth open. Then I thought, it's now or never, so I asked her for a drink.'

Clare laughs, 'And told me to never leave you.' She tugs on his sleeve. 'Didn't you tell Jo we'd met, that we were going out?'

He blinks. 'Um . . . No.' His face says it all – I'm a man, why would I?

'Aah,' Clare says, as if a lot of things are now becoming clear, 'so you thought me and Eric . . .'

'You say he really wants to ask me out?' Jo needs to know this, urgently.

'Yes, of course. He can't talk about anything else. He thinks you just . . . hated the idea.'

'I thought you two . . .'

Clare laughs. 'I kind of get that now. No, we just get on really well. We're friends.'

Jo can't help it. 'Oh my God,' she says, and now she has her head in her hands. What must he have thought of her? But then she looks up and beams at Lucy. 'Eric the Viking likes me.'

Clare touches her arm, smiling. 'Well, you two have a nice lunch, and have a happy Christmas, Jo,' She leans down and hesitantly kisses Jo on the cheek.

Jo barely acknowledges it. At one level she knows she is being rude (and is about to be a whole lot ruder), but she can only think of one thing.

'Luce, I'm so sorry – I've got to go to London.'

'Of course you have,' Lucy says, smiling at her.

And Jo knows, this is why no one but Lucy will ever be her best friend.

Jo stands up. She sits down. Then stands up again.

Lucy watches her, grinning. 'What are you doing, idiot?'

'Am I mad? What about you guys? And will he even be there?'

Lucy reaches up and pulls her down into the chair. 'Look it's not even one o'clock yet. It's – what? – a four-hour drive to London? What time does he shut the shop?'

Jo searches in her bag for her phone – she could Google this. With her hand in the bottom of her bag, a clear image appears in her mind of her phone charging on the dresser in her mum's kitchen. Lucy takes over, pulls out her own phone and within a few seconds has established the optician's is shutting early today – 5 p.m. rather than 7 p.m. She tells Jo it is a huge oversight that there is no photo of Eric the Viking on his website.

'I could just about make it in time,' Jo says, still sitting.

'Yes, you could,' Lucy assures her.

Jo now looks directly at her best friend. 'But what about you, and . . . am I completely mad?'

'Yes, undoubtedly,' Lucy says, while at the same time pulling Jo to her feet and dragging her to the exit. At the door to the pub, Jo asks Lucy to let her mum know. 'Say I'll call her from the flat when I get to London. And tell her that I'm sorry. And I'm sorry to you, too. Look, I don't have to go – Lucy, if you want me to stay, I will.'

'I know you would,' says Lucy, smiling. 'But you really, really like this guy, don't you? So just *go*. I'll be fine.' She grins. 'But you have to phone me as soon as you know what's happening with Eric the Viking. And I want a photo of him. No excuses.'

'But he might not be . . . I don't even know if he still . . .' Jo pauses.

'Just go. You'll never find out unless you do,' her best friend tells her.

So in the end she hugs Lucy and does as she's told.

48

The road to London

After about half an hour of driving, her heart has stopped racing and she is concentrating hard on the here and now. She may have no phone but she has her purse, plus the overnight bag she was taking to Lucy's. She is sidetracked for a moment – she still has all their presents in the car. Then she is back to focusing on the road. And it needs all her attention. Sleet is blurring her vision and her windscreen wipers are on full-speed. She sends a silent message of thanks to her dad. Whatever the weather is like, she knows her little car will cope. Everything has been checked. Twice.

She thinks of her mum. There is no doubt she will be worrying about the weather – the radio is predicting more snow – but she knows she can rely on her dad to reassure her. Hasn't Jo been driving on the farm since she was fourteen. Although, perhaps best not mention that one – she's not sure her mum knows her dad let her drive his old Land Rover around the farm.

By Wetherby, they are at a standstill. Her radio tells her (in between a Slade Christmas classic and Bing Crosby's 'White Christmas') that a lorry has jack-knifed and is blocking both carriageways. The sleet has stopped but snowflakes are fluttering slowly down. They melt as soon as they settle on her bonnet, but the edge of the dual carriageway is turning to an off-white slush.

She's glad her car's heating is so good, but is suddenly hungry. She thinks of Lucy; did she stay for lunch in the pub? Jo smiles – of course she did. She would have joined Clare and Finn and pumped them for information. She is probably looking at Eric the Viking's Instagram feed right now.

Jo is flooded with doubts. This is madness. She could get stuck here for hours. And if it really starts to snow, she could be stuck overnight. Happy bloody Christmas.

She tells herself she is feeling this way because she's hungry. But there is nowhere to stop, and anyway she's not even moving.

Then she remembers her present for Sanjeev. She knows he will forgive her (in the same way he knew she would fight his corner with his wife). She reaches into the back and rummages in the tote bag filled with their Christmas presents. She bought an old-fashioned stocking filled with Cadbury's confectionery for Sanjeev – she does this each year, ever since he told her that as a boy it was always his favourite present. She tears open the paper and packaging and starts eating.

Once she is on to her second bar of chocolate, she feels better and the traffic has started to move. As a mantra to reassure herself she repeats out loud: 'Eric the Viking likes me'; 'I am not Average Jo, I am on an adventure.'

It doesn't take her long to get bored of this. She thinks of Claudia Jones; hadn't she said the same thing about her campaigning? *I even bore myself.* Jo reaches for the radio controls and clicks a few buttons until she finds a Radio 4 Christmas play. Perfect. The play makes her think of her mum at home in the kitchen, and this calms her.

When she nears London, she is heartily sick of every radio station and all her Spotify choices. There have been more delays at Loughborough, and by Luton the sheer volume of traffic into London is keeping the average speed at under thirty miles an hour. It is at this point she finally admits to herself there was no possible chance of her getting to Highgate for 5 p.m. She thought everyone left London for Christmas; apparently not.

Things improve after crossing the M25, but then heavy snow slows her progress. Now the flakes are falling, big and fat. She tries to think of how many children will be delighted, but mainly she feels foolish and tired and hungry. All she can do is concentrate on the road, lanes blurred by settling snow, until they are crawling in a single file towards the capital.

It is past 8 p.m. before she reaches North London, and she is conscious she still has to find somewhere to park. After a few false starts she finds a multi-storey car park, and then she starts the trudge through the gathering snow to Uncle Wilbur's flat. She has very little hope that there will be anybody else in the alleyway, and she envisages a lonely Christmas Eve in a cold flat. Then she thinks of Malcolm. Won't he be at home? She could always call on him.

Her spirits lift and she finds pleasure in the sight of so many people out celebrating. The snow lends an additional vibrancy to the Christmas mood; some people are throwing snowballs, some just walking hand in hand, faces upturned to the sky. The couples make her think of Eric the Viking and she picks up her pace. Just maybe . . .

The alleyway is dark and still. The streetlamp nearest the High Street is out. In the distance she sees movement and hurries towards it. A figure is backing out of a doorway, key in hand.

The figure turns.

'Jo! What are you doing here?'

'Lando, how are you?' She tries to swallow her disappointment. 'Have you seen Eric?'

He shakes his head. 'Sorry, he headed off hours ago. I just popped back as I'd left Sacha's present here. Merry Christmas, though! Got to rush, Ferdy is waiting for me. We need to put the carrots out for the reindeer.'

Jo wishes Lando a Happy Christmas and turns away. Snow is now gathering on her lashes, making her blink. She had better get into Uncle Wilbur's shop and make the best of it. The inside of the shop is cold and still. She picks up the post lying on the old indigo and bronze tiles, and puts the bundle on the nearest shelf. The white sheets of paper across the windows give the interior an eerie glow, like snow is already piled up high against the windows. She tries the light switch beside the door, but nothing happens.

At the back of the shop, she sees a pale orange glow and

she remembers the timer Kendrick set up for her. She goes to get the lamp, clicking the switch on the kettle as she passes. She doesn't have any milk, but there will be coffee. She is suddenly conscious of how little she has with her – she doesn't even have her phone – but then reminds herself: this is London, there will always be shops open late. A wave of loneliness washes away any desire for food and she pushes her bags out of the way and takes up her place on the stool behind the counter. She leans down, plugs in the lamp and at the same time turns the blow heater on, shifting it with her foot so it is throwing all its warmth in her direction. She spots something part hidden under the counter. She picks it up and brushes off the dust. It is a pen-and-ink drawing of a Viking.

Looking at it, she feels foolish and lonely in equal measure.

Sitting in a faint pool of light, she stares at the blank whiteness of the windows. Now what should she do?

Suddenly the answer is so obvious, she can't believe she didn't think of it before. She wonders if part of her (and the gods, maybe?) always knew where she was heading; even when she was procrastinating back in the pub. And she has time. It is only 9 p.m. The ghosts won't be out and about until ten o'clock.

After all, those are the rules.

49

Christmas Eve in Highgate Cemetery

Jo raids her Uncle Wilbur's cupboards and drawers for all his warmest clothing. She puts on several layers of socks until her feet are the right size for his heavy boots – she thinks they may be ex-Army issue. Then she pulls on jumpers, scarves and gloves, and finally, his long winter overcoat and a grey wool hat. Dressed in his clothes, she feels a closeness to her favourite uncle and sends him a silent message of thanks – not just for this moment, this sharing of his belongings, but for what the last few months have given her and for all the childhood memories.

At the back of the wardrobe she finds a stout stick and, as she drags it out, a memory tumbles out with it. She sees her maternal grandfather leaning on this stick, both hands clasped over the top, eyes half closed in contemplation of the mountains sweeping down to Ullswater. So, Karl Marx kept his father's picture in his breast pocket; Uncle Wilbur kept his father's stick.

Thoughts of family remind her she hasn't yet called home, so she takes off her gloves and rings her parents. Luckily her dad answers and, without asking for any more details, agrees that he will tell her mum she is safe, and also get her to call Lucy.

Outside, the snow has stopped falling but the ground is icy and slippery – even in Uncle Wilbur's boots and using her grandfather's stick to steady her. It is easier once she gets away from the High Street. Fewer people have walked here, and the fresh snow gives her more purchase. She heads for the narrow lane that will lead her down to the cemetery.

Houses are aglow with Christmas lights and she is grateful to those residents who have left their curtains open, allowing her a glimpse of the warmth within. From somewhere come the strains of a cello being played, the faint rasp of the bow wrapped within the full richness of the melody. And then it stops. A dog barks.

From the High Street, Jo can make out distant laughter, and then she is navigating her way down the narrow lane and all she can hear is the scrunch of her boots and the short puffs of her breath. It is easier than she expected, but she goes slowly, holding onto fences and lampposts, until she reaches the gates to the Eastern Cemetery.

They are locked.

She hadn't thought of this. They were usually guided by Malcolm as to when to visit the cemetery, and so in her mind it was always available, always there for them.

She swings the backpack she has brought with her off her shoulder and searches for her torch. Then, clicking on the strong beam, she makes her way further down the lane, examining the wall of the cemetery. It is a low wall, topped with tall railings; it is well maintained and there are no obvious gaps. Her heart sinks.

But she has come this far; she can't go back now. She thinks of John Lobb, walking all the way to London from Cornwall. The least she can do is keep going. It is easier to walk now, as the snow is deeper and there are railings to hold on to.

She doesn't have to go far before she sees them. Footprints leading across the lane to a point further down the hill. They come to a halt by the wall, between a stone post and a streetlight. One set of prints is small, hopping bird-like across the snow; the other is from a larger foot (possibly encased in a John Lobb boot). Jo is flooded with an elation far greater than when she plunged into the Hampstead Ladies' Pond.

Of course they have come. In her heart she knew they would. And Malcolm was prepared. Through the railings, between the post and the streetlamp, she spots a stepladder.

She finds them on the bench near Karl Marx's tomb. They turn, startled, at the crunch of her boots in the snow.

Malcolm springs to his feet, then she sees him relax. 'Joanne? Joanne! Is that really you?' He peers at her and Jo widens the gap between her woolly hat and her scarf to reveal her face. It is then that she is hit full in the stomach by a barrelling vicar.

Ruth wraps her in a comprehensive hug. Over her shoulder, Jo can see Malcolm – who she now realizes doesn't quite look like Malcolm – clapping his hands together. 'I thought you would come. When you didn't answer your phone, I wondered, I hoped,' he says, delightedly.

Ruth lets go of her and, stepping back, looks up at her. 'You are a sight for sore eyes. And *thank you*, Jo. You and Angela. I can't tell you what a difference it made to me.' She turns to Malcolm. 'Room for one more, do you think?'

'Yes, indeed,' and Malcolm steps aside so Jo can see the bench. It appears to have been covered in a tarpaulin of sorts (or maybe it's Ikea bags?) on top of which are layered blankets and cushions. Jo spots the green and cream tartan blanket from Malcolm's ottoman. In front of the bench is a small, fold-out camping table. On it is a large lantern, a thermos flask, two cocktail glasses and a cocktail shaker. A round basket is sitting beside the table. Malcolm reaches into the basket and retrieves a third glass. 'Shall we?' he says, gesturing to the bench.

Ruth lets out a snort of laughter. 'You put in a third glass?' She looks suspiciously at Malcolm. 'Did you know she was coming?'

'No,' Malcolm says, 'but I knew you would be praying for a safe deliverance when we couldn't get hold of her.'

Ruth looks even more suspicious, 'And . . . ?' she says.

Malcolm then repeats what he once told Jo. 'Reverend Ruth, I will never believe in God. But I do believe in you.'

'Oh, Malcolm,' Ruth says, reaching out her hand to him.

No one has made any mention of Malcolm's appearance. He is wearing a purple beret, a vermillion scarf and a long turquoise afghan coat embroidered with flowers.

A few minutes later, they are all tucked up on the bench, blankets wrapped around them, glasses in hand. Malcolm has mixed his traditional Christmas cocktail. The thermos, which Jo had imagined might contain tea, is full of enough cocktail for a second, or possibly third glass. Reverend Ruth is sitting squeezed between Jo and Malcolm. Jo lets out a contented sigh.

'I have some sausage rolls in my basket. I think they should still be warm. Would anyone like one?' Malcolm offers, and Jo remembers just how hungry she is.

As they sit eating sausage rolls and some brie and cranberry tartlets that Malcolm forgot he had packed, the snow starts to fall again. Slow, lazy flakes flutter around them. The position of the bench means they are sheltered from the gathering snow, but the tombs circling them look as if they have been iced with it. Jo uses her torch to illuminate more of the graveyard. The stone angels are cloaked in white and Karl Marx is wearing a toupee of snow.

Jo doesn't know whether it is the sight of Karl Marx looking ridiculous, or the sheer joy of being here with these two people, but she starts to laugh. The sound is caught up and echoed by her companions and Jo remembers dancing with them around Uncle Wilbur's kitchen.

'What are we like?' she eventually says. 'I mean, look at us,' and she starts to laugh again.

'I must say,' Malcolm says, 'I do think it is rather marvellous.'

Ruth joins in, 'I know what you mean, Jo – the three of us. I don't know quite how you would describe this.'

Malcolm's breath clouds the cold air as he speaks. 'I suppose, Reverend Ruth, I would say that we are simply friends and leave it at that.'

Jo wonders if that is it. She knows friendship can be complex, and, thinking of Lucy, it can make you feel physically ill when it goes wrong. But at its best, wasn't it joyfully uncomplicated? Someone was simply your friend. And that was that.

They sit in silence for some time, and then Jo asks, 'If you don't mind telling us, Ruth, what happened when you went to see your brother?'

'Ah, yes, Don. Good heavens, that was tough. He just repeated what my parents had told me over the years: that I was too full of myself, too different. Just not what they wanted.' Ruth's voice is strained, 'But I can't say I regret it. Well, not now. I tried and I will always know that. I can't deny it knocked me for six, but then you sent me the link to that wonderful forum you and Angela had set up.' This time Ruth leans over and kisses Jo on the cheek. 'I will never be able to thank you enough for that.'

Malcolm tops up their cocktail glasses, shaking back the sleeve of his turquoise afghan coat so as not to dribble drink on his cuff. 'And now, Reverend Ruth, I think you should tell Joanne and me how you came to be the Runaway Vicar.'

It seems to Jo that Malcolm has borrowed a certain direct-ness from his friend, the Reverend Ruth Hamilton.

50

The secret of the Runaway Vicar

'Oh, must I?' Ruth complains. 'I should have known you two would figure out I hadn't told you everything.'

But from her tone, Jo knows that she is going to tell them. She tucks her arm into Reverend Ruth's and waits.

'Oh Malcolm, I feel such an idiot,' Ruth confesses.

'Better get it over with, otherwise Joanne and I will think the worst, and I am sure it really isn't that bad,' Malcolm insists.

'Well, I feel it is,' Ruth states, almost grumpily.

'You are only human, Reverend Ruth,' Malcolm says, soothingly.

'I know, Malcolm – I really do know that – but I felt like I had let myself down, and my calling.' She continues, and Jo thinks she detects a hint of humour in her voice, 'And it is *so* embarrassing, when I look back.' Ruth sighs. 'Okay then. Let me tell you the story of Stan . . . I mean, what a name – it's not very romantic, is it?'

Malcolm and Jo stay silent. It doesn't seem to them as if there is any possible response to this.

'Well, Stan Pickwell was a newcomer to our community. He was originally from Liverpool.' Ruth groans. 'A bookie.'

Jo smiles.

Ruth seems to get some sense of this. 'Yes, I know, I know. Well, he had bought the old Manor House. Threw money at it. I think he was trying for a bit of gentrification.' Ruth snorts. 'That was never going to work.' Jo thinks she says this with a marked degree of affection.

'I called in, as I always would to anyone new to the parish, and, of course, we were always on the lookout for funds for the upkeep of the church.'

Jo can hear real humour return to Ruth's voice.

'Well, I walked around the house, and it didn't seem like anyone was in. I eventually found Stan in the annexe where the swimming pool was. He was having a dip. Anyway, I introduced myself and, as I'm chatting, it dawned on me that the man didn't have a stitch on.' Ruth laughs. 'He was butt naked. Of course I should have left. But he was very jolly and just . . . well, the upshot was that he said he would give the church a very large donation if I would join him in the pool.'

'And did you?' Jo is laughing.

'Of course! It was a challenge. I know it was mad, but he was funny and treated me like a woman rather than a reverend. I just liked him. There was this . . .'

'Chemistry,' Jo supplies.

'Exactly,' Ruth says, squeezing her arm.

'And oh my goodness, it was fun. Well, that is where it started. And the sex! I have never had such a good time. I didn't think I could do half of what I ended up doing.' Ruth says this with some pride – and with no embarrassment. 'We just couldn't get enough of each other . . .

'There was only one problem,' Ruth says more seriously.

Ah, a married man, Jo thinks.

'I feel a bit shy saying this. I have never told anyone this. I mean, I'm not a prude. But, well, it didn't feel right.'

Jo's mind is working at a million miles an hour. What the hell had this man asked her to do?

'It wasn't so much what we did . . .'

'Yes?' Jo and Malcolm say slowly in unison.

Ruth then says, 'Don't look at me when I say it.'

Jo and Malcolm automatically look at her, then both look quickly away.

'Well, when Stan . . . you know . . . umm . . .'

This is so unlike Ruth, who is normally so direct.

'Well, when he . . . well . . . when he came,' Ruth says quickly, 'he used to call out, very loudly, "Sweeet Jeeesuuus!"'

There is complete silence for a second and then the bench is rocking with Jo and Malcolm's laughter. Ruth eventually joins in. 'I know not everyone has my faith, but *really!*'

It takes a while for the laughter to die down as Malcolm and Jo keep muttering 'Sweeet Jeeesuus!' and it starts them off again. Eventually they are quiet, and Ruth adds, quite matter of factly, 'There was also the problem, of course, that he was married. Somehow he had forgotten to mention that. He talked of his ex-wife but not the current one, who was spending the summer in France, as it turned out.'

'Oh, Ruth,' Jo says, with sympathy.

'Maybe my own fault . . .'

'No, it certainly was not,' Malcolm insists.

'I think I just got carried away. It was *so* good between us – I mean so much fun. Work was so stressful – all the things I told you before: they were all true. Life was hard. So it was wonderful to forget my calling and just be a woman for once. And really . . .' Ruth says this with relish, 'the sex was quite extraordinary.'

'Is the affair the reason you ran away?' Jo asks, hugging Ruth's arm.

'Yes and no,' Ruth says, turning her head from side to side. 'It came to a head one day. I was sitting at home thinking about what to do. I knew by then I had to finish it with Stan. I had found out about his wife, you see. Then I saw Colin Will-kill-soon coming up the path. I just couldn't face him. I wasn't sure what it would be this time, but there was always something he wasn't happy about. So when he knocked, I didn't answer. Then I heard him trying the front door and I realized I hadn't locked it, so there he was heading down the hall to the kitchen. I grabbed my bag from the back of the door and just stepped out into the garden. I thought if I was there, I could pretend I'd been out and was just coming in.'

'Good plan,' Jo comments.

'Well, there I was in the garden, in the shadow of the laurel bush, looking in on Colin in my kitchen. And suddenly I was watching my life from the outside. I saw the piles of paperwork on the table, the calendar crammed with events. And there was Colin, ferreting around, picking up letters, reading the notes in my church diary. He even opened the fridge and had a good look inside. I heard him harrumph when he saw the bottles of wine in the door.'

'I would have hit him with one,' Malcolm says, and Jo knows the peace-loving man beside her means it.

'The final straw was when he went upstairs. I just stood stock-still, shocked. Now I can't believe I didn't rush in and scream at him, but it felt unreal, like I was watching someone else's life. It was then I heard him opening up drawers in my bedroom.'

'The bastard,' Jo exclaims.

'Quite,' Malcolm says, with satisfaction.

'And that was it. I saw the work, the endless problems; but most of all I saw myself as this person that people felt they could make comments about; someone whose letters they could read; drawers they could rifle through. What was worse, I knew *what* he would find in my bedroom drawer. It was *so* humiliating.'

'You don't have to tell us if you don't want to,' Jo assures her.

'Oh, you know so much,' and despite herself, Ruth starts to laugh again. 'I suppose it was quite a compliment.' There is a long pause and a covering of snow slips from a nearby tomb with a swoosh and a thud. 'The thing was, Stan had quite a thing for my . . . well . . . for my breasts.'

Jo can't help it; she is grinning openly now.

'He wrote me a poem, and I was pretty certain Colin would have found it and I . . . couldn't bear it.'

Jo is no longer smiling, 'Of course not. The *bastard*,' she says, with real venom.

They sit in silence and then Ruth says, much more cheerfully, 'Want to hear it?'

'Yes!' is the immediate chorus from both Jo and Malcolm.

'Oh, well, in for a penny,' Ruth says, reaching for her phone. She scrolls through some photos, 'I took a picture of it,' she explains. The graveyard is quiet and then the Reverend Ruth Hamilton speaks formally, as if addressing a congregation.

The cassock you wear with so much pride
Covers perfections, you should not hide.
Your breasts are a wonder, beyond compare,
I thank the Lord for the joy found there.
Who knew that we would find such bliss,
In the intimacy of our first kiss.
Now is the agony of being apart,
For you and your breasts have stolen my heart.

They do laugh, but they also squeeze tight to the Reverend Ruth. 'I think that is rather marvellous,' Malcolm declares. 'You clearly inspired the man.'

'What happened next?' Jo asks. 'After you saw Colin in your house?'

'I just . . . turned around and started walking. I got down to the dual carriageway out of town and a lorry stopped and gave me a lift. It was an Italian driver, so I suppose he never saw the news story. After that, I just . . . couldn't bear to go back.'

Jo nods her understanding and remembers Malcolm's comment: *Ah, going back, finding the will to do that, now that is a much more difficult endeavour.*

'So has anything happened since? I mean, have you heard from Stan?'

'Oh, no, that's all over.'

'And the press?' Jo asks.

'Well it's a pretty old story by now. But my bishop and I came up with an idea and a week ago I gave a press conference about my disappearing to the local media.'

'I haven't seen anything in the news,' Jo says.

'Oh, you wouldn't,' Ruth chuckles.

'What?' They both ask this.

'Do you remember how I deal with scam calls?' Ruth asks Jo.

'Oh, definitely,' she replies.

'Well, imagine that multiplied by ten. I talked about theology, about my doubts about the scriptures. I went on for hours discussing the minutiae of faith and my way back to the Lord.' Ruth laughs. 'Of course, no one wanted to write about that, so I am pretty certain the story is dead in the water,' Ruth declares with satisfaction.

Jo can hear the sizzle of the candle flame against the deep silence of fallen snow.

'So that,' Ruth concludes, 'is pretty much it.'

Jo relaxes back on the bench. So that was Reverend Ruth's

THE BOOK OF BEGINNINGS

secret. But is that the end of Ruth's tale? She feels there must be more. 'So what next?' she asks.

'I'm going to a new parish.'

Jo can't help thinking of Angela, of all those people on the message board. Everyone would be so disappointed.

'I did think about going back,' Ruth says, as if reading Jo's thoughts, 'but in the end the bishop put his foot down and reminded me I was only human.'

'Quite right,' Malcolm says, kicking at the snow with the toe of his boot. 'No need to have to deal with the likes of Colin Will-kill-soon any more.'

'Oh, I think the bishop has put a stop to his gallop.' Jo can tell from her voice that Ruth is pleased. 'You can only serve for six years as a churchwarden unless you get a suspension to this rule. Colin was trying to organize that, but a phone call here, a glass of sherry there and . . . well, let's just say, the bishop will be first in line to thank him profusely for his services when he has to step down.'

Malcolm chuckles over this, then says, thoughtfully, 'There is one thing, Ruth, I have been meaning to ask you. You once told us there were two things you tried to live your life by. I appreciate one was the – do unto others – but I just wondered what the second was?'

'Oh, must we, Malcolm?' Ruth says, shaking her head.

'I'd like to hear it too, Ruth, if you don't mind,' Jo says.

'Oh, all right. But I know what you're going to say, Malcolm. The second thing is, to love God,' Ruth carries on quickly, 'and before you start on me, Malcolm, I know it sounds obvious, but I don't think of it like you might suppose. To me it is about humility. Just acknowledging and reminding myself that there is something else that is much more important than I am. For me, it's the Christian God, but for others it could be Allah, or Buddha – whatever it is that reminds you that you don't have every answer, and you're not the be-all and end-all.'

'No, I understand that,' Malcolm says, softly.

'But where are you going?' Jo wants to know, 'where's your new parish?'

'Richmond.'

'A very pleasant place,' Malcolm says. 'It is lovely there by the Thames in summer.'

'No, not Richmond in Surrey,' Ruth says, with a chuckle. 'Richmond in Yorkshire.'

'You're kidding!' Jo exclaims. 'Oh Ruth, that's amazing.' She thinks of Uncle Wilbur. Perhaps he had been right after all when he said the Runaway Vicar needed to find her place. (*A place for everything and everything in its place.*)

'Well, you rather sold the idea of the North-East to me,' Ruth declares, 'so I wanted a new start and I thought I would give it a go.'

'You'll love it. And I'll have you nearby . . . ish.'

'Really?' Ruth says, the word pregnant with questions.

Malcolm lets out a slow. 'Aah.' This, however, is filled with sadness.

Jo turns to him. 'What about you, Malcolm?'

'Well, I have rather taken up Reverend Ruth's advice. Highgate Cemetery is very well supported but I find that there are many other cemeteries that are under threat from the developers. I have joined a Save our Souls campaign. For me, it is as much about saving the wildlife habitats as preserving history. I have even bought some handcuffs in case I need to attach myself to any railings,' he adds, cheerfully.

'I expect there are many such graveyards that need saving in Yorkshire,' Ruth suggests, innocently.

Malcolm sits completely still for several moments.

'And you think . . .' he muses.

'I do indeed,' Ruth says, borrowing one of Malcolm's phrases.

'So do I,' Jo adds, with enthusiasm. In her heart she is sure the three of them are meant to be on stage together for a few more scenes.

'Shall we drink to the future?' Ruth suggests, reaching for the thermos of cocktails. She insists they all get to their feet as she tops up their glasses. The snow has stopped falling but the thick covering smothers the sound of the city beyond the walls. Jo feels this is a moment captured in time that she will never forget. They are cocooned in the light of the lantern, the circle of snowy, ghostly tombs guarding their little group. For her, this will always be an important meeting point: of herself, the Reverend Ruth Hamilton, and the campaigner, Malcolm Buswell.

'I feel we should say something,' Ruth says, raising her glass, and cocking her head towards Malcolm.

Malcolm gives a slight shake of his head. A brave man, but still a reserved man.

Jo hears her own voice, strong in the darkness, and watches her breath mist the air. 'I would like to say something.'

They both look to her.

It came to her as she gazed out into the darkness of the cemetery.

'To the three of us.' She pauses and then adds the words that George Eliot wrote: 'It is never too late to be what you might have been.'

The three of them raise their glasses in unison.

51

Jo Sorsby makes plans

They settle back on the bench, a quiet, thoughtful trio. Jo's reverie is interrupted by Reverend Ruth: direct as (almost) always, she gets straight to the point.

'Now then Jo, enough about us – tell us all about your plans. What are you doing back in London for Christmas Eve?'

'Before we go into all that, shall we have a walk around the cemetery?' Jo suggests. She feels the need for a pause, a chance to gather her thoughts. 'We're never likely to be here like this again.'

'You're right, Joanne. As much as I would like to make this an annual convening with the ghosts each Christmas Eve, I do worry about those railings. Even with a stepladder,' Malcolm admits.

Ruth is already up on her feet and pulling something from her pocket.

Jo's impressed. 'Good head torch.'

The torch certainly has a very powerful beam, and Ruth leads the way, Jo taking up the rear. First they visit George Eliot's grave and stand in silence for a few moments, before moving on deeper into the graveyard. The path squeaks under their feet and their bodies, brushing the branches, dislodge snow, which falls with a slithering sigh.

As they walk, they talk about their ghosts; where they are now and what they might be doing. Jo thinks William Foyle and John Lobb will be on their second pint. Those two ghosts, who reminded her of the importance of friendship. Malcolm suggests that, even now, Issachar is showing George Eliot the display of her novels in the window of Waterstones. Something, Issachar tells her (loudly, so passers-by can hear), that he has arranged just for her.

Ruth is quieter about her ghosts. Eventually she says, she hopes they have more success than she did, reconciling with their pasts and their families.

Malcolm reaches out and pats her shoulder. 'You did everything you could, Ruth. No one could have done more. Sometimes it is time to move on.'

Jo wonders if Malcolm is also talking about himself.

It strikes Jo that anyone overhearing them would think they are quite mad. Yet she knows for the three of them – right here, right now – their ghostly Christmas Eve story has become a reality.

'Will you write your ghost story, Malcolm?' Jo asks.

'Most assuredly. Maybe I will start after I move house. I hear Yorkshire is nice.'

Jo hears a quiet, 'Ah, wonderful,' from Reverend Ruth.

Now they are deeper into the graveyard, the boughs are bent low with the weight of snow. It feels as though they have entered a smaller world, a cave of branches, ivy and ice. It is darker and there is a new depth to the silence.

Jo's torch beam picks up a headstone of a private who died aged 19 in 1917.

Malcolm sees it too. 'Joanne, it is most remiss of me. I should have thanked you for your wonderful gift. I spent the whole afternoon reading the airmen's stories.'

After half an hour wandering through the cemetery, they are back at their bench. Karl Marx is still glowering at them, but it is difficult to take him so seriously with his toupee of snow. Malcolm walks over and clears the snow off Claudia Jones's grave. Meanwhile, Jo tucks herself in under the blankets. She picks up her cocktail glass and, while Malcolm and Ruth study the gravestone, she tips some Christmas cocktail onto the earth. Well, she presumes the gods like cocktails too.

'So out with it,' Ruth says, sitting down. 'What are you going to do, Jo?' She holds the blanket out for Malcolm to tuck himself under.

Jo smiles, remembering the decision she reached on the moors a few days ago. 'I'm going to start my own stationery shop.'

'Ah,' says Ruth, beaming. 'Good for you.'

'Delightful,' says Malcolm. 'Then you don't intend to continue with your Uncle Wilbur's establishment?'

'I did think about it, but no. I want to live closer to home. Nearer to the hills.' Near to Lucy and to Mum and Dad, she thinks.

Ruth and Malcolm nod.

'Uncle Wilbur is definitely helping me, though,' she says. 'His flat and shop have been left to Mum, and they are worth a ridiculous amount of money. She wants me to have some of this to help me start. Plus I still have my redundancy money. I thought I would take up the bronze and indigo floor tiles that are in the doorway and put those in my new shop, oh, and keep the oak cabinet. And the noticeboard, of course.'

'And your uncle's armchair was exceedingly comfortable . . .' Malcolm reflects.

Jo grins. 'Yes, I've got my eye on that too,' she confesses.

She wants to always have something of the spirit of Uncle Wilbur in her new shop. Her favourite uncle walking beside her, never forgotten. She is going to call her shop Dear Wilbur, and she is planning a website, too – a way to keep in touch with her tribe of Stationery Lovers.

'Where will your new shop be?' Ruth asks.

'I'm not sure yet,' Jo says, reflectively. 'I think these last six months have made me realize I need a new start. But somewhere closer to home.' She smiles. 'My heart will always be in the North-East, but I don't want to just go back to the old places.' And she thinks, the old habits. 'So I've been looking at towns like Ilkley – it's about an hour from my parents and not too far from where my best friend, Lucy, lives.' She nudges Ruth's arm, 'I guess it would be about an hour from Richmond too.'.

'Excellent.' Ruth says this first, but Jo notices there is a quiet echo from Malcolm.

Jo tries to find the words to describe her walk up on the moors and all she had thought about. 'I think being in London made me see that you can find communities, and friendship, anywhere.'

'Go on,' Ruth prompts.

'I realized that you can make friends in unexpected places. When I had to shut up Uncle Wilbur's shop, I had so many messages of support from customers via Twitter – people who love stationery. They spread the word about what was happening, and now I feel like I'm getting to know some of them too.'

The candle in the lantern is burning low, and it won't be long before they have to leave. The thought of Eric the Viking starts to intrude, but there is more Jo wants to say.

'When I was home, it made me realize I wanted a new start where I wasn't just Average Jo—'

'You certainly are not . . .' her friends begin.

But Jo stops them. 'I've always been somewhere in the middle when it comes to most things, and though it isn't necessarily a bad thing, I think it became a problem for me.'

'How?' Ruth asks.

'I guess I settled for things when I shouldn't have done.' Jo thinks of James, taking over her life. Of her job at the bank, which she liked but never loved. 'And because I thought of myself as average and ordinary, I was always looking at people who seemed to be doing better than me, thinking maybe I should try to be more like that, but doing nothing about it.' Jo thinks specifically of the 'popular crowd' who she started to hang out with.

'So,' Jo continues, 'I ended up feeling inadequate, and then bad, because I didn't do anything to change it.'

'And now you want to change something?' Malcolm asks.

'Well, yes and no,' Jo laughs. She looks out into the cemetery for inspiration. And she finds it. 'I am glad that there are people who can write like George Eliot; who have huge brains like Marx; are campaigners like Claudia; have the skill of John Lobb, the business acumen of William Foyle; people who can sing and play like Hutch, and who have big ideas like Issachar. But I'm not one of them. And I'm okay with that. I now know what I want.

'I'd like to run a stationery shop. I need to be able to walk out onto the hills. But I've also found I like cities. So I think Ilkley could be perfect – it's on the edge of the Yorkshire Dales, but not that far from Leeds. And it's okay to not want much more than that.' Jo doesn't mention her longing for a family. One of the things she realized up on the moors was that, for her, this really was up to the gods. She continues, 'So, I don't need to be extraordinary. I want to run a small shop, I want to spend time with my friends and family, I want to walk, go to the pub, cook, write with a fountain pen.' She smiles. 'I think I might like to try some more wild swimming . . .'

Ruth nudges her. 'I might even come with you.'

'. . . but that's about as adventurous as it's going to get. And that's okay.'

'I would say that it is more than okay,' Malcolm agrees.

'So you'll have no regrets about leaving London?' Ruth asks, pointedly.

What can she say? She has no idea. Here in Highgate Cemetery it has been magical; she will treasure the memory of this Christmas Eve for ever.

But . . . Eric the Viking? Her stomach lurches. Where is he? When will she see him again? Has she left it too late?

'Has Eric the—' But Ruth gets no further.

'Oh course!' Jo exclaims. 'He's helping Crisis at Christmas.' And she recalls Lando saying that Eric always turned up to do eye-tests for the homeless on Christmas Eve. Was he still there now? Could she find out where that was?

'Joanne, I think there is something you are not telling us,' Malcolm says.

And so she tells them. Explains about Caramel Toffee Clare, about Finn, and how she left Lucy in the pub and drove through the snow to get here. But that when she got to the alleyway, there was no Eric the Viking.

'What are you going to do now?' Malcolm asks.

'I have no idea.'

'Want me to light a candle for you?' Ruth says, with a grin.

'Will you?'

'Of course.'

'You know, another thing I thought about up on the moors,' Jo interjects. 'Some customers in the shop would always take the fountain pens apart. They needed to know how they worked. I think some people look at life and religion in the same way – they need to dissect it to make sense of it. I'm just not one of them. I don't think I need to keep pulling apart what I believe. I just know how I feel. And that's enough.'

She understands now that she is a woman who will light a candle for a friend; wish them well in her thoughts; swim in a freezing pond in memory of a good woman she never knew . . . and from now on, she will also thank the gods sometimes with wine poured on the earth. She also believes that a fox could visit a grieving man, and that by saying goodnight to her absent uncle each night, she is connecting with him somehow.

It may not make sense to anyone else, but it makes sense to her. She looks at the two figures beside her, bundled up in coats and blankets, faces half lit by the guttering candle, and is overwhelmed by her love for them. They are her dear friends.

They sit in silence for some time. Then the candle eventually fizzes and dies.

'Time to go home, I think,' Malcolm's voice sounds in the dark.

Ruth switches on her torch and together they gather all the blankets and cushions, stuffing them into the Ikea bags they have been sitting on. They make their way cautiously towards the stepladder. There is no one about, and the streetlamp throws an orange glow over the fresh snow. Their footprints from earlier have all but disappeared. With lots of encouragement and laughter, they get over the railings without mishap. Malcolm then tucks the stepladder and lantern out of sight behind a hedge, saying he will collect them later.

'There we go, two less things to carry back. What are our plans now?' he asks.

'Well, I am going to midnight mass with Reverend

Abayomrunkoje – he has promised there will be mulled wine and mince pies. Would you care to join me?'

Jo is astounded when Malcolm says, 'Yes, I believe I would like that.'

They look at him in astonishment. He adds a caveat: 'But do not for a moment think that I am changing my views on God.'

'Oh, I will have you running the cake stall before you know it,' Ruth jokes.

And Jo thinks, she probably will. God or no God.

'And you, Joanne, will you join us?' Malcolm asks, bowing his head slightly, in the old polite manner.

'No. I think I'll go back to the flat. I should call Lucy and . . .' She doesn't know what else to say, as she has no clear idea of what she intends to do.

Ruth picks up the two Ikea bags filled with blankets and cushions. 'Well, you make sure you call us. And if you stay in London, come to us for Christmas Dinner. Malcolm has invited me to stay with him.'

Jo is pleased to see Reverend Ruth is back to organizing them all, but with none of her previous slump into anxiety. Malcolm then retrieves a pen and scrap of paper from the bottom of his basket, so he can write down their phone numbers for Jo. They part with hugs and kisses – Jo getting tangled up in the Ikea bags – then Ruth and Malcolm tramp off down the lane.

Jo watches them go, the tall figure in an afghan coat striding easily; the smaller figure throwing up a flurry of snow with small, deliberate steps. As they disappear from sight she thinks she hears the words, 'Sweeet Jeeesuus!' drifting back to her, and the sound of laughter.

Up the hill the snow lies drifting against the cemetery wall. No cars have braved the steep slope. The scene ahead is pristine white, apart from a line of small paw prints – a fox? Jo fleetingly thinks of Eve Buswell.

Using her grandfather's stick like a staff, Jo starts to make her slow ascent up the hill.

52

The Christmas Eve ghosts

Two men watch her as she passes the gates of Highgate Cemetery. Both are wearing three-piece suits: one has a large beard and a trilby perched on the back of his head; the other has longish grey hair swept back from his face, a small pair of spectacles balanced on his nose. Despite the snow, they do not appear to feel the cold.

'Wha' ye be thinking, Will?' the man with the beard asks the other.

His companion thinks he's laying the Cornish accent on a bit thick tonight. But that's John for you. Soon he'd be calling him, 'My lover.'

'Tha' we should get ourselves down the rub-a-dub for a pint.'

The other man nods, and pulls his hat forward on his head.

William Foyle thinks he made that too easy, and racks his brain for some cockney rhyming slang John Lobb won't know. He perks up. He could always invent a few phrases. That'd get him.

'Well, what ye be thinking of them three?' John asks, as they turn in the direction of their favourite pub.

'Not so bad,' William replies. 'They got us pegged,' he laughs.

'Not so far out on old Issy either,' John agrees. 'Where be he tonight?'

William snorts. 'To Shabby with Georgie. Saw 'em 'eading for a bus.'

John wants to know but hates to ask. In the end, curiosity gets the better of him. 'Shabby?'

William chortles, 'Shabby . . . Westminster Abbey. Said summat about giving old Georgie the last laugh. Said as 'ow they'd have a picnic in Poet's Corner.'

Both of them chuckle at this, and William links his arm with John's.

''ow about Karl?' William asks.

'Off with Claudia, as per,' John replies. 'Them two, they don't 'alf fight. But he says to me, he does, "That woman never bores me." Can't say fairer than tha' I tell him.'

'And 'utch?' William enquires.

'Same as last year,' John nods. And from somewhere in the cemetery (if you listen very carefully) comes the soft tinkling of a piano.

'Off with George Michael again, then,' William concludes.

'Tha' be right,' John agrees. He then recalls something much more important. 'Remember it be your round.'

'Na, you got that arse about tit, my son,' William replies.

The argument continues all the way down the hill.

53

Christmas Day

By the time Jo gets to the top of Highgate High Street, she begins to think she has made a mistake. How will she ever track Eric the Viking down? Perhaps he works all night? Where will she even start? She could be inside a warm church with mulled wine – or curled up by the fire – with Ruth and Malcolm. She thinks of the woodland sitting room. Instead of this comfort (and probably more nibbles and a whisky), she is heading back to a cold shop and flat. And some of the electrics are definitely not working – maybe she could lose power in the flat too? In the distance, she hears the faint peel of church bells. Then, closer by, the sonorous tolling of midnight.

It is Christmas Day.

As she turns into the alleyway, she sees the glow. Instead of the blank white of her makeshift cover, the shop window is patterned with flickering orange. Had she left the heater on? She should have checked the fuses, the wiring, when the lights didn't work. She runs to the door, scrabbling for her keys. Is she burning her mum's inheritance to the ground? She thinks of all that paper. And wooden shelving. She pushes open the door, and suddenly realizes this is a mistake. Brendan (fire and safety officer at the bank) always said, 'Let the oxygen in and you feed the fire.' Jo instinctively steps back, fully expecting the backdraught that Brendan had promised would kill her.

There is nothing. Just the gentle sound of classical music. It reminds her of the cello she heard playing earlier. There is a piano playing along with it. A memory of a melody she may have heard as she passed by the Highgate Cemetery gates comes back to her.

Cautiously, she peers around the door. The lamp is lit, and arranged on the shelves and windowsills are dozens of glasses. All sizes: wine, pint, tumbler. Each glass has a candle burning within it. The twinkling of the Christmas tree lights adds to the soft glow. Behind the counter, seated on her stool, is Eric the Viking, a book open in front of him.

She has never seen a Viking cry before. He doesn't cry like he laughs, with big noisy sobs; he just lets the tears fall. He looks tired, and scruffy, but there is something else. He is looking at her like his life depends upon this moment – on her. And she knows, as her mum knew in that out-of-season coffee shop, that she loves this man.

'You came.' He tries to grin, but his face crumples and he rubs a big paw of a hand across his eyes. 'Gets me every time,' he says. And she can see him trying once more to smile. He nods down at the book. 'Can't help it. Poetry. Sets me off.'

She takes a step towards him, but he holds up a hand. 'I thought you weren't coming. Clare texted me and Lando did too. I used your key, and saw your bag. But I thought I'd left it too late. So I wrote you something.' He looks briefly behind him, at her wall of words, now curling with cold and damp. 'I pinned it there. But really I wanted to read it to you.'

'Read it now,' she says, staring back at him, taking him all in.

His old grin is back this time, 'I'll cry,' he tells her.

'That's okay – I will too.' She is already. She pulls off her woolly hat and unwraps her scarf, but doesn't move from where she is standing.

And the Viking from Birmingham pulls down a piece of paper from the wall behind him and in the flickering candle light reads what he has written out for her:

Time was away and she was here
And life no longer what it was,
The bell was silent in the air
And all the room one glow because
Time was away and she was here.

His voice falters on the last line, and the fragile vulnerability of this releases something in her. And then she is around the side of the counter – boots, jumpers, coat and all – and he pulls her to him. The stool is knocked over, but it doesn't matter. When he kisses her, she can feel his hand in her hair and then on her cheek. She reaches up her own hand and interlaces her fingers with his. And then he has his arms wrapped tight around her and Jo sinks into the certainty that she has found her home.

(*A place for everything and everything in its place.*)

Eventually the stool is righted, she is sitting on her side of the counter (still in her uncle's coat, face red from the cold and crying. And from the Viking's beard), and he is on his side, in his normal spot.

'Where have you been Stationery Girl? I thought you were never coming.'

So she tells him about it all; her friends and the Highgate Cemetery ghosts.

'So you broke in?' and the walrus laugh is back.

'Yes, I suppose we did,' she says, in some surprise, wondering why she ever thought she was average.

He wants to know about all the characters they have researched, and their ideas for conversations, only stopping her briefly so he can nip next door to his shop. He brings back a bottle of champagne, some smoked salmon, and two boxes of biscuits – presents from patients (including Dwayne, who can now see straight, but as Eric the Optician predicted is attending all his Christmas parties wearing a patch). They drink the champagne from mugs.

At the end of her recital he says, 'It just proves your Uncle Wilbur was right.'

She looks at him enquiringly.

'He'd seen this area change a lot over the years, but he always said people are much the same and more alike than they think.'

Jo nods, thinking of her favourite uncle and of the ghosts, picked at random, who all found something to share.

'So, you think Lando and I spend all our time scrapping . . .' Eric starts, in mock protest.

Soon after, Jo asks to borrow Eric's phone and takes a selfie of the two of them, which she sends to Lucy. She feels it is the least she owes her. Eric also forwards the photo on to Lando and Clare.

'You have no idea how many people have been bugging me about where you had got to.'

This reminds her she needs to speak to her mum but, looking at the time, she decides it is too late to call now. She will ring her in the morning – and then realizes it is the morning; it is nearly two o'clock.

After this, Jo borrows the phone again and sends the photo and a message to Ruth and Malcolm. She has a feeling they will be waiting up to hear from her. She sends her apologies, that she won't be joining them for Christmas Day. It seems Eric the Viking has other plans. She just hopes it is a Nordic tradition to stay in bed all Christmas Day.

They blow out all the candles, and Eric picks up her bag. As he opens the door, she sees it has started to snow again. He holds his hand out to her.

'Okay, Jo Sorsby, Stationery Girl, shall we go home?'

Sometimes a heartbeat is all the time it takes to reach a decision.

Epilogue

Two years later

THE ILKLEY GAZETTE

Eric and Jo Sveinbjörnsson announce the birth
of their son, Eliot.
    Born 24 December.

Acknowledgements

This is a book, primarily about friendship. I could not have written it without the support of my friends – they really are too numerous to mention (for which I count my blessings). But you know who you are, and be sure that you have my gratitude and my love.

Like Jo, I am fortunate enough to have a best friend. When Rev. Ruth says, *There is a fundamental truth, comfort and joy in having a best friend*, I could not agree more. In fact, I was thinking of you, Pip, as I wrote this.

Within the story, the lines sometimes become blurred between who is family and who is a friend, which, of course, happens in life. My friends, Sally and Michael have become family. And my sister-in-law, Judith, is not only family, but a dear friend. Thank you.

Dear to me, as always, are my daughters Alex and Libby. Thank you for your endless support and encouragement and for introducing me to the joys of wild swimming.

What can I say about the Reverend Anne Heywood?! She really did inspire this book. I have learnt so much from observing her approach to people and life. Thank you, Anne, for sharing your stories and your philosophy with me. May we continue to share much more wine and laughter.

Thank you to Fiona who lent me her poetry skills. And apologies to her husband Neil who could not understand why she had written a poem about breasts.

Thank you to the staff and volunteers of Highgate Cemetery. I would recommend anyone take the time to visit (but please don't break in on Christmas Eve night!). In thinking of Malcolm's ghosts and wondering who would meet on Christmas Eve, I wrote out some names of those buried in the cemetery and put these in a hat. I then drew them out at random (just like Jo, Malcolm and Ruth). So, who met who really was a matter of chance. I think it proves that Uncle Wilbur was right: people are more alike than we might at first suppose, and people will always find things to share.

As for the rest of Highgate and Hampstead, as mentioned in the book, forgive me for taking liberties – I added alleyways and shops as I fancied – but I hope I have kept true to the atmosphere of the area. Regarding the geography and landscape of the North-East I also hope I have got these right. It is an area very close to my heart, but I am aware I am a visitor rather than a resident.

I would also like to thank the team at Robert Frith's in Gillingham, Dorset. You were so patient in answering my questions about the life and trials of an optician. (Eric the Viking says thank you, too.)

Any author will tell you there is a whole team that craft and support a book on its journey to readers. Thank you to my agent, Tanera Simons. And to the team at HarperFiction who devoted so much time and passion to the editing process: Martha Ashby, Lucy Stewart and Belinda Toor – with a special thanks to Katie Lumsden.

I would also like to thank those in the team who do so much to get my book into readers' minds and into their hands. Alice Gomer, Harriet Williams and Bethan Moore from the sales team. Jo Kite and Sophie Raoufi from the marketing team. Fliss Denham and Sofia Saghir from the publicity team. And Ellie Game who did such an amazing job creating the cover design.

And finally, I would like to mention Charlotte Ledger from HarperCollins. She was the publisher who gave me a break with my first book, *The Keeper of Stories*. I do not forget it – or that her dog is called Betty. Charlotte, I hope you didn't mind me borrowing her name for Angela Green's dog.

Bibliography

In researching the historical aspects of this book I turned to some of the excellent biographies that have been written about those who ended their days in Highgate Cemetery. These include:

Abel, E. Lawrence, *Lincoln's Jewish Spy: The Life and Times of Issachar Zacharie* (Jefferson, US, 2020)

Breese, Charlotte, *Hutch* (London, 1999)

Davies, Carole Boyce, *Left of Karl Marx: The Political Life of Black Communist, Claudia Jones* (Durham, US, 2008)

Dobbs, Brian, *The Last Shall be First: The Colourful Story of John Lobb the Bootmakers of St James's* (London, 1972)

Hughes, Kathryn, *George Eliot: The Last Victorian* (London, 1999)

Samuel, Bill, *An Accidental Bookseller: A Personal Memoir of Foyles* (Puxley, 2019)

Wheen, Francine, *Karl Marx* (London, 1999)

Whittell, Giles, *Spitfire Women of World War II* (London, 2021)

Thank you so much for helping to bring Malcolm's ghosts to life.

The extract on page 55 –

I have known the silence of the stars, and of the sea.
And the silence of a city when it pauses.

– is from the poem 'Silence' by Edgar Lee Masters.

The extracts from the poem 'Meeting Point' by Louis MacNeice are reproduced with kind permission of David Higham Associates, Ltd.